WHAT
DARKNESS
BRINGS

A Sebastian St. Cyr Mystery

C. S. HARRIS

D0348423

AN OBSIDIAN MYSTERY

OBSIDIAN
Published by the Penguin Group
Penguin Group (USA) LLC, 375 Hudson Street,
New York, New York 10014

USA | Canada | UK | Ireland | Australia | New Zealand | India | South Africa | China
penguin.com
A Penguin Random House Company

Published by Obsidian, an imprint of New American Library, a division of Penguin Group (USA) LLC. Previously published in an Obsidian hardcover edition.

First Obsidian Mass Market Printing, March 2014

ISBN 978-0-451-41818-0

Printed in the United States of America
10 9 8 7 6 5 4 3 2 1

continued . . .

"Harris combines all of the qualities of a solid Regency in the tradition of Georgette Heyer by pairing two strong characters trying to ignore their mutual attraction while solving a crime together. Anyone who likes Amanda Quick and/or is reading the reissued Heyer novels will love this series."
— *Library Journal* (Starred Review)

"[The] seductive antihero [is] at his swashbuckling best."
— *Publishers Weekly*

WHERE SERPENTS SLEEP

"C. S. Harris's attention to historical detail and sense of adventure combine to make a ripping read . . . captivated me to the final page."
— Will Thomas, author of the Barker & Llewelyn novels

"An intriguing mix of bloody murder, incest, and brutality. The author, who has done her historical homework, makes a fascinating focus of her book in Hero Jarvis, a young woman whose uncompromising independence puts her far ahead of her time."
— *The Washington Times*

"[Sebastian and Hero] are a perfect hardheaded match as they lead Harris's romping good story."
— *The New Orleans Times-Picayune*

"Harris does an excellent job of interweaving the mystery in this book with the larger story arc of the series . . . solidly written."
— *St. Petersburg Times*

"Outstanding. . . . Harris does a nice job of weaving the many plot strands together while exploring the complex character of her protagonist."   — *Publishers Weekly* (Starred Review)

WHY MERMAIDS SING

"A serial-killer thriller set two hundred years ago? . . . It works, thanks to Harris's pacing and fine eye for detail. A real plus: the murk and stench of the age only heighten the suspense."
— *Entertainment Weekly*

"Thoroughly enjoyable . . . moody and atmospheric, exposing the dark underside of Regency London . . . deliciously ghoulish . . . kept me enthralled."
— Deanna Raybourn, author of *The Dark Enquiry*

WHEN GODS DIE

"Like Georgette Heyer, Harris delves deep into the mores of Regency England, but hers is a darker, more dangerous place."
— *Kirkus Reviews* (Starred Review)

"Deftly combines political intrigue, cleverly concealed clues, and vivid characters . . . a fast-moving story that will have readers eagerly anticipating future volumes in the series."
— *Publishers Weekly* (Starred Review)

"Harris knows her English history and has a firm grasp of how a mystery novel is supposed to play out . . . a crescendo of suspense and surprise. . . . Fans of historicals, especially those set in Regency-era England, will snap up this triumph."
— *Library Journal* (Starred Review)

WHAT ANGELS FEAR

"Perfect reading. . . . Harris crafts her story with the threat of danger, hints of humor, vivid sex scenes, and a conclusion that will make your pulse race. Impressive."
— *The New Orleans Times-Picayune*

"A stunning debut novel filled with suspense, intrigue, and plot twists galore. C. S. Harris artfully re-creates the contradictory world of Regency England as her marvelous characters move between the glittering ballrooms and the treacherous back alleys of London. . . . Start this one early in the day—you won't be able to put it down!"
— Victoria Thompson, author of the Gaslight Mystery series

"Appealing characters, authentic historical details, and sound plotting make this an amazing debut historical."
— *Library Journal* (Starred Review)

"An absorbing and accomplished debut that displays a mastery of the Regency period in all its elegance and barbarity . . . will grip the reader from its first pages and compel to the finish."
— Stephanie Barron, author of the Jane Austen Mystery series

"The combined elements of historical fiction, romance, and mystery in this fog-enshrouded London puzzler will appeal to fans of Anne Perry."
— *Booklist*

"A masterful blend of history and suspense, character and plot, imagination and classic mystery. A thoroughly intriguing, enjoyable read."
— Laura Joh Rowland, author of the Sano Ichiro Mystery series

Books in the
Sebastian St. Cyr Mystery Series

For

Helen Breitwieser

The gaudy, blabbing and remorseful day
Is crept into the bosom of the sea;
And now loud-howling wolves arouse the jades
That drag the tragic melancholy night;
Who, with their drowsy, slow and flagging wings,
Clip dead men's graves and from their misty jaws
Breathe foul contagious darkness in the air.

—William Shakespeare, *Henry VI*,
PART 2, ACT 4, SCENE I

Chapter 1

London
Sunday, 20 September 1812

The man was so old his face sagged in crinkly, sallow folds and Jenny could see pink scalp through the thin white hair plastered by sweat to his head.

"The irony is delicious; don't you agree?" he said as he slid a big, multifaceted piece of blue glass down between the swells of her breasts. The glass felt smooth and cool against her bare skin, but his fingers were as bone thin and cold as a corpse's.

She forced herself to lie still even though she wanted desperately to squirm away. She might be only seventeen, but Jenny Davie had been in this business for almost five years. She knew how to keep a smile plastered on her face when inside her guts roiled with revulsion and an exasperated urge to say, *Can't we just get this over with?*

"Think about it." He blinked, and she noticed he had no lashes fringing his small, sunken eyes, and that his teeth were so long and yellow they made her think of the ratty mule that pulled the dustman's cart. He said, "Once, this diamond graced the crowns of kings and nestled in the silken bosom of a queen. And now here it lies . . . on the somewhat grubby breasts of a cheap London whore."

"Go on wit' you," she scoffed, squinting down at the pretty glass. "Jist because I'm a whore don't mean I'm stupid. That ain't no diamond. It's *blue*. And it's bigger than a bloody peach pit."

"Much bigger than a peach pit," agreed the old man as the glass caught the flickering light from a nearby brace of candles and glowed as if with an inner fire. His dark eyes gleamed, and Jenny found herself wondering what he needed a whore for since he seemed more excited by his big chunk of blue glass than he was by her. "They say that once, this stone formed the third eye of a heathen—"

He broke off, his head coming up as a loud pounding sounded at the distant front door.

Before she could stop herself, Jenny jerked. She was lying on her back on a dusty, scratchy horsehair sofa in the cavernous, decrepit parlor of the old man's house. Most men took their whores in the back rooms of coffeehouses or in one of the city's numerous accommodation houses. But not this man. He always had his whores brought here, to his cobweb-draped old mansion in St. Botolph-Aldgate. And he didn't take them upstairs either, but did his business here, on the couch—which suited Jenny just fine, since she never liked being too far from a way out of trouble.

He muttered something under his breath she didn't understand, although from the way he said it she figured it was some kind of curse. Then he said, "He wasn't supposed to be here this early."

He reared up, straightening his clothes. He'd had her strip down to her stockings and shift, which he'd untied so that it gaped open nearly to her waist. But he hadn't taken off any of his own clothes, not even his fusty, old-fashioned coat or shoes. He glanced around, the blue chunk of glass held tight in one fist. "Here," he said, gathering her stays, petticoat, and dress and shoving them into her arms. "Take these and get in—"

The knocking sounded again, louder this time, as she slid off the couch with her crumpled clothing clutched to her chest. "I can leave—"

"No." He moved toward the looming, old-fashioned chimneypiece that stood at one end of the room. It was a fantastical thing of smoke-darkened wood carved into tiers of columns with swags of fruit and nuts and even animals. "This won't take long." He pressed something in the carving, and Jenny blinked as a portion of the nearby paneling slid open. "Just get in here."

She found herself peering into a dark cubbyhole some six or eight feet square, empty except for an old basket and a couple of ironbound trunks lined against one wall. "In there? But—"

His hand closed around her bare upper arm tight enough that she squealed, "Ow!"

"Just shut up and get in there. If you let out a peep, you won't get paid. And if you touch anything, I'll break your neck. Understood?"

She supposed he saw the answer—or maybe just her fear—in her face, because he didn't wait for her reply but thrust her into the little room and slid the panel closed. Whirling around, she heard a latch click as a thick blackness swallowed her. She choked down a scream.

The air in the cubbyhole was musty and old smelling, like the man and the rest of his house, only nastier. It was so dark she wondered how the blazes he thought she was going to steal something when she couldn't see anything but a tiny pinprick of light about level with her head. She went to press one eye against the speck of light and realized it was a peephole, contrived to give a good view of the room beyond. She watched as he nestled his pretty piece of glass inside a velvet-lined red leather box. Then he shoved the box in the drawer of a nearby console and yelled, "I'm coming, I'm coming," as the knocking at the front door sounded again.

Jenny took a deep, shaky breath. She'd heard about some old houses having hidden cupboards like this.

Priests' holes, they called them. They had something to do with Papists and such, although she'd never quite understood what it was all about. She wondered what would happen to her if the old goat never came back to release her. And then she wished she hadn't wondered that, because it made the walls seem to press in on her, and the blackness became so thick and heavy it felt as if it were stealing her breath and sucking the life out of her. She leaned her forehead against the wooden panel and tried to breathe in sucking little pants. She told herself that if Papists used to hide their priests in these cubbyholes, then they must have contrived a way for the panel to be opened from the inside. She began feeling around for the catch, then froze when she realized the voices from the front hall were coming closer.

Pressing her eye to the peephole again, she watched as the nasty old codger backed into the room. He had his hands raised queerly, sort of up and out to the side, like a body trying to ward off a ghost or something. Then she saw the pistol in the hands of the old man's visitor, and she understood.

The old cove was talking fast now. Jenny held herself very still, although her heart thumped in her chest and her breath came so hard and fast it was a wonder they couldn't hear it.

Then she heard a new pounding on the front door and someone shouting. The visitor holding the gun jerked around, distracted, and the old goat lunged.

The gun went off, belching flame and pungent smoke. The old man staggered back. Crumpled.

Jenny felt a hot, stinging gush run down her legs and realized she'd just wet herself.

Chapter 2

"*B*ut it was supposed to be *mine*," wailed George, Prince Regent of Great Britain and Ireland, his plump, feminine face florid with rage as he paced wildly up and down the marble-floored room. "What the devil was Eisler thinking, getting himself murdered like this before he could deliver it to me?"

"Shockingly inconsiderate of the man," agreed the King's powerful cousin, Charles, Lord Jarvis, without the slightest betraying hint of amusement in his voice. "Only, do calm yourself, Your Highness; you don't want to bring on one of your spasms." He caught the eye of the Prince's private physician, who was hovering nearby.

The doctor bowed and withdrew.

Jarvis's immense power did not derive from his kinship with the King, which was distant. It was his peerless blend of stunning intelligence and unswerving dedication to the preservation of the monarchy combined with a cold, unblinking ruthlessness that had made him indispensable first to George III, then to the Prince Regent. For thirty years, Jarvis had maneuvered from the shadows, deftly blunting the inevitable repercussions of a dangerous combination of royal weakness and incompetence complicated by a hereditary tendency toward insanity. If not for Jarvis's capable stewardship, the English monarchy might well have gone the way of the French, and the Hanovers knew it.

"Any idea who is responsible for this outrage?" demanded the Prince.

"Not yet, my lord."

They were in the Circular Room of Carlton House, where George had been hosting a musical evening when some fool carelessly dropped the news of the murder of Daniel Eisler within the Prince's hearing.

They'd had to clear the room quickly.

The Regent continued pacing, his movements surprisingly quick and energetic for a man of his girth. Once, he'd been a handsome prince, beloved by his people and welcomed with cheers wherever he went. But those days were long gone. The Prince of Wales—or Prinny, as he was often called—was now in his fiftieth year, grown fat with self-indulgence and dissipation, and despised by the nation for his spiraling debts, his endless extravagant building projects, and his increasing fondness for expensive jeweled trinkets.

"I've already commissioned Belmont to design a special piece around it," said the Prince. "And now you're telling me the diamond is gone? Vanished? Where am I to find another blue diamond of such size and brilliance? You tell me that! Hmm?"

"When the murderer is apprehended, the diamond will presumably be recovered," said Jarvis as the Prince's physician reentered the room, a small vial in his hand. Behind the doctor came one of Jarvis's own men, a tall, mustachioed ex–military officer of the type with whom Jarvis liked to surround himself.

"Well?" Jarvis demanded of his henchman.

"They've nabbed the murderer," said the officer, leaning forward to whisper in Jarvis's ear. "I think you'll find his identity interesting."

"Oh?" Jarvis kept his gaze on the Prince, who was obediently swallowing his doctor's potion. "And why is that?"

"It's Yates. Russell Yates."

Jarvis tipped back his head and laughed.

※

Jarvis held a scented pomander to his nose, the heels of his dress shoes clicking on the worn paving stones as he strode down the frigid, rush-lit prison corridor. Normally, he ordered prisoners brought to his chambers at the Palace. But under the circumstances, seeing this man in his cell seemed more . . . delectable.

The stocky turnkey paused outside a thick, nail-studded door, the heavy iron key raised, one bushy eyebrow cocked in a wordless question.

"Well, go on, then; open it," said Jarvis, breathing in the scent of cloves and rue.

The man fit the key in the large lock and turned it with a click.

The feeble light of a single smoking tallow candle filled the narrow room beyond with dark shadows. A man standing beside the cell's barred window turned abruptly, chains clanking, as the draft of the opening door caused the flame to flicker and almost go out. He was a young man, in his thirties, his body powerful and well muscled, his handsome face filled with an expression of anticipation that faded when his gaze fell on his visitor.

Jarvis wondered whom the man had been expecting. His lovely wife, perhaps? The thought made Jarvis smile.

The two men regarded each other from across the width of the small room. Then Jarvis drew a jeweled snuffbox from his pocket and said, "We need to talk."

Chapter 3

*T*he morning dawned dull and overcast, the air crisp with an unseasonably sharp reminder of winter days to come. Sebastian St. Cyr, Viscount Devlin, drew up on the verge of the carriageway, the breath of his elegant, high-bred chestnuts showing frosty white as they snorted and hung their heads. It was nearly seven, and they'd been out all night.

For a moment, Sebastian paused, his gaze narrowing as he studied the cluster of constables near the bank of the canal. They were on the southwestern edge of Hyde Park, far from the carefully groomed fashionable rides and promenades favored by the residents of Mayfair. Here, the grass grew rough, brush choked the clusters of trees, and what few paths existed were narrow and seldom traveled.

He handed the reins to his tiger, a half-grown groom named Tom who scrambled forward from his perch at the rear of the curricle. "Best walk 'em," said Sebastian, dropping lightly to the ground. "There's a nasty bite to that wind, and they're tired."

"Aye, gov'nor." Tom's scattering of freckles stood out stark against his pale skin. He had a sharp-featured face, held tight now with exhaustion and suppressed emotion. He was thirteen years old, a onetime street urchin and pickpocket who had been with Sebastian for nearly two years. They were master and servant, but they were also more than that, which was why Tom felt compelled to add, "I'm sorry 'bout your friend."

Sebastian nodded and turned to cut across the meadow, the soles of his Hessian boots leaving a faint trail of crushed grass behind him. He had spent the past ten hours in an increasingly concerned search for his missing friend, a devil-may-care, charming scapegrace of a Taffy named Major Rhys Wilkinson. At first, Sebastian had wondered if Wilkinson's wife might be overreacting when she asked for his help; he'd suspected Rhys simply popped in for a pint someplace, fell in with old friends, and forgot the time. But Annie Wilkinson kept insisting Rhys would never do that. And as night bled slowly into dawn, Sebastian himself had become convinced that something was terribly wrong.

As he approached the stand of oaks near the canal, a familiar middle-aged man, small and bespectacled and wrapped in a greatcoat more suited to the dead of winter than a chilly September morning, broke off his conversation with one of the constables and walked forward to meet him.

"Sir Henry," said Sebastian. "Thank you for sending me word."

"Sorry news, I'm afraid," said Sir Henry Lovejoy. Once of Queen Square's public office, Sir Henry was the newest of Bow Street's three stipendiary magistrates, a man who undertook his responsibilities with a seriousness born of his own personal tragedies and a dour religious outlook. He and Sebastian might be unlikely friends, but friends they were.

Sebastian gazed beyond the magistrate, to where the lifeless body of a tall, dark-haired man in his early thirties lay curled on its side next to a rustic bench. "What happened to him?"

"Unfortunately, that's not readily apparent," said Lovejoy as they walked toward the body. "There are no discernable signs of violence. He was found lying much as you see him. It's as if he sat down to rest and then collapsed. I understand he has been ill for some time?"

Sebastian nodded. "Walcheren fever. He fought it as long as he could, but in the end he was invalided out of the service."

The magistrate tut-tutted softly. "Ah, yes; terrible business, that. Terrible." The 1809 assault on the Dutch island of Walcheren was the kind of military debacle most Englishmen tried to forget. The largest British expeditionary force ever assembled up to that time had embarked with the ambitious aim of taking first Flushing and then Antwerp, in preparation for a march on Paris. Instead, they'd been forced to withdraw from the island after only a few months, in the grip of a medical disaster. In the end, more than a quarter of the forty thousand men involved succumbed to a mysterious disease from which few ever recovered.

Sebastian hunkered down beside his friend's body. The two men had met nearly ten years before as subalterns, when Sebastian bought his first commission as a raw cornet and Wilkinson had just won promotion to the same rank. The son of a poor vicar who'd served with the common soldiers as a "gentleman volunteer" for three long years before a vacancy opened up, Wilkinson made no attempt to hide his good-humored scorn for the young Earl's heir, whose wealth enabled him to step straight into a rank Wilkinson himself had had to fight to earn. Sebastian won the older man's respect only slowly; friendship between them had taken even longer. But it had come.

Wilkinson still wore the proud swooping mustache of a cavalry officer. But his clothes were those of a gentleman down on his luck, the cuffs of his shirt neatly darned at the edges, his coat showing the effects of one too many brushings. Once, he'd been a strapping officer, tanned dark by the sun and full of life. But years of illness had wasted his once powerful body and left his skin sallow and sunken. Reaching out, Sebastian touched his friend's cheek, then brought his hand back to rest on his own thigh, fingers curled. "He's stone-cold. He must have been here all night."

"So it would seem. Hopefully Paul Gibson will be able to tell us for certain after the postmortem."

Like Sebastian and Wilkinson, Gibson had once worn the King's colors. A regimental surgeon, he'd honed his craft on the charnel-house battlefields of Europe. No one was better at ferreting out the secrets a dead body might have to tell—which was why Gibson was the last person Sebastian wanted examining this body.

He swiped one hand across his beard-roughened face. "Is that necessary? I mean, if he died of the fever . . ."

Lovejoy looked vaguely surprised. Normally, Sebastian was a vocal proponent of the still relatively new and highly controversial practice of autopsying the bodies of victims of murder or suspicious death. "Still best to be certain—wouldn't you say, my lord? Although I don't doubt you're right. From the looks of things, he sat down on the bench to rest and suffered a seizure of some sort. Poor man. One wonders what possessed him to push himself by walking so far. And at night, after the park was closed."

Sebastian was afraid he knew only too well why Wilkinson had chosen to lose himself in the farthest reaches of the park, after hours. But he felt no need to share that fear with Lovejoy.

He pushed to his feet. "How's his wife taking it?"

Lovejoy cleared his throat uncomfortably. "Badly, I'm afraid. I understand he also leaves a child?"

"Emma. She's only just turned four."

"Tragic."

"Yes." Sebastian was suddenly aware of an intense exhaustion combined with an urgent need to hold his own wife in his arms and simply bury his face in the soft fragrance of her dark hair. He was a man who had been married less than six weeks, and he'd just spent the entire night away from his wife's bed.

Nodding to the magistrate, he turned toward his waiting curricle. The larks in the nearby elms were in full throat, the light strengthening, the mist beginning to lift. But as he crossed the meadow, he noticed a familiar figure walking toward him with a dark top hat and greatcoat glistening from the morning dew.

Tall and barrel-chested, with a big head and blunt features, Alistair St. Cyr, Fifth Earl of Hendon and Chancellor of the Exchequer, was in his late sixties now. Once, Hendon had boasted of three strong sons. Then death had taken the eldest, Richard, and the middle son, Cecil, leaving Hendon with only the youngest, Sebastian—the son who was least like the Earl and who had always seemed to confuse and dismay him.

The son who was not, in fact, Hendon's child, although that was a truth only lately and disastrously revealed.

Sebastian was still the Earl's heir and, as far as the world knew, his son. The few who knew otherwise had their own reasons for keeping quiet. But since the truth's painful revelations that May, Sebastian and Hendon had publicly exchanged only the most formal and brief of greetings. In private, they had not spoken at all. For Hendon to seek Sebastian out now could only mean trouble. Sebastian's thoughts flew, inevitably, to his new wife and the child she carried within her.

"What is it? What's wrong?" he demanded without preamble as the men came up to each other.

Hendon swiped one meaty palm across his lower face, and Sebastian realized with shock that, like Sebastian, the Earl had yet to shave that morning. "I take it you haven't heard the news?"

"What news?"

"Russell Yates has been committed to Newgate to stand trial for murder."

Sebastian exhaled a long breath and stared out over

the nearby, breeze-ruffled treetops. He had only a passing acquaintance with Yates, a flamboyant and somewhat enigmatic ex-privateer who'd taken London society by storm. But Yates's wife . . .

The beautiful, talented, vital woman who was Yates's wife had once been the love of Sebastian's life—until he lost her to Hendon's twisted trail of lies and half-truths and soul-shattering revelations.

"Murder?" said Sebastian. "Of whom?"

"A diamond merchant by the name of Daniel Eisler."

"Never heard of him."

Hendon shifted his lower jaw from side to side in that way he had when considering a problem or when dealing with something or someone who violated his carefully drawn moral codes. "In that, you are fortunate. The man was vile."

"Have you seen Kat?"

Hendon nodded. "She came to me at once, hoping that I could somehow use my influence to intervene. But this is beyond me, I'm afraid." He paused, as if considering his next words carefully. "I've never claimed to understand this marriage of hers to Yates. But I do know she has become exceedingly close to the man this past year. She's . . . worried."

"Kat?" Kat Boleyn was not a woman who frightened easily.

Hendon said, "I realize that in the past I have been critical—perhaps even dismissive—of your obsession with murder and justice. All of which makes it rather hypocritical of me to be asking for your help in this now. But from what I've been able to discover, the case against Yates is strong. There'll be a coroner's inquest sometime this week, but there's no doubt but what they'll support the magistrate's findings."

"Are you certain he didn't actually do it?"

"Kat insists he is innocent. Although from the looks of things, the only hope he has of escaping the hangman's noose is if you can somehow manage to figure out who the real killer is." Hendon cleared his throat uncomfortably, his voice tense. "Will you do it?"

"I'd do anything for Kat. You know that."

For Kat. Not for you. The unsaid words hung in the air between them.

Hendon's vivid blue eyes blinked. St. Cyr eyes, they called them, for they had been the hallmark of the family for generations. Kat had eyes like that.

Sebastian's own eyes were a strange, feral-like yellow.

Hendon said, "I must make it clear that she did not want me to ask you to do this."

"Why the hell not?"

"You know why."

Sebastian met the Earl's frank gaze. He knew it wasn't simply Sebastian's own recent marriage that had given Kat pause; it was a matter of whom he had married.

And it troubled him profoundly to realize that the woman he'd loved for most of his adult life had felt she couldn't come to him when she needed him the most.

Chapter 4

$\mathcal{R}$ussell Yates was one of those rare men who defied both the expectations and the conventions of his world and yet somehow still managed to prosper.

He had been born to a life of ease and luxury, the son of an East Anglian nobleman. But one frosted, wretched night in the winter of his fourteenth year, Yates stole from his father's high-walled, sprawling home and ran away to sea. When asked the reason for such a bold but undeniably rash impulse, Yates typically laughed and cautioned his listeners against the dangers of allowing impressionable young lads to read too many stirring tales of high adventure. But Sebastian had long suspected that the true reasons were much darker and could at times be glimpsed lurking behind the laughter in the man's mocking hazel eyes, like the shadowy ghosts of childhood's worst nightmares.

No one knew all that had occurred during the man's years at sea. There were whispered tales of shipwrecks and pirates and daggers stained with the blood of both innocent and evil men. All that could be said with certainty was that Yates had risen from his precarious beginnings as a cabin boy to become captain of a privateer that terrorized the shipping of England's enemies from the Spanish Main to the East Indies. By the time he returned to take his place in London society, he was a wealthy man.

He bought a grand house in Mayfair and quickly set about scandalizing the more sanctimonious members of the ton. Broad shouldered and sun bronzed, his dark hair worn too long and with the wink of pirate's gold in his left ear, Yates moved through London society like a sleek tiger on the prowl at a garden party. His well-muscled body kept toned and hard by regular workouts at Jackson's Boxing Salon and Angelo's fencing parlor, Yates exuded unabashed virility and an aggressive masculinity in a way that was rare amongst the sophisticated, mannered men of the ton. The high sticklers would always look askance at him, but London's most popular hostesses loved him. He was wellborn but deliciously unique, endlessly amusing—and very, very rich.

Yet Sebastian sometimes found himself wondering what had brought Yates back to London after so many years. There was a coiled restlessness about the man, a recklessness born of a mingling of boredom and despair that Sebastian both recognized and understood. Was it boredom or an urge to self-destruction that drove Yates to risk everything for the transient, meaningless thrill of running rum and the odd French agent beneath the noses of His Majesty's Navy? Sebastian could never decide. But whatever Yates's reasons for dabbling in smuggling and espionage, his most dangerous activities were actually those of the boudoir. For the truth was that London's most virile, most ostentatious Corinthian preferred the sexual pleasures to be found with those of his own gender.

It was an inclination more dangerous than smuggling, viewed by society and the law as a crime on par with treason. For in an age given over to vice and excess, love of one's own kind remained the ultimate unforgivable sin, punishable by a hideous death.

It was his fear of that death—a fear increased by the enmity of the King's powerful cousin, Lord Jarvis—that had driven Yates into a marriage of convenience with the most beautiful, the most desirable, the most sought-after actress of the London stage: Kat Boleyn, the woman Sebastian had loved, and lost.

※

Yates's prison cell was small and stone-cold, the air thick with the pervasive stench of effluvia and rot. A tumult of raucous voices and laughter rose from the crowded yard below the room's small barred window, but Yates himself sat silently on the edge of his narrow cot, elbows propped on splayed knees, bowed head clutched in his hands. He didn't look up when, keys rattling, the turnkey pushed open the thick door.

"Jist bang on the door when ye need me, yer lordship," said the turnkey with a sniff.

Sebastian slipped the man a coin. "Thank you."

Yates lifted his head, his fingers raking through his long dark hair to link behind his neck. A day's growth of beard shadowed the man's dark, handsome face; his coat was torn, his cravat gone, his breeches and shirt smeared with blood and dirt. Yates obviously hadn't come here without a struggle.

"So have you come to gloat too?" he said, his voice rough.

"Actually, I'm here to help."

An indecipherable expression flitted across the man's face before being carefully hidden away. "Did Kat ask you—"

Sebastian shook his head. "I haven't seen her yet." He pulled forward the room's sole chair, a straight-backed spindly thing that swayed ominously when it took his weight. "Tell me what happened."

Yates gave a bitter laugh. "You're married to the daughter of my worst enemy. Give me one good reason why I should trust you."

Sebastian shrugged and pushed to his feet. "Suit yourself. Although I will point out that Jarvis happens to be

my worst enemy too. And from what I'm hearing, the
way things stand now, I'm the only chance you have."

For a long moment, Yates held his gaze. Then he blew
out a painful breath and brought up a hand to shade his
eyes. "Sit down. Please."

Sebastian sat. "They tell me you were found bending
over Eisler's body. Is that true?"

"It is. But I swear to God, he was dead when I found
him." He scrubbed his hands down over his face. "How
much do you know about Daniel Eisler?"

"Not a bloody thing."

"He is—or I suppose I should say, he was one of the
biggest diamond merchants in London. Prinny did business with him, as did most of the royal dukes. I've heard
it said he even sold Napoléon the diamond necklace he
presented to the Empress Marie Louise as a wedding
present."

"So he still traded with the French?"

"Of course he did. They all do, you know. The Conti-
nental System and the Orders in Council are inconve-
niences, but nothing more." Yates summoned up a ghost
of a smile. "That's why God invented smugglers."

"Which is where you come in, I presume?"

Yates nodded. "Most of Eisler's diamonds came from
Brazil, through a special arrangement he had with the
Portuguese. But he also had agents buying up gems
across Europe. A lot of once-wealthy people there are
facing ruin, which means they're looking to raise money
any way they can."

"Selling the family jewels being one of those ways?"

"Yes."

Sebastian studied the other man's tired, strained face.
"So what happened last night?"

"I went to Eisler's house to finalize the details of an
upcoming transaction. I'd just knocked on the door
when I heard the sound of a pistol shot from inside the
house. The door was off the latch, so I pushed it open
and like a bloody fool went rushing in."

"Why?"

"What do you mean, *why*?"

"Why put yourself at risk of being shot too?"

Yates stared back at him, his eyes narrowed, the muscles along his jaw working. "If you were standing on the steps of a business acquaintance's house and heard the sound of a shot from inside, would you run away?"

Sebastian smiled. "No."

"Exactly."

"Where were Eisler's servants while all this was going on?"

"The man was a bloody miser. He lived in a decrepit old Tudor house that was falling down around his ears and retained only an ancient couple who tottered off to bed every night after dinner. Campbell, I think their name is. As far as I know, they slept through the whole thing. I sure as hell never saw them."

"What time did this happen?"

"About half past eight."

"So it was dark?"

"It was, yes. He'd left one measly candlestick burning on a table in the entry, but I could see more light coming from the parlor just to the right of the stairs. That's where I found him, sprawled some eight or ten feet inside the room. His chest was a bloody mess, but I went to see if by some chance he still lived. I was just leaning over him when a man came barreling in behind me and started screeching, 'What have you done? Good God, you've killed him!' I said, 'What the devil are you talking about? I found him like this.' But the bloody idiot was already rushing off yelling 'murder' and calling loudly for the watch. So then I did the second stupid thing of the evening: Rather than stick around to explain myself to the constables, I ran. I didn't realize the bastard knew who I was."

"And who was he?"

"Turns out he's Eisler's nephew—a man by the name of Samuel Perlman."

Sebastian went to stare thoughtfully out the small, high window.

After a moment, Yates said, "It doesn't look good, does it?"

Sebastian glanced back at him. "To be frank? No, it doesn't. Can you think of anyone who might have had reason to kill Eisler?"

Yates laughed. "Are you serious? You'd be hard-pressed to find anyone who ever did business with Eisler and *didn't* want to kill the bastard. He was a mean, nasty son of a bitch who enjoyed taking advantage of other people's misfortune. Frankly, it's amazing the man managed to live as long as he did—and I suspect that was only because people were afraid of him."

"Afraid of him? Why?"

Yates twitched one shoulder in a shrug and glanced away. "He had a bad reputation for being vindictive. I told you: He was an ugly bastard."

"And did you have a reason to want to kill him?"

Yates was silent a moment, worrying his lower lip between his teeth. Then he turned his head to look straight at Sebastian. And Sebastian knew even before the man opened his mouth that he was lying. "No. No, I didn't."

Chapter 5

Sebastian studied Yates's strained, beard-shadowed face. "You know, unless you've a hankering to dance the hempen measure to the toll of St. Sepulchre's bell, you're going to need to be honest with me."

Yates's jaw hardened. "I told you: I'd no reason to kill the bastard. I didn't like him, but if we all took to killing people we don't particularly fancy, London would soon be mighty thin of company."

Sebastian pushed away from the window and went to signal the turnkey. "If you think of anything useful, let me know."

Yates stopped him by saying, "Why are you doing this?"

Sebastian paused to look back at him. "You know why."

The two men's gazes met and held. Then Yates looked away, and Sebastian knew a moment of deep disquiet.

Sebastian said, "Any chance Jarvis could be behind this?"

Sebastian might not know the cause of the animosity between the two men, but he knew it ran deep and deadly. Thus far, Yates had managed to survive the enmity of the King's powerful cousin only because he had in his possession evidence that would destroy Jarvis if it ever came to light. What that evidence was, Sebastian had never discovered. But because of it, the two men lived in an uneasy state of check, neither able to make a move to destroy the other without destroying himself.

It was a situation that Sebastian suspected could not persist indefinitely. And although it troubled him to admit it, if Sebastian were a betting man, he would put his money on Jarvis.

Yates said, "The last thing Jarvis wants is to see me hanged. He knows the consequences."

"So I would have thought. In which case the question then becomes, why isn't he doing something to prevent it?" If anyone had the power to see the charges against Yates dropped, it was the King's Machiavellian cousin.

But Yates only shook his head and shrugged, as if the answer escaped him.

⁂

Pushing his way back through the prison's crowded Press Yard and labyrinth of corridors, Sebastian found he had to close his mind to the sea of pale, desperate faces, to the endless, plaintive chorus of, "Have pity on poor little Jack!" and "Gov'nor, can ye spare a farthing? Only a farthing!"

Once, just twenty months before, he had found himself in much the same desperate position as Russell Yates. Accused of murder, he'd chosen the life of a fugitive in a desperate attempt to catch a twisted killer and clear his own name. Sebastian knew only too well how British "justice" worked.

Yates's chances of being declared innocent were slim.

The heavy, ironbound main door of the prison slammed shut behind him, and Sebastian paused on the pavement outside to suck a breath of clean air deep into his lungs. All the turmoil of the street known as the Old Bailey swirled around him: Axles creaked as wagon drivers cursed and whipped their teams; a pie man shouted, *"Fresh and hot. Hot! Hot!"* The scent of ale wafted from a nearby tavern. And still the smell of the prison seemed to cling to him, a foul, oily stench of decay, hopelessness, and looming death.

The relentless pounding of hammers drew his attention to the spot outside the Debtors' Door where a crew of workmen were knocking together the scaffold and viewing platform that would be used for the execution of two highwaymen scheduled for tomorrow morning. Until recently, London had hung her condemned prisoners at Tyburn, to the west of the city, with the doomed men, women, and children drawn through the streets in open carts surrounded by a raucous, drunken mob. But as the fields around Hyde Park filled with the elegant homes of the wealthy, Mayfair's aristocratic inhabitants took exception to that endless, malodorous parade. And so the exhibition was shifted here, to the street outside Newgate Prison. Sebastian had heard that when a notorious murderer — or a woman — was hanged, choice viewing spots at the windows of the surrounding buildings could rent for as much as two or three guineas.

Someone with Russell Yates's colorful background could easily attract a crowd of twenty thousand or more.

Sebastian became aware of Tom sitting motionless on the curricle's high seat, his solemn gaze on a workman who was climbing up on the platform to lever into place a stout beam studded with massive iron hooks. Tom's own brother had been hanged here for theft at the age of just thirteen.

It had been Sebastian's intention to drive to St. Botolph-Aldgate and take a look at the scene of Mr. Daniel Eisler's murder. But he was suddenly aware of a profound exhaustion he saw mirrored in his tiger's face, of his rumpled clothing and day's growth of beard, and of the need to offer his condolences to the grieving widow of an old friend.

He ran a hand down the nearest chestnut's sweat-darkened neck and told Tom, "Go home, see the chestnuts put up, and then take the day off to rest."

Tom's face fell. "Ne'er tell me ye'll be takin' a *hack-*

ney?" That peerless arbiter of taste and deportment, Beau Brummell himself, had decreed that no gentleman should ever be seen riding in a hackney carriage, and Tom had taken the Beau's strictures to heart.

"I am indeed. To drive this pair back out to Kensington again, after all they've been through, would be beyond cruel."

"Aye, but . . . *gov'nor*. A hackney?"

Sebastian laughed and turned away.

✢

Sebastian had known Annie Wilkinson for as long as he'd known Rhys—except that when he'd first met her, she'd been Annie Beaumont, the plucky, freckle-nosed, seventeen-year-old wife of a dashing cavalry captain named Jake Beaumont. Few officers' wives chose to "follow the drum" with their husbands, for the life could be both brutal and deadly. But Annie, the daughter of a colonel, had grown up in army camps from India to Canada. She took the hardships and dangers of a campaign in stride, without ever losing her ready laugh or cheerful disposition. He remembered once, in Italy, when a brigand caught her in the hills outside of camp and she coolly shot her would-be assailant in the face. When her first husband died from a saber wound complicated by sepsis, she married again, to a big, rawboned Scotsman who succumbed to yellow fever in the West Indies just months after their wedding.

Rhys Wilkinson might have been Annie's third husband, but Sebastian had never doubted the strength of her love for the easygoing Welshman. And of her three husbands, only Wilkinson had succeeded in giving Annie a child. Now, as Sebastian mounted the steps to the couple's cramped lodgings in a narrow street called Yeoman's Row, just off Kensington Square, he found himself wondering if that made this husband's death easier or harder for Annie to bear.

He had intended only to send up his card along with

a note of condolence. But he was met at the door by a breathless, half-grown housemaid who dropped a quick curtsy and said, "Lord Devlin? Mrs. Wilkinson says to tell you she'd be most pleased to see you, if'n you was wantin' to step upstairs?"

And so he found himself following the housemaid up the bare, narrow set of stairs that led to the shabby apartment to which Rhys Wilkinson's continued illness had reduced his young family.

"Devlin," said Annie Wilkinson, both hands extended as she came forward to greet him. "I was hoping you'd come. I wanted to thank you again for trying to—for looking—" Her voice cracked.

"Annie. I'm so sorry." He took her hands in his, his gaze hard on her face. The freckles were still there, although faded to a sprinkling of cinnamon dust across the pale flesh of her high cheekbones and the thin arch of her nose. As a girl, she'd been awkward and almost funny-looking, all skinny arms and legs and a wide, toothy grin. But she'd grown into a delicate beauty, her form tall and willowy, her features unusual but exquisite, her hair a rich strawberry blond. "Tell me what you need me to do," he said, "and I'll do it."

He felt her hands tremble in his. "Sit and just talk to me, will you? Most of my acquaintances seem to assume that I've either dosed myself senseless with laudanum, or that since this is my third experience with widowhood, then I must be taking it comfortably in stride. I can't decide which is most insulting."

She led him to a sagging, aged sofa near where a curly-headed little girl was playing with a scattering of toy horses. "Come and make your curtsy to his lordship, Emma," she told the child.

Pushing to her feet, the little girl carefully positioned one foot behind the other and bobbed up and down with a mischievous giggle. She was tall for her age, and skinny like her mother, with her father's dark hair and gray eyes, and a roguish dimple that was all her own.

"Hello there," said Sebastian, hunkering down beside her. "Remember me?"

Emma nodded her head vigorously. "You gave me my *Aes-hop's Fables*," she said, stumbling over the pronunciation of the name. "Daddy tells me a story every night." A faint frown tugged at her gently arched eyebrows. "Only, he didn't come home in time last night."

Sebastian glanced up at Annie's stricken face. He had brought the child the book some months before, when Rhys invited him to dinner one evening. "I could read you a story now," he said, "if you'd like."

"That's all right," said Emma with a wide smile that was more like Annie's than that of her dead father. "But thank you." She dropped another curtsy and went back to her horses.

Sebastian rose slowly.

Annie said, "I told her, but I don't think she really grasps what has happened. How much of death do we understand at the age of four?" Her voice quavered again, and Sebastian reached out to recapture one of her hands.

They sat for a time in silence, their gazes on the child, who was now whispering, "Clippity-cloppity, clippity-cloppity," as she pushed a small bronze toy horse mounted on wheels along the pattern of the threadbare carpet. Then Annie said, her voice low, "Did he kill himself, Devlin? Tell me honestly. I wouldn't blame him if he did—he's been so dreadfully unwell. I don't know how he stood it so long."

Sebastian knew a moment of deep disquiet. It was one thing to harbor such suspicions himself, and something else again to hear them voiced by Wilkinson's own wife. "I didn't see anything to suggest it, but it's impossible at this stage to tell."

Her freckles stood out, stark, against the pallor of her face. "There'll be a postmortem?"

"Gibson is doing it. I can stop by his surgery and let you know what he's found, if you like."

Nodding, she swallowed hard before answering. "Yes. Please. I'd like to hear it from you . . . if it's true."

"Annie . . ." He hesitated a moment, then pressed on. "I know things have been hard for you, since Wilkinson was invalided out. I wish you'd let me—"

"No," she said forcefully, cutting him off. "Thank you, but no. I've a grandmother in Norfolk who offered years ago to take me in, should I ever find myself homeless. When this is all over, Emma and I will go to her."

He studied her tightly held face. "All right. But promise me that should you ever find yourself in need, you'll let me know."

"I'll be fine, Devlin; don't worry."

He stayed talking to her for some time, of happier days with the regiment in Italy and the Peninsula. But when he was leaving, he touched his fingertips gently to her cheek and said, "You didn't promise me, Annie."

She crinkled her nose in a way that reminded him of the near child she'd been when they first met. "I'll be fine, Devlin. Truly. "

He forbore to press her further. Yet as he hailed a hackney and headed toward home, he could not shake the conviction that he was somehow failing both her and his dead friend.

Chapter 6

Sebastian lived in a bow-fronted town house on Brook Street, near the corner of Davies. The house was elegant but small. Once, it had suited him just fine. But since his marriage six weeks before to Miss Hero Jarvis, he'd been thinking he ought perhaps to consider moving to something larger, grander. Only, when he'd mentioned it to Hero, she'd simply looked at him steadily in that way she had and said, "I like our house."

He found her now seated sideways at the bench before her dressing table. She wore a very fetching emerald green walking dress trimmed with navy braid and had her head bowed as she worked at closing the fastenings of a smart pair of navy half boots. He paused for a moment, one shoulder propped against the doorframe, and watched her. Just for the pleasure of it.

She was a woman in her twenty-sixth year, generally described as more handsome than pretty and taller than most people thought a woman ought to be. She had inherited her aquiline profile, fierce intelligence, and a certain chilling ruthlessness from her powerful father, Charles, Lord Jarvis. But her Enlightenment-inspired beliefs—and her conviction that with affluence and privilege came an obligation to fight for the rights of society's underdogs—were unique to her.

Sebastian hadn't liked Hero much when they first

met. Since he'd been holding a gun to her head at the time, he suspected the antipathy had been mutual. Respect had come gradually, even grudgingly; the intense physical attraction that accompanied it had surprised—and dismayed—them both.

Their marriage was as complicated as the reasons that had brought it about, and they were still working their way toward understanding and something else, something deep and powerful that both beckoned and scared the hell out of him. Passion came easily; trust and openness took time and effort and a leap of faith he wasn't certain either of them was yet ready to make. There was still so much she didn't know about him, or he about her. And it occurred to him now that he was about to jeopardize all that they had so far managed to build between them by what he was about to do.

Just as he knew he had no real choice.

She looked up, caught him watching her, and smiled. "It's a nasty habit you have," she said, "sneaking around, spying on people."

"I wasn't sneaking. I made quite a bit of noise, actually."

She let out a genteel huff. "We don't all have the eyes and ears of a bird of prey." Still smiling, she rose to her feet and came to rest her hands on his shoulders, her gaze on his face. Her smile faded, and it occurred to him that perhaps she knew him better than he thought she did, because she said, "Your friend is dead, isn't he?"

"A keeper found the body this morning in Hyde Park."

"Oh, Devlin; I'm so sorry."

He bracketed her face with his palms and kissed her once, long and hard. Then he rested his forehead against hers and took a deep breath before letting her go. "More interviews today?" he asked lightly.

She nodded, turning away to tuck a small clothbound notebook into her reticule. "I've found another crossing sweep who's agreed to talk to me."

"I should think they'd all be eager to talk, given that you pay them handsomely for nothing more than the

privilege of listening to them natter on about themselves."

"You'd be surprised how many of these children are
afraid to open up," she said, hunting for something
amidst the litter of hair clips and books on her dressing
table. "And I don't blame them. From what I'm hearing,
their distrust of authority figures is more than justified."

Sebastian found himself smiling. After working on
everything from Catholic emancipation and the slave
trade to labor laws and the economic causes of the current proliferation in the number of prostitutes in London, Hero was now writing an article on the poor
children who eked out a meager living by sweeping London's street crossings. She was so taken with the project
that she was thinking about doing a collection of such
articles to be gathered into a book entitled *London's
Working Poor*.

"Ah, here it is," she said, coming up with a pencil. She
straightened, caught him smiling, and said, "You're
laughing at me."

"Yes. But that doesn't mean I don't admire what you do."

She poked the pencil into her reticule and reached for
her gloves. "My father, needless to say, is scandalized.
I'm not certain which concerns him more: the possibility
that I might contract some dread disease from one of the
wretches or the lowering suspicion that I'm turning into
a maudlin lady bountiful."

"Surely he knows you better than that."

She gave a soft chuckle. "He should by now. I'm far
too much his daughter to ever take to ladling out soup or
teaching Sunday school." She looked up from pulling on
her gloves, and whatever she saw on his face stilled her
amusement. She said, "There's something more, isn't
there? Something besides Rhys Wilkinson's death."

He nodded. "Have you seen this morning's papers?"

"Not yet. Why? What has happened?"

"Russell Yates has been arrested for the murder of an
Aldgate diamond merchant."

She kept her features carefully composed. She was very good at hiding what she was thinking. "And did he do it?"

"He says he didn't. I believe him."

"Can you prove it?"

"I don't know. All I know is, if I don't, he'll hang."

She reached for her hat and turned away, her attention all for her reflection in the mirror as she settled the velvet-trimmed confection on her head. Like most of London society, Hero knew only too well that the woman who was now Yates's wife had once been Sebastian's mistress. She knew, too, that something had happened between them the previous autumn, something that ended in Kat Boleyn's marriage to Yates and sent Sebastian into a brandy-soaked downward spiral from which he had with difficulty only recently emerged. But that was all she knew, and he wasn't sure he was ready to tell her the rest.

He said, "This is something I must do."

He watched while she positioned her hat just so, then pivoted slowly to face him again. "Are you concerned that I might object? Pitch a fit and take to sulking in my room in a jealous pique?"

He gave a rueful laugh. "No. But—"

"You told me just now that you admire my work. Do you think I don't admire what you do? Do you imagine I'm the kind of woman who would begrudge your efforts to save a man's life simply because you share a past with that man's wife?"

He shook his head. Reaching out, he cupped his hand beneath her chin, tipped his head to brush her lips with his. "You're a wonder to me, Lady Devlin," he said, his breath mingling with hers.

She smiled. But he saw the shadow in her fine gray eyes, and he knew that while she could never begrudge him what he was about to do, that didn't mean the situation didn't worry her.

Just as it worried him.

Chapter 7

The boy looked to be eight or nine years old at most, his face round, with widespread eyes and a short upper lip, his sandy hair as dirty and matted as moldy hay.

He sat on the bottom step of the Church of St. Giles, a cheap, ragged broom clutched in one fist, his head tipped back as he peered up at Hero. He wore tattered corduroy trousers and a threadbare man's coat so big its tails hung down to his ankles and he'd had to roll up the sleeves like a washerwoman. His hands, like his feet, were bare, and every inch of visible skin so grimy as to resemble aged oak in hue. But his light brown eyes were bright and lively, his features mobile and expressive as he let his gaze take in the glory of Hero's braid-trimmed gown and plumed, broad-brimmed velvet hat.

"Are you really a viscountess?" he asked, lisping slightly.

"I am, yes." Hero nodded to the elegant equipage drawn up at the kerb beside them. "See my carriage?"

The urchin—who said his name was Drummer—stared at the shiny, yellow-bodied carriage with its team of restless, highbred blacks, its liveried coachman and footman waiting impassively. "And ye want to talk to *me*?" said the boy on a rapt exhalation of breath.

"I do, yes. I want to know how long you've been working as a crossing sweep."

The lad screwed up his features with the effort of thought. There were thousands of poor boys and girls like him across London—children who made their living by sweeping the mud and manure from the city's street crossings. In a sense, it was a form of begging, although the children did perform a service. Since they staked out a site and worked the same location for years, the trustworthy ones soon became known in a neighborhood and could also earn extra money by running errands, holding horses, or carrying packages for the area's inhabitants.

"Well," he said, "I started at it right after me da died, the winter I turned ten. I'm twelve now, so it's been more'n two years, I guess."

Hero made a surreptitious adjustment to the notes she was taking in her notebook. "And is your mother still living?"

"No, m'lady. She died o' the flux just six months after me da. He used to be a bricklayer, ye know. But he fell off a scaffold and broke his leg so bad he died from it. At first I tried tatting hair nets, like me mum used to do. But I weren't no good at it. Then I seen other children getting money for sweeping the crossings, so I bought meself a broom and took it up. I usually work this corner with another boy named Jack, but he ain't been well lately."

"Where do you live?"

"Usually I takes a room with some other lads in a lodging house up the lane there. But it's thruppence a night, and with winter comin' soon, I'm saving me money so's I can buy me a pair o' boots."

"So where are you sleeping now?"

"Here, m'lady. If I rolls up in a tight ball in the shadows by the door, the charlie don't usually see me. And even if he does rouse me, I just come back once he's gone."

Hero refused to let herself think about the fear, loneliness, and hunger that must haunt this child as he curled up for the night on the cold stone steps. Yet she found she still had to clear her throat before she could ask, "And how much do you earn, on average, with your sweeping?"

The boy looked confused. "On average?"

"How much do you usually make a day?"

"Yesterday I only took in tuppence ha'penny, it was so dry. Dry days is always the worst. We likes it when it rains— particul'rly a hard wettin' what makes lots o' mud but then clears up, so that folks come out again. On a good day, I can make as much as tenpence. But the brooms wear out faster when it's muddy. A broom costs tuppence ha'penny, and it'll only last four or five days in wet weather, where's I can get a fortnight out o' one if things is dry."

Hero glanced down at the boy's broom, which was basically a bundle of twigs lashed to a stout stick. He might lack an understanding of the concept of averaging, but he obviously had a solid grasp of the economics of his business—and the forethought to forgo lodgings on an autumn night in order to save for the boots he knew he'd be needing in the coming winter.

"What hours do you normally work?"

"The take is best here between nine and seven, al-though I know some lads what work Mayfair, and they don't usually start till noon or even one, when the nobs come out. I wish I could get in with them," Drummer added wistfully. "They can take as much as a shilling a day, only their spots is all full up right now. But I goes with them at night to the opera and tumbles."

"You tumble?"

"Aye. We do cat'un-wheels and flips, and the gentlemen comin' out o' the opera'll laugh and give us a few pence, especially if they've a girl on their arm. There's one boy by the name o' Louis who gets e'en more tin give him, on ac-count of he can do backflips. Me, I ain't so good even at the cat'un-wheels. I get giddy after jist two or three."

"So you don't go to sleep until after the opera lets out?"

"Oh, no, m'lady. Then we goes to the Haymarket— 'cept on Sundays, when we goes there earlier."

"What do you do there?" Hero asked. An ancient thoroughfare running from Piccadilly to Pall Mall, the Haymarket was crowded with theaters, hotels, supper houses—and prostitutes.

"Well, sometimes a gentleman'll drive up in a carriage and tell us to bring him a girl. We can get as much as five or sixpence for that. If the gentleman is dressed nice, we'll fetch him a real pretty girl."

Hero stared at the guileless young pimp before her in horrified fascination. "And if he's not 'dressed nice'?"

The boy grinned. "Well, then we'll fetch him one o' the girls what ain't so young and pretty. But sometimes, we gives the best chances to girls what've been kind to us. Sometimes a girl'll go by and we'll shout out, 'Good luck to you!' and she'll give us a copper."

"These girls whom you, um"—Hero hesitated, searching for an appropriate word—"supply," she said finally, "do you find them walking in the street?"

"Sometimes. But if we don't find any girls walking, we know what lodging houses to go to, to get 'em. And the next day, they'll usually give us a copper or two, by way o' thanks."

"So at what time do you finally quit working?"

"We all meets at three o'clock, on the steps o' St. Anne's, and reckon up what we've taken."

Good heavens, thought Hero; the child worked from nine in the morning to three the next day. She said, "And then you come here to sleep?"

"Aye. Although I gots to move when the sun comes up." The fatigue that shadowed the boy's eyes and sagged his jaw was obvious. "I'll be glad when I saves up enough to buy them boots. Last night was nippy."

Hero pressed a coin into the sweeper's palm and closed his fist around it. "Here's a guinea for you, my little man. Thank you for agreeing to talk to me."

Then she turned and walked rapidly back to her carriage, before she was tempted to empty her purse into his thin, grubby hands.

Chapter 8

Squashed between a grimy brick warehouse and a chandler's shop, the dilapidated home of Daniel Eisler lay on a narrow, crooked street called Fountain Lane, just off the Minories. Built of dressed sandstone blocks darkened and crumbling with age, the house looked as if it might once have been surrounded by extensive gardens. Now rampant ivy covered its gabled end, while rusty iron bars disfigured the mullioned windows.

St. Botolph-Aldgate was a long, narrow parish that stretched all the way from the Thames up to Aldgate High Street, so that it actually straddled the boundary between the City of London and Middlesex. Dominated by the vast presence of the East India Company, it was mainly given over to gunsmiths and the various maritime trades, especially slaughterhouses and breweries. And here, in the narrow lanes off the Minories, had settled a number of refugees from the Netherlands and the various German states.

Pausing on the flagway opposite the old house, Sebastian let his gaze travel over the sagging eaves, the dusty broken glass of an attic window. He was close enough to the river that he could smell the scent of tar and brine and dead fish, hear the dull roar from the seamen and dockworkers who crowded the taverns and ale shops along Whitechapel to the east. But here, the cobbled street was quiet, with many of the old shops and houses being replaced by warehouses. At eight or nine in the evening—the time of Eisler's death—the lane would probably have been deserted.

A man pushing a cart piled high with scrap iron cast him a curious look but kept going. Stepping wide to avoid a gutter clogged with sodden refuse, Sebastian crossed the street to rap sharply on the house's worn but stout front door. He had to bang the knocker twice more before the door swung inward less than a foot, then stopped.

An old man's pale, gaunt face appeared in the crack. Thin tufts of soft gray hair stuck out at odd angles from a narrow, bony head; his cheeks were sunken, his skin yellow and wrinkled with age, his black butler's coat rusty and threadbare and too large for his shrunken frame. He blinked several times, as if disconcerted by the overcast day's flat white light. "If you are looking for Mr. Eisler," he said in a thin, quavering voice, "I regret to inform you that he is not at home. In point of fact, he is dead."

He made as if to shut the door.

Sebastian deftly inserted one boot in the opening, stopping him. "Actually, you're the one to whom I wished to speak. I take it you're Mr. Eisler's butler—Campbell, isn't it?"

The aged retainer dropped his gaze to Sebastian's foot, then looked up again. "You're not from Bow Street, are you? Because Mr. Leigh-Jones said we wasn't to speak to anyone from Bow Street."

"Mr. Leigh-Jones?"

"The chief magistrate at Lambeth Street. Called us all down to the public office as witnesses, he did, late last night when he committed that Yates fellow to Newgate to stand trial for murder. Mr. Leigh-Jones warned us most particularly not to go blabbing to anyone from Bow Street."

Bow Street had been the first of the public offices

formed, and still retained an exalted position that gave it
authority over crimes and criminals not just in the metropolis but in all of England. It wasn't unusual for magistrates from the lesser public offices to resent the
prominence of Bow Street and seek to forestall any possible interference in their districts.

Sebastian said, "Do I look like a Bow Street runner?"

Campbell studied Sebastian's exquisitely tailored coat
and flawlessly tied cravat, his doeskin breeches and polished Hessians. "You don't, no. But you could be one of
those fellows from the newspaper offices. Mr. Leigh-
Jones also directed us most particularly not to be talking
to any of them either."

Sebastian extracted a card from his case and held it
out between two fingers. "I am Devlin. I trust Mr. Leigh-
Jones didn't direct you not to speak to me?"

The butler held Sebastian's card at arm's length and
squinted. "No. No, he did not." Not a single muscle in the
old man's face altered, but he opened the door wide and
executed a somewhat creaky bow. "How may I be of assistance to you, my lord?"

Sebastian stepped into a soaring, medieval-style hall
with darkly paneled walls, an uneven, badly cracked
flagged floor, and an elaborately coffered, smoke-
blackened ceiling. The space was vast, yet hopelessly cluttered with an odd assortment of dusty but exquisite
furniture: sandalwood consoles with delicate inlay; a dark
Renaissance chest carved with mythical beasts; gilded
chairs that looked as if they might have come from Versailles. Row after row of dark paintings in heavy, mildew-
flecked gilded frames filled virtually every wall surface,
while on the far side of the hall, a worn, steep staircase
angled toward the first floor. Through a limestone-cased
archway beside it, Sebastian could see a dark passage that
disappeared toward the rear of the house. A second arch,
also framed in chipped, grimy stone, led to what looked
like an old-fashioned parlor. The tattered brocade drapes
at the window were tightly drawn, but as Sebastian's eyes

adjusted to the gloom, he could easily make out the stain that disfigured the parlor's threadbare carpet.

"Mr. Eisler was found in there," said Campbell, nodding toward the parlor as he carefully closed and locked the front door behind him. "Took the shot square in his chest. Made ever such a mess."

"You were here last night, were you?"

"I was, my lord. Only, as I told Mr. Leigh-Jones, it is the practice of Mrs. Campbell and I to retire to our rooms by eight o'clock. The first we knew anything was amiss was when the constables came pounding on our door in the attic."

"So you didn't hear the shot?"

"No, my lord. My hearing's not what it used to be— nor Mrs. Campbell's."

Sebastian let his gaze drift, again, around the old hall, assessing the distance from the front door to the staircase and the passage beyond. If Yates had been standing on the stoop as he claimed when he heard the shot, and then rushed inside to find Eisler dead, would the killer have had time to escape the parlor and run down the shadowy passage—or up the stairs—without being seen?

Sebastian doubted it.

He said, "Is there a door that leads from this floor to the rear yard?"

"There is, yes. At the end of the passage there."

"May I see it?"

The butler gave another of his creaky bows. "If you will follow me, my lord?"

Moving with doddering slowness, he led the way down a narrow corridor made even narrower by more furniture lined up on either side. Sebastian counted four doors opening off the passage, plus a set of steep, narrow steps leading down to what he assumed was the basement kitchen. The entire house reeked of decay and stale cooking grease mingled with the smell of an old man's unwashed clothes and some other, indefinable odor to which Sebastian could not put a name.

"I've heard of you, you know," said the butler, drawing back a heavy iron bolt on the door at the end of the passage. It was an old door, Sebastian noted, shrunken and warped by age, so that it did not fit its frame. "In fact, I've followed your career with a certain morbid fascination. And I must say, it's interesting you should ask about this door."

"Oh? Why's that?"

"After the constables left last night, I naturally checked to make certain that all the windows and doors were secure."

"And?"

"This door was open."

"You mean, the bolt was drawn?"

"More than that, my lord. The door itself was standing quite ajar. It's possible, of course, that the constables threw it open in their search for the suspect—he ran off, you know, as soon as Mr. Perlman came and discovered him standing over the body. But I did find it peculiar. I mean, I myself heard Mr. Perlman say the blackguard ran out the *front* door. So why would they bother? And if it was the constables who opened the door, then why didn't they close it? Shockingly bad form, if you ask me." Campbell dragged open the door and bowed as a chorus of birdsong filled the air. "After you, my lord."

Sebastian stepped onto a terrace of uneven slates strewn with dead leaves and broken branches and crowded with row after row of birdcages. In the largest cage near the door, half a dozen black crows flapped their wings in frustration. Other cages held everything from sparrows and doves to a white owl and one very disgruntled-looking, long-haired black cat with a long bushy tail and glinting green eyes.

"Mr. Eisler was fond of birds?" said Sebastian, going to stand before the cat's cage. The cat blinked and stared back at him in sulky discontent.

Campbell cleared his throat. "I don't know as I'd say he was exactly *fond* of them, my lord. But he was always buying them."

Sebastian glanced over at the wooden-faced butler. "And doing what with them?"

The butler stared out over the overgrown ruin of a garden, toward a crumbling brick wall and the collapsed roof of what might once have been a stable. "That I couldn't say, my lord."

Sebastian studied the aged retainer's carefully composed features, then turned back toward the house. "Do you know if Mr. Eisler was expecting any visitors last night?"

Campbell waited until they were back inside and the door was carefully relocked before saying, "Mr. Eisler frequently had visitors."

"Oh? Anyone in particular you remember?"

"I'm afraid my memory isn't what it used to be, my lord."

"Like your hearing."

Campbell slid the bolt home with quavering fingers. "Just so, my lord."

Sebastian let his gaze drift around the cluttered space. Many of the paintings, he now realized, were priceless; he spotted a Van Eyck, a Fouquet, and, half-hidden behind the open door to the kitchen stairs, a massive Tintoretto. "The only staircase to the first floor is the one in the hall?"

"Yes, my lord." Frowning, the butler leaned toward him, a suddenly arrested expression sharpening his features as he peered up into Sebastian's face.

"What is it?" Sebastian asked.

"Have you by chance been here before, my lord?"

"No. Why do you ask?"

"You're quite certain you didn't come one day last week, to see Mr. Eisler?"

"Quite certain."

The butler pursed his lips, his brow furrowing as he subjected Sebastian to a narrow-eyed study. "Yes, you're right, of course. Now that I think about it, I believe the gentleman in question was slightly darker and perhaps a few years older—*and* not exactly a gentleman, if you get my drift, my lord? But for all that, there's no denying the individual in question looked enough like you to be your own brother.... If you don't mind my saying so, my lord?"

Chapter 9

Sebastian was aware of a strange sensation, like a rush of burning liquid that coursed through his veins, tingling his fingertips and dulling all external sound. As if from a long way off, he heard the old man say, "You don't by chance have a brother, do you, my lord?"

"A brother?" Somehow, Sebastian managed to keep his voice calm and even. "Not living, no." *At least, not to my knowledge,* he thought, although he didn't say it. He turned deliberately toward the darkened parlor beside them. "You say Mr. Eisler was found in here?"

"He was, my lord." Campbell went to open the faded drapes at the front windows, filling the room with dust and a dim light half-obscured by thick wavy glass coated with the grime of ages. "Sprawled on his back just there. Quite ruined the rug, I'm afraid."

The chamber was long and narrow and crowded like the rest of the house with a discordant jumble of furniture and art. Sebastian recognized a Rembrandt self-portrait and a Madonna by Fra Filippo Lippi. The carpet on the floor looked like a priceless seventeenth-century silk Isfahan, its far edge disfigured by a large dark stain no one had yet made any effort to clean.

Hunkering down beside it, he breathed in a cloying mixture of dust and blood and a faint but unmistakable whiff of stale burnt powder. Mr. Eisler's wound had ob-

viously bled profusely. Yet there were no splatters of
blood on the nearby wall or on any of the furniture. Sebastian looked up. "How, precisely, was the body ori-
ented?"

The butler came to stand beside him. "He was on his
back, as I said, my lord."

"Yes, but was he facing toward the door? Or away
from it?"

"Well, his head was just here"—the old man moved
with ponderous slowness, his thin arms waving as if to
sketch the position of the body in the air—"with his feet
there, nearer the door. So I suppose he must have been
turned in that direction when he was shot—wouldn't you
say, my lord?"

"Probably," said Sebastian, although he'd seen enough
men shot in the war to know the force with which a bullet could spin a man around and send him staggering.

He pushed to his feet, his gaze drifting over the
strange, shadowy chamber. With its collection of furniture, statues, porcelains, and paintings, the place more
closely resembled a storeroom or auction house than a
home. "Are all the rooms like this?" Sebastian asked.
"Full of furniture and piles of art, I mean."

"Most of them, yes. Mr. Eisler was something of a collector, you know. I'm afraid Mrs. Campbell gave up trying to fight the dust quite some time ago. People were
always . . . giving him things."

From here, Sebastian could make out at least two
more Rembrandts, a Caravaggio, and a nearly life-sized
marble statue of a horse that looked as if it might have
been looted from Constantinople by the knights of the
Fourth Crusade. "Mr. Eisler's friends appear to have
been quite generous," he said, picking his way through
the clutter to the far end of the room. Nearly the entire
back wall was taken up by a massive old-fashioned fireplace topped by a magnificent chimneypiece carved
with mythical beasts and garlands laden with fruit and
flowers.

"An interesting piece," said Sebastian, pausing before it.

"Mmm. They say this house dates back to the time of the Tudors, although for all I know that could just be so much talk."

Sebastian let his gaze drop to the worn black horse-hair sofa pulled up at an angle beside the cold hearth. He could just see the toes of a pair of blue satin slippers peeking out from beneath the bottom cushions.

"Know who those might belong to?" he asked, nodding toward them.

The aged retainer's jaw sagged. "Good heavens. No." Bracing his weight on one of the sofa's rolled arms, he bent to come up with a cheap pair of women's shoes decorated with gaudy paste buckles and somewhat the worse for wear.

"I take it at least some of Mr. Eisler's visitors were ladies?" said Sebastian, reaching for one of the shoes. Its owner must have been a tiny thing; the slipper was practically small enough to fit a child.

Campbell cleared his throat and looked decidedly uncomfortable. "Some ladies, some . . . not ladies, if you get my drift, my lord?"

Sebastian studied the shoe with a growing sense of puzzlement. He could understand a woman inadvertently leaving behind a hair ribbon or a bangle. But her shoes? How could a woman forget her shoes?

"Were any of Mr. Eisler's female visitors notice-ably—," he began, only to be interrupted by a thunderous banging on the front door.

"Excuse me, my lord." Campbell gave a painful bow and moved away to open the front door.

Sebastian let his gaze drift once more around the room. There was another door, he now realized, half-hidden by a curtain and just to the left of the fireplace wall, that looked as if it might lead back to the passage. He was moving to investigate when a man's gruff, booming voice filled the entry.

"Where is he? I heard he was seen coming here. By God, if he thinks he's—"

A burly, middle-aged figure appeared in the doorway. He was big and sweaty and bursting with self-importance, his hair prematurely silver but still thick, his full face pink and unlined, his ponderous girth a testament to a life of ease. "Ah! So it's true." He brought up a thick hand to point an accusatory finger at Sebastian. "I knew it. I *knew* it! You're Devlin, aren't you? I'd heard you were at Newgate, visiting that bloody scoundrel. Well, let me tell you right now, we don't need your interference around here. This is Aldgate, not Bow Street; do you hear? Sir Henry Lovejoy might welcome your meddling, but Bow Street has no interest in this case—none at all! So I'll thank you not to be interfering in what's none of your business. Do I make myself clear?"

Sebastian calmly raised one eyebrow. "Have we met?"

The man's lips tightened into a hard, straight line. His eyes were a pale hazel, his cheeks full and crisscrossed with tiny red veins, his neck wreathed with rolls of fat. "I am Leigh-Jones. Bertram Leigh-Jones, chief magistrate at Lambeth Street Public Office. And you, sir, are not welcome here. You're not welcome here at all. We already caught the scum who did this; you saw him yourself at Newgate."

"He says he didn't do it."

Leigh-Jones let out a rude laugh. "Of course he says he didn't do it. They all say they didn't do it. There's not a guilty man in Newgate, to listen to 'em." The laugh turned into a sneer. "Your man Yates is no different. Found standing over the body, he was. Oh, he'll hang, all right. No doubt about it."

With deliberate, provocative slowness, Sebastian let his gaze slide over the man before him, from his mottled, sweat-streaked face to his clumsily tied cravat and the egg stain on the garish waistcoat that pulled too snugly across his protuberant belly. He watched the magistrate's complexion darken and his jaw harden until the man was virtually shaking with fury. Then Sebastian nodded to the old butler and said, "Thank you for your time."

He turned toward the door, quietly tucking the blue satin slipper out of sight. He'd already made up his mind to return to the house later that night under the cover of darkness, when Campbell and his wife were asleep in their attic rooms.

"You're not to come back here," Leigh-Jones shouted after him. "You come back here, and I swear to God, I'll have you up before me on charges of trespass—viscount or no viscount. You hear me? *You hear me?*"

Sebastian kept walking.

Chapter 10

Sebastian had first learned of the existence of another dark, lean young man with yellow eyes from a Chelsea doctor who'd lost his watch and pocketbook to such a man at the point of a gun one stormy night on Hounslow Heath. And then, just that August, Sebastian and the man had come face-to-face.

His name was Jamie Knox, and he'd once served as a rifleman with the 145th. A crack shot with an almost mythical reputation for accuracy over long distances and in the dark, he was discharged when his unit was reduced after the disastrous defeat of the English forces under Wellington at Corunna. What he'd done after that was a matter of dispute. Sebastian was inclined to believe the tales that said he'd taken to the high toby and become a highwayman, a legendary figure in black who preyed on the coaches of those foolish enough to venture unescorted across the wasteland of Hounslow Heath after dusk.

Aided by what was reputed to be an animal-like sense of hearing and a preternatural ability to see in the dark, Knox had quickly accumulated the resources to purchase a Bishopsgate public house known as the Black Devil. Although there were others who said Knox had in fact stolen the pub—and murdered its previous owner.

Sebastian had never discovered which version of the tale was true. But he had it on reliable authority that the

French wine and brandy in Knox's cellars found its way across the Channel in the holds of darkened ships that plied their dangerous trade on moonless nights. . . .

And that one of Knox's associates in that shadowy world was a certain aristocratic ex-privateer named Russell Yates.

The Black Devil was a half-timbered relic from an earlier age, built against one of the few remaining stretches of London's old Roman walls. Popular with Bishopsgate's shopkeepers, clockmakers, and tailors, it was marked by a faded wooden sign depicting a black devil dancing against a background of flames. Like its exterior, the inside of the house had changed little over the centuries. The heavily beamed ceiling hung low; the flagged floor was uneven and covered with sawdust to catch spills; a heavy, smoke-blackened stone hearth took up a significant portion of one wall. When Sebastian pushed open the taproom door, he found the public room crowded with a typical noontime assortment of journeymen and apprentices from the surrounding streets.

A few of the nearest men glanced up, curious, then went back to their beer. Caught in the midst of drawing a tankard of ale, the young woman behind the counter froze as Sebastian walked toward her.

"Bleedin' hell," she said, tossing her head to shake back a heavy lock of dark hair that had fallen into her face. "Not you again."

Sebastian gave her a smile that showed his teeth. "Where is he?"

Setting aside the tankard, she rested one hand on her hip and hardened her jaw. Her mouth was wide and full, her cheekbones high, her dark eyes almond shaped and exotically tilted. She was beautiful and voluptuous, and she knew it. "Think I'd tell ye?"

A low laugh came from behind him. "Pippa has a tendency to hold grudges, I'm afraid," said Knox. "She somewhat resents your threat to see me hanged."

"Only if I discover that you're guilty," said Sebastian, turning.

The tavern owner stood with one hand propped against the frame of a doorway that opened off the end of the taproom. He might have left the high toby behind, but he still dressed all in black, like the devil that danced before the flames of hell on the sign hanging outside his tavern. Black coat and waistcoat, black trousers and boots, black cravat. Only his shirt was white.

He was older than Sebastian by a few years, darker, and perhaps a shade taller. But he had the same leanly muscled frame, the same fine-boned face, the same feral yellow eyes. As far as Sebastian knew, the two men were not related; yet Knox looked enough like Sebastian to be his brother.

Or at least a half brother.

"I didn't kill your damned Frenchman," said Knox. The smile on the man's face remained, but his eyes had hardened. Just six weeks before, Sebastian had accused Knox of killing a paroled French officer named Philippe Arceneaux. Knox denied it. But Sebastian was never completely convinced of the man's innocence.

"How about a diamond merchant named Daniel Eisler?"

The faintest flicker of surprise crossed the tavern owner's features, then disappeared. It could have meant anything. "You've been busy, haven't you? From what I hear, the man's barely been dead twelve hours." His gaze shifted, significantly, to a nearby table of leatherworkers who were suddenly looking interested. Pushing away from the doorframe, he took a step back. "Pippa? If you'll bring us a couple of pints?"

Following him into the inner room, Sebastian found himself in a small, neat office sparsely furnished with the unpretentious functionality of a campaign tent.

"Please, sit," said Knox, indicating the plain gateleg table that stood near a window overlooking the cobbled rear yard.

Sebastian sat and waited while the woman, Pippa, banged two foaming tankards down on the tabletop, threw him a malevolent glare, then slammed the door behind her as she returned to the taproom. He said, "Somehow, I expected you to deny knowing Eisler."

Knox came to sprawl in the opposite chair. "Why should I? Because he's dead? Are you imagining I killed him too?"

"Where were you last night around eight or nine?"

Knox took a long, slow sip of his ale and set it down before answering. "Here, at the Black Devil. And damn you to hell for asking."

Sebastian looked at the dark, handsome face of the man across from him and said, "You went to see Eisler last week. Why?"

"How do you know I went to see him?"

"His butler remembered you."

For a long moment, the other man stared back at him. Then he pushed up from his chair and crossed the room to unlock a small chest. He withdrew a flat rectangular object wrapped in oilcloth, locked the chest again, and came to lay the article on the table before Sebastian.

Roughly bound with cord, the bundle was some fifteen inches long, slightly less wide, and two or three inches thick. "What is it?" asked Sebastian.

"Open it."

Sebastian untied the cord that held the oilcloth in place and peeled it back to reveal a crumbling brown calf-bound book. Opening the tattered cover, he found himself staring at a handwritten script that was neither Roman nor Greek, but something at once strange and vaguely familiar. Puzzled, he ran his fingertips over the page. The book was definitely made of paper rather than vellum, yet it had been written by hand, not printed on a press.

"How old is it?" he asked.

"Late sixteenth century, I'm told," said Knox, resuming his seat.

"It's in Hebrew?"

"So they say."

Carefully turning the brittle, foxed pages, Sebastian studied the cramped script illustrated with curious geographical shapes and strange images. He looked up. "What does this old manuscript have to do with Eisler?"

Knox reached for his tankard, but he didn't drink from it. Instead, he turned his head to stare out the window beside them. Watching him, Sebastian had the impression he gazed beyond the cobbled yard and the shady elms of the ancient churchyard that bordered it. Far beyond, to a distant, sun-blasted land, dry and stony and ravaged by war. In Sebastian's experience, most ex-soldiers carried their past with them always, like a dark vision of hell that, once glimpsed, is never forgotten.

"To men like you and me," said Knox, his voice rough, "war means burned villages, dead women and children, and fields plowed by cannonballs. It means fruit rotting in orchards because there's no one left alive to pick it, and wells fouled by the stinking bodies of pigs and goats and dogs. It means men with their bellies ripped open and their faces shot off. But that's because we're just the poor sods who fight and bleed and die. For some men, war is an opportunity."

"You're saying Eisler was one of those men?"

A faintly derisive smile curled the tavern owner's lips. "There were very few opportunities Daniel Eisler missed."

"I'm told he kept agents on the Continent to buy the jewels of families that found themselves in strained circumstances."

"So I've heard, although I never dealt with them myself. But Eisler also had another man in his employ, a defrocked Spanish priest by the name of Ferdinand Arroyo. Arroyo's mission was to acquire a certain type of manuscript of interest to Eisler—mainly in Greek, Latin, and Hebrew, but sometimes in Old French, Italian, or German."

Sebastian stared down at an age-mottled page half-filled by a curious representation of a winged angel holding what looked like Saturn and breathing fire. "This being an example?"

"Yes."

"So how does it come to be in your possession?"

"It was brought to London by gentlemen with whom I do business. I was to deliver it to Eisler today."

"Why show it to me?"

Knox hesitated. "Let's just say I consider Russell Yates something of a friend."

Sebastian studied the other man's hard, sun-darkened face. He didn't doubt for a moment that Knox had a damned good reason for showing him the manuscript, although he suspected friendship wasn't part of it. But all he said was, "Who do you think killed Eisler?"

Knox leaned back in his seat and crossed his outthrust boots at the ankles. "I'd say there's probably somewhere between five hundred and a thousand men—and women—in this town who wanted to see that bastard dead. With odds like that, it's inevitable that he was eventually going to run up against someone willing to do more than just wish. But if you're asking me for names . . . I haven't any."

"Except for Señor Ferdinand Arroyo?"

Knox brought his tankard to his lips and drank. "Last I heard, Arroyo was in Caen."

Sebastian closed the aged manuscript's fragile cover and rose to his feet. "Thank you."

"Take it," said Knox, leaning forward to push the manuscript across the table toward him. "I've no use for it. It's not like I read Hebrew."

"You could sell it."

"The old-book business never appealed to me. Take it. If you can find someone to read it for you, you might find it . . . useful."

Sebastian wondered what a three-hundred-year-old manuscript could tell him about last night's murder of a diamond merchant. But he wrapped the aged volume in its oilcloth covering again and tucked it beneath his arm. "I'll see it's returned to you."

Knox shrugged. "Suit yourself."

Sebastian had almost reached the door when Knox stopped him. "You said Eisler's butler remembered me."

Sebastian paused to look back at him. "That's right."

"I never gave him my name."

"He didn't know your name. But he remembered what you looked like."

Knox widened his eyes. "His powers of description must be something to be wondered at."

"He said you looked enough like me to be my brother."

"Ah."

The two men's gazes met and held. Neither spoke, for there was no need. One might be the son of the beautiful, faithless Countess of Hendon, while the other was the bastard child of a Ludlow barmaid, but the resemblance between them was as undeniable as it was inexplicable.

Chapter 11

Sebastian walked out of the Black Devil to find a woman waiting for him in a fashionable high-perch phaeton drawn by a dainty white mare. She had her famous auburn-shot hair tucked up beneath a shako-style hat, and a veil hid most of her face. But he would have recognized Kat Boleyn anywhere.

He paused for a moment, aware of an unpleasant tightening in his chest. Then he stepped up to the kerb. "How did you know where to find me?" he asked.

Rather than answer, she turned to the liveried groom at her side. "Wait for me here, Patrick."

"Yes, ma'am," he said, yielding his place to Sebastian.

"Yates told me you'd been to see him this morning," she said as Sebastian vaulted up into the high seat beside her. "I wanted to thank you for offering to help."

"For God's sake, Kat. As if I wouldn't? Why the bloody hell didn't you come to me instead of Hendon?"

She gave her horses the office to start, her gaze on the lane ahead. "You know why."

"If you're worried about Hero, I think you underestimate her."

She remained silent, her attention all for the task of guiding the mare between a brewer's wagon and a coal cart.

He said, "You didn't tell me how you knew where to find me."

"It was more in the order of a good guess. Yates says Knox was involved in smuggling goods into the country for Eisler. Only, he doesn't know what."

Sebastian shifted his grip on the oilcloth bundle in his hands. "According to Knox, it was books. Strange old manuscripts written mainly in Greek, Latin, and Hebrew."

She threw him a quick, incredulous glance. "Old books? But . . . why?"

"He seems to have been something of a collector, our Mr. Eisler."

"The man was a bastard."

"That too."

She swung sharply around the corner. "Does Knox know anything about Eisler's death?"

"He says he doesn't."

"But you don't believe him?"

"He's not exactly a pillar of rectitude and responsibility."

"True."

Sebastian let his gaze travel over her exquisite, familiar features. He had fallen in love with her when she was sixteen and he barely twenty-one. So long ago now, long before Hendon's machinations had driven them apart not once, but twice. Before Sebastian joined the army and saw death, destruction, and savage cruelty on a scale that had come close to expunging his humanity and withering his soul. Before Kat began feeding information to the French in an effort to aid Ireland, the land of her birth. Before she'd married Russell Yates in a desperate maneuver to save herself from the vindictive wrath of Charles, Lord Jarvis, who'd promised her torture and an ugly death.

Sebastian knew her marriage to Yates had never been—could never be—more than one of convenience. Yates's association with the most beautiful, most desirable woman of the London stage was for him a tactic to quiet the whispers about his sexuality, while Kat, in exchange, gained the protection of whatever damaging information Yates held against Jarvis. It was a marriage devoid of both sexual attraction and romantic love. But Sebastian knew that over the past year the two had nevertheless become friends—good friends. And Kat had always been fiercely loyal to her friends.

Yet Sebastian couldn't shake the feeling there was something more to her concern, a subtle nuance that eluded him.

He said, "You told me once that Yates has evidence against Jarvis—evidence of something that would ruin him if it became known."

"Yes."

"It should be in Jarvis's best interest to see that no harm comes to Yates. If anyone has the power to get the charges against him dropped, it's Jarvis. So why hasn't he done it?"

She drew in a deep, troubled breath, a subtle betrayal that was unusual for her.

"What?" he asked, watching her.

"Jarvis visited Yates in his cell last night. Yates says he came to reassure him that he was in no danger."

"But you don't believe him?"

She shook her head, her lips pressed into a tight line as she turned her horse back onto Bishopsgate. "Yates used to think the evidence he has against Jarvis could protect us both. Only, I'm not so sure."

Sebastian knew a sense of profound disquiet. If given a choice between saving Kat and saving himself, he had little doubt which Yates would choose.

But all he said was, "How well did you know Eisler?"

"I didn't. But I've been asking around. Word on the street has it he was killed by a Parisian named Jacques Collot. Collot likes to claim he fled France during the Revolution because his monarchist principles were revolted by the excesses of republican and democratic fervor. But from what I'm hearing, the truth is probably considerably less flattering."

Sebastian frowned. "What was his connection to Eisler?"

"Let's just say Eisler wasn't exactly careful about the origins of the jewels he bought. He also had a tendency to cheat the people he did business with."

"You think he cheated Collot?"

She drew up outside the Black Devil again, where her groom was rushing to finish eating a paper-wrapped sausage he'd bought from a nearby cart. "They say Collot was heard raging about Eisler in a tavern just two nights ago—swore next time he saw the man he was going to kill him."

"Drunken talk is cheap."

"True. But it's a place to start, isn't it?"

"It is, yes. Do you know where I can find this man?"

She shook her head. "Sorry."

He dropped lightly to the paving, then paused with one hand on the seat's high railing. He had the unsettling sense that there were unseen but powerful forces at work behind all this. Powerful and dangerous. He glanced over at her groom. "Is your man armed?"

She pressed her lips into a thin, tight line and shook her head. "I refuse to allow Jarvis to frighten me."

"Jarvis frightens me, Kat. Please, just . . . be careful."

⁂

Returning to Brook Street, Sebastian sent for his valet and asked without preamble, "Ever hear of a somewhat unsavory Frenchman named Jacques Collot?"

Most gentlemen's gentlemen would be outraged by their employer's suggestion that they consorted with or were in any way familiar with the members of London's vast criminal class. But Jules Calhoun was not your ordinary gentleman's gentleman. Small and lithe, with a boyish shock of flaxen hair and a roguish smile, he was a genius at repairing the ravages the pursuit of murderers could at times inflict on Sebastian's wardrobe. But he also possessed certain other skills useful to a man with

Sebastian's interests—skills that had their origins in the fact that he began life in one of the worst flash houses in London.

"I have heard of him, my lord," said Calhoun. "I believe he arrived in London some ten or fifteen years ago. But I can't say I know much about him."

"Know where he lives?"

"No. But I can find out."

⚜

Several hours later, Sebastian was seated at the desk in his library with Knox's manuscript open before him when Hero came in.

She still wore her emerald green carriage dress, although the plume in her jaunty hat was now sadly drooping, for it had come on to rain. "Ah, there you are," she said, taking off her hat to frown down at the bedraggled feather.

"So, did your crossing sweep talk to you?" he asked, leaning back in his chair.

"He did. And you would not *believe* some of the things he told me." She came to peer over his shoulder at the manuscript. "I didn't know you read Hebrew."

"I don't. I'm looking at the pictures. They're . . . strange."

She let her gaze run over the page, her eyes widening slightly at the illustration of what looked like a spinning wheel surrounded by odd symbols. "Where did this come from?"

"I'm told it was smuggled into the country for Daniel Eisler, although he died before he could take delivery. And I haven't the slightest idea what it is."

She turned the pages, pausing to stare at an illustration of a fanged demon with the wings of an eagle. "I could be wrong, but it looks as if your Mr. Eisler was interested in the occult."

"What makes you think—" He broke off as Calhoun appeared in the doorway.

"I beg your pardon, my lord," said the valet, beginning to back away. "I'd no notion her ladyship—"

"That's quite all right," said Sebastian. "Did you find Collot?"

"I did, my lord. I'm told he keeps a room at the Pilgrim in White Lyon Street."

"Good God."

The valet's eyes danced with amusement. "I take it you're familiar with the establishment?"

"I am."

Calhoun cast a significant glance at Hero, who was busy thumbing through the tattered old manuscript. "Shall I have Tom bring the curricle around, my lord?"

"No; after last night, I told him I wanted him to rest today. Send Giles."

"Yes, my lord."

"Who's Collot?" Hero asked after Calhoun had gone. "And what is so nasty about the Pilgrim that neither you nor Calhoun care to sully my lady's delicate ears with it?"

Sebastian gave a soft laugh. "Collot is a reputedly unsavory Frenchman who may have had something to do with Eisler's death, while the Pilgrim is a den of vice and iniquity in Seven Dials."

"Hmm. You'll take a pistol with you, of course?"

"My dear Lady Devlin, are you perhaps worried about my safety?"

"Not really," she said, a smile flickering around her lips as she turned back to the book. "Do you mind if I look at this while you're gone?"

"You don't by any chance read Hebrew?"

"Sadly, no. But I know someone who does."

Chapter 12

A quarter of an hour later, Sebastian walked down the steps of his house to find the curricle waiting, with Tom standing at the grays' heads.

"What the devil are you doing here? I told you to take the day off and rest. Where's Giles?"

"Giles is feeling peakish. And I done rested—for *hours*."

Sebastian leapt up to take the reins. "I don't recall hearing anything about Giles feeling 'peakish.'"

Tom scrambled onto his perch. "Well, he is."

Sebastian cast the tiger a suspicious glance.

But Tom only grinned.

❧

Lying just to the northwest of Covent Garden, the nest of fetid alleys and dark courts known as Seven Dials had once been a prosperous area favored by poets and ambassadors and favorites of Good Ole Queen Bess. Those days were long gone. The once grand houses of brick and stone lining the main thoroughfares were now falling into ruin, their pleasure gardens and parks vanished beneath a warren of squalid hovels built of wood and given over to beggars and thieves and costermongers of the meanest sort.

The Pilgrim, on a narrow lane just off Castle Street, was

technically licensed to sell beer as well as spirits but appeared to cater mainly to those who preferred their alcohol in the form of cheap gin.

"A go of Cork," said Sebastian, walking up to the counter.

The gin slinger, a stout, aging woman with a massive bosom swelling out of the bodice of her ragged, dirty dress, looked at him through narrowed, suspicious eyes as she splashed gin into a smudged glass. "Wot ye doin' 'ere? We don't need yer kind 'ere. Yer kind is always trouble."

"I'm looking for Jacques Collot. Know where I might find him?"

"Collot?" She sniffed and shook her head. "Never 'eard o' 'im."

Sebastian laid a half crown on the stained countertop. "If you do happen to see him, tell him I have a job he might be interested in, would you?"

"I told ye, I ain't never 'eard o' 'im." But the coin disappeared.

Sebastian went to settle at one of the rickety tables at the rear of the room, the glass of pungent gin twirling back and forth between his fingertips. He even raised it as if to drink a few times, although he was careful not to let it touch his lips.

A sluggish fire burned on the shallow hearth, filling the room with a bitter smoke that didn't encourage many of the patrons to linger. Sebastian watched a steady stream of men file into the low-ceilinged chamber, throw down a shot of gin at a penny a glass, then leave again. As far as he could tell, the glasses were never washed.

After some five or ten minutes, a stocky, middle-aged man with graying side-whiskers and one strangely wayward eye walked through the door. Bypassing the counter, he came straight to pull out the chair opposite Sebastian and sit.

They say Collot's got a wandering eye, can't control which way it looks, Calhoun had told Sebastian before he left Brook Street. *He's maybe forty or forty-five; about my height but carrying more flesh.*

"I hear that you search for Collot," the man with the faulty eye said in a heavy French accent. "I am not he, *mais je puis*—er, I can perhaps find him for you, if you wish. Yes?"

Sebastian nodded to the slatternly barmaid, who slapped a shot of gin down in front of the Frenchman, exchanged a veiled glance with him, and went away again.

The man downed his gin in one long pull and licked his lips. "You have a job, yes?"

"For Collot."

"Collot, he is my good friend since many years. You tell me, I tell him."

"You knew him in Paris, did you?"

"*Mais oui.* We were the children together. In Montmartre. You know Paris?"

"I heard Collot was a jewel thief in Paris."

The man leaned back in his seat, his mouth hanging open in a parody of shock. "A thief? *Non.* Who says such a thing?"

"The same people who say the nob in Newgate didn't kill Daniel Eisler. They say Collot did it."

The man shoved up from his chair, ready to run, his wandering eye rolling wildly. *"Monsieur!"*

"I suggest you sit down," said Sebastian quietly. "There are two Bow Street runners waiting out the front for you, and two more out the back." He punctuated the lie with a smile. "You can talk to them if you prefer, but I suspect you might find it more pleasant to deal with me."

Collot sank back down into his seat, his voice hoarse. "What do you want from me?"

"How did you know Eisler?"

"But I didn't say I—"

"You knew him. Tell me how."

Collot licked his lips again, and Sebastian signaled the barmaid for another shot of gin.

"How?" Sebastian repeated after the woman left.

"I knew him years ago."

"In Paris?"

Collot downed the second gin and shook his head. "Amsterdam."

"When was this?"

"'Ninety-two."

"You sold him jewels?"

The Frenchman's lip curled, his nose wrinkling like that of a man who has just smelled something foul. "He was scum. The worst kind of scum. He'd as soon cheat you as look at you, and then he'd laugh in your face and call you a fool."

"Did he cheat you?"

As if aware of the pit yawning before him, Collot drew himself up straighter in his chair. "Me? *Mais non.* Not me."

Sebastian tilted his gin back and forth between his fingertips, aware of the Frenchman's eyes upon it. "The jewels you sold to Eisler in Amsterdam in 'ninety-two, where did you get them?"

"My family. For generations, the Collots have been lapidaries. Ask anyone who knew Paris, before. They'll tell you. But by the autumn of 'ninety-two, things were bad—very bad. We could not stay. We took refuge in Amsterdam."

"And sold Eisler your jewels?"

"Yes."

"And you've had no dealings with him here in London?"

"No."

"That's not what I'm hearing."

"Perhaps people have me confused with someone else. Some other émigré."

"Perhaps." Sebastian shifted in his seat so that he could cross his outthrust boots at the ankles. "Who do you think killed Eisler?"

Collot touched the back of one hand to his nose and

sniffed. "What you trying to do to me, hmm? People see me talking to a Bow Street runner, what are they to think? You try to get me killed?"

"I'm not a runner, and everyone in here thinks I'm offering you a job. What kind of jobs do you do, exactly?"

Collot sniffed again. "This and that."

Sebastian shoved his own untouched gin across the table. After a moment's hesitation, Collot picked it up and raised the glass to his lips, his hand shaking so badly he almost spilled it.

"You're afraid of something," said Sebastian, watching him. "What is it?"

Collot drained the glass, then leaned forward, his lips wet, the veins in his forehead bulging against his sweat-slicked skin. Sebastian could smell the fear roiling off him, mingling with the stench of stale sweat and cheap gin. The Frenchman threw a quick glance around, his voice dropping to a whisper. "Eisler was peddling a big diamond. A big *blue* diamond."

"How large of a diamond are we talking about?"

"Forty-five or fifty carats. Perhaps more."

"Where did it come from?"

"Only one big blue diamond I know about, and that's the one belongs to the banker, Hope."

"Henry Philip Hope?"

"No. The other one. His brother, Thomas."

"I haven't heard anything about a big blue diamond being associated with Eisler's death."

"That's my point. No one has heard about it. So I ask you, where is it? Hmm?" He wiped a trembling hand across his mouth and said it again. "Where is it?"

Chapter 13

Sebastian figured he could automatically discount upward of ninety percent of what Jacques Collot had told him. But the Frenchman's fear, at least, had been real. And his reference to the Hopes was so unexpected, so outrageous, that Sebastian decided it just might be worth looking into.

A respectable old family of Scottish merchant bankers, the Hopes had settled in Amsterdam in the previous century and prospered there for generations. The family business, Hope and Company, was the kind of financial establishment that lent money to kings. Just ten years before, they had put together the financial package that enabled the fledgling United States to purchase the Louisiana Territory from Napoléon's France—thus, coincidentally, helping to fund the continuing French war effort.

But the Hopes were, predictably enough, not particularly anxious to experience republican principles firsthand. When the French armies marched on Amsterdam and The Hague, the Hopes packed up their vast collection of paintings and sculptures and gems and scurried back across the Channel to England.

Sebastian's acquaintance with the Hopes was limited to desultory state dinner parties and crowded ballrooms and various similar functions of the kind he generally preferred to avoid. If he had been in Thomas Hope's vast museum-like house in Duchess Street, he didn't recall it. But when Sebastian sent up his card, the Hopes' very proper English butler quickly showed him in. One did not turn away the heir of Alistair St. Cyr, Earl of Hendon and Chancellor of the Exchequer.

Thomas Hope greeted him with a wide smile and firm handshake. But his small eyes were hooded and wary, and Sebastian found himself wondering why.

"Devlin! Good to see you. This is a surprise. Please, have a seat." A short, ungainly man in his forties with a craggy, almost brutish-looking face, he stretched out a hand toward a yellow satin-covered settee that looked like something Cleopatra might have reclined upon while awaiting Mark Antony. "And how is your father?"

To a casual observer, the remark might have seemed innocent; it was not. Everyone who was anyone in London knew that a deep and lasting estrangement had grown up between the Earl of Hendon and his heir.

"He is well, thank you." Sebastian returned the banker's practiced smile. "And you?"

As they exchanged the customary polite nothings, Sebastian let his gaze drift around the room, taking in the mummy cases painted on the ceiling, the alabaster vases, the regal, Egyptian-style cats, the life-sized portrait of a beautiful, dark-haired, sloe-eyed woman painted on worn boards that looked very much like part of an ancient sarcophagus.

"Is that from a Ptolemaic tomb?" Sebastian asked, staring at it.

Hope appeared delighted. "You recognize it! It is, yes. This is what I call my Egyptian Room. The piece you're sitting on was manufactured to my own design, based on drawings I did of a similar relic discovered in a tomb near the Nile while I was there."

Sebastian glanced down at the settee's black wooden frame, which was decorated with paintings of the jackal-headed god Anubis and had bronze scarabs for feet.

Thomas, he now remembered, was the Hope brother with little interest in the actual business that generated the family's fortune. Leaving his relatives to mind the bank and mercantile empire, he'd spent much of his youth on an extended Grand Tour, visiting not only Europe but Africa and Asia, as well. Now confined to Britain by the disruptions of war, he devoted himself largely to increasing his stature as a patron of the arts. Lately he'd also taken to his pen, publishing a folio volume entitled *Household Furniture and Interior Decoration*, followed shortly by *Costumes of the Ancients*. His newest project was reportedly a grandly ambitious philosophical work on the origins and prospects of man, although he was said to despair of ever finishing it.

"Have you been to Egypt?" he asked eagerly, nodding discreetly to the butler, who moved to open a bottle of wine.

"Once, although quite a few years ago."

"Splendid! And Istanbul? Damascus? Baghdad?"

"I'm afraid not."

Hope's face fell. "Ah. What a pity. I once spent an entire year in Istanbul, sketching the ruins and palaces. If you ever find yourself presented with an opportunity to visit the city, you must seize it. There is no place quite like it."

"My wife has always been anxious to travel, so perhaps one day we shall make it there." Sebastian paused to accept a glass of wine from the butler's tray, then said casually, "I wonder, were you acquainted with Daniel Eisler?"

Thomas Hope was no fool. He took his time accepting his own wine, using the delay as a cover for thought. He had a big mouth, loose and wet, and a habit of flexing it in a peculiar way right before he began to speak. He flexed it now, like a sleek, wily fish considering and then rejecting a juicily baited hook.

"Eisler? Of course. He was in Amsterdam with us, you know." He sipped his wine, his eyes above the glass downcast. "His death is shocking, is it not? I do believe that one of these days the English simply must agree to the formation of a proper police force, lest we all find ourselves murdered in our beds."

"Did you ever buy jewels from him?" Sebastian asked, refusing to be distracted by what was a popular, perennial topic.

"From Eisler? You must be thinking of my brother, Henry Philip. He's the family jewel collector, not I. You really must ask to see his collection sometime. He keeps it in a great mahogany cabinet with sixteen drawers, one for each category of specimen. He has a pearl that is said to be the largest saltwater pearl in existence—nearly two hundred grams, and two inches long. It's lovely—quite spectacularly so."

"What about big blue diamonds? Do they interest him?"

"Blue?" Thomas Hope sipped his wine and pursed his lips so that he now resembled nothing so much as a frog. "I couldn't say, actually. I know the red ones are the rarest. And of course, the ladies generally like the pink ones."

"Daniel Eisler wasn't trying to sell a large blue diamond for your family?"

Hope laughed out loud. "Good heavens, no. Now is the time to be buying jewels, not selling them. The prices are quite depressed. It's all these émigrés, you know. Henry Philip was telling me about a twenty-five-carat square white table-cut diamond he bought recently from some old Frenchwoman who was so desperate, she was willing to part with it *for a song*."

A light step sounded in the hall. Hope turned his head, his mouth puckering feverishly as a woman appeared in the doorway. She was considerably younger than Hope, perhaps by as many as fifteen or twenty years. She wore her dark hair styled short, so that it curled fashionably around her face and showed off her long neck and sloping white shoulders. Her eyes were dark and luminous, her nose perfectly straight, her mouth full lipped and rosebud pink.

"Ah, Louisa, dear," said Hope, working his mouth into a smile. "How kind of you to join us. I believe you've met Lord Devlin? Devlin, this is my wife."

"Mrs. Hope." Sebastian rose to his feet and sketched a bow.

La Belle et la Bête, society called them. Beauty and the Beast. It wasn't hard to see why. Beauty extended her hand for Sebastian to kiss, her face glowing with the kind of smile that inspired poets and painters. "Lord Devlin. What a pleasant surprise."

She wore a simple gown of white muslin caught up beneath her full breasts with a pink satin ribbon; a simple gold chain and locket encircled her neck. She was one of those women who had about her an air of gentle repose and serenity that made one think of Evensong and incense and sunlight streaming through stained-glass windows. But Sebastian knew the impression of gentle beatitude was deceptive. A professional killjoy in the mold of Hannah More and the Clapham Saints, she was an active member of the Society for the Suppression of Vice, a nasty organization dedicated to stamping out dancing, singing, card playing, and just about any other pleasure and amusement that might gladden the hearts and ease the sorrows of the city's laboring poor.

She did not urge him to sit again, so that Sebastian found himself wondering with some amusement if she'd been lurking outside the drawing room door, ready to rush in and put an end to any conversation that threatened to stray into unwanted channels.

"You must come see us again, with Lady Devlin," she said, her laced fingers coming up to rest charmingly against her chin, her gentle smile never slipping.

The thought of the two women together—Hero with her forthright, radical principles and Louisa Hope with her self-satisfied, sanctimonious moralizing—threatened to overset Sebastian's gravity. He reached for his hat. "I will, yes. In the meantime, I won't intrude on you any longer." He bowed again. "Servant, Mrs. Hope. Don't bother ringing; I can see myself out."

"I'll walk with you to the door," said Hope, as if vaguely embarrassed by his wife's maneuvers. "You really must come back with Lady Devlin and see the rest of the house. I'm doing each room in the style of a different country, one for each of the various places I've visited."

They descended the grand wide staircase, their footsteps echoing as if in a vault. Sebastian said, "If Eisler were trying to sell a large blue diamond, where do you think it might have come from?"

Hope paused at the base of the stairs, his mouth puckering as if it were a necessary prelude to thought. "Hmm. Difficult to say, really. The provenance of so many of these large specimens is . . . well, shall we say *shaky* at best?"

"You're not familiar with such a gem?"

"I am not, no. But then, as I said, my brother is the family's amateur lapidary. He might have heard of such a piece. Unfortunately, he's in the country at the moment." Hope nodded to the butler, who moved to open the front door.

"When was the last time you saw Eisler?"

"Good heavens, I'm not certain I can answer that. It's been some time, though; that I do know."

"Can you think of anyone who might have wanted to kill him?"

Thomas Hope's rubbery lips twisted. "Russell Yates, from what the papers tell us. Dreadfully bad ton, that man. I always thought he'd make a sorry end."

The butler stood, wooden, beside the still open door. A wind had kicked up, sending a loose handbill down the street and carrying the sharp, biting promise of more rain.

"They haven't hanged him yet," said Sebastian.

"No, but they will soon enough."

A man's ringing laughter sounded on the footpath outside, his voice cultured but tinged with a vague Irish lilt as he said, "The devil fly away with you, Tyson! I tell you, the horse is sound—as sound as the Bank of England."

Another man answered, his tones those of Hereford and Eton rather than Irish, and so familiar that Sebastian found himself stiffening.

"This is supposed to reassure me, is it?"

Sebastian could see him now. Tall and broad shouldered, the man filled the doorway. He was half-turned, still looking back at the unseen Irishman on the footpath below him. In his mid-twenties, he wore the typical rig of a town beau: dark blue, carefully tailored coat by Schultz, boots by Hobbs, hat by Lock. But his powerful build and military bearing told their own story. He turned, still smiling as he reached the top step. Then his gaze fell on Sebastian, and the laughter died on his lips.

"Ah, how fortuitous," said Hope. "Devlin, do allow me to introduce Lieutenant Matt Tyson and my wife's young cousin, Blair Beresford."

Tyson's clear gray eyes met Sebastian's. His hair was chestnut brown, his cheeks strong boned, his jaw square and marked by a rakish scar across his chin that enhanced rather than detracted from his rugged good looks.

"The lieutenant and I have met," said Sebastian evenly.

"Excellent, excellent," said Hope, beaming and utterly oblivious to the powerful undercurrents of animosity that crackled between the two men.

Tyson's companion—considerably younger and fairer—took off his hat and shook Sebastian's hand with boyish enthusiasm. From the looks of things, Louisa's Irish cousin couldn't have been more than twenty or twenty-two, with a head of soft golden curls, merry blue eyes, and the face of an angel. "Devlin?" said Blair Beresford. "Oh, by Jove. This is an honor, my lord, an honor indeed. Did you know Matt in the Peninsula, then?" He glanced laughingly at his friend. "And here Matt never told me."

"Our acquaintance was . . . brief," said Tyson, a muscle bunching along his powerful jaw.

Sebastian was aware of Tom, waiting with the curricle below, his slight form motionless as he stood at the grays' heads, his face a mask as his gaze traveled from one man to the other.

"Gentlemen," said Sebastian, tipping his hat.

Without looking back, he descended the stairs to vault up to the curricle's high seat and gather his reins. "Let 'em go," he told Tom.

The grays sprang forward, the boy scrambling to take his perch at the rear of the carriage. "You know that cove from somewhere?" Tom asked as Sebastian sent the grays dashing up the street at a shocking pace. "The big one, I mean."

"Spain. He was with the 114th Foot, although from the looks of things, he's sold out."

"'Peared to me 'e weren't exactly pleased to see you," observed Tom. "In fact, I'd say 'e weren't weery pleased to see you atall."

"Perhaps that's because the last time he saw me, I was sitting on his court-martial board."

"What 'ad 'e done?"

"According to the decision of my fellow officers, nothing. He was found innocent. But he was accused of robbing and killing a young Spanish woman and her two children."

Chapter 14

*H*e'd been avoiding it all day. But the time had come, Sebastian knew, to visit the Tower Hill surgery of his old friend Paul Gibson.

Once a regimental surgeon with the Twenty-fifth Light Dragoons, Gibson had learned many of the secrets of life and death from his close observation of the countless shattered, slashed, burned, and maimed bodies strewn across the world's battlefields. Then a French cannonball took off the lower half of one of his own legs, leaving him racked by phantom pains and with a weakness for the sweet relief to be found in an elixir of poppies. He now divided his time between sharing his knowledge of anatomy at the teaching hospitals of St. Thomas's and St. Bartholomew's, and tending his own small surgery near the looming bastions of the Tower of London.

Leaving the curricle in Tom's care, Sebastian cut through the narrow passage that ran alongside the surgeon's ancient stone house to the small outbuilding at the base of the unkempt yard where Gibson performed his autopsies. It was here that he also practiced surreptitious dissections on bodies filched from London's churchyards by gangs of unsavory characters known as resurrection men. By law, the dissection of any human corpse except that of an executed felon was forbidden, which meant that if a surgeon wanted to perfect a new technique or further expand his understanding of human anatomy or physiology, he had little choice but to trade with the body snatchers.

Sebastian was aware of thunder rumbling in the distance and a patter of scattered raindrops as he followed the beaten path through the rank grass. The air filled with the smell of damp earth and death. Gibson had left the outbuilding's door open; through it, Sebastian could see the pale body of a man stretched out on the surgeon's granite slab. It was Rhys Wilkinson, and from the looks of things, Gibson was only getting started.

"There you are, me lad," said Gibson, looking up with a grin as Sebastian paused in the doorway.

"Find anything?" he asked, careful not to look too closely at what Gibson was doing to the cadaver before him. Sebastian had spent six years fighting the King's wars from Italy to Spain to the West Indies; he had seen death in all its ugliest, most heartbreaking and stomach-churning manifestations. He had even killed men himself, more times than he cared to remember. But none of that had left him with Gibson's calm insouciance when it came to viewing the dissected, mangled, or decomposing bodies of the dead. . . . Particularly when the body belonged to someone he'd called friend.

"We-ell," said Gibson, drawing out the word into two syllables, "I've only just begun, I'm afraid. Had a coroner's inquest that lasted far longer than it ought to have. About all I can tell you at this point is the liver and spleen are enlarged. But then, that's typical for someone with Walcheren fever."

"He told me just a few weeks ago that he thought he was getting over the worst of it."

"No one ever really gets over Walcheren fever, I'm afraid," said Gibson. He was a few years older than Sebastian, in his early thirties now. But chronic pain had etched deep the fan of laugh lines beside his green eyes, touched the temples of his dark hair with silver, and left him thin and wiry. "I'm not saying for certain that's what killed him, mind you. I've a few things to look at yet." He paused. "How's Annie taking it?"

"Badly."

Gibson shook his head. "Poor girl. She's been through so much."

"She's game," said Sebastian.

"Aye, that she is. But she was looking rather worn down last I saw her."

"Things have been difficult for them, what with Wilkinson invalided out and too ill to hold a position. I offered to help, but she would have none of it."

"I'm not surprised. She was always a proud woman." Gibson limped out from behind the slab, his peg leg tapping on the uneven paving. "I take it you've heard about Russell Yates?"

"I have. You wouldn't by chance know who's doing Daniel Eisler's postmortem?"

Gibson smiled. "I thought you might be interested, so I asked around. Seems there wasn't one. I gather the magistrate involved doesn't hold with such outlandish modern practices. I did, however, manage to speak to a colleague of mine—a Dr. William Fenning—who was called to confirm the man's death at the scene. He said Eisler had been shot at close quarters in the chest. Death was likely virtually instantaneous."

"Did he notice anything else?"

"You mean, at the house?" Gibson shook his head. "I'm afraid not. He was brought in to view the body; he gave his opinion and left. I gather he was late for a dinner party."

The two men went to stand outside, their backs to the close room and its grisly contents, the damp wind clean and cool in their faces. Sebastian said, "Do you remember Matt Tyson?"

Gibson looked over at him. "You mean the lieutenant from the 114th Foot who was court-martialed after Talavera?"

"That's the one. I ran into him just now. From the looks of things, he's sold out."

"I'm not surprised. He might have been acquitted, but those kinds of accusations leave an opprobrium that lingers."

"Justifiably, in his case," said Sebastian dryly.

Gibson shook his head. "I've never really believed in evil—at least, not as something with a finite existence outside ourselves. But when I run across someone like Tyson, it makes me wonder if the good nuns might not have been right after all."

Gibson fell silent, his gaze on the bunching, heavy gray clouds bearing down low on the surrounding rooftops and on the soot-streaked white bulk of the old Norman keep. And Sebastian knew without being told that the surgeon's thoughts had returned, like his own, to the man on the slab behind them.

Sebastian said, "Annie wanted me to tell her the results of the autopsy. You'll let me know when you're finished?"

"Of course." Gibson hesitated, then said, "You do realize that when one dies of something like an overdose of laudanum, it doesn't show up? Perhaps someday science will learn how to detect these things, but at the moment it's beyond us."

Sebastian met his friend's gaze but said nothing.

Gibson continued. "It just looks as if the body's systems shut down, which would also be consistent with someone who had long been in ill health."

Sebastian blew out a harsh breath and nodded. "That's good. Annie's suffered enough."

Neither of them said, *She doesn't need the shame of her husband's suicide added to everything else.* But then, they didn't need to.

The knowledge of it was there, in the storm-charged air.

Chapter 15

Charles, Lord Jarvis, lounged comfortably in an over-stuffed armchair beside his host's hearth, a glass of good French brandy cradled in one palm, his head tipped back to rest against the seat's high back as he watched his host pace across the carpet. The sound of wind-driven rain slapping against the windowpanes and drumming on the leaves of the trees outside filled the room.

"The brandy is undeniably excellent," said Jarvis, pausing to take a delicate sip. "But I don't think you invited me here for my opinion on your cellars."

Otto von Riedesel, the man pacing the room, whirled to face him. Big boned and stocky, and well into his fifth decade, he wore the black broadcloth dolman and black trousers of a colonel in the Black Brunswickers, a volunteer corps who fought the French at Britain's side. Although the Duke of Brunswick was, technically, Britain's ally, von Riedesel's position as the Duke's representative in London was nevertheless delicate. For while Brunswick was both first cousin and brother-in-law to the Prince Regent, Prinny had long been estranged from Princess Caroline, his plump, slightly mad wife, who was the daughter of the late Duke of Brunswick and sister to the present one.

"This murder is troubling. Most troubling," said the colonel, smoothing his hand down over his flowing black mustache. His cheeks were full and ruddy, his nose a bulbous, unrefined blob. Despite his uniform and rank, the colonel's days of active campaigning were now over. He'd grown soft and, Jarvis was beginning to suspect, dangerously timid.

"Really? I wouldn't have said so."

The Brunswicker's heavy brows drew together in a frown. "You vould have me believe all is under control?"

"It is, yes. Although if you show the world that worried face, you will only succeed in focusing attention on that which you wish to conceal, thus bringing about precisely what you would prefer to avoid."

"Easy for you to say." Von Riedesel brought his own brandy to his lips and drained the glass. "It is not you who vill be ruined if the truth gets out."

"It won't get out," said Jarvis.

Chapter 16

*T*he rain was coming down hard by the time Sebastian walked in his front door. "Is Lady Devlin at home?" he asked, handing his hat and gloves to his majordomo, a former gunnery sergeant named Morey.

"She is, my lord," said Morey, carefully wiping the moisture from Sebastian's top hat. "I believe you will find her in the drawing room with an elderly gentleman, one Mr. Benjamin Bloomsfield. I've just taken up some tea."

"Thank you."

Sebastian could hear the low drone of an elderly man's quavering voice as he mounted the stairs to the first floor.

"I don't think you'll find many in London who are mourning his passing," he heard the man say.

"He was a shrewd bargainer?" asked Hero.

"Shrewd? That's one word for it."

Sebastian could see their visitor now, seated in a chair drawn up beside the hearth. The man was indeed aged, his long flowing beard as white as Eisler's snowy owl, the bony fingers he held templed before him gnarled with arthritis and palsied with age. He wore an ill-fitting black coat, old-fashioned in cut and somewhat the worse for wear. But his light brown eyes were still sharp with intelligence, the sallow, lined flesh of his face settled into a pattern of gentle good humor that spoke of a life spent laughing at the vicissitudes of fate and the absurdities of his fellow men. No one seeing his scuffed shoes and darned stockings would ever imagine that he was one of the wealthiest men in London, with interests that ranged from banking and shipping to fur, wheat . . .

And diamonds.

"The truth is that Daniel Eisler was a vicious, unscrupulous scoundrel, and the world is a better place with him out of it." The old man turned his head as Sebastian paused in the doorway and made a motion as if to push himself out of his chair.

"No, please, sir, don't get up," said Sebastian, going to clasp the old man's hand. "We've never met, Mr. Bloomsfield, but I've heard much of your charitable work. It's an honor to meet you."

"The pleasure is mine, young man. I've known Miss Jarvis here—excuse me, *Lady Devlin*, for years now, although I must admit I'd quite despaired of ever seeing her settled with a family of her own. You are to be congratulated for both your good fortune and your good sense."

Sebastian glanced over at Hero in time to see a faint flush of color darken her cheeks. Then she looked pointedly away and said with painful politeness, "Would you like some tea, Devlin?"

He swallowed a smile. "Yes, please."

Bloomsfield said, "Your wife tells me you believe this young man the authorities have arrested is innocent."

"I do, yes." A small fire had been kindled to chase away the evening's growing chill, and Sebastian went to stand before it. "You knew Eisler, did you? I gather he was a widower."

Bloomsfield shook his head. "To my knowledge, the man never married. Lived alone for years in that wreck of a house with only two old servants to wait on him."

"I've seen the house. It's somewhat overflowing with furniture and art."

Bloomsfield huffed a mirthless laugh. "You mean it

looks like a glorified pawnshop. Which is essentially what it was."

"Do you mean to say Eisler was in the habit of giving loans?" asked Hero, handing Sebastian a cup of tea.

"I don't know if I'd call it a habit, exactly. 'Business' is more like it. His rates were ruinous and his terms outrageous. He used to insist that his victims—excuse me, his clients—leave several valuable items with him as collateral. Paintings, statues . . . even furniture, if it was fine enough."

"And gems?"

"Oh, yes, he was especially fond of gems. Needless to say, very few of his clients ever managed to reclaim their property—even when they paid off their loans."

Sebastian took a sip of his tea. "Someone told me there must be any number of people in London who are glad to see Eisler dead. I'm beginning to understand what they meant."

Bloomsfield nodded. "I heard recently of a young nobleman who took the family's emeralds to have them cleaned before presenting them to his new wife, only to discover they were all paste. His mother'd had them copied and hocked the original stones to Eisler to pay her gambling debts. The young marquis threatened Eisler with legal action—they weren't hers to sell, after all. But in the end he gave it up."

"Why?" asked Hero.

Bloomsfield lifted his shoulders in a shrug. "I never heard. But it's not unusual. Did you know that more than half the gems in the British Crown Jewels are paste? The originals have been pawned over the years to pay for our various illustrious monarchs' wars."

"Not to mention their mistresses," said Hero.

Bloomsfield's soft brown eyes danced with amusement. "That too."

Sebastian said, "I understand Eisler was handling the sale of a large diamond for someone. Did he do that sort of thing? Negotiate the sale of jewels for other people?"

"Frequently, yes."

"Why?" asked Hero. "I mean, I can see why Eisler would do it, since he'd obviously make a fat commission on the transaction. But why wouldn't a gem's owner simply sell it openly?"

"Typically because they don't want anyone to know that they're selling. In general, if you hear a collector is selling one or more of his specimens, it's a fairly good indicator that he's found himself in financial difficulties. And that's the kind of information most men don't care to make common knowledge."

"Do you know of any gem collectors who are selling at the moment? Particularly someone with a large blue diamond?"

Bloomsfield shook his head, although he looked vaguely troubled. "I haven't heard of anyone, no."

"What?" asked Sebastian, watching him.

"Did you say a large *blue* diamond?"

"That's right. Why?"

"It's just . . . They're very rare, you know. The only specimen I can think of that might fit such a description—" He broke off and shook his head again. "No, that's impossible."

"So you do know of such a diamond?"

The old man leaned forward in his seat, his hands gripping the chair's arms, a surge of excitement quickening his voice. "I'm not aware of a large blue diamond currently in anyone's collection. But I do know of such a specimen that was lost. And what is interesting is that it was lost exactly twenty years ago this month. Are you familiar with *le diamant bleu de la Couronne*?" He glanced from Sebastian to Hero.

Both shook their heads. "No."

"In English it's known as the 'French Blue.' It was once part of the French Crown Jewels. They say it came out of India as an enormous roughly cut triangular stone of over a hundred carats. Louis XIV bought it for the French Crown and had it recut and set, I believe, into a cravat pin."

"Must have made a very large cravat pin," said Hero.

Bloomsfield's eyes twinkled. "True. But then, Louis XIV was quite a large man. His successor Louis XV had it remade as the focal point of a magnificent Emblem of the Golden Fleece."

"What happened to it?"

"It disappeared along with the rest of the French Crown Jewels during the Revolution—the week of 11 September 1792, to be exact. It has never been recovered."

"The twenty years is significant," said Sebastian. "Why?"

"Because in 1804, Napoléon passed a decree establishing a twenty-year statute of limitations for all crimes committed during the Revolution—although I've no doubt the French royal family would dispute the sale of the diamond and claim ownership, if they heard about it."

Hero set aside her teacup. "Which would be another good reason for trying to sell the diamond quietly."

"True," said Bloomsfield.

Thunder rumbled in the distance, growing louder and louder as the wind dashed a driving rain against the drawing room's windowpanes.

Sebastian said, "If Eisler were peddling the French Blue, who would the likely buyers be?"

Bloomsfield sat in thoughtful silence for a moment, then dropped his gaze to the fire and blew out a long, troubled breath.

"Who?" asked Hero, watching him.

He looked up, his features drawn. "Prinny. That's who I would try to sell it to, if I were Eisler. The Prince Regent."

Chapter 17

After Bloomsfield's departure, Sebastian stood with his back to the fire and watched as his wife calmly poured herself another cup of tea. Both her posture and occupation were typically feminine and domestic. Only, he knew there was nothing typical about Hero.

She set aside the heavy silver pot and reached for a spoon to stir her tea. "I gather it's the Frenchman Collot from the unsavory Pilgrim in Seven Dials who told you about this mysterious blue diamond?"

"It was, yes. He claims Eisler was selling the gem for Thomas Hope."

She looked up. "Thomas, not Henry Philip?"

"That's right. Hope denies it, of course."

"But you don't believe him."

Sebastian smiled. "I'm afraid I don't have a very trusting nature." He felt his smile harden.

"There's something else," she said, watching him. "What?"

"Am I so transparent?"

"At times."

He shifted his gaze to the burning coals beside him. "I ran into a man coming out of Hope's house—a lieutenant in the 114th Foot named Matt Tyson. I knew him in Spain."

"I take it he was not exactly one of your boon companions?"

"He was not. I sat on his court-martial board."

"What had he done?"

"He was accused of murdering a Spanish woman and her two children so that he could steal their gold and jewels. Their throats were slit."

"Did he do it?"

"He claims he did not. He says he happened upon the scene just in time to see another man—an ensign— commit the crime. Unfortunately, since Tyson shot the man dead, the ensign was not in any position to defend himself against the charge. Personally, I think Tyson and the ensign committed the murders together, and then Tyson killed his accomplice when he realized they were about to be discovered by a British patrol."

"What makes you think that?"

"Tyson and I might not have been boon companions, but he and the ensign were."

"Ah. Yet Tyson was acquitted?"

"He was, yes. A sergeant with the riflemen came forward to testify that he heard the woman screaming and then saw Tyson rush into the house in a futile attempt to save her. My fellow officers believed him."

"Yet you did not. Why?"

"The patrol that came upon the murder scene said Tyson was covered with blood; the ensign was not. I think Tyson bribed the sergeant to perjure himself."

She took a slow sip of her tea. "What manner of man is he, this Tyson?"

"About twenty-five, remarkably handsome. He comes from an old, respected family in Hereford. Did well at Eton. On first meeting, he comes off as affable. Engaging. Frankly likeable. But it's all a carefully calculated facade. Beneath it lies one of the coldest, most brutally self-interested men I've ever met."

"You think he could be Daniel Eisler's killer?"

"I don't know. There is no doubt in my mind that Matt Tyson is a killer and a thief. But that doesn't mean he's necessarily behind this killing." He hesitated, then said,

"Interesting that Mr. Bloomsfield should choose this particular moment to pay you a visit."

She set aside her teacup. "Actually, I went to see him this afternoon, but he was out. So technically, he was returning my call."

"Ah." His gaze went beyond her, to where Eisler's tattered old manuscript lay on the table near the bowed front window. "I take it you showed him the manuscript?"

"I did. He says it's called *The Key of Solomon* and it does indeed appear to be some sort of magic handbook."

"So you were right," said Sebastian, going to pick it up.

"I was, although I'm afraid poor Mr. Bloomsfield was quite shocked by the contents. He translated a few passages for me, then refused to have anything more to do with it."

"Had he heard of it before?"

She shook her head. "No. But he found an inscription inside the frontpiece that indicates it was copied in Amsterdam. He says it's written in Sephardic cursive script." She came to watch as he leafed through the strange text. "I have a friend named Abigail McBean who is something of an expert on these old magic texts. She told me once that they're called 'grimoires' and—" She broke off, her eyes narrowing as he looked up at her and smiled. "What's so funny?"

At that, he laughed out loud. She was friends with a motley collection of brilliant, fascinating, and decidedly unfashionable people, from scholars and poets to reformers and artists. She knew geologists and architects, antiquaries and engineers; he should have expected that she'd be acquainted with at least someone whose specialty was ancient magic texts.

The amusement faded as it occurred to him that there was something decidedly off about a man accepting his wife's help in his attempts to prove the innocence of his former mistress's new husband. He said, "You don't need to be doing this."

She reached over to tweak the manuscript from his grasp. "Yes, I do."

She started to turn away from the window, the book in her hands, then paused, her gaze on the darkening scene outside.

The rain had settled into a steady downpour, the clouds hanging dark and low to steal whatever light had been left in the sky. Women with shawls pulled over their heads hurried through the gathering gloom, their pattens clicking, the murky glow from the oil lamps reflecting in a dull gleam off rain-washed paving stones. A landau emblazoned with a coronet and drawn by a matched team of dapple grays dashed past, its spinning red wheels throwing up a fan of water from the gutter to spray over the footpath. It wet the trouser legs of a man standing near the area steps of the house across the street, his slouch hat pulled low over his face. He neither flinched nor moved but simply stood, his gaze fixed on their house.

"What is it?" Sebastian asked, watching Hero's expression change.

"That man. He's been standing there staring at the house for nearly an hour. I noticed him when I was showing Mr. Bloomsfield the manuscript. We brought it here to the window so that he could catch the last of the daylight and—"

But Sebastian was already pushing away from the window to stride rapidly toward the door.

Chapter 18

Sebastian walked out of the house into a wild wind that threw rain in his face and flapped the tails of his coat. A whip cracked, a shaggy team of shire horses filling the road in front of him so that he had to pull up sharply at the edge of the footpath, swearing impatiently as he ducked around the laden coal wagon. He half expected the slouch-hatted watcher to have disappeared into the mist by the time he reached the far side of the street. But the man was still there, his rain-darkened coat huge on his skeletally thin frame, his mouth pulled wide into a madman's grin as he waited for Sebastian to walk up to him.

"Who the bloody hell are you and why are you watching my house?" Sebastian demanded, coming to a halt in front of him.

"It's funny you should be asking that, you see," said the man, "because I was wanting to pose the same question to you."

His hair was a greasy dark tangle heavily threaded with gray that hung too long around a face with hollowed cheeks and sunken, watery black eyes. At sometime in the distant past, his nose had been badly broken, and a puckered red scar distorted one side of his face. In age he could have been anywhere between thirty-five and fifty, exposure to the elements and ill-health having roughened his skin and dug deep grooves beside his mouth. For a moment, Sebastian thought he looked vaguely familiar; then the haggard face twitched and the impression vanished.

Sebastian frowned. "What question?"

"Who are you?"

"You're telling me that's why you're standing here in the rain? Because you want to know who I am?"

"It is, yes."

The rain poured around them, dimpling the puddle in the gutter at their feet, pinging on the iron railing of the steps that led down to the kitchen, and running in rivulets down the smiling man's face.

The man's grin widened. "She's a fine-looking woman, your wife. Very fine-looking."

A powerful surge of fear-fueled rage coursed through Sebastian. He slammed the man back against the brick wall of the house behind him, one forearm pressed up tight against his skinny throat. "What the devil is that supposed to mean?"

The man shook his head, his grin still eerily in place. "Didn't mean nothing by it."

"Why the bloody hell do you want to know who I am?"

The man's eyes squeezed shut as he gave a strange, half-strangled laugh. "I saw you. Saw you coming out of his house."

"Whose house?"

The man flattened his hands against the brick wall behind him, his stringy muscles tense, his fingers splayed. Then he opened his eyes, and they were like the eyes of a child or of the very old, when the mind begins to lose its ability to comprehend and simply stares out at the world in helpless confusion and need. "Oh, I can't tell you that."

Sebastian took a step back and let the man go. "You stay away from my wife. Is that understood? You stay away from my house, and you stay away from my wife. I see you hanging around here again, I'll have you taken up by the watch."

He realized the man was no longer looking at him but

at something beyond him. Turning, Sebastian saw Hero calmly crossing the street toward him, the hem of her delicate white muslin gown lifted above the mud- and manure-strewn paving.

When Sebastian looked back, the man was gone.

"So, who is he?" Hero asked, her gaze following the skinny man's retreating figure as she stepped up onto the flagway beside him. A gust of wind blew the rain in stinging, swirling sheets around them.

"Someone who belongs in Bedlam."

She brought her gaze back to Sebastian. "Oh? You mean like a man who charges out into the rain with neither hat nor cloak?"

He swiped the water out of his eyes and looked at his wife. Rain dripped from her wet hair, ran down her cheeks, soaked the wet muslin of her elegant gown so that it clung to every swell and hollow of her magnificent body. He said, "You mean like you?"

Her face lit up with surprised delight and she let out a peal of laughter that tilted her head up to the sky.

※

The rain eased up later that evening, only to sweep back in just after midnight.

Lying awake in his wife's bed, Sebastian could see streaks of strange green lightning illuminating the churning clouds that pressed low over the fetid alleyways and rain-lashed docks to the east. There came a moment's breath-stealing pause; then the rumble of the thunder began, building louder and louder into a window-rattling crescendo that bled seamlessly into memories he would rather have forgotten.

He sensed a subtle shift beside him, heard a whisper of movement. A soft, warm hand crept across the bare flesh of his chest. Hero said, "You're not sleeping."

He smiled into the darkness. "And you are?"

She rolled over to press her long body against his side as he brought his arms down to gather her to him.

She said, "You're worried about that man, the one who was watching the house."

He stroked his hand down her back and over the swell of her hip. "I keep thinking I've seen him before, only I can't place where."

"A beggar on a street corner, perhaps? A face glimpsed in the desperate crowds outside St. Martin's poorhouse?"

Sebastian shook his head. "I don't think he's a beggar."

"You said yourself he sounds as if he belongs in Bedlam."

"That doesn't mean he isn't somehow involved in Daniel Eisler's death."

"I don't see the connection."

"Why was he here, now, watching the house? Watching you? Not me. You."

She propped herself up on one elbow so she could look down at him. "I can take care of myself."

Her words echoed those Kat had said to him earlier that day. Only, in that instance she had been referring to the threat posed by Jarvis . . . Hero's own father.

He caught the dark fall of hair curtaining her face and swept it back with his splayed fingers. He had seen her shoot a man point-blank in the chest and barely register any reaction, either horror or remorse. There was a hard edge to this woman that he knew came to her from her father, Jarvis. It was leavened by her sense of justice and a measure of compassion for the suffering of those less fortunate that Jarvis had never experienced. But Sebastian knew she could still kill without hesitation or compunction to protect herself or others, just as he knew that none of that might be enough to keep her safe.

He said, "We're all vulnerable. Especially when dealing with a madman."

She was silent a moment, her face solemn, a frown digging a furrow between her eyebrows. "Do you think I don't worry about you?"

"That's not—"

"Not the same? Because you are a man and I am a woman?"

"No. Because it's one thing for me to make the choice to put my own life in danger and something else entirely when my actions endanger someone else."

She touched her fingers to his lips. "I knew what I was letting myself in for when I married you, Devlin."

He smiled against her hand. "I'm not sure I did." It was the closest he'd ever come to speaking of the profound shifts in their relationship and the unexpected, life-altering deepening of the ties that bound them.

She let her hand slide down his chest, down over the tender flesh of his belly. His breath caught, and he saw her eyes darken with want.

He rolled her onto her back, rising above her. The wind drove the rain against the windowpanes. The green glow of the lightning flickered in ethereal pulses around them. He kissed her cheek, her eyelids, her hair, the delicate hollow at the base of her throat. His world narrowed down to the rasp of flesh against flesh, hands reaching, fingers clenching. The softness of her lips. The whispered urgency of her desire.

And his.

❧

Sebastian was easing his breeches up over his hips when he became aware of Hero coming to stand in the doorway of his darkened dressing room. She'd drawn a blanket over her shoulders against the chill, but otherwise she was naked, her body long and pale, her rounded belly silhouetted against the throbbing electric light of the storm.

She said, "I suppose there's a good reason you're sneaking away from my bed at one in the morning."

He smiled and pulled a shirt over his head. "I want to have another look at Eisler's house—alone, and with no interruptions."

"Unless someone interrupts your housebreaking with a blunderbuss."

"Do you think me so careless?"

"No. But you didn't get any sleep last night. You need to rest, Devlin."

He bent to pull on his boots. "How much rest do you suppose Russell Yates is getting tonight?"

"There will always be innocent men in danger of being hanged."

He knotted a casual kerchief around his neck and reached for his coat. "True."

"You said the doors were bolted and the windows barred. So how will you get in?"

"I've an idea."

"Well, it's reassuring to know that should we ever find ourselves in dire straits, you could make a credible living as a burglar."

He grunted and caught her to him for a quick kiss, but she surprised him by holding him close and hard.

She said, "You'll be careful." In typical Hero fashion, it was more of a command than a request.

He kissed her again, on her nose. "Good God. You sound just like a wife."

"Don't be insulting." She adjusted the set of his hat. "What exactly do you expect to find?"

"Answers, hopefully."

"To precisely which questions?"

"I haven't figured that out yet."

Chapter 19

$\mathcal{A}$ single oil lamp mounted high on the wall of the corner greengrocer's shop cast a small, murky puddle of light. But the rest of the crooked lane lay still and quiet in the wet darkness.

Pausing in the shadow of a recessed doorway that smelled strongly of urine, Sebastian watched as the gusting wind ruffled the rain-drenched ivy that draped the scarred stone facade of Eisler's house and half obscured the ancient leaded windows. Like the warehouses and shuttered shops around it, the house was dark. He had no way of knowing if the aged retainers employed by Eisler were still in residence, but if so, they would long ago have retired to their attic bedchamber for the night. Casting a quick glance around, he crossed the street to duck down the narrow, malodorous passageway that ran along the south side of the house.

Vennels, he'd heard them called in Scotland and the north of England. This one was barely wide enough for a man turned sideways and terminated in an old gate made of thick, vertical planks studded with clavos and hinged with iron straps. But the wood was crumbling with rot, the rusted mountings flaking and so thin they snapped easily when Sebastian leaned his weight against the boards. He caught the gate before it could clatter

onto the weed- and leaf-strewn paving and set it carefully to one side.

What must once, two hundred years or more earlier,
have been a delightful Renaissance garden of rose-
shaded walks bordering parterres of comfrey and cham-
omile, tansy and feverfew, was now a dark, overgrown
tangle hemmed in by the looming, grimy brick walls of
its neighbors. Massive elms, their spreading limbs heavy
with rain, had grown up near the terrace. Any other man
would have been blind. But Sebastian moved easily,
picking his way over downed rotting branches, tangled
wet vines, and broken masonry.

It was a gift, his mother had told him, this catlike ability to see clearly in all but the complete absence of any
light, to hear sounds too subtle or high-pitched for most
human ears. The trait was shared by no one else in his
family, and he still remembered the look on his mother's
face when she first discovered the strange, almost ani-
malistic quality of his senses.

She'd come upon him unexpectedly one evening,
when he was curled up on a bench in the summerhouse
reading a book long after the sun had set. He realized
now that she had surely known then, even if Sebastian
himself had not, that this gift came to him from his
father. . . .

The father who was not the Earl of Hendon.

He pushed the memory from his thoughts and quietly
mounted the shattered steps to the terrace, stepping
carefully to avoid the telltale clatter of broken stones
shifting beneath his boots. The rows of ratty wooden
cages were still there to the left of the door, their forlorn
feathered occupants huddled against a damp wind that
carried with it a foul stench of neglect and misery. Nearly
every food bowl was empty, the water vessels scummed.

Moving purposefully from cage to cage, he quickly
unlatched one door after the other, rattling the slats of
those whose occupants appeared too weakened or mo-
rose to seize the freedom offered them. In a whirl of

wings, they rose against the night sky, first sparrows, doves, and larks; then, once the smaller birds had flown to safety, the goshawks and owls. Sebastian stood at last before the cage of the disgruntled, long-haired black cat, which looked up at him with slitted green eyes. Sebastian swung open the cage door, its hinges squealing loud enough to make him wince.

"Well, go on, then," he whispered when the cat remained motionless. "What are you waiting for? An invitation from the King?"

The cat blinked.

Sebastian tipped the cage forward, upending the cat, which dropped lightly onto the pavement beside him with an indignant yowl.

"Shhh," hissed Sebastian.

The cat streaked into the night, its ridiculously long, bushy tail lashing back and forth.

Sebastian watched it for a moment, ears straining for any sound that might indicate that his presence had been detected. The wind gusted up again, thrashing the creaking limbs of the old elms.

He eased the knife from his boot and crossed to the back door.

The gap between the door and its frame was not as wide as he'd hoped, but it was enough. Slipping the blade through the opening close against the frame, he pressed down until the hard steel of the knife sank into the softer iron of the bolt with enough purchase to enable him to slide the bolt a fraction to the right. Then he freed the blade, eased it in close to the frame again, and pressed down.

He did this again and again, working the bolt back bit by bit. The work was excruciatingly slow. It would have been much easier to simply knock out the bars on one of the windows and break the glass, but he preferred to leave as little sign of his entry as possible. He was aware of a soft patter as the rain started up again, and the distant cry of the watch shouting, *"Two o'clock on a rainy night and all is well."* Then the bolt cleared the frame with a soft click, and the door creaked inward perhaps six inches.

Sebastian pushed it open wider, took a step, and nearly tripped as something warm and furry threaded between his legs.

"Will you go away?" he whispered.

The cat let out a soft mew.

Bloody hell.

Slipping the knife back into its sheath, Sebastian stepped over the cat, then quickly shut the door in its face.

"Meow," complained the cat, caught on the outside.

With the door closed, the corridor lay in near total darkness, the only illumination a faint glow that spilled through the archway from the windows of the vast hall beyond. The rows of heavy paintings on the walls and stacks of fine furniture loomed out of heavy shadows. The smell of mold and rot hung thick in the air.

Moving quietly, he opened the first door to his right and found himself staring at a dining room that looked as if it hadn't been used for its intended purpose in decades. The velvet curtains at the windows hung in tatters; a long Jacobean table and a dozen chairs with barley-turned legs, so darkened by centuries of smoke and old wax as to be nearly black, stood in the center of the room. All were so buried beneath piles of furniture and stacks of paintings and *objets d'art* that it would take a man a week to search the room, clearing a path for himself as he went.

Closing the door, Sebastian turned to the opposite side of the corridor, only to draw up short at the sight of a pair of green eyes gleaming at him from out of the darkness.

"How the devil did you get in here?" he whispered to the cat. Then a waft of wind scented by wet pavement and sodden earth caused the heavy door from the terrace to shift with a loud creak, and he realized that, without the bolt, it had swung open again.

He used his boot to nudge the cat out of his way. "Just be quiet, will you?"

The next door opened to reveal a chamber only slightly less cluttered than the dining room, although this space was obviously used for more than storage, for there was a clear path from the door to a beautiful ebony desk inlaid with ivory and piled high with papers. From the looks of things, someone had been going through them — no doubt Eisler's heirs or their solicitors. Beyond the desk stood a massive safe, its heavy iron door hanging open, its shelves empty. Whatever gems, stacks of currency, and other secrets it might once have contained were now gone.

He moved on.

As he had suspected, the next door proved to be a second entrance to the long parlor where Eisler had been shot. This, obviously, was how the murderer had managed to flee the house without being seen by Yates . . . *if* Yates was telling the truth about what had happened that night.

It bothered Sebastian that he was not as convinced of that as he would like to have been.

There remained only one more door on this floor, not far from where the set of narrow steps led down to the basement kitchen. Crossing back across the corridor, he pressed down on the door latch.

It was locked.

At his feet, the black cat settled on its haunches and let out a soft mew.

"Yes, it is puzzling, isn't it?" Sebastian said to the cat. "But I wish you would—"

He broke off as a muffled thump sounded from below.

Sebastian drew back from the top of the stairs, his spine pressed against the wall, the dagger from his boot in his hand. A faint glow, as if from a lantern, illuminated the stairwell leading up from the basement and threw the long shadows of two men across the far wall. A heavy footstep sounded on the stairs, then another.

"Meow," went the cat.

The footsteps stopped.

"Meow." Stretching to its feet, the cat arched its back and went to stand at the top of the stairs, its enormous fluffy tail lashing back and forth, green eyes glinting in the darkness.

"What in the name of all that's 'oly is that?" demanded one of the men in a frightened whisper.

The second man answered, his voice older, harsher. "It's a cat, you damn fool." Sebastian heard a whacking sound, as if the older man had walloped his companion with his hat.

"Ow. What was that for?"

"Jist shut up and keep goin'."

The footsteps resumed their cautious ascent.

Sebastian eased sideways deeper into the shadows cast by the open stair door and a massive bureau piled high with everything from a marble bust and Grecian urn to a jumble of elegant walking sticks. But there was no place to hide, and he couldn't cross in front of the stairs or even slide back toward the dining room without moving into the men's line of vision.

"Where do we look first?" whispered the younger man, his voice cracking with nerves.

"The parlor, I should think," answered his companion.

"And if we don't find it there?"

"Then we go through every bleedin' room in the house till we do find it. What do ye think? Ye want to be the one to tell the gov'nor we failed?"

"No. But . . ." The footsteps halted again. "Morgan?"

"What? Now what are ye stoppin' for?"

"Why's the back door standin' open?"

Sebastian could see the first housebreaker now. A tall, skinny lad dressed in a brown corduroy coat and baggy trousers, he held a shuttered horn lantern in one clenched fist, the muted light glowing golden on the smooth, unlined features of a youth probably no more than sixteen or eighteen. His gaze riveted on the open back door, he swallowed heavily, the movement visibly bobbing his Adam's apple up and down. The lantern light quivered as his hand shook.

"What the 'ell?" said the older man, pausing on the step behind him.

"Ye think maybe the wind blew it open?"

"How the 'ell would I know? Go look."

"Give me the pistol."

"Why? Ye think Rawhead and Bloodybones are gonna git ye?"

"Stop laughin' at me and jist give me the pistol."

The older man grumbled but handed over a heavy horse pistol that looked like a relic of the Thirty Years' War.

Sebastian held himself utterly still as the young housebreaker passed in front of him, the light from the lantern playing over the walls and jumbled treasures of the corridor. If the man had simply glanced around, he would have seen Sebastian quite easily. But the lad's attention was fixed on the open door and the windswept terrace beyond. He was so nervous, Sebastian could see the barrel of his gun shaking; the lantern light danced and quivered.

"Well?" demanded the older man, reaching the top step. He was slightly shorter than his companion but considerably bulkier, with a thick neck, a powerful chest, and heavily muscled arms and legs. His features were blunt, his nose large and crooked, his beetle-browed gaze fixed, like the younger man's, on the door to the terrace.

Then he turned his head and saw Sebastian standing no more than five feet away from him.

Chapter 20

"*What the 'ell!*"

Jerking a large, curving knife loose from the sheath at his side, the ruffian rushed at Sebastian, the blade held over his head in a backhanded grip.

Seizing a heavy brass walking stick from the clutter atop the bureau beside him, Sebastian swung it up to block the blade's vicious downward slash. Metal clanged against metal. But the power behind the blow was so intense that the impact reverberated down Sebastian's left arm, and he staggered.

The housebreaker recovered instantly, his lips curling away from his teeth in a fierce rictus, his grip on the knife shifting. "Shoot 'im!" he yelled to the younger man by the door.

"I can't! Yer in the way," he screeched, the gun held straight out in front of him in a trembling grip, his voice rising an octave as he fumbled to set down the lantern.

"Bloody bastard," growled the thick-necked man. He lunged again, driving the knife straight toward Sebastian's heart.

Dancing sideways an instant too late, Sebastian felt the blade slice through the flesh of his ribs as he pivoted and drove his own dagger deep into the ruffian's chest.

"Morgan!" cried the man from the doorway.

For one suspended moment, the ruffian froze, his heavy features a study in astonishment. Then he crumpled.

Sebastian tried to wrench his dagger free and felt it catch on the man's ribs as he fell.

"You killed my brother!" screamed the young man at the door, the pistol held before him, his left hand coming up to steady his grip. His finger was just tightening on the trigger when the black cat stretched up and sank the claws of both front paws into his leg.

The man let out a sharp yelp. Belching flame, the pistol exploded in a deafening roar that filled the corridor with pungent smoke and a shower of pulverized plaster as the shot buried itself in the ceiling.

His jaw sagging in fear and fresh horror, the younger man threw away the now useless pistol and bolted out the door.

Sebastian wrenched his dagger free from the dead man's chest with a violent shove that sent the body tumbling and thumping down the stairs. He could hear the younger man crashing through the overgrown wreck of a garden, frantic, stumbling blindly. By the time Sebastian erupted out the door into the wet, windblown night, the housebreaker was nearly to the ruined stables.

Gripping the gory dagger in his fist, Sebastian dashed across the terrace and leapt down the steps. A sharp branch snagged his coat; he jerked and heard the cloth rip as he pushed on. He could see the young housebreaker's slim frame silhouetted against the night sky as he scrambled up the pile of fallen bricks that marked the crumbling wall at the base of the garden.

"What do ye want from me?" he screamed, pausing to grab one of the loose bricks and chuck it at Sebastian's head.

Sebastian ducked. "I want to know who sent you."

"Go to 'ell."

Collecting his feet beneath him, the lad jumped. Sebastian heard his body hit the other side with a splat, then the plopping squish of running feet flailing through mud.

Sebastian climbed after him, the half-collapsed wall shifting ominously beneath him as he dropped lightly onto the far side.

He found himself in a muddy, rubbish-strewn alley hemmed in by high walls on either side. He could see the lad dashing frantically for the distant street, his feet slipping and sliding in the muck as he ran.

Sebastian pelted after him, then drew up sharply as the dark outline of a carriage loomed at the end of the alley. The near door flew open, the long, dark barrel of a rifle poking out into the night.

"Shit," he swore, instinctively ducking his head as he dove into the shadows of the wall beside him. He hit the cold mud and said, *"Shit,"* again as he slid face-first through what smelled like a heap of rotting cabbage leaves mingled with a pile of fresh horse dung. Looking up, he saw a spurt of flame, heard the crack of a rifle shot cut through the night.

But the unseen man in the carriage was not shooting at Sebastian.

Some twenty feet from the end of the alley, the young housebreaker stumbled, his body jerking, his torso twisting, his knees buckling beneath him. The carriage's driver whipped up his horses; the vehicle lurched into the night, trace chains jangling, wheels clattering over the cobbles.

Swiping at the mud and muck on his face, Sebastian went to hunker down beside the boy and draw his trembling, bloody body into his arms. "Who hired you?" Sebastian asked, lifting him.

The lad shook his head and coughed, his eyes scared, one clawlike hand digging into Sebastian's arm.

"Tell me, damn it! Don't you understand? Whoever they are, they just killed you."

But the light was already fading from the boy's eyes, the tension in his body easing, the fierce grip on Sebastian's arm loosening, falling.

"Son of a bitch," swore Sebastian. Heedless of the mud, he sank back on his haunches, the dead boy still gripped in his arms. "Son of a bitch," he said again.

And then he said it a third time. "Son of a bitch."

※

Hero was dressed and seated beside the fire in her bedchamber, the ancient Hebrew manuscript open on her lap, when Devlin walked in, bringing with him a pungent odor of rotten cabbage, horse manure, and mud. He'd already stripped off his coat and boots, but his face, waistcoat, and breeches were liberally smeared with muck, and he held a longhaired black cat tucked up under one arm.

The manuscript slid to the floor, forgotten, as she stared at him. "*Devlin.* Good God. Are you all right?"

"What are you doing up?" he asked as the cat gave a disgruntled howl and leapt from his arms.

"I couldn't sleep. What happened? And what are you doing with that cat?"

"He claims I owe him since he saved my life, although I maintain he was only returning the favor."

She started to laugh. Then she noticed the dark red sheen mingled with the muck on his waistcoat and the laughter died on her lips. "Is that your blood?"

"Only some of it." He headed for his dressing room, stripping off clothes as he went.

She followed him. "How much of it?"

He yanked off his ruined waistcoat, his nose wrinkling as he tossed it aside. "My apologies for the aroma. I fear I slid through someone's garbage pile. Calhoun isn't going to be happy. I think that waistcoat was his favorite."

"How much of it?" she demanded again, helping him ease his ripped shirt over his head. He tried to turn away, but she saw the long purple slit that cut across his ribs and caught his arm. "Devlin—"

He squinted down at it. "It's not deep."

"Why didn't you go to Gibson and get it sewn up?"

"It's not that bad."

"You could get lockjaw from it!"

"Sewing it up wouldn't prevent that, now, would it?"

She gave him a look that needed no accompanying words and turned toward the bellpull. "If nothing else, you need to wash it well with hot water. I'm ringing for Calhoun."

"Good God, no; it's nearly four in the morning."

She let her hand fall to her side and turned toward the door. "Very well. I'll go down into the kitchen and heat some water myself."

He let her ring for Calhoun.

Afterward, she curled up on the rug beside his chair while he sat before the fire, a glass of brandy in his hand, and told her what had happened.

"What do you think those men were looking for?" she asked when he had finished. "The blue diamond Collot told you about?"

He took a long, slow sip of his brandy. "I suppose it's possible, but I doubt it. I think whatever is going on here is far more serious than some diamond—however big it might be."

"Are you certain the rifleman in that carriage was shooting at the young housebreaker and not you?"

"If he was aiming at me, he's an appalling shot."

"Most people are."

"Not this one. He hit the lad square in the chest, killing him almost instantly."

She kept her gaze on the cat, who was giving himself a long, fastidious bath beside the hearth. "You think he was killed to keep him from revealing who hired him?"

"I think it likely, yes."

"But . . . why? Why not simply haul the lad into the carriage and whisk him safely away?"

"He said the man I killed in the house was his brother. I suppose that once we learned the identity of the dead man, it wouldn't have been hard to track down the lad and find whoever was behind the attempted burglary."

"But the man in the carriage had no way of knowing the older man was dead."

"They could have heard the shot. And they knew that only one of their men came out of that house, chased by me."

"True," she conceded. "You didn't see anyone around before you went inside?"

"No. But that doesn't mean they weren't there."

"Do you think they recognized you?"

"Well enough to know that I wasn't their hireling, obviously. But probably not so well as to know who I was. Most people don't see well in the dark."

"Some do."

He met her gaze, and she knew he was thinking the same thing she was. He said, "The lad was no more than twenty feet away from the rifleman when he was hit. It wasn't a difficult shot."

"True." She watched the cat curl itself into a ball, sigh, and close its eyes. The milk bowl and plate of minced beef beside it—provided by Calhoun—were now empty. She said, "Did you go to the authorities?"

"I did not. I took to my heels and fled."

"With the cat."

"He was insistent."

"Is it a he?"

"It is. I checked." Bending forward, he picked up the manuscript from beside her. "If you were looking at this, no wonder you couldn't sleep."

"It is . . . bizarre. I'm anxious to hear what Abigail Mc-Bean can tell me about it in the morning." She leaned back against his chair, felt his fingers brush her flesh as he played with the curls at the nape of her neck.

He said, "I have a bad feeling about this."

Her gaze met his, her expression solemn. "So do I."

Chapter 21

*I*n the fashionable world, where balls lasted until nearly dawn and breakfasts were held at midday, morning calls began at three in the afternoon. Fortunately, Hero knew that Miss Abigail McBean had long ago resigned herself to being hopelessly outré and did not keep fashionable hours.

A confirmed spinster well into her thirties, Miss Mc-Bean now shared her small but comfortable Camden Town house with a young niece and nephew orphaned some six months before by the sudden, tragic death of their parents. Hero could hear the children's laughter coming from the rear garden when, carrying the battered old manuscript, she arrived at her friend's house the next morning.

She was met at the door by a young, flaxen-haired housemaid who was so flustered to find a real viscountess ringing the bell that she escorted Hero immediately to her mistress, who was, as the girl cryptically announced, "Upstairs."

Upstairs proved to be in the attic. As they neared the top of the narrow attic steps, Hero could hear her friend's voice coming from behind a half-open door at the end of the corridor, chanting, *"Angeli supradicti."*

The housemaid, a slim slip of a girl who couldn't have been more than fifteen or sixteen, hesitated on the last stair, her eyes growing wide as she swallowed, hard. "Miss McBean is in there, m'lady," she whispered, her chest jerking with her suddenly agitated breathing as she pointed one shaky hand toward the far door. "I kin knock for you if you want, but . . ." She sucked in an audible gasp of air, her voice trailing off into nothing.

"I'll announce myself," Hero told the girl, who dropped a quick, relieved curtsy and bolted back down the stairs.

"Agla, On, Tetragrammaton," exclaimed the voice at the end of the hall.

Biting her lip to keep from laughing, Hero pushed the door open wider.

A short, plump figure shrouded in a white linen robe, her face hidden by a deep, monklike cowl, circled the room in slow, measured steps. She held an open book in one hand, in the other a flask of holy water such as a Catholic priest might use. *"Per sedem Adonay, per Hagius, o Theos,"* she intoned, punctuating each phrase with a flick of the holy water. On the room's scrubbed wooden floor was drawn a circle upon which were positioned a strange assortment of objects: an earthenware vessel filled with glowing coals; a naked sword blade; flasks of perfume. The pungent scents of myrtle and musk permeated the room. The robed figure was so focused on reading the incantations from her book and stepping precisely around the circle that she didn't notice Hero until she was nearly upon her. Then she looked up, her step faltering, her jaw sagging, before she clamped it shut and went off into a peal of laughter.

"Losh!" she exclaimed in a pronounced Scottish brogue. "Frightened the sense out of me, you did. For one hen-witted moment, I actually feared all the laws of the universe had reversed themselves and the silly spell worked."

"What? You were trying to conjure me, were you?"

Miss Abigail McBean pushed back her cowl and set aside her holy water. "Not you, exactly." She pointed to a woodcut illustration in her book. "The angel Anael, who rules the tenth hour of Tuesday—or at least, he does according to Peter de Abano, who wrote this thing back in 1496."

Hero studied the illustration. "You think I look like that, do you?"

In mock seriousness, the Scotswoman held up the open book with its illustration beside Hero, as if comparing the two. "Hmm. Well, you're female, of course. And you don't have black hair or six-foot gray wings. Not to mention a wand tipped with a pine cone and decorated with ribbons."

Hero tweaked the book from her friend's grasp and studied the title. *"Heptameron,"* she read aloud. "I take it this is one of your grimoires?"

"It is." Miss McBean pulled the linen robe off over her head, transforming herself from an exotic, vaguely menacing figure into a plump woman in a simple sprigged muslin gown. She had a pretty round face with a small nose, full, rosy cheeks, and a head of riotously curling rust-colored hair that she'd tried rather unsuccessfully to contain in a bun. "Its English title is *Magical Elements*. I've been wanting to try this incantation for weeks, only I just got the hyssop."

Hero studied her friend's unlined, pleasant face. "If you don't believe in these spells, why do them?"

"Because I know of no better way to understand what these men were trying to do and how they felt when they did it." She nodded to the calfskin-bound manuscript Hero had tucked beneath her arm. "What's that?"

Hero held it out to her. "I'm told it's called *The Key of Solomon.* Ever hear of it?"

Miss McBean took the manuscript with a hand that was suddenly not quite steady. "I've heard of it."

Chapter 22

Sebastian was careful to wait until after twelve o'clock to pay a call on the Park Street home of his aunt, the Dowager Duchess of Claiborne. The house was not, technically, the property of the Dowager but belonged to her son, the present Duke of Claiborne. But the Duke, a stout, mild-mannered man well into his middle years, knew himself to be no match for his formidable mother. Rather than assert his rights of ownership, he simply lived with his growing family in a much smaller house in Half Moon Street, leaving Henrietta in possession of the grand pile over which she had reigned as mistress for more than half a century.

Born Lady Henrietta St. Cyr, the elder sister of the current Earl of Hendon, she was one of the few people who knew that she was not actually Sebastian's aunt, although the world believed her to be. But neither Sebastian nor Henrietta was the type to allow technicalities to interfere in their affections.

He found her seated at her breakfast table, a half-eaten piece of toast and a cup of tea before her. Like her brother, she was big boned and fleshy, with a broad, plain face and the piercing blue eyes that were the hallmark of the St. Cyr family. She had never been a pretty woman, even when young. But she was every inch the earl's daughter and made a splendid duchess. Always exquisitely groomed and imperious in manner, she was one of the grandes dames of society. And if at all possible she never left her dressing room before one o'clock.

"Good heavens, Aunt," said Sebastian, bending to kiss her rouged cheek. "The clocks have barely struck twelve and I find you already on the verge of setting forth into the world. How . . . dreadfully unfashionable."

She rapped him affectionately on the ear, chuckling as she straightened the towering purple turban he'd knocked slightly askew. "Impertinent jackanapes. As it happens, I did not sleep well last night. All that banging and booming; I swear it was enough to wake the dead. Now, stop looming over me and sit down and tell me why you are here. No, don't bring him a cup of tea, you foolish man," she told the hapless footman who was about to do just that. "Get him some ale."

Sebastian drew out the seat beside her. "What makes you so certain I'm not here simply for the pleasure of your company?"

"Because I know you. And because I read the papers." She paused, a hint of apprehension tightening the lines around her mouth. Henrietta might be leery of his recent marriage to the daughter of Lord Jarvis, but she had never approved of his relationship with Kat either. Sebastian knew she would frown on anything likely to bring him once more into the orbit of his ex-mistress.

She leaned forward, her gaze hard on his face. "But first, I want you to tell me how your new bride gets on. Is she well?"

"Hero? I doubt she's ever been sick in her life. I wanted to ask—"

"I saw her in Bond Street the other day," said Henrietta, ignoring his attempt to change the subject. "She looked ravishing—positively *glowing*, in fact, which is not a word I ever thought I would use to describe Hero Jarvis. She's not by chance increasing, is she?" She looked at him archly.

Sebastian stared back at her. Her capacity to ferret out

other people's secrets had always struck him as bordering on the uncanny. He said, "Bit soon for that, isn't it?"

"Is it?"

Sebastian paused while her man placed a tankard of ale before him, then drank deeply. "I'm here to ask what you can tell me about the Hopes."

A faint, enigmatic smile touched her lips. She took a delicate sip of her tea, then said, "Which ones?"

"Henry Philip and Thomas."

"Ah. Well, there isn't much to say about Henry Philip. He's never married, you know, and seldom ventures out into company. Queer little man."

"I understand he's something of a gem collector."

"He is, yes. I've heard it said he has the largest private collection of jewels in Europe, although I've never seen it personally."

"What about Thomas? Does he share his brother's interest in gems?"

"Not to my knowledge. Oh, he buys the odd piece for that wife of his." Henrietta's nose quivered in a way that told him Louisa Hope was not one of her favorites. "But for the most part he fancies himself something of an antiquary and patron of the arts."

"Tell me about his wife."

"Louisa de la Poer Beresford. Her uncle is the Earl of Tyrone and the Marquis of Waterford."

"And her father?"

"Some clergyman. In Ireland, of all places."

"So Thomas Hope was quite a catch for her."

"He was, yes. Although I've heard there were tears when the match was first suggested to her."

"He is rather . . . unattractive. Even if he is staggeringly rich."

"True. But I believe there was more to it than that. She had formed a previous attachment to someone who was most unsuitable—a by-blow of her uncle or some such thing. There was no question of the family ever al-

lowing anything to come of *that*. So in the end she gave
up and married Hope."

"Admirable," said Sebastian with heavy sarcasm.

His aunt frowned at him. "Realistic."

"A pity she doesn't appear to have much of a fondness for Egyptian sarcophagi—or for Thomas Hope, for
that matter."

"Indeed. I fear she has turned into one of those fe-
males who seems to believe that just because they are
unhappy they must needs devote their lives to an attempt to make the rest of the world miserable, as well."

Sebastian smiled. "Not fond of the Society for the
Suppression of Vice, are you, Aunt?"

"I always say there's nothing wrong with a bit of vice
as long as it's not taken to the extreme. Give me someone with a touch of vice over someone with an excess
of sanctimonious hypocrisy any day."

He laughed and took another swallow of ale. "I understand she has a young cousin staying with her from
Ireland. Have you met him?"

Henrietta's scowl cleared. "I have, yes. Blair Beresford. Charming young man. As attractive as his cousin
but with none of Louisa's self-righteous drivel. I must
say, however, that I do not care for that military man he
has taken up with."

"You mean Lieutenant Tyson?"

"I do, yes. He may be a fine figure of a man, and I
know the Tysons are an old, respected Hereford family.
But there's something not quite right about him. And
don't ask me to explain it, because I can't."

She drained her teacup, set it aside, then fixed him
with a level stare. "Now, not another word will you get
out of me until you tell me how the Hopes could possibly
be involved in Eisler's murder. And there is no point in
trying to deny that's what this is all about, because I
know you."

"I don't know that they are involved."

"Huh. Well, I certainly trust you don't intend to start

suspecting everyone who ever bought jewels from that dreadful man."

"Good heavens," said Sebastian, opening his eyes a little wider. "Aunt Henrietta. What did you buy from him?"

She put up a hand to straighten her turban again, although it was not in need of adjustment. "That lovely little diamond bracelet I wore to the Queen's Drawing Room recently—the one Claiborne made such a fuss over when he saw it. Mind you, I didn't deal with Eisler directly. But I had no doubt where the piece came from."

"So with whom did you deal?"

"A lapidary named John Francillon. He has an establishment on the Strand. I actually saw him there a few days ago."

"You mean you saw Francillon?"

"No. I mean that I saw Eisler in Francillon's shop."

"What day was this?"

"Saturday, I believe. The two were huddled together in the back when I first walked in. I wouldn't have paid much attention if Eisler hadn't been acting positively furtive about the entire affair."

Sebastian smiled. "So naturally then you did pay attention."

"I did, yes. Although I managed to get only a glimpse of the stone involved—what looked like an enormous blue sapphire. After Eisler left, I asked Francillon if the item was for sale. He became quite flustered when he realized I'd seen it and begged me not to tell anyone about it. Which I would have done," she added, "if Eisler weren't dead."

Sebastian stood and planted a loud kiss on her cheek. "Aunt Henrietta, I don't know what I'd do without you."

"Where are you going?" she asked as he headed for the door.

"To pay a call on your Mr. Francillon."

Chapter 23

The rain started up again long before Sebastian reached the Strand, the low-hanging clouds robbing the city of color to leave only gray: gray wet streets, flat gray light, gray sky. The air was heavy with the dank scent of wet stone and coal smoke and the pungent odors of the nearby river.

Leaving his horses in Tom's care, Sebastian ducked beneath a trim black awning with the name FRANCILLON neatly lettered in gold. He pushed open the door, the shop bell jangling. An older man behind the counter paused in the act of hanging a botanical illustration of an exotic lily and turned.

He looked to be somewhere in his late sixties, his dark hair silvered at the temples, although his movements were full of energy, his small, wiry form still trim and upright. He had the high forehead, tight lips, and thin Gallic nose of his ancestors, French Huguenots who had fled their homeland after the revocation of the Edict of Nantes more than a hundred years before. The Francillons had plied their trade in London for generations, yet his voice still carried a faint inflection when he asked, "May I help you?"

Sebastian went to rest his hands on the counter and lean into them. "My name is Devlin. I'm looking into the circumstances surrounding Daniel Eisler's death, and

I'm interested in the large blue diamond he was selling. I understand you saw it."

Something flickered in the depths of the Huguenot's pale brown eyes, only to be quickly hidden when he lowered his lashes. "I'm sorry. I don't know what you're talking about."

"You're quite certain of that?"

"Yes."

Sebastian let his gaze travel, deliberately, around the small shop. A variety of gems, some cut, polished, and set, others still in the rough, crowded the cases. But the walls above were filled with paintings of birds and insects and shadow boxes displaying everything from exotic beetles to enormous, brilliantly colored butterflies. Francillon might have been trained as a lapidary, but his interests obviously included all aspects of natural history.

Sebastian said, "I would imagine the prosperity of an establishment such as this relies quite heavily on its reputation for honesty and integrity. Unfortunately, a good name, once lost, can be nearly impossible to reclaim."

"Francillon has been a respected name for over a hundred—"

"So I am told. Which is why, I should think, it would be in your best interest not to have the name of your establishment linked to a notorious incident of theft and murder."

The tactic was heavy-handed and crude, but effective. Francillon stared back at him, his jaw set hard, his voice tight with suppressed indignation. "Precisely what do you wish to know about the stone?"

"First of all, I'm curious as to why Eisler brought it to you."

"I was asked to prepare an illustrated sales prospectus."

"And did you?"

"I did."

"What exactly does that involve?"

"Generally? Tracing around the stone, weighing it,

and preparing a colored rendering. In this case, both a plan and an elevation."

"So you can describe it to me."

"I could. However, I am not entirely convinced that I should." —

Once more, Sebastian let his gaze drift significantly around the shop.

Francillon cleared his throat. "The specimen in question was a brilliant-cut diamond of an extraordinary shade of sapphire blue, unset at the time of my inspection and weighing in at over forty-five carats."

It was the first real confirmation Sebastian had received that such a diamond actually existed. He said, "To whom was Eisler planning to sell it?"

"I do not know. I was not made privy to that information."

"Did he mention where it came from?"

"He did not."

"But you have some ideas, don't you?" said Sebastian, watching the lapidary's face.

Francillon swallowed but remained silent.

Sebastian said, "I'm told large blue diamonds are quite rare. So rare in fact that an experienced lapidary such as yourself would surely be aware of all such gems in existence."

"I am unaware of any forty-five-carat blue diamond in any known collections."

"What about a collection that has been lost?"

"I beg your pardon?"

"The French Blue was a large, sapphire-hued diamond, was it not? It disappeared along with the rest of the French Crown Jewels exactly twenty years ago this month. That doesn't strike you as rather . . . coincidental?"

"The French Blue was larger—over sixty-seven carats. And of a different cut."

"Diamonds can be recut, can't they? It seems to me that anyone trying to sell the French Blue might well find it expedient to alter it."

Francillon's gaze met Sebastian's before skittering away. "I don't understand why you are here, asking me these questions."

"I am here because Daniel Eisler is dead and I am beginning to believe it more and more likely that the French Blue had something to do with his murder."

"But the authorities have already captured the man responsible!"

"They have committed a man to Newgate, yes. I don't believe he's guilty. And I have a fundamental objection to seeing innocent men hang."

Francillon hesitated a moment, then reached below the counter to come up with a large folio, which he laid open atop the case. He flipped through the volume for a moment, as if looking for something, then swung the book around to face Sebastian. "There." He pointed to a full-page colored illustration. "You see? Here is Louis XV's insignia of the Golden Fleece."

Sebastian found himself staring at a gaudy confection of gold and priceless gems. At the center of the piece coiled a magnificent red dragon exquisitely carved from a long oxblood-hued stone. Scores of what looked like small, clear diamonds formed the dragon's wings and tail; above him rested an enormous clear hexagonal diamond, with a slightly smaller yellow stone above that. But the emblem's true focus was the enormous deep sapphire blue diamond that nested in the tongues of flame shooting from the dragon's mouth. From below that, nearly dwarfed by the big blue stone, dangled a golden ram, its fleece formed by dozens of small yellow stones set in gold.

"What's the big clear diamond at the top, here?" asked Sebastian, pointing to it.

"That was called the Bazu. At nearly thirty-three carats, it was second in size only to the French Blue. The large yellow stones you see here"—he pointed to them— "and here are yellow sapphires, ten carats each. The five brilliant-cut diamonds were five carats each. And there were literally dozens of smaller stones. These here in the fleece were all yellow diamonds."

"And none of these gems has ever been recovered?"

"Only the carved red dragon—known as the Côte de Bretagne. It was found almost by accident not long after the theft."

"So we know the piece was broken up."

"Yes." Francillon closed the book and tucked it out of sight beneath the counter. "But you must understand that all of this is nothing more than sheer speculation on my part. Eisler said nothing—*nothing*—to lead me to suspect the diamond he showed me was the French Blue, recut."

"Who was the sales prospectus intended for?"

"I told you, Eisler never said. But . . ."

"But?" prompted Sebastian.

"It is not hard to guess."

"You mean Prinny, don't you?"

Francillon shrugged and rolled his eyes but said nothing.

Sebastian studied the small Frenchman's tightly held face. "When you first heard Eisler had been murdered, who did you think killed him?"

Francillon let out a startled huff of laughter. "You can't be serious."

"Oh, but I am."

Francillon cleared his throat again and looked pointedly away. "Well, then, if you must know, I naturally assumed Perlman might have had something to do with it."

"Who?"

"Samuel Perlman. Eisler's nephew."

"Isn't he the nephew who found Russell Yates standing over Eisler's body?"

"There is only the one nephew, which is why he is Eisler's sole heir."

"I didn't know that."

Francillon nodded. "He is Eisler's sister's son. Eisler never made any secret of the fact he despised the lad. He was always threatening to disinherit him and leave his money to charity."

"Exactly what did Perlman do to incur his uncle's displeasure?"

"Mr. Eisler always considered his nephew ... profligate."

"Is he?"

Francillon scratched the tip of his nose. "Let us say simply that Mr. Perlman's attitudes toward money and expenditures were considerably different from Mr. Eisler's own. But there was more to the disaffection than that. Mr. Eisler was also beyond incensed by the lad's recent marriage. He actually told me on Saturday that it was the last straw with him. The last straw."

"His wife is unsuitable?"

"Eisler considered her so." A faint smile tightened the skin beside the lapidary's eyes. "Her father is the Archbishop of Durham."

"Ah," said Sebastian. "Tell me: Was Mr. Perlman in any way involved in his uncle's diamond business?"

Francillon shook his head. "I'd be surprised if Mr. Perlman ever expressed any desire to become involved. But even if he had, Eisler would never have agreed."

"Because he considered his nephew incompetent? Or dishonest?"

"Because Mr. Eisler never trusted anyone, even his own kin. In my experience, we all view the world through the prism of our own behavior. If a man is honest, he generally assumes that those he meets will deal honestly with him. As a result, he trusts people and takes them at their word—even when he should not. Since he does not lie or cheat himself, it does not occur to him that others might lie or deceive him."

"And Eisler?"

"Let's just say that Daniel Eisler went through life in terror of being deceived."

"Did anyone ever succeed in deceiving him?"

The smile lines beside the lapidary's eyes deepened.

"Even the wiliest of men are sometimes deceived. But if you are asking me for names, I can't give you any. Eisler kept his secrets well."

Sebastian inclined his head and turned toward the door. "Thank you for your help."

Francillon bowed and went back to tidying the wall behind his cases.

Sebastian walked out of the shop and stood beneath the awning, looking out at the rain. A housemaid hurried past, a shawl drawn up over her head, her pattens clicking on the pavement; at the corner, an urchin with a broom was working hard at clearing a pile of wet manure from the street.

Sebastian turned and went back into the shop.

"Can you think of anyone Eisler was afraid of?"

Francillon looked around again, his face pinched with thought. Then he shook his head. "Only dead men."

It struck Sebastian as a peculiar statement.

But no matter how he pressed Francillon, the lapidary refused to be drawn any further.

Chapter 24

Paul Gibson sat with his hands wrapped around a frothy tankard of ale and his head tipped back against the old-fashioned settle of his favorite pub on Tower Hill. His eyes were sunken and dark with exhaustion, his cheeks covered by a day's growth of beard. Seated across from him, Sebastian took a sip of his own ale and said, "You look like hell."

The surgeon gave a hoarse chuckle. "Sure then, but I must be getting old. Time was, I could spend all night fighting to save some poor lad's life and then turn out to play a fine game of cricket early the next morning. Now I deliver a contrary babe in the wee hours and find I've a hard time crawling out of bed before Evensong."

"And how did your contrary babe fare?"

"Mother and child are doing just grand, thank you." Gibson's eyes focused on Sebastian's face. "You don't exactly look too chipper there yourself, you know."

Sebastian grunted. "The more I find out about Daniel Eisler, the more of a tangled mess events surrounding his murder appear to be." He told Gibson of his previous night's visit to the ancient house in Fountain Lane, of the young man who died in his arms, and of his interesting conversation with the lapidary, Francillon.

"Have you spoken to this nephew, Perlman?" asked Gibson.

Sebastian shook his head. "Not yet. I wanted to drive out to see Annie again first. I take it you've finished Wilkinson's autopsy?"

"I have."

"Anything?"

Gibson shook his head. "I've listed the likely cause of death as Walcheren fever."

Sebastian hadn't realized he'd been holding his breath until he let it ease out in a long, forceful exhalation. "Annie will be glad to hear that."

"Think she'll believe it?"

Sebastian met his friend's troubled gaze. "Are you saying it isn't true?"

"It could be. I did say 'likely.' The truth is, I simply don't know for certain." He took another deep draft of ale. "It must have been a living hell for a man like Wilkinson, to find himself reduced to a weak invalid."

"Yet he told me recently he thought he was getting better."

Gibson met Sebastian's gaze and held it. "He lied."

❧

Leaving Tower Hill, Sebastian drove down to Kensington, where he found Annie Wilkinson seated on a bench in the small walled garden of the square near her lodgings, her gaze resting thoughtfully on Emma, who was sailing a small red boat in a puddle left by the rain. The day was misty and cool, but both mother and child were wrapped up warmly, and Sebastian thought he could understand the need that had driven them here, away from the memories that surely haunted their small rooms down the street.

"Devlin," said Annie, rising quickly to her feet when she saw him. "Have you heard anything?"

"I've just spoken to Gibson. He says he'll be reporting to the coroner that Rhys died of Walcheren fever."

She pressed the fingers of one hand to her lips. "Thank God."

They turned to walk together along the path, with Emma skipping happily ahead of them, her little wooden boat clutched in one fist. He said, "Annie, you told me Rhys went for a walk that night at around eight or nine. Do you know why?"

"He did sometimes, right before bed." She looked over at him, her soft gray eyes narrowed. "Why?"

"Had he seemed unusually troubled by anything that day?"

She drew up short, her head jerking back, her features tightening. "If he had, do you think I would tell anyone?"

"Annie," he said gently. "I'm on your side. I just want to make certain we're not missing anything."

She brushed a soft tendril of hair off her forehead with a shaky hand. "I'm sorry." She hesitated a moment, as if considering his question, then said, "Rhys hadn't been himself for some time now. It can't be easy, watching your health crumble, finding yourself unable to do even the simplest things. But he seemed no different Sunday than he had the day or the week before."

"Had he any enemies that you know of?"

"Rhys? Good heavens, no. You knew him. He could sometimes be quick to judge, but he was never the kind of man who collects enemies. What are you suggesting? Surely you don't think someone could have . . . that someone might have murdered him?"

"I don't think it, no. But I wanted to be certain."

They paused again as Emma squatted down to launch her boat in a new, larger puddle that ran along the edge of the path.

Watching her, Annie said quietly, "She remembers Rhys now, but she won't for long. Soon he'll just be someone she hears her mother talking about, someone no more real to her than the tortoise and hare in that book of fables you gave her."

"She might remember him—or at least the warm glow of his love for her, even if it's only because she grows up hearing you speak of it."

"But she'll never actually know *him*, just as he'll never have the joy of watching her grow up into the woman she will become. And when I think of it, it's almost more than I can bear."

He wanted to say, *Then don't think about it. Dwelling on it now will only twist the pain of his death that much deeper.* But he kept the thought to himself because he knew the truth was that no newly bereaved woman could help thinking these things.

As if echoing his thoughts, she said, "How dreadfully maudlin and female I must sound."

"You're one of the strongest women I've ever known, Annie. It's all right to give yourself time to grieve."

She shook her head, her throat working as she swallowed hard. "You know what one of the worst parts of all this is? I find myself thinking that in some ways I lost Rhys—the Rhys I fell in love with—three years ago, when he sailed for that damned, diseased-ridden island. He was never the same afterward. Only, then I feel so small and selfish and contemptible that I can't stand myself."

"Annie, I understand."

She pulled a face that reminded him so much of the girl she'd once been that he found himself smiling. "Listen to me," she said. "More maudlin pap. And I haven't even thanked you for coming all the way out here again to see me."

"I'll come again tomorrow, if I may. Perhaps next time Emma will let me read her a story."

"I think she'd like that."

He was aware of mother and child watching him as he let himself out of the garden and climbed up to his curricle's high seat. But when he looked back, it was to see Annie hunkering down beside her daughter, the hem of her black mourning gown trailing unheeded in the puddle as she gave the small red boat a powerful push that sent it skimming across the water before an ever-expanding wake.

Chapter 25

*B*y the time Sebastian finally tracked Samuel Perlman to Tattersall's Subscription Rooms, he had learned much about Daniel Eisler's flamboyant nephew.

Despite Francillon's use of the term "lad," Perlman was actually forty-two years old. A patron of the most exclusive establishments in Bond Street and Savile Row, he lived with his new bride in a lavish mansion on the north side of Hanover Square. The source of his wealth was a vast mercantile empire he had inherited from his own father some ten years before and then immediately turned over to competent managers, preferring to devote himself to a life of pleasure and excess. As far as Sebastian could discover, he did not gamble, he kept no mistress, and he was not in debt.

Perlman was looking over the points of a delicate white-stockinged bay mare in Tattersall's yard when Sebastian walked up to him. The rain might have eased off, but the colonnaded open market still glistened with scattered puddles through which men and horseflesh splashed. For one intense moment, Perlman's gaze met Sebastian's over the back of the mare. Then he rolled his eyes, blew out a weary, bored sigh, and said, "Oh, God, you've found me."

"Were you hiding from me?" Sebastian asked pleasantly, propping one shoulder against a nearby column and crossing his arms at his chest.

Perlman huffed an incredulous laugh and returned his attention to the mare. "Hiding? What a fatiguing—not to mention decidedly plebian—activity. Hardly."

He was tall and gangly, with curly dark hair framing a balding pate, and a sadly receding chin—a defect unfortunately accentuated by the excessively high shirt points and extravagantly tied cravat he affected. His coat was made skintight and nipped in at the waist; his pantaloons were of the palest yellow, his waistcoat of figured silk. Daniel Eisler's extravagant nephew obviously had pretensions to dandyism.

Sebastian smiled. "If you know I've been looking for you, then I assume you also know why."

"I gather you've taken an interest in my uncle's murder. Although to be frank, I can't imagine why, given that the brute responsible is already locked up fast in Newgate awaiting execution."

"You mean awaiting trial."

Perlman waved one long-fingered, exquisitely gloved hand through the air. "Technicality. The man is clearly guilty. I myself found him standing over my poor uncle's lifeless body."

"So I'm told. I was wondering: Why were you there?"

Perlman froze. "I beg your pardon?"

"Why did you choose to visit your uncle that night?"

"Why not? He is—or, I suppose one should say, he was—my only near relative."

"And he disliked you excessively."

Perlman gave up inspecting the horse and turned toward him. "I don't know if I'd go that far, although I won't deny we weren't close. Still, one must do one's duty to one's elderly relatives, you know."

"Especially when one has expectations from those elderly relatives."

"What a decidedly vulgar consideration."

"The truth frequently is rather vulgar, I'm afraid." Sebastian reached out to run his hand down the mare's white-blazed nose. "I'm told your uncle threatened to disinherit you."

Perlman gave a tight-lipped smile. "Only every other day. He swore if I didn't mend what he liked to call my 'extravagant ways' that he'd leave everything he owned to charity. But it was never going to happen."

"So certain?"

"My uncle didn't believe in charity. He'd burn down his house and everything in it before he'd give one penny to the poor and needy." He drawled the words "poor and needy" the way another man might say "flotsam and jetsam."

"He could always have decided to leave his fortune to someone else. Someone he liked . . . better."

"He didn't like anyone better. Yes, my uncle despised me, but then, he despised everyone. The difference is, I am his sister's son. And when all was said and done, that mattered to him. Not much, mind you. I doubt he'd have walked across the street to save my life. But he believed in keeping money in the family. So if you're trying to insinuate that I might have had reason to kill my uncle, I'm afraid you're sadly wide of the mark—in addition to being damned insulting."

"I would imagine Russell Yates finds your accusation of murder rather insulting, as well."

Perlman's nostrils flared, his fashionably pale face now infused with angry color. Every affectation of boredom and insouciance had disappeared, leaving him trembling with fury and something else, something that looked very much like fear. "I walked into my uncle's house and found Yates standing over the body. How the devil are you imagining I might have been the one who shot him?"

"It's fairly simple, actually. You shoot him. Yates knocks at the door. You panic, run out the back, and then nip around to come charging in the front and accuse Yates of what you yourself have done."

"That is the most preposterous thing I have ever heard. I know nothing about guns. I've received no military training. I'm not even a sporting man!"

"You don't need to be an expert shot to hit someone who is standing right in front of you."

The rain had started up again, pounding on the gallery roof and rapidly clearing the yard of men and horses. Perlman squinted up at the lowering sky. "Enough of this nonsense. I'm not going to stand here and listen to this drivel." He nodded curtly to the mare's handler and started to turn away.

Sebastian stopped him by saying, "Tell me about the blue diamond."

Perlman pivoted slowly toward him again. If his face had been red before, it was now white. "I beg your pardon?"

"The big, brilliant-cut blue diamond your uncle was selling. You do know about it, don't you? I would imagine it's worth a tidy sum."

"My uncle had no blue diamond."

"Oh, but I'm afraid he did. At least, he had it in his possession while he arranged a sale for its proper owner. You're not telling me it's been lost, are you?"

The tip of Perlman's tongue flicked out to wet his lips. "I'm afraid you've been misinformed, or perhaps you have simply misunderstood something that was said to you."

"Perhaps." Sebastian smiled. "I hope for your sake that's true. Otherwise, things might become . . . awkward, hmm? I mean, when the diamond's original owner attempts to reclaim his property from the estate?"

Still vaguely smiling, Sebastian walked away, leaving Perlman standing in the open yard, oblivious to the driving rain that splattered mud on his pale yellow pantaloons and melted the high starched points of his ridiculous collar.

Chapter 26

"*I*t's an interesting copy," said Abigail McBean, carefully turning the manuscript's worn, browned pages.

They had settled in a crowded room on the first floor overlooking the wet garden. Hero suspected the chamber had probably been designed as a morning room. But Abigail had turned it into a combination morning room/library, with most of the walls covered by towering bookcases stuffed with old books and a curious assortment of objects. She had *The Key of Solomon* open on the table and apologized to Hero for failing to offer her refreshment by saying, "I make it a practice never to have food or drink around while viewing a valuable old manuscript."

"I quite understand," said Hero, watching her friend. "*Is* it valuable?"

"From a scholarly standpoint, yes. Monetarily? I'm not the one to judge. Going by the writing style, I'd say this copy probably dates to the middle of the sixteenth century."

"Which is a century after the invention of the printing press. So why is it handwritten?"

Miss McBean turned the next page and frowned down at an illustration of strange geometric design. "*The Key of Solomon* has been translated into Greek, Latin, Italian, French, and to a lesser extent into English. But to my knowledge it has never been published. Even grimoires that have been printed are frequently also found as manuscripts. There is a belief that handwritten texts contain inherent magical forces of their own, so they're considered more powerful than the printed versions."

"So it's—what? Basically a magic textbook?"

"Yes. It tells you how to make talismans and amulets, how to cast magical spells, how to invoke angels or demons—that sort of thing."

"For what purpose?"

"The usual: sex, money, and power."

"What about revenge?"

"That too."

"All the typical motives for murder," Hero said softly.

"I hadn't thought about it that way, but I suppose you're right." Miss McBean's hand stilled on the pages. "Where did you get this?"

"It was smuggled into England for a man who was murdered last Sunday."

"You mean Daniel Eisler?"

"You knew him?"

Miss McBean carefully closed the manuscript's worn leather cover and set it aside. "I did, actually. He was obsessed with the occult. And I don't mean in a scholarly sense—although he did try at first to convince me that that was his motive."

"You mean he believed in it?"

"I eventually came to realize that he did, yes. He was continually approaching me for assistance in translating some difficult passage or tracking down obscure references."

"You're saying you helped him?" Hero asked, not quite managing to keep the surprise out of her voice.

Miss McBean went off into one of her hearty gales of laughter. "If you're asking did I assist him in summoning demons and casting spells of ruination and destruction, the answer is no. What I was doing up there"—she nodded toward the attic room above—"was just my way of wrapping my head around what the writers of these texts were up to."

She was silent for a moment, her gaze on the scene outside the window, where her towheaded niece and nephew, umbrellas in hand, could be seen splashing gleefully through rain puddles under the watchful eye of a nursemaid. The girl looked to be about eight, the boy perhaps three or four years younger. The boy squealed with delight, the girl shouting something Hero couldn't quite catch.

Abigail smiled; then her smile faded. "I suppose in a sense I did help him at first, inadvertently. When he told me his interest was scholarly, I naturally believed him. I mean, why wouldn't I? It was only gradually I began to realize he was deadly serious about what he was doing. He actually *believed* in the power of the old rituals and incantations. He had an extensive collection of grimoires."

Hero nodded to *The Key of Solomon* on the table between them. "What can you tell me about this one?"

"Well . . . it's generally considered one of the most—if not the most—important of all the grimoires. It purports to date from the time of Solomon, although in reality it was probably written during the Renaissance. Most of them were."

"For some reason I always tend to associate magic with medieval times, not the Renaissance."

Miss McBean nodded. "Folk magic was widespread during the Middle Ages. But by the Renaissance there was a growing sense that magic had degenerated since the days of the Egyptians and Romans. Then, with the fall of Constantinople and the expulsion of the Jews and Moors from Spain, places like France, Germany, and England saw a huge influx of some of the truly ancient magic texts that had been lost to Europe. As a result, in the fifteenth century there was a veritable explosion in the writing of new grimoires. You'll find a lot of Jewish kabbalistic magic, Arab alchemy, and Greco-Roman-Egyptian influence in these works."

She ran her fingertips over the edge of the battered old manuscript, then sat staring at it thoughtfully.

"What is it?" Hero asked, watching her.

"I was just thinking. . . . The newspapers said Daniel Eisler was shot. Is that right?"

"Yes. Why?"

"It doesn't sound to me as if his interest in the occult had anything to do with what happened to him. I mean, it's not as if he were found spread-eagled on a pentacle with a Hand of Glory burning on his chest."

"A hand of what?"

Abigail McBean's eyes crinkled in quiet amusement. "You don't want to know." The amusement faded. "Do you really think this"—she indicated the old grimoire— "has something to do with his death?"

"Probably not. But there might be something here we're missing. Something important."

Hero was aware of Abigail fixing her with a steady stare. "I gather Lord Devlin has taken an interest in Daniel Eisler's death?"

Hero nodded. "He doesn't believe that Russell Yates— the man who has been arrested for the crime—is guilty."

"Ah." Her friend's gaze shifted again to the children playing in the garden. For a moment, Hero thought she was about to say something. But she didn't.

Hero said, "Do you know where I could find an English version of *The Key of Solomon*?"

Miss McBean rose to her feet in a waft of lavender mixed oddly with musk. "I have several. I'd be happy to lend you one."

"Thank you, but I couldn't let you do that."

"No, please; none of the copies I have are especially valuable. Let me do this."

"All right. Thank you."

The version she lent Hero was smaller, only about eight inches tall, but written in a beautiful, flowing hand and exquisitely illustrated in rich shades of ultramarine and cinnabar and vermilion. Hero glanced through it, her eyes widening. "You said most spells deal with wealth, sex, power, or revenge. Which would you say interested Eisler the most?"

Miss McBean thought about it a moment. "He seemed particularly obsessed with invocations to constrain the spirits of the dead."

"Invocations to— Good Lord."

"I'm not so sure the good Lord has aught to do with any of this," said Abigail McBean, her plump, pretty face taking on an oddly pinched look, her frizzy red hair like a flame in the rainy day's gloom. "Read the book. You'll see."

※

Outside Abigail McBean's deceptively normal-looking little house, a faint drizzle was still falling from the gray sky. The air hung heavy with the smell of wet grass and fading roses and the acrid bite of smoke from the endless rows of chimneys. As she walked down the short garden path to where her carriage waited at the kerb, Hero's attention was all for the task of keeping the rain off the two manuscripts in her arms. She didn't notice the dark-haired man in the slouch hat and too-big coat until he reared up before her.

"There y'are. Been waitin' for you, I have," he said, his grin wide and vacuous, like a man who laughs at his own private joke—or long ago took leave of his senses.

Hero's gaze flew to her yellow-bodied carriage, the horses' hides gleaming blue-black in the rain. She saw her footman, George, start forward, face going slack with sudden alarm. She knew she was in no real danger. Yet she felt her skin crawl, her breath quicken in that way common to all living things when confronted with evidence of madness.

"Excuse me," she said, making to go around him.

Bony and filthy, his hand snaked out, his fingers digging into the sleeve of her carriage dress. "Don't go yet. Got a message for the captain."

Quivering with revulsion, Hero jerked her arm away from the man's grasp with such force that she nearly sent the two manuscripts in her hands flying. "What captain?"

"Captain Lord Devlin. Tell him I'm owed what I'm owed, and he ought by rights to see that I get it. Maybe he don't remember Jud Foy. But he should. Oh, yes, he should."

"My lady?" said George, coming up beside her. "Is this person bothering you?"

Foy held his splayed hands up and out to his sides. His grin never faltered and his gaze never wavered from Hero's face. "You tell him. Hmm?"

Then he thrust his hands into the pockets of his coat and sauntered away, elbows swinging, lips puckered into a tuneless whistle quickly lost in the patter of the rain.

Chapter 27

Sebastian arrived back at Brook Street to find Hero seated at the library table calmly cleaning a tiny muff flintlock with a burnished walnut stock and engraved gilt mounts that had been a gift from her father.

He said, "Is this general maintenance, or did you shoot someone?"

She looked up at him. There was no humor in her face, only a cold purposefulness that reminded him disconcertingly of Lord Jarvis. "Ever hear of a man named Jud Foy?"

He thought about it a moment, then shook his head. "I don't believe so. Why do you ask?"

"Because he was waiting for me when I came out of Abigail McBean's house today—the same man who was watching this house last night. He said his name is Jud Foy, and he wanted me to give you a message."

"*Bloody hell.* How did he know where you were?"

She shook her head. "I've no notion. But he called you 'captain.' He said, 'Tell the captain I'm owed what I'm owed.'"

"'Owed'? What does he think he's owed?"

"He didn't specify. Whatever it is, though, he seems to believe it's your responsibility to see that he gets it. You may not remember him, but he obviously thinks you should."

Sebastian walked over to where a bottle of burgundy stood with glasses on a tray. He poured himself a drink, then stood with the glass in one hand, his thoughts far away.

Jud Foy. *Jud Foy?* He tried to put the name together with the wet, disheveled, skeletally thin man from last night, and knew it again, that vague sense of an elusive memory gone before it was quite grasped.

Hero said, "You told me last night that you thought he looked familiar."

"He did. But I still can't place him." Sebastian took a slow sip of his wine. "I thought last night that he must have something to do with my investigation into the murder of Daniel Eisler. Now I'm not so sure."

"Because he knows you were in the army?"

Sebastian nodded. "Although I suppose it's possible he's linked in some way to Matt Tyson. When he said, 'I saw you coming out of his house,' I assumed he was talking about Eisler's house. But he could have meant Hope's house."

She listened to him, her face impassive, while he told her of his conversations with Francillon and Perlman. Then she said, "Is it possible Foy could have something to do with your friend Rhys Wilkinson? You've visited his lodgings several times in the last few days, haven't you?"

"I suppose that's possible too, although I doubt it." He set aside his glass and reached for his hat and gloves.

"Where are you going?"

"To ask Sir Henry to look into this Foy. And then I think it's time Lieutenant Tyson and I had a little talk."

※

"Jud Foy?" Sir Henry Lovejoy frowned, his lips pursing thoughtfully as he shook his head. "The name's not familiar to me. But I can ask one of the lads to look into him. Do you want him arrested?"

"He hasn't exactly done anything," said Sebastian.

They were walking down Bow Street. The rain had eased up again, but the narrow lane was dark and wet and crowded with a crush of ragged costermongers and squeaky carts overflowing with produce from the nearby market of Covent Garden. The scent of damp earth and sweaty, unwashed bodies hung thick in the air.

Sir Henry said, "I had a visit yesterday evening from Mr. Bertram Leigh-Jones."

Sebastian looked over at him. "Oh?"

"Your name came up in conversation. He made a number of demands." Sir Henry pulled at his earlobe, the faintest hint of a smile playing about his normally serious features. "Unfortunately, I can't seem to recall what any of them were."

"He's a very prickly magistrate, Mr. Leigh-Jones."

"Most West End magistrates are—with good reason."

"Oh? Why's that?"

They turned down the short stretch of Russell Street that led to the open market square. The press had become a nearly intolerable squeeze, and Sebastian noticed that Lovejoy was careful to keep his hand in his pocket, guarding his purse.

The magistrate sniffed. "Let's just say that a parliamentary inquiry into the licensing of pubs in a number of parishes might uncover a pattern of irregularity."

"Interesting."

"Mmm. After he left, I decided to send one of my lads over to Fountain Lane to make a few inquiries. Given the quick apprehension of Mr. Yates, I suspected Lambeth Street might have neglected to interview some of the locals not directly involved."

Sebastian huffed a soft laugh. Leigh-Jones should have known better than to demand that Bow Street stay out of his district's affairs. "And?"

"The constable couldn't find anyone who would admit to being in the area at the time of the murder." Sir Henry cast Sebastian a quick sideways glance. "You've heard that two men were found dead at Eisler's house early this morning? One stabbed in the house, the other shot down in the rear alley."

"I'd heard, yes."

"You wouldn't happen to know anything about that, would you?"

Sebastian kept his gaze on the crowded market square before them, its rickety stalls piled high with turnips and potatoes, cabbages and squash. "Have they been identified?"

Sir Henry nodded. "They have, yes. The ruffian in the house was Morgan Aldrich, a man well-known to the authorities in the area, whilst the body in the alley belonged to his young brother, Piers."

"How did they manage to enter the house?"

"I understand they worked the bars loose at a window in the basement light well, then used a diamond-tipped blade to cut the glass."

"Unusually sophisticated for common ruffians."

"It is, yes. Curiously, however, the bolt on the back door also appears to have been tampered with. It was very subtle—so subtle I suspect most people would have missed it entirely. Only, Eisler's old retainer, Campbell, noticed it."

"He would," said Sebastian.

"One suspects," continued Sir Henry, looking at Sebastian intently, "that some unknown personage, desirous of concealing his illicit entry, gained admittance through the back door, and that unknown personage is the one responsible for the deaths of the Aldrich brothers, who came in through the basement with no regard for whatever evidence of their housebreaking they were leaving behind."

"An interesting theory. Only, how likely is it that two different sets of ruffians would break into the same house at the same time, and take to murdering one another?"

"I suppose that would depend on what they were looking for. You wouldn't happen to have any ideas, would you?"

Sebastian kept his features carefully schooled. "Mr. Eisler was known to possess a number of valuable items."

"So he was." Lovejoy paused, his attention momentarily caught by a Punch and Judy professor set up beneath the nearest arcade, then walked on. "Ah, I almost forgot; my constable did uncover one interesting piece of information. One of the individuals with whom he spoke—a chandler's apprentice—recalled seeing Mr. Yates standing on the pavement before the victim's house the morning of the murder. Eisler himself was in his open doorway, and the two men were engaged in what the apprentice described as a 'right royal row.'"

Sebastian felt his jaw tighten with a spurt of quiet rage. Yates had assured him quite emphatically that he'd had no quarrel with Eisler. "The apprentice knew Yates by name?"

"No. But his description of the man involved was unmistakable. There can't be many sun-darkened gentlemen in London who wear their hair long and affect a gold pirate's hoop in one ear."

"And the apprentice was certain the argument he witnessed occurred Sunday morning?"

"He was, yes. Seems he encountered the altercation on his way home from services at Holy Trinity."

"Did he happen to hear the subject of their quarrel?"

"He did not. He did, however, catch the final, heated exchange of words. Seems Eisler told Yates, 'Don't even think about crossing me. I can destroy you and you know it.'"

Sebastian squinted up at the templelike facade of the church overlooking the square. "And did he manage to catch Yates's reply?"

"I'm afraid he did. He says Yates laughed out loud and said, 'I can split your gullet from stem to stern quicker than a Haymarket whore can pick your pocket, and don't you forget *that*, you bloody little bastard.'" The magistrate paused to look out over the churchyard's jumble of gray, moss-covered tombstones. "Of course, Eisler was shot, not stabbed. But still . . . it doesn't look good for Mr. Yates."

"No," said Sebastian, drawing up beside him. "No, it doesn't."

Chapter 28

*R*ussell Yates had drawn his cell's slat-backed chair up to a small table and was busy writing when the turnkey opened the iron-banded oak door for Sebastian. In the last twenty-four hours, the ex-privateer had managed to shave and change into clean clothes. A feather bed and warm blankets softened his cot; a pitcher of water and a basin stood on a plain shelf beside a bottle of good cognac and a crystal glass. Prison could be surprisingly comfortable for those wealthy enough to make the appropriate arrangements.

But it was still prison.

"I ought to let you hang," said Sebastian without preamble as the turnkey locked the heavy door behind him. "I swear to God, if it weren't for Kat, I would."

Yates pushed awkwardly to his feet, his leg irons throwing him off balance. "What the bloody hell does that mean?"

"It means that if you can't be honest with me, then you're just wasting my time—and yours. And the way I see it, you don't have much time left to waste."

A muscle ticked along the ridge of the man's jawbone. "What do you think I'm lying to you about?"

Sebastian gave a humorless laugh. "Have you told me so many bouncers that you can't be certain which ones I've caught on to? I'm talking about last Sunday morning. When you stood in the middle of Fountain Lane and threatened to gut Eisler from stem to stern. The chandler who witnessed the exchange will doubtless be testifying at your trial. What do you think the chances of your acquittal are now?"

Yates simply stared at him, his face pale.

Sebastian said, "You claimed you had no quarrel with Eisler. What the hell was it about?"

Yates sank into his chair again, one splayed hand pressing against his cheek with such force that it distorted his features.

"What was the quarrel about?" Sebastian demanded again when the other man remained silent.

Yates shifted his hand so that it covered his lower face and mouth. "The old bugger was trying to cheat me. He'd somehow managed to acquire certain information. . . . I don't suppose I need go into detail as to its nature. He thought he could use it to his advantage."

"Why the devil didn't you tell me this before?"

A faint flush darkened the other man's face. "I suppose I thought if you knew I had a reason to kill him, you wouldn't help me. But I didn't shoot him. I won't deny that I considered it. But I didn't actually do it."

Sebastian studied the other man's pinched features. The ponderous British legal system called men such as Yates "sodomites" and punished them with a rare viciousness. But they tended to call themselves "mollies." They had created a shadowy culture of their own in London, a hidden but vibrant subworld of pubs and coffeehouses called molly houses where they felt free to mingle and meet, to dance and cut up a lark. Yet the threat of disgrace, imprisonment, and death hung over them always. The men who moved through that world lived in constant fear of both detection and extortion.

Sebastian said, "Where did Eisler acquire this information?"

"The bastard traded in other people's secrets, the same way he traded in gems and fine furniture and art objects. He was always getting nasty bits of information out of people who owed him money."

"You mean he was a blackmailer?"

"Not in the strictest sense. He was more subtle than that. But he certainly used what he knew about people to his own advantage."

"Exchanging shouted threats in the street doesn't exactly sound subtle to me."

Yates gave a ghost of a smile. "True. But then, I was refusing to play his game."

"You weren't afraid?"

The privateer's jaw hardened. "Men have tried extortion with me before."

Sebastian had heard about the schemes often run against the mollies. Two confederates would cruise the parks and byways known to be frequented by London's mollies. Then they'd separate, with one of the pair— usually young and attractive—approaching a likely target to "make a bargain." Once the target was in a compromising position, the second confederate would rush in on the couple and threaten to denounce the extortion victim to the authorities unless he paid them. Handsomely and repeatedly.

"And what did you do to those who thought you a likely victim for extortion?" asked Sebastian. "Kill them?"

Yates simply stared back at him.

"Bloody hell," swore Sebastian.

"Would you have me believe you wouldn't do the same, in my position?"

The two men's gazes met. Clashed.

Yates said, "If I'd killed Eisler, I would tell you. *I didn't kill him.*"

Sebastian went to stare out the small barred window overlooking the Press Yard below. They called it the Press Yard because, until recently, it was where those who refused to enter a plea against charges were literally *pressed*: Increasing loads of weights were placed upon the accused's chest until he—or she—agreed to plead.

Or until they were crushed to death, at which point the legal niceties were no longer relevant.

He said, "I'm told Daniel Eisler was in the process of trying to sell a large blue diamond—a very large blue diamond. Do you know anything about that?"

"No."

"What about a man named Jud Foy? Ever hear of him?"

"Foy?" Yates shook his head. "I don't think so. What does he look like?"

"Thin. Disheveled. Like he belongs in Bedlam."

A smile flickered across the ex-privateer's features. "Really, Devlin, I'll admit I associate with some rougher sorts, but I do draw the line somewhere."

"What about a former army lieutenant named Tyson?"

"You mean Matt Tyson?"

"So you do know him."

"I've met him a few times, here and there. Why?"

"Know if he had any dealings with Eisler?"

Yates thought about it a moment, then said, "He must have. I remember running into him once in Fountain Lane, although it was some time ago now. Perhaps as much as a month or so ago."

"Do you know why he was there?"

"No. Why? What does Tyson have to do with this?"

Sebastian pushed away from the window. "I don't know. But I intend to find out."

                                 ✻

Lieutenant Matt Tyson was about to enter Gentleman Jackson's Boxing Salon when Sebastian walked up to him and said, "We need to talk. Come walk with me."

Tyson paused, the faintest hint of a smile tightening the sun-darkened flesh beside his thin lips as he shook his head. "Sorry; I'm meeting someone here at four."

Sebastian kept his voice pleasant. "We can have our conversation inside, if you prefer. I've no doubt Jackson's other patrons would find the sordid details of your court-martial fascinating."

Something flashed in the lieutenant's eyes, something almost immediately hidden by his carefully lowered lids. "I was acquitted; remember?"

"Not by me."

Without glancing at him again, Tyson resettled his hat on his head and turned his steps toward Piccadilly. A thick bank of dark clouds still hung low over the sodden city. Water dripped from overhanging eaves and misted windowpanes; the pavement glistened dark and wet.

"When did you sell out?" asked Sebastian, falling into step beside him.

"A couple of months ago, if you must know. What the devil difference does it make to you?"

"Curious timing."

"What is that supposed to mean?"

"Only that after all these years, it looks as if Wellington is finally turning the tide against the French. I should think it would be a time of great opportunity for a man of your . . . talents."

Tyson's eyes narrowed. But all he said was, "Sometimes a man just gets tired of killing."

"Not all men."

Tyson threw him a quick sideways glance. "You did."

It had been two years now since Sebastian had sold out for a complicated crescendo of reasons he'd yet to come to grips with. But then, he had never been the kind of man who took pleasure in killing.

Tyson had.

Sebastian said, "What was your business with Daniel Eisler?"

The man's faint smile broadened. "My, my, you have been busy, haven't you?"

"What was it?" Sebastian said again.

Tyson shrugged. "Eisler bought jewels. I had some to sell. And no, I didn't slit some señorita's throat or rape a convent full of nuns to get them. I took them off a dead

French colonel at Badajoz. Where he got them is really none of my affair, now, is it?"

The bodies of the French dead were routinely stripped of their valuables, uniforms, and boots before being buried or burned. The spoils of war had long been considered a natural supplement to the King's shilling. Officers didn't usually join in the looting of the dead, although some did.

But the systematic looting of civilians was something else again. Wellington had always discouraged the age-old tradition of subjecting a conquered city to three days of ritual pillage by marauding, drunken soldiers—both because it was bad for discipline and because the British liked to portray themselves as saviors rather than conquerors. But Badajoz would remain forever a stain on the honor of the modern British army, for the fortified Spanish frontier city had endured days of savage rape, murder, and pillage after being stormed by Wellington's troops last March. Tyson might claim his booty came from the body of a French colonel, but Sebastian suspected otherwise.

He said, "And did Eisler give you a fair price for your 'items'?"

"He did, yes. Otherwise, why would I have done business with him?"

"Who suggested him to you? Thomas Hope?"

Tyson shook his head. "A friend from Spain. And I haven't been anywhere near the old goat in weeks, so if you're looking for someone besides Yates to pin this murder on, you're just going to have to keep looking."

In Sebastian's experience, most people had a tendency to fidget when they lied; they hesitated, or their voices rose in pitch, or their demeanor shifted in some subtle way. But there were those who could meet your gaze, smile, and lie with a careless grace born of a complete absence of either guilt or fear of detection. Matt Tyson was one of those men.

"I might actually believe you," said Sebastian, "if I hadn't sat on your court-martial board."

A quick flare of anger tightened the lieutenant's features before being carefully smoothed away. He turned his head to watch an elegant red barouche dashing up the street. After a moment, he said, "I did see something at Eisler's house the last time I was there, which you might find relevant."

"Oh? What's that?"

"A woman was leaving Fountain Lane just as I arrived. A young, nicely dressed gentlewoman. I couldn't tell you who she was—she was heavily veiled and got into a hack that was waiting for her. I assumed at first she was there for much the same reason I was—to sell Eisler a piece of her jewelry, probably to pay off a gaming debt. Then I saw Eisler."

"And?"

"The old goat had his flap buttoned awry. He must have taken her right there in the parlor because I could still smell the stink of his lust in the air. I've since heard it's where he always took his women—whores and ladies alike."

"You're saying he made a practice of it?"

"Didn't you know?" Smug amusement bordering on derision suffused the other man's face. "He was quite the nasty old sot, your Eisler. He'd loan money to pretty young things, and then when they couldn't pay his ruinous interest rates, he'd offer them a choice: Either let him tumble them on that ratty old couch or have whatever trinket they'd pledged declared forfeit. He offered the same deal to men who were late on their payments—if they had a pretty wife."

When Sebastian remained silent, Tyson laughed out loud. "Don't believe me? Ask that sybaritic nephew of his."

"You mean Perlman? What would he know of it?"

"Far more than you might think. I've heard that one of the ways Perlman kept in his uncle's good graces was by providing him with whores." Tyson paused as the church bells of the city began to chime the hour, one after the other ringing out over the wet streets. "And now, you really must excuse me. I did mention I was meeting someone at four."

Sebastian let him go.

Under ordinary circumstances, he'd have been inclined to doubt just about anything a man like Tyson said. But he kept remembering that dank, foul room with its heavy, old-fashioned chimneypiece and a small pair of cheap blue satin slippers peeking out from beneath a worn horsehair sofa.

Chapter 29

*T*he discovery that Eisler had been engaging in a nasty combination of blackmail and sexual exploitation had the potential to open up a vast array of new suspects, most of them unfortunately both nameless and faceless. If Yates and Tyson were telling the truth — and Sebastian suspected that in this, at least, they were — then London must be so full of men and women who'd nursed a secret but powerful reason to murder the old bastard that it was difficult to know where to start.

Sebastian was seated in the drawing room, the blue satin slipper held thoughtfully in his hands, when Hero came in yanking off her wet bonnet and gloves.

"I've been looking for the black cat," she said. "I can't find him anywhere."

"Calling what? 'Here, cat, cat, cat'? You need to give him a name."

"He's not my cat; he's yours." She went to stand at the window, her gaze on the rain-washed pavement below. "One of the housemaids saw a man hanging around who sounds like Foy. She said he was trying to coax the cat to come to him with what looked like sardines."

Sebastian knew a moment of disquiet. But all he said was, "The cat's probably just taken shelter from the rain someplace. He'll be back. Where else is he likely to get roast chicken and a bowl of cream?"

She gave him a tight, strained smile and nodded to the slipper in his hand. "What's this?"

Sebastian held it up. "It's one of a pair that I found tucked beneath a tattered old horsehair sofa in Daniel Eisler's parlor."

She lifted the shoe from his hand. "This is not a lady's slipper."

"No, it is not."

She looked up at him. "You say both shoes were still there?"

"Yes."

"How odd. I wonder if he gave their owner a new pair and she simply left the old ones."

"Eisler? I suspect that old bastard never gave anyone anything—excepting perhaps an inclination for suicide."

"Then I'd say the shoes' owner must have left the premises precipitously." She handed the shoe back to him. "Somewhat like Cinderella."

"Only, I doubt this Cinderella was worried about her coach turning into a pumpkin at the stroke of midnight."

Hero said, "Apart from the fact that walking in one's stocking feet would be decidedly uncomfortable, these shoes—however cheap I might consider them—would nevertheless represent a significant investment for their owner. I doubt she left them behind willingly."

"I'm thinking she might have been there when Eisler was shot."

Hero frowned down at the tiny, worn shoe. "And ran away in fear?"

"That's one possibility."

"Are you saying you think your Blue Satin Cinderella might have shot him?"

"Perhaps."

"So who is she?"

"I have no idea. But I know someone who might."

"Oh, God. Not you again," exclaimed Samuel Perlman when Sebastian came upon him in the showrooms of Christie's in Pall Mall.

Sebastian ran his gaze over the framed sepia-colored drawing of a woman's head that Perlman was examining. "I'd have thought you just inherited enough of this sort of thing from your uncle to satisfy the acquisitive urgings of even the most ardent collector."

"I like to keep an eye on what's available," said Perlman, leaning forward to squint at the drawing's signature. "Do you think it's really a Leonardo?"

"You tell me."

Eisler's nephew had changed into tight, buff-colored trousers, a claret-and-white-striped waistcoat, and a monstrously wide cravat meticulously arranged in a complicated style known as the Waterfall. He straightened. "After our previous conversation, I'd hoped I'd seen the last of you."

Sebastian showed his teeth in a smile. "Let that be a lesson to you: If you don't care to see me again, you might consider being a bit more forthcoming in your answers to my questions."

Perlman breathed a resigned sigh. "What now?"

"I've been hearing some interesting tales about your uncle and women."

"Women?" Perlman gave a high-pitched titter. "Don't be ridiculous. My uncle was an old man."

"Not that old."

Perlman moved on to a massive, heavily framed oil that took up a considerable section of one wall, his attention all for the darkly swirling scene before him.

Sebastian said, "I'm told you used to provide your uncle with whores."

Perlman cast him a quick sideways glance. "And precisely who, one wonders, told you that?"

"Does it matter?"

When Perlman remained silent, Sebastian said, "I think your uncle may have had a woman at his house the night he was shot. Did you send her to him?"

"I did not."

"But you're not denying that you did sometimes act as his procurer."

Perlman kept his gaze on the vast oil. "What an ugly little word."

"You have one you prefer?"

"I won't deny I did occasionally perform certain . . . commissions for him."

"Define 'occasionally.'"

"Every few weeks . . . or so."

"Where did the women come from?"

"The Haymarket. Covent Garden. Really, Devlin, you know as well as I do where to find women of that sort."

"Are you saying you supplied him with common women you picked up off the street?"

Perlman swiped the tip of his nose between one pinched thumb and forefinger and sniffed. "That's the kind he liked."

"I've heard he also liked another kind of women. Pretty young gentlewomen who owed him money—or whose husbands owed him money."

"I wouldn't know anything about that," said Perlman loftily.

"You wouldn't?"

"I would not." He cast a quick glance around, but the auction rooms were nearly deserted in the gloom of the rainy afternoon. "Listen: I am not denying my uncle had an appetite for women. He did. It was . . . unseemly. But to my knowledge he satisfied those needs with whores. Now, if you'll excuse me? You are distracting me. This is not a leisure activity, you know. Art collecting is serious business."

"In a moment. So you would have me believe you never heard of him coercing a gentlewoman to share his couch?"

"I have not, no."

Sebastian smiled. Unlike Tyson, Samuel Perlman was a terrible liar. "Then tell me this: Who owed your uncle money?"

Perlman gave a tsking huff of derision. "That sort of information is privileged. I couldn't tell you, even if I knew."

"Are you saying you don't know?"

"As a matter of fact, I don't. The bastard must have written it all down somewhere, but I'll be damned if I can find his ledgers. He obviously hid them."

"That's one possibility," said Sebastian.

"Are you suggesting there's another?"

"Whoever shot Eisler could have taken them."

Perlman gave another of his derisive little laughs. "My uncle was shot by Russell Yates. And everyone in London knows it ... except you, apparently."

Sebastian shifted his gaze to the large canvas beside them, a biblical scene complete with plumed Roman soldiers, fainting women, and an angry bearded man with a bare, heavily muscled chest who may or may not have been Samson. "Looks like a Van Dyck."

Perlman opened his eyes in astonishment. "Impressive."

"But that doesn't mean it is."

Sebastian turned toward the door.

He'd taken two steps when Perlman stopped him by saying, "I do know the name of one man who owed my uncle money. Beresford. Blair Beresford."

Sebastian paused. "I thought you said you consider that sort of information privileged."

A gleam of what looked suspiciously like sly triumph flared in the other man's eyes. "I know I can rely upon you to exercise the utmost discretion with the information I have provided you."

"Have something against Beresford, do you?"

But Perlman only smiled faintly and returned to his study of the oil.

❧

It took Sebastian a while, but he finally tracked Blair Beresford to Bond Street, where the Irishman waited outside the bow-fronted establishment of one of London's most fashionable milliners. The rain had finally eased up, the clouds breaking apart to show pale aquamarine streaks of clear sky above. Beresford was leaning against the side of Louisa Hope's elegant barouche, his arms folded at his chest, his chin sunk in his cravat, his thoughts evidently far, far away.

"Ah, there you are," said Sebastian, walking up to him.

Beresford straightened with a jerk, his eyes going wide in a way that told Sebastian the young Irishman had obviously at some time in the past several hours had an interesting conversation with his friend Matt Tyson. "Actually, I was just about to go see if Louisa—"

"Not to worry," said Sebastian, ruthlessly turning the younger man's steps toward Oxford Street. "I won't take but a moment of your time. I'm just wondering if you could explain something for me."

Beresford cast an apprehensive glance over his shoulder, toward the milliner's shop. "I can try."

"Good. You see, I've been wondering: Why would someone whose cousin is married to one of the richest men in England need to go to a bloodsucker like Daniel Eisler to borrow money?"

Sebastian watched as all the color drained from the younger man's face to leave him pale and visibly shaken. "I'm afraid I don't know what you're talking about." He drew up abruptly. "And now, if you'll excuse me, I really must—"

"Cut line," said Sebastian, swinging to face him. "You can answer the question, or I can ask it of Louisa Hope. Which do you prefer?"

Beresford met his gaze, then looked away, his lower jaw thrust out as he exhaled a long, painful breath. "Louisa doesn't know anything about any of this," he said quietly.

"Why Eisler? Why not go to Hope?"

Beresford continued walking, his soft blue eyes fixed on the wet pavement before them. "I did. The first time."

"Go on."

"It all happened one night right after I first came to London. I fell in with some friends from Oxford. They wanted to try a gaming hell near Portland Place, so I went with them. The stakes were . . . high. Almost before I knew it, I'd lost a thousand pounds." He gave a nearly hysterical laugh. "A thousand pounds! My father only clears twelve hundred pounds in a good year."

"So you went to Hope?"

Beresford nodded. "He behaved remarkably well, under the circumstances. Read me a lecture, of course, but nothing I didn't deserve. When he handed me the money, he warned me there would be no second time."

"Don't tell me you went back to the same hell again?"

Beresford's lips crimped into a painfully thin line. "Hope told me I didn't need to repay him. But . . . it didn't sit right with me to just take his money. The problem was, I knew the only way I could ever get my hands on that much blunt would be to win it."

"How much did you lose the second time?"

"Five hundred pounds. I was winning at first—"

"You always do."

"But then my luck turned. Quite suddenly and rather disastrously. I did have the sense to quit. Only, not soon enough."

"If you'd had any sense, you wouldn't have gone back there at all."

Beresford's eyes flashed with resentment. "You think I don't know that now? I came damned close to putting a pistol in my mouth. There was no way I could go to Hope and admit I'd lost another five hundred pounds."

"So you went to Eisler instead. How the devil did you imagine you would ever repay him? Were you planning to take to the high toby next?"

The rat-a-tat-tat of a drum sounded from the top of

the street, accompanied by the tramp of marching feet. Beresford glanced toward the sound, a deep stain of shame spreading across his fair cheeks. "He . . . I . . . That is to say, I agreed to perform certain services for him."

Sebastian was beginning to understand at least part of Perlman's motivation in sending him to Beresford. "You mean, you undertook to regularly provide him with whores."

Beresford's eyes widened, his throat working painfully as he swallowed. "How did you know?"

"Call it a good guess. Did you provide Eisler with a whore last Sunday?"

"Sunday? No. But I know he had at least one other person doing the same thing I was."

Sebastian studied the younger man's handsome, strained face. He struck Sebastian as earnest and basically decent, if dangerously inexperienced and naive. For the most part, he was probably telling the truth.

But only for the most part.

Sebastian said, "Where were you that evening?"

"You mean when Eisler was shot? I was with Matt Tyson, at his rooms in St. James's. We were drinking wine . . . playing a friendly game of whist . . . that sort of thing."

Not for the first time, Sebastian found himself wondering at the friendship between the older, battle-hardened lieutenant and this young, fresh-faced Irish boy barely down from Oxford. "How long have you known Tyson?"

"Six weeks or so, I suppose. We met at a musical evening given by a mutual acquaintance." His gaze darted back to where his cousin had appeared in the doorway of the milliner's shop, her head turned as she conversed with someone behind her. "There's Louisa. I really must—"

"One more question," said Sebastian as a column of soldiers swung into view, red uniforms clean and new, brass buttons glinting in a gleam of sunshine. "What can

you tell me about the blue diamond Eisler was selling
for the Hopes?"

The younger man's features slackened in a convincing
expression of puzzlement. "Blue diamond?" He shook
his head. "I'm sorry. I don't know anything about it.
Henry Philip Hope is the one who collects gems, and I've
only met him a few times."

"It's possible Thomas Hope purchased this diamond
five or six years ago, perhaps for your cousin."

Beresford looked thoughtful. "I know he gave Louisa
some ridiculously expensive pieces when he was courting
her—I remember my mother referring to them rather
sardonically as 'bribes.' But I couldn't say exactly what
they were. I never saw them. And Louisa actually prefers
to wear smaller, more delicate jewelry."

Louisa Hope's voice floated across to them. "Blair?"

Beresford gave a quick, flustered bow. "Excuse me.
Please."

Sebastian let him go.

He stood and watched the young man lope back
down the street, dodging two turbaned matrons making
their slow, ponderous way arm in arm up the flagway,
and nearly colliding with a liveried footman burdened
with a pile of packages. He was aware of the column of
soldiers drawing abreast of him, side drum tapping, boots
tramping out their familiar cadence. They looked to be
new recruits, probably on their way to the port, where a
ship would carry them away to as-yet-unfought battles in
distant lands.

He turned to watch them, his gaze studying the rows
of freshly scrubbed faces. Most appeared pathetically
eager and excited; a few were anxious. But one or two
bore the distant, focused stare of a man who has seen his
own death and yet marches inexorably toward it.

Chapter 30

*I*n Sebastian's experience, men like Blair Beresford rarely committed murder. There was something sad and gentle—almost fragile—about the young man that argued against the kind of passion and violence that murder usually entailed. But he'd learned long ago that most people, however calm and tender, however controlled and even-tempered, were capable of murder if pushed hard enough or put in the wrong situation.

He couldn't see Beresford killing Eisler over a debt of five hundred pounds, although he had only Beresford's word for it that the debt actually was five hundred pounds and not ten times that. Would Beresford kill for five thousand pounds? Ten thousand?

Sebastian still didn't think so. But if Eisler had goaded or taunted the young man? If he had threatened to expose Beresford's debt and the way in which he was repaying? Was Blair Beresford capable of killing a nasty, evil old man while in the grip of a rage born of fear and shame?

Sebastian couldn't be certain, but he thought it possible.

Turning toward his own curricle, Sebastian found himself wondering once again why Samuel Perlman had given him Blair Beresford's name. And it occurred to him now that the object of Perlman's animosity might not be Beresford himself so much as Thomas Hope. If whoever killed Daniel Eisler also stole the valuable blue diamond Eisler was handling, then as Eisler's heir, Perlman would be responsible for compensating the diamond's owner for its loss—assuming, of course, that the owner could prove Eisler had had the gem in his possession.

Sebastian suspected a man as astute as Hope would have kept detailed records of any such transaction.

But if the blue diamond was indeed the motive for Eisler's murder, that would require the killer to have known that the old man had the gem in his possession. So how many people would have been privy to that information? Francillon, obviously, and Hope—if the diamond was truly his. Samuel Perlman? Perhaps. Blair Beresford? Possibly. Matt Tyson? Again, possibly, if Beresford knew.

Only, how had Jacques Collot come to hear of it? And who else might have known?

Sebastian started to head back toward Brook Street. Then he changed his mind and turned his horses toward the Strand and the discreet establishment of the lapidary John Francillon.

⁂

The shutters were already up on the windows of Francillon's small shop on the Strand when Sebastian pushed open the door, the jingle of the brass bell filling the air.

Francillon was behind the counter, his back turned, his head bent as he slid a tray into a tall wooden cabinet. "Sorry, we're closed," he said without even bothering to look up. "You can come back in the morning, if you like. We open at ten."

Sebastian said, "I have a few more questions I need to ask you."

Francillon spun around, the shop's single oil lamp throwing his lithe shadow across the counter and up over the rows of paintings and specimens on the far wall. "But I have already told you everything!"

"This isn't about Eisler's diamond, exactly." Sebastian placed his forearms on the polished countertop and leaned into them. "I want you to tell me about the theft of the French Crown Jewels."

Francillon turned to carefully close the cabinet door behind him. "What makes you think I know more than what I have already told you?"

"Because jewels are your business, and this was probably the greatest jewel theft in history. Because your people came from France, so I would imagine you've watched the events unfolding there very carefully. And because I don't think you're the kind of man who's comfortable with the idea of letting someone who's innocent hang for a murder he didn't commit."

Francillon smoothed his hands over his hair, as if to reassure himself of its neatness, although there was not a strand out of place. Then he came to rest one hip on a high stool, his laced fingers resting against his thigh, his gaze far, far away. "Very well. Let me see. . . . You know that the revolutionary government confiscated the Crown Jewels from Louis XVI after he attempted to flee the country with his family in the summer of 1791?"

"Yes."

"To give you an idea of the amount of treasure involved, an inventory was made at the time. It ran to something like fifty pages."

"That much?"

Francillon nodded. "The Bourbons had what was probably the largest collection of jewels in Europe. All together, they were valued at more than twenty-four million livres; the French Blue alone was estimated to be worth three million livres."

"So what did the revolutionary government do with them?"

"The Crown Jewels were declared the property of the people and placed under guard in the Hôtel du Garde-Meuble on the Place Louis XV—what later became the Place de la Révolution." He paused, a spasm crossing his face. The Place de la Révolution had become famous as the site of the guillotine.

"Go on," said Sebastian.

"The jewels were then put on display. The thinking was that since they belonged to the people, the people ought to be allowed to see them. So every Monday, the *hôtel* was opened to the public. The jewels remained on display for over a year, until August of 1792, when a decision was made to close the exhibit due to the growing instability in Paris."

"But they were still kept in the Garde-Meuble?"

"Oh, yes. In locked cabinets in a chamber located just above the ground-floor entrance. The chief conservator responsible for the treasures complained constantly that he needed more guards, but . . ." Francillon shrugged. "It was September of 1792; the entire nation was falling apart."

"So at the time of the theft," said Sebastian, "the exhibition was closed?"

"It was. But before the visits were suspended, a man named Paul Miette had gone to the Garde-Meuble every Monday for weeks, studying the habits of the guards, the various approaches to the treasure room. There is some evidence he also managed to acquire inside information about the habits of the guards, but that was never proven."

"So what happened?"

Francillon pulled at his earlobe. "On the night of 11 September, Miette and some half a dozen of his cohorts simply propped a ladder against the wall at the front of the building, cut a hole in an upstairs window, and climbed inside. There was so much to steal that they couldn't carry it all away with them. But when they realized the theft had not been noticed, they came back two nights later, and again two nights after that. By their fourth visit, they'd become so bold that they turned the theft into a drunken revelry, complete with whores, food, and wine. Everything from jeweled swords to statues to bells was simply tossed out the windows to friends waiting in the street below."

"You can't be serious," said Sebastian.

Francillon sighed. "I wish I were not. They were finally spotted by an officer of the National Guard, who sounded the alarm. But it took him so long to convince the building's watchmen to open the chamber's doors—which were, of course, still sealed—that the thieves managed to escape."

"You're saying none of them were caught?"

"One or two who were too drunk or too stupid to run were taken up at the scene; a few more were arrested later. But none of the actual ringleaders were ever apprehended. In the end, several men were executed. A few were given short prison sentences and then quickly pardoned."

"That sounds rather suspicious."

"It does, does it not?" Francillon cleared his throat. "At the time, the public was naturally outraged by the theft of the nation's treasure. Some tried to place the blame for the theft on the Queen, Marie Antoinette—which was ridiculous, given that she was under guard herself at the time. Others thought it was a counterrevolutionary plot to destroy the Revolution by stealing France's wealth. But there were those who suspected that forces within the revolutionary government itself had been responsible. You see, the Minister of the Interior had actually suggested back in August that the Crown Jewels be sold and the proceeds used to support the Revolution's paper currency and defray other expenses—in particular the looming war with Austria and Prussia. But there was such an outcry that the scheme was abandoned."

"At least publicly," said Sebastian.

Francillon met his gaze, his expression solemn. "Exactly." His eyes slid away. "One interesting point is that the thief who is credited with devising the scheme in the first place—Paul Miette—was actually imprisoned in La Force until shortly before the theft, as were nearly a dozen of his colleagues. There have been suggestions that their release was arranged by men within the government."

"You say Miette was never captured?"

"Never. He simply disappeared. Some of the smaller stones were recovered in Paris in the days and weeks following the theft. But the major pieces—the French Blue, the Bazu, and many, many others—have never been seen again."

"Do you know the names of any of Miette's colleagues?"

Francillon frowned with the effort of memory. "Let me see. . . . There was Cadet Guillot; he is probably the best known, along with a man named Deslanges. And, of course, Collot."

"Collot?" said Sebastian sharply. "You mean Jacques Collot?"

Francillon looked at him in surprise. "You have heard of him?"

"I have. He claims he comes from a long line of Parisian lapidaries."

Francillon threw back his head and laughed. "I suppose he can certainly claim to come from a long line of ancestors with a marked interest in jewels. But I'm afraid the Collots' talents have never been those of a lapidary."

"Meaning?"

"The Collots are thieves," said Francillon, his lean features hardening. "And they have been for a hundred and fifty years or more."

※

Sebastian was in his dressing room rubbing ashes into his face when Hero came to stand in the doorway behind him, the black cat perched regally in her arms.

He looked over at her and smiled. "So, where was he?"

"He'd somehow contrived to get himself shut in the tack room in the stables."

"Someone needs to tell him about curiosity and the cat."

With a contemptuous lashing of its long, fluffy tail, the cat jumped from her arms and ran off. "I did," she said. "He didn't appreciate it."

She brought her gaze back to his worn breeches and leather waistcoat, the disreputable coat and grimy shirt gleaned from the secondhand clothing stalls in Rosemary Lane. He'd also wrapped padding around his waist that effectively altered both his silhouette and his gait. "Do I take it you're not planning an evening at your club?"

He leaned forward, his gaze on the mirror as he dabbed more ashes mixed with grease from the kitchen onto the dark hair at his temples. "I've just had an interesting conversation with the lapidary, Francillon."

"Oh?"

"He tells me there's a strong possibility the theft of the French Crown Jewels was actually engineered by the revolutionary French government."

Pushing away from the doorframe, she wandered the room, fiddling first with a box of collars, then with one of the ragged coats Calhoun had assembled for Devlin's selection. "What makes you so certain this blue diamond is in any way connected to Eisler's death?"

"At this point, I'm not certain it is. I'm also hearing credible stories about the man's cutthroat lending practices and certain aberrant sexual practices that could very well be what ended up getting him killed."

She glanced over at him. "Define 'aberrant.'"

"Compelling attractive young women to lie with him when they—or their husbands—fell behind on interest payments."

A wave of revulsion flickered over her face. "I'd say that goes beyond aberrant, all the way to downright evil. The more I hear about Eisler, the more I think whoever killed him deserves a reward rather than punishment."

Sebastian wiped his hands on a towel. "I might agree, except for one thing."

"What's that?"

"Whoever murdered Eisler is about to let an innocent man hang for what he did."

"True." She hesitated a moment, then said, "So why this continuing interest in the French Crown Jewels?"

"Because for some reason, the more I look into Eisler's affairs, the more the French Blue keeps coming up. It obviously fits into all this somewhere; I just can't figure out where or how."

"Which is why you're dressed like a fat publican down on his luck?"

Sebastian reached for a battered black hat and settled it low on his forehead. "I've decided I need to have another conversation with my friend Jacques Collot. A candid conversation."

Hero smiled. "And what do you expect him to tell you?"

"Mainly, what happened to the French Blue between the time it disappeared from the Garde-Meuble in Paris and when it reappeared in Daniel Eisler's possession shortly before his death." Propping one foot on the edge of a bench, Sebastian loosened the dagger he kept in a sheath in his boot, then straightened to slip a small double-barreled pistol into the pocket of his tattered greatcoat. "And maybe—just maybe—where the bloody diamond is now."

Chapter 31

*B*y the time Sebastian reached the parish of St. Giles, the darkness of the night was complete, the sickle moon and few dim stars that had been visible earlier at dusk hidden now by a haze of coal smoke and scattered clouds. The smell of cook fires and a pervasive dampness left from the day's rain hung heavily in the air, underlain by the inevitable stench of effluvia and decay. As he paid off his hackney driver, a tousle-haired woman in a tawdry, low-cut red gown emerged from the shadows of a nearby doorway to smile archly. "Lookin' fer some fun, gov'nor?"

Sebastian shook his head and turned to push his way through the raucous, drunken crowds of costermongers and day laborers, thieves and pickpockets, doxies and beggars, his gaze carefully scanning the sea of rough, dirty faces.

The East End of London was choked with men like Collot: raised in want and desperation, uneducated, angry, and long ago cut loose from the moral underpinnings that typically anchored those who looked askance at them. Most were English or Irish, but in their midst one also found many French, Danes, Spaniards, even Africans. Living precariously from day to day, subsisting largely on potatoes and bread and crammed as many as five or ten to a room, they wreaked their own kind of vengeance on a system that viewed them as a permanent "criminal class," impervious to improvement and suitable only for containment. Those who didn't die young or violently could generally look forward to being either hanged or transported to the nasty new penal colony at Botany Bay that had replaced the earlier hellholes in Georgia and Jamaica.

With each step he took, Sebastian allowed himself to sink deeper and deeper into a persona he had affected often during the war, when he'd served as an exploring officer in the hills of Iberia. It was Kat who'd first taught him, long ago, that there was more to carrying off an effective disguise than a dirtied face and old clothes; successful deception lay in recognizing and altering the subtle differences in movement and posture, mannerisms and attitude that distinguish us all. Gone were the upright carriage, the easy confidence and demeanor of the Earl's son. Instead, he moved from one public house and gin shop to the next with the stooped shoulders, ducked head, and furtive sideways glances of a man who had never known command, who had been forced to claw and bluff his way through life, who could rarely be certain where his next meal would come from, and who always knew that the heavy hand of vengeful authority could fall upon him at any moment.

It was in a public house just off Great Earl Street that Sebastian finally spotted his quarry in earnest conversation with three cohorts huddled around a battered table. Ordering a pint of ale from a barmaid who couldn't have been more than fourteen, Sebastian stood with his back to the counter, one knee bent so that the sole of his boot rested against the rough planking behind him. The close atmosphere smelled of spilled ale and tobacco and unwashed men. Narrowing his eyes against the smoke, he watched Collot nod to his cohorts and rise from the table to walk toward him.

Sebastian held himself very still.

But the Frenchman brushed past Sebastian without a

flicker of either recognition or suspicion and pushed open the door. His companions remained at their table.

Setting aside his tankard, Sebastian followed Collot out into the dark coolness of the night.

He trailed the Frenchman down a crooked lane lit only by a rare torch flaring in a rusted sconce fastened high to the side of a crumbling wall, or by whatever dim light filtered through the thick, grimy panes of old glass in the windows of the occasional coffeehouse or gin shop. Quickening his pace, he caught up with Collot just as the Frenchman was passing a narrow alley between a pawnshop and a tallow-candle maker.

As if sensing the danger behind him, Collot half turned as Sebastian plowed into him.

"Mon Dieu!" he cried as the force of Sebastian's momentum carried the two men deep into the fetid darkness of the alleyway.

Sebastian slammed the Frenchman face-first against a rough brick wall, one hand tightening around Collot's right wrist to yank his arm behind his back and lever it up, effectively holding him pinned in place.

"Bête! Bâtard!" swore Collot, his gray-whiskered face twisted sideways, his hat askew, his one visible eye opened so wide Sebastian could clearly see the white rimming his dark, dilated iris as he struggled against Sebastian's hold. "Put a hand on my purse, you whore's son, and I'll—"

"Shut up and listen to me very carefully," hissed Sebastian, every affectation gone from his manner.

Collot stilled. "You?"

Sebastian drew his lips back into a smile. "Yes, me."

"What is this? What do you want?"

"Two rules," said Sebastian softly. "Rule number one: Don't even think about lying to me again. Lies have a tendency to make me cranky, and I'm already not in the best of moods at the moment."

"But I did not lie—"

"Rule number two," said Sebastian, increasing the

pressure on the Frenchman's arm in a way that made him grimace. "Don't waste my time. There's an innocent man in Newgate who's liable to hang for a murder he did not commit. Which means that when you waste my time, you're helping to kill him."

"Are you so certain, *monsieur*, that he is indeed innocent of what he is accused? Perhaps you—"

"You're forgetting rule number two," said Sebastian evenly.

Collot fell silent.

Sebastian said, "I learned something interesting today. It seems that, far from coming from a family of Parisian lapidaries, you are actually descended from a long line of Parisian thieves."

Collot huffed a nervous laugh. "Jewel thieves, jewelers— is there such a difference?"

Sebastian was not amused. "Tell me about the theft of the French Crown Jewels from the Garde-Meuble in Paris."

"But I never—"

Sebastian tightened his grip. "Now you're forgetting both rule number one and rule number two. You told me you sold jewels to Daniel Eisler in Amsterdam in 1792. What I want to know is, was one of them the French Blue?"

Collot gave a snort of derision. "You think they would allow us to keep something as valuable as the Emblem of the Golden Fleece?"

"Who is 'they'?"

"Danton." Collot spit the word out as if it were a bite of tainted old mutton.

The name caught Sebastian by surprise. A coarse, physically ugly mountain of a man, Georges Danton had initially fled the Revolution, only to return and rise to prominence as one of the architects of the Revolutionary Tribunal and the Reign of Terror. "Danton? Not the Minister of the Interior, Roland?"

"They were both in on it—the two of them, Danton and Roland, working together."

Sebastian said, "It was Danton who eventually sent Roland to the guillotine."

"Eventually, yes. But in September of 1792, Danton and Roland were allies. Danton and Robespierre were also allies at one time; remember? Only, that didn't save Danton's head when Robespierre eventually decided to move against *him*, now, did it?"

Sebastian shifted his grip to swing Collot around to face him. In the flickering light thrown by a distant torch, the Frenchman looked pale and slack-jawed, his wayward eye more noticeable than ever. "Why should I believe you?"

Collot turned his head and spat. "Why should I care whether you believe me or not? I am telling you, Danton and Roland wanted to sell the Crown Jewels because the government needed the money. Only, the other members of the government would not agree. So Danton arranged to have the jewels 'stolen' instead."

"And the French Blue? What happened to it?"

A distant burst of laughter jerked Collot's attention, for a moment, to the lane at the end of the alley. Then he brought his gaze back to Sebastian and smiled.

"You don't know anything, do you? That was September of 1792, when the combined armies of Austria and Prussia were camped at Valmy, just a hundred miles from Paris. Together, they outnumbered the French troops facing them nearly two to one. If they had advanced on the city then—in the middle of September—they could have taken Paris. The Revolution would have been over. Finished. That's what Danton was afraid of. He knew what his life would be worth if Louis were restored to the throne."

"What are you suggesting? That Danton used the French Crown Jewels to bribe the Prussian and Austrian armies not to attack Paris?"

Collot gave a harsh, ringing laugh. "Not the Prussians and the Austrians; their commander."

Sebastian's eyes widened, for Collot's words opened

up an entirely new angle on Eisler's murder. He took a step back and released Collot so suddenly the Frenchman sagged and almost fell.

For the man commanding the Prussian and Austrian armies at Valmy was none other than Carl Wilhelm Ferdinand, Duke of Brunswick, husband to George III's sister, the English Princess Augusta, and father to Princess Caroline....

The estranged wife of George, the Prince Regent.

Chapter 32

Finding himself unexpectedly free, Collot took off in a stumbling trot down the alley, his hands splayed out awkwardly at his sides, the tails of his tattered coat flying in the damp breeze.

Sebastian let him go.

He was remembering a dark carriage looming out of the night, a frightened young man running toward those whom he believed were his allies, the deadly spurt of flame from the end of a darkened rifle barrel. Who would do something like that?

The obvious answer was people without conscience or scruples.

People who see their own agents as expendable.

People with far more at stake than a mere diamond, however big and rare.

Still turning Collot's revelations over in his mind, Sebastian emerged from the alley into the raucous turmoil of the street beyond. Someone was scraping on a fiddle, and half a dozen Irishmen were dancing a jig, cheered on by a circle of laughing, ragged women. Beyond them, he could see a lithe, pockmarked man wearing a small-brimmed, dented hat and standing by himself on the far side of the street. He had one shoulder propped against a rough brick wall, his hands thrust in his pockets, his gaze seemingly directed toward a saucy redheaded bit o' muslin who was smiling at him. But when Sebastian turned south, toward Covent Garden, the man readjusted his hat and pushed away from the wall to follow him.

As he wound his way up the crowded street, Sebastian was aware of the pockmarked man behind him. The man hung well back, always careful to keep some distance between them. But when Sebastian paused to gaze through the misted window of a coffeehouse, his shadow paused too. The man had a lean, sharp-boned face with a small nose, a pointed chin, and dark hair. His clothes were those of a day laborer or apprentice. . . .

Or someone considerably more unsavory.

Whistling softly, Sebastian continued on.

The pockmarked man fell into step behind him.

As they neared Long Acre, the crowds became more scattered, the neighborhood less depraved. Sebastian quickened his pace, his footsteps and those of his shadow echoing dully in the narrow streets. He turned right onto Long Acre, then immediately drew back into the darkened doorway of a button shop. The pockmarked man rounded the corner and continued past Sebastian some three or four paces before becoming aware that his quarry had suddenly vanished. He abruptly drew up.

Sebastian stepped from the doorway into the light of a street lamp and said, "Who are you and why the hell are you following me?"

The man whirled. Rather than dissembling or startling in any way, he whipped a nasty knife from beneath his coat and lunged forward to slash the blade across Sebastian's stomach with enough force to have disemboweled him if the steel had cut flesh. Instead, the knife ripped through the covering of the bolster Sebastian had used to pad his torso. A cascade of white feathers spilled around them, fluttering in an airy flurry to the wet pavement.

"Qu'est-ce que c'est?" For one unguarded moment, the man stared at him, confused.

"You son of a bitch," swore Sebastian, his boot lashing out to smash into his assailant's wrist.

The impact sent the knife careening into the darkness. Sebastian followed the kick with a jab of his right fist that caught the man high on the cheekbone and spun him half around. A second blow glanced across his ear and knocked the dented hat flying.

With an angry roar, the assailant lowered his head and charged, fists flailing. But the feathers were slick underfoot, the soles of his shoes slipping, throwing him off balance. Sebastian landed another punch against his assailant's temple. The man broke and ran.

Leaping off the flagway into the street, he nearly collided with a hackney drawn by a skittish chestnut. The horse reared, neighing in alarm as the man dashed down the narrow lane that led to St. Paul's and Covent Garden Market.

Sebastian pelted after him.

They erupted out of the lane into the broad market square, its stalls now shuttered in the darkness. During the day, the piazza before St. Paul's was the site of London's largest produce market. But at night, it was given over to the city's demimonde. Painted women in low-cut gowns hissed and whistled as the two men pelted across the square, sliding awkwardly on the mushy cabbage leaves and smashed rotten fruit underfoot.

The man was lithe and agile and amazingly fleet-footed. Rather than gaining on him, Sebastian soon found himself having a hard time keeping up. They raced between rows of shuttered stalls, leapt over piles of refuge, and dodged sleepy, ragged little boys who crawled out from beneath the dark counters to holler at them. On the far side of the square, an aged landau pulled by a mismatched team of bays dashed past, its gray-bearded coachman clad in worn livery, its sole passenger a turbaned dowager either too financially pressed or too cheap to employ a footman to ride up behind her. With a running jump, Sebastian's assailant leapt up to catch hold of the rear bar, his feet scrabbling for purchase on the platform.

"God damn it," huffed Sebastian as the landau bowled

on up the street, carrying its uninvited hanger-on away with it. The pockmarked man pivoted agilely, one hand still grasping the bar, the other raised to his forehead in a mocking salute.

Sebastian sprinted after the landau for another two blocks. Then the carriage turned onto the Strand, picking up speed as it rolled away toward the west.

He gave it up.

Hunching over, he braced his hands against his thighs, his body shuddering as he drew air into his aching lungs. A few last feathers fluttered down around him like the downy flakes of winter's first snow.

⁂

"So who was he?" asked Hero, pausing in the doorway to Sebastian's dressing room.

The house was quiet around them, the room lit only by a brace of candles on the dressing table. He pulled the ruined shirt off over his head and unwound the bindings that held what was left of the padding around his waist. "I don't know. But he was French." He frowned down at the flesh revealed beneath the bindings. The tip of the man's blade had cut through the padding enough to leave a long, angry weal across his lower abdomen.

"You're acquiring an impressive collection of cuts on your torso," said his wife, pushing away from the doorframe. "All you need now is a slice along the right side of your ribs and the symmetry will be complete."

"Huh," he grunted, and tossed the shredded padding at her.

She ducked, laughing, then went to uncork a flask of alcohol and liberally soak a folded cloth. "Whoever he was, he must have been watching Jacques Collot rather than you; otherwise, he would have known your protuberant belly began life as a feather pillow."

"You're probably right. In which case the question then becomes, who is watching Jacques Collot? And why?"

She came to press the alcohol-soaked pad to his cut. He sucked in his breath in an audible hiss.

"Stings, does it?" she said, her voice pleasant.

"If I didn't know better, I'd suspect you of deriving some sort of fiendish delight from this."

She grunted, her head bent as she focused on her task. "Tell me again what Collot said about the theft."

He told her. He watched the way the flickering light from the nearby candles danced across her face, watched as she gripped her lower lip between her teeth while she worked.

He said, "Why do I get the distinct impression that none of this is exactly news to you?"

She set the pad aside and carefully recorked the flask. "How much do you know about Princess Caroline's father, the Duke of Brunswick?"

"Not much, I'm afraid."

"He was a surprisingly accomplished and unusual man—very much a student of the Enlightenment. They used to call his court at Wolfenbüttel the 'Versailles of the North.' It was a center for poets and artists and men of letters, and filled with an exquisite collection of books, paintings, and fine furnishings."

"Sounds like Daniel Eisler would have loved it," said Sebastian.

"Napoléon certainly did."

"He ransacked it?"

"I think 'stripped it' would be a more accurate term." She perched on the edge of the bench while he poured warm water in the basin. "Napoléon had something of a grudge against the Duke. You see, in addition to being the brother-in-law of the King of England, father-in-law to the Prince of Wales, and a patron of artists and scholars, he was also considered one of Europe's best generals. When the American colonists revolted against us, good ole King George actually asked Brunswick to lead Britain's forces. He refused."

Sebastian looked over at her. "Any particular reason?"

"Some say it was because he wanted King George to fail—that he was sympathetic to the Americans' cause."

"Was he?"

"I suspect he was. In 1792, the French revolutionary government in their turn approached Brunswick and asked him to take command of their army. He refused them as well, but not without expressing his support for the reforms they were enacting."

Sebastian scrubbed at his face and hair, rinsing away the ashes and grease. "So why did he agree to take command of the combined armies of Austria and Prussia instead?"

"I don't know. Perhaps they gave him no real choice. But his distrust of the Austrians was well-known, as was his belief that the Prussian King—also his cousin, by the way—was a fool."

Sebastian reached for a towel. "According to Collot, Brunswick's army was within a hundred miles of Paris at the time of the theft of the French Crown Jewels."

She nodded. "That's right, at Valmy. It's well-known that the revolutionary government tried to negotiate with Brunswick—to persuade him to withdraw. A meeting was actually held."

"And?"

"Supposedly, the negotiations failed."

Sebastian frowned. "But Brunswick still didn't attack Paris."

"No, he didn't. And every day he held off was one more day the French were able to use to build up their own forces. Did you know that Johann Wolfgang von Goethe was with the Prussian Army at Valmy?"

"I did not."

"His account of those days makes interesting reading. He was convinced some sort of treachery was afoot. He says there was no conceivable reason why an attack on Paris wasn't launched immediately."

"But there was eventually a battle."

"Eventually. Although it was more in the nature of a

small skirmish. And after that, Brunswick simply . . . withdrew. The next day, the National Convention abolished the monarchy and declared France a republic. And barely four months after that, Louis XVI was beheaded."

"You're saying Collot was right—that Brunswick was bribed?"

"According to the rumors, his price was five million livres."

"With part of the payment being delivered in the form of the French Blue?"

"That's the rumor."

He looked over at her. "And is the rumor true?"

"I've never been told."

Which did not, he realized, exactly answer his question.

Their gazes met. And he knew it again, that awareness that no matter how close they might become, Jarvis's shadow—and Hero's loyalty to her father—would always be between them.

She said, "After everything you've learned about Eisler—the blackmail, the financial exploitation, the sexual debauchery—you still think the mystery surrounding this blue diamond is somehow involved in his death?"

"Somehow, yes."

She nodded as if coming to a decision and rose to her feet. "Then you might find it useful to speak to a certain colonel in the Black Brunswickers named Otto von Riedesel. He was in Spain with Wellington up until a few months ago, when he was wounded. But before that he served the old Duke of Brunswick."

Sebastian swiped the towel at a drop of water running down his cheek, then tossed it aside. A corps of volunteers raised by the current Duke of Brunswick to fight against Napoléon, the Black Brunswickers were known for their brutality.

And for their fierce desire for revenge.

Chapter 33

At dawn the next morning, Colonel Otto von Riedesel was exercising a magnificent black Hanoverian on the Row in Hyde Park when Sebastian brought his own Arab mare in beside him.

The colonel glanced over at Sebastian, then looked away, his jaw set hard. A big man with a full ruddy face, small brown eyes, and a swooping mustache, he wore the uniform of the Black Brunswickers—or the Black Horde, as they were sometimes called. As a symbol of their state of mourning for the occupied Duchy of Brunswick—now under the control of Napoléon—the corps' entire uniform was black: black boots, black trousers, black dolman, black shako. The only touches of color came from the blue of his dolman's collar and the Brunswicker silver death's-head on his black shako.

The two men trotted along in a strained silence filled with the creak of saddle leather, the pounding of their horses' hooves on the wet earth, the chorus of birdsong rising from the sparrows waking in the misty elms lining the path. At last, as if goaded beyond endurance, the Brunswicker exclaimed, "Vhat the hell do you vant from me?"

"I think you know the answer to that."

Von Riedesel gave a loud snort.

Sebastian said, "When Daniel Eisler was murdered, he had in his possession a large blue diamond. I'm told that diamond was previously held by the late Duke Carl Wilhelm of Brunswick."

"I am a simple soldier. Vhat makes you think I know of such things?"

"The diamond in question is in all probability a recut version of a stone that once formed part of the French Crown Jewels."

The colonel reined in hard, the red of his cheeks darkening to an angry hue, his horse chafing at the bit. "If you mean to suggest that the present Duke's father allowed himself to be bribed into—"

"I'm not suggesting anything," said Sebastian calmly. "I frankly couldn't care less how the Duke came into possession of the French Blue. I want to know what happened to the gem between the time it was acquired by Carl Wilhelm and when it showed up in the possession of Daniel Eisler."

"I told you; I know nothing of this." Von Riedesel set his spurs to his horse's sides, and the black Hanoverian leapt forward.

Sebastian kept pace with him. "You're quite certain of that, are you?"

"Yes!"

"I suppose you're right; I should have directed my questions to the Prince Regent. As the Duke's son-in-law and executor of his will, Prinny would surely know what happened to the diamond after the Duke's death." Sebastian showed his teeth in a smile. "Sorry to have troubled you, Colonel. Good day."

He was turning his horse's head toward the gate when von Riedesel stopped him. "Wait!"

Sebastian paused, one eyebrow raised in inquiry.

"Ride on vith me a moment," snapped the Brunswicker.

Sebastian fell in beside him again.

Von Riedesel said, "Vhat I have to tell you is in the strictest confidence."

"Of course."

The Brunswicker set his jaw. "Six years ago, vhen it became obvious that Napoléon was liable to overrun Brunswick, Duke Carl Wilhelm decided to send his jewel collection to his daughter for safekeeping."

"You mean to Princess Caroline."

"Yes."

Sebastian studied the Colonel's tight red face. "He entrusted you to bring it here, did he?"

Von Riedesel nodded. "I carried it in my personal luggage. Unfortunately, it wasn't long after I arrived in London that word reached us of the Duke's death in battle. His vidowed Duchess—your own English Princess Augusta—fled to London and sought refuge with her daughter." He hesitated, then said, "This was in 1806. You know of the shameful straits under which the Prince forced his wife to live?"

"I know," said Sebastian.

It was in 1806 that the Prince first instituted a governmental inquiry against Caroline in an attempt to rid himself of the wife he'd loathed at first sight. He accused her of everything from witchcraft to adultery, but in the end the "delicate investigation" failed in its objective. In retaliation, the Prince—spoiled, petulant, and endlessly indulgent of himself and his string of mistresses—cut off virtually all funds to his wife's household, leaving her in near poverty.

"In other words," said Sebastian, staring off toward the river, where the early morning mist was beginning to lift as the sun rose higher into a soft blue sky, "Caroline began selling her father's gem collection to pay for her and her mother's living expenses."

"Discreetly, of course."

"She must have been very discreet, if Prinny never caught wind of it."

Von Riedesel gave a slight bow. "Just so."

It suddenly struck Sebastian as deliciously ironic that the rare blue diamond now reportedly coveted by the Crown Prince had been previously sold behind his back by his own wife. "And the French Blue?"

"I never said Duke Carl Wilhelm possessed the French Blue. He did, however, have in his collection a large diamond of the darkest sapphire."

Sebastian ducked his head to hide his smile. "Who bought this large blue diamond from Caroline?"

"You don't seriously expect me to tell you that, do you?"

"No. But you can tell me if I'm wrong. It was Hope, wasn't it? Not Henry Philip Hope, but Thomas."

Wordlessly, the Black Brunswicker kept his gaze fixed straight ahead, his body rising and falling in tireless synchronicity with his horse's motion.

⁂

Hero was standing in the entry hall, her head bowed as she worked at buttoning her gloves, when Sebastian walked in the house.

"Another crossing sweep interview?" he asked, handing his riding crop, hat, and gloves to Morey.

She wore a white cambric walking dress with a high-collared spencer of blue silk ruched down the front. "Yes," she said, her attention all for her buttons, which were extensive. "I'm particularly looking forward to this one. It's a little girl." She looked up, her eyes narrowing as she studied his face. And he found himself wondering again, unpleasantly, just how much — and what — she knew that she wasn't telling him. She said, "Discovered something interesting, have you?"

He cast a significant glance toward the library, and she walked ahead of him into the room, going to stand beside the empty hearth while he quietly closed the door.

He said, "How did you know that the late Duke of Brunswick sent his jewel collection to his daughter the Princess of Wales for safekeeping?"

"You know I can't tell you that."

He studied her flawlessly composed face. The problem was that the most obvious explanation—that she had heard it from her father—made no sense. Jarvis had always served the King and the Crown Prince; yet von Riedesel and Caroline had maneuvered behind the Prince on this. So why had Jarvis kept their secret?

She said, "Was von Riedesel able to tell you who bought the French Blue?"

"He claims the big blue diamond from the Duke's collection did not come from the French Crown Jewels. But the gem in question was indeed purchased by Thomas Hope."

"So Collot told you the truth?"

"He did. The problem is, I don't understand how Collot could have come to have that interesting piece of information. I'm also puzzled as to why Hope would be selling the stone now. He told me himself that this is not a good time to be selling gems. So why is he putting one of the most famous diamonds in the world on the market?"

"There are rumors. . . ."

"Yes?" he prompted when she hesitated.

"The wars are putting an increasing strain on both international merchants and the old-style banking companies. The disruption of trade has simply been too extensive and gone on far too long."

"Are you saying Hope and Company is in financial trouble?"

She nodded. "I understand things have reached such a pass that they may soon be forced to sell to the Barings. They're trying to hold off, but I suspect it's only a matter of time."

"The sale of a large, rare diamond might conceivably raise enough to keep the company afloat."

"It might . . . if the value of gems weren't so sadly depressed at the moment."

Sebastian went to lean one hip against the edge of his desk, his arms crossed at his chest.

"What?" asked Hero, watching him.

"Now, there's a motive for murder I hadn't considered."

Hero shook her head. "I don't understand."

"Eisler was more than just a diamond merchant; he was a wealthy man in his own right. What if he was unable to sell the diamond for the price Hope wanted? Hope might have decided to kill Eisler and steal his own gem so that he could claim the estimated value of the stone from Eisler's estate *and* still keep the diamond."

She huffed a disbelieving laugh. "Thomas Hope? You can't be serious."

"You'd be surprised at the things men will do when they get desperate."

She shook her head. "No. I don't believe it. He's not that kind of man."

"I must admit it seems an unlikely explanation to me, although for a different reason."

"What's that?"

Sebastian pushed away from the desk. In his mind's eye, he again saw a desperate figure running down a muddy alley, heard the crack of a rifle, felt the spill of warm blood over his hands as he raised a dying boy into his arms.

"The shooter in the carriage."

Chapter 34

*T*homas Hope was supervising a couple of workmen repairing the skylight in his fifty-foot-long picture gallery when Sebastian paid a call on the banker's Duchess Street mansion.

"I ask you," exclaimed the little man in disgust, his mouth puckering furiously, "how difficult can it be to construct a skylight that doesn't leak?"

Sebastian squinted up at the ornately plastered ceiling, its lavish, pale-blue-and-white-swagged medallions marred by an ugly brown stain. "I suppose that depends on how much it rains."

Hope grunted. "Fortunately, the gallery is wide enough that none of the paintings were damaged. But look at what it's done to the upholstery of the banquettes! And I only just had them recovered in this lovely pale blue fabric."

"Tragic," agreed Sebastian. "Could I speak with you a moment in private?"

"Of course," said Hope, padding flat-footedly beside Sebastian toward the far end of the gallery. "I take it you're still looking into the death of Daniel Eisler?"

"I am." Sebastian hesitated. The man was so earnest and eager that it seemed the height of incivility to accuse him even of dissembling, let alone of something as sordid as murder. "I had an interesting conversation this morning with an individual who contradicted some of the things you told me the other day."

"Oh?"

"In fact, he confirmed the information I was originally given." Sebastian paused to rub the back of one knuckle against the side of his nose. "When one person tells me something, I generally try to keep an open mind about its veracity. But when two completely disparate individuals provide the same information, I'm inclined to believe them."

Hope stared back at him, his eyes narrowing, his face hardening. The man might come across as affable and effete, but it would never do to forget that he owned a company that lent money to kings and emperors. "I don't know what you're talking about."

"Then let me be more blunt. I think the blue diamond Daniel Eisler had in his possession when he was killed was recut from the French Blue, and he was selling it for you. I can promise to try to keep the transaction private, but not at the expense of an innocent man's life."

Hope walked over to stand before a massive Rubens, his head tipping back as he stared up at the towering canvas. "I don't think you quite understand what's at stake here," he said quietly. "This isn't about the possibility of a legal challenge from the Bourbons. If the diamond is indeed the French Blue—and I'm not saying that it is—then it has been recut. So while there might be speculation, the association could never be proven."

"True. But I don't think it's the Bourbons you're worried about, is it?"

Hope cast a quick glance over his shoulder at the workmen on the scaffold and shook his head. His voice dropped even lower. "Napoléon Bonaparte has spent the last eight years in a determined effort to reassemble the French Crown Jewels. He sees the treasure's loss as a blow to France's honor, to the point that its recovery has become an obsession with him. And the most precious of all the French Crown Jewels was the *diamant bleu de la*

Couronne. It's why he was so determined to overrun the Duchy of Brunswick and ransack the palace—because he was convinced he'd find the French Blue there. And he was furious when he didn't."

"So Napoléon knows the revolutionary government bribed the Duke?"

"I doubt the world will ever know the truth of what happened at Valmy in 1792. But there have always been rumors. And one must remember that Napoléon is himself a general. I've heard it said that in his opinion, a bribe is the only explanation that makes sense out of what happened at Valmy. All I know is that, somehow, he found out Eisler had a large blue diamond for sale."

"You know this for certain?"

Hope nodded. "One of his agents approached Eisler last Saturday morning."

"Who?" asked Sebastian sharply. "Who was this agent?"

"Eisler wouldn't say. He was very nervous, for obvious reasons. When it comes to the search for the French Crown Jewels, Napoléon has proven himself utterly . . ." Hope hesitated, as if searching for the right word, then settled for: "Ruthless."

"Not to mention lethal," said Sebastian. "So why not agree to sell him the stone?"

Hope gave a low laugh that rumbled in his chest. "The Emperor has a bad reputation when it comes to paying for his purchases. You've heard that Eisler provided the diamond necklace Napoléon presented to Empress Marie Louise as a wedding gift?"

"Yes."

"The final payment was never made. Eisler lost a small fortune on the transaction. Napoléon's attitude is that the honor of supplying his exalted personage should be reward enough."

"It's a tendency he unfortunately shares with the Prince Regent," said Sebastian dryly.

"True. But anyone selling jewels to Prinny learned long ago to require payment up front and in cash."

"So why not do the same with the Emperor?"

"Because Prinny's agents don't generally kill recalcitrant sellers and steal their merchandise. Napoléon's do."

"Are you suggesting that is what happened to Eisler?"

Hope gave another quick glance around. "It makes sense. Don't you think?"

"So you're saying the diamond is missing?"

Hope's features contorted with a spasm of anxiety. "It is, yes."

Sebastian studied the small man's mobile, expressive face. "Who besides you knew Eisler had the blue diamond?"

"It's difficult to say with any certainty. People talk. *Someone* obviously did, or else how did Napoléon's agent know to approach Eisler?"

"And did this French agent know the identity of the stone's true owner?"

"No. How could he? Unless Eisler told him."

"Are you so certain that he did not?"

Hope looked momentarily confused. "Why would Eisler tell him?"

"In an attempt to save his own life, perhaps?"

Sebastian watched the banker suck his lower lip between his teeth as the color drained from his homely face. Taking pity on the man, Sebastian said, "If Napoléon's agent did kill Eisler and recover the diamond, then the French would have no reason now to come after you."

"Yes. But what if the French don't have the diamond? What if someone else murdered Eisler and stole the gem? Or what if Eisler was murdered for some other reason entirely and Samuel Perlman now has the diamond?"

"Does Perlman know his uncle was handling the diamond for you?"

"Of course he does. I immediately laid claim against the estate for its value."

"He's refusing to pay, is he?"

Hope worked his mouth furiously back and forth.

"He is trying." He frowned down the length of the gallery, to where the workmen were resetting a pane of glass. Then he leaned in closer to ask quietly, "Do *you* think the French have recovered the diamond?"

"Actually, I'd be very surprised if they have."

Hope looked surprised. "What makes you so certain?"

"Because I think they're still looking for it."

Chapter 35

*S*amuel Perlman was watching a cricket match at an oval near Sloane Square when Sebastian walked up to him.

He glanced sideways at Sebastian and exhaled in exaggerated exasperation. "You do realize this is getting tiresome, don't you?"

"For both of us," agreed Sebastian, pausing beside him, his gaze on the batsman. "Let me give you a hint: It's never a good idea to lie when there's a murder involved. It tends to give people the impression you've something to hide. Something like guilt."

Perlman laughed out loud. "Surely you aren't still suggesting I had something to do with my uncle's death?"

"You might. I don't know yet. But as it happens, I was referring to a certain large, rare gem that's gone missing. You remember the one—the big blue diamond you told me you'd never heard of, despite the fact you were already vociferously denying Thomas Hope's claim against the estate for its value. Now, it's always possible that whoever murdered your uncle also took the diamond. Or, you could simply be pretending that he did."

Perlman's dark curly hair quivered against his fashionably pale cheeks. "Don't be insulting. If I had any desire to acquire that diamond, I would simply have purchased it."

"Ah. So you admit you did know about it."

"All right. I did, yes. But I certainly did not *steal* it. To even suggest such a thing is ridiculous. I'm a wealthy man."

Sebastian kept his gaze on the pitch. "The problem with wealth is that appearances can be deceptive. Trade is always so fickle, is it not? Particularly in time of war. I suspect that between the depredations of Napoléon and the Americans, your interests have not been performing well lately."

"My holdings and investments are performing just fine, thank you. So if you're looking for some poor sod to pin this murder on, you're going to need to look elsewhere."

Sebastian gave a slow, nasty smile. "If that's the way you want to play it. I hope you have your affairs in order." He bowed and started to move away.

Perlman raised his voice. "Wait! What does that mean? What are you going to do?"

Sebastian pivoted to face him again. "I don't need to do anything. I wouldn't be surprised if the French already suspect that the stone they're looking for might now be in your possession. You see, Napoléon is under the impression Hope's diamond once formed part of the French Crown Jewels. And as you know, the Emperor is not averse to killing in order to get the jewels back."

"But I don't have it!"

"Somehow, I suspect Napoléon's agents won't be content to simply take your word for it."

Perlman threw a quick glance around and lowered his voice. "Someone's been watching me."

"Really?"

Perlman nodded solemnly. "I've seen them once or twice. But usually it's just a feeling I get. It's unpleasant. Not to mention . . . unsettling."

"Have you told the authorities?"

"So they can laugh at me? Hardly." Perlman licked his lips. "Listen; I'll tell you what I know. But if you try repeating anything I say in a court of law, I'll deny it to your face."

"Go on."

"You're right; Uncle was selling the diamond for Hope. He even showed it to me several days before he was killed."

"Why?"

"What do you mean, *why*?"

"I was under the impression your uncle didn't like you much. So why did he show it to you?"

"You didn't know my uncle, did you?"

"Fortunately, no."

"He was obsessed with beauty and inordinately proud of the items that came into his possession—even if they belonged to someone else. He liked to show them off."

"So where is the diamond now?"

"I don't know. He had it in a red Moroccan leather presentation case when he showed it to me. I found the empty case on the floor of the parlor the morning after the murder. Presumably, Yates took it when he killed my uncle."

"Except that Yates didn't kill Eisler."

A condescending smirk spread across the other man's face. "The authorities seem to disagree with you."

Sebastian ignored the jibe. "Have you searched the house for it?"

"Of course I've searched for the damned thing! You think I want to pay what Hope is demanding for it?"

"Did you ever find your uncle's account books?"

"No, I haven't found those either." A tart edge had crept into Perlman's voice.

"Did it ever occur to you that both the diamond and your uncle's books could very well be hidden in the same place?"

"Yes, it has occurred to me. Do you take me for a fool? I tell you, I've looked everywhere. I've even started sorting through stuff that obviously hasn't been shifted in decades."

"Do you mind if I have a look around the house my-self?"

Perlman laughed. "You can't be serious."

"Why not?"

The other man stared thoughtfully into the distance for a moment, then shrugged. "Have a go at it, if you like. I'll send a message to Campbell, telling him to expect you. But don't say I didn't warn you."

"Warn me about what?"

"Uncle had some peculiar interests."

"What kind of interests?"

But Perlman simply shook his head and said, "You'll see."

❧

"I don't get why this nephew fellow 'as suddenly up and decided to be all cooperative like," said Tom as Sebastian turned his horses toward Holburn.

"Perhaps because he's afraid that whoever killed his uncle might try to kill him too." Sebastian guided his horses around a brewer's wagon drawn up before the pub at the corner. "Or it could be because he killed his uncle himself, and now he's afraid he's got Napoléon's agents after him. Fear can be a powerful motivator."

Tom opened his eyes wide. "Ye reckon 'e might be next?"

"It's certainly possible. We seem to be dealing with some decidedly lethal-minded people."

Tom lapsed into a thoughtful silence but broke it only a few minutes later, saying, "What ye expectin' to find in that old house? Ye already been there twice."

"True. But my previous ventures were both interrupted."

"What ye think ye mighta missed?"

"At this point? Far too much."

❧

Sebastian was raising his hand to rap Eisler's tarnished knocker when the door was jerked open and held wide by a beaming Campbell.

"I've just received Mr. Perlman's message," said the aged retainer with one of his trembling bows. "And may I say, my lord, how thrilled I am to be allowed to assist you with one of your investigations? Positively *thrilled*."

"Ah ... excellent," said Sebastian, stepping inside. He was beginning to realize that an overly enthusiastic witness could in its own way be as much of a problem as a stubbornly taciturn one.

Campbell beamed. "Where shall we start? The attics? The basement? The parlor?"

"How about back here?" said Sebastian, crossing the jumbled old hall to the low archway beside the stairs. Reaching out, he turned the handle of the first door on his left. It was still locked.

"Do you have the key to this room?"

"Unfortunately, no, my lord. Mr. Eisler always kept the key to this particular room. Neither Mrs. Campbell nor myself was ever allowed inside it."

"When Mr. Perlman searched the house, did he have a key?"

"He did, my lord. I believe he discovered one in Mr. Eisler's office safe. But I'm afraid he carried it away with him."

"I see." Sebastian took off his driving gloves and thrust them into a pocket. "Very well. Thank you. I'll ring if I need you."

Campbell's face fell with disappointment. But he bowed with a sigh of resignation and tottered away.

Sebastian waited until the old man had shuffled out of sight. Then he removed from his pocket a set of metal shafts on a ring. It was called a picklock, a device with which Sebastian had become adept during his time as an exploring officer. It required only a keen sense of hearing and a deft touch, both of which Sebastian possessed. Easing the appropriate bent tip into the lock, he carefully slid aside the lock's gates.

The door popped open.

The room beyond lay in near total darkness. Closing

the door behind him, Sebastian crossed to the window to jerk open the thick curtains, then turned.

The chamber was empty except for a trunk and a long table upon which a small number of objects were neatly arranged. Unlike the rest of the house, this room was scrupulously clean, the walls freshly painted, the worn flagstone-paved floor well scrubbed. There was no rug. Instead, a design had been traced onto the floor with what looked like chalk.

His muscles oddly tense, Sebastian walked slowly toward it.

He was standing on the edge of an enormous circle superimposed on a square, with three smaller circles inside it. Four even smaller circles occupied what he suspected were the compass points, each containing a strange geometric symbol within it. More symbols were strategically placed between the second and third inner circles, along with what looked like a verse written in a strange script. At the very center of the figure stood an earthenware vessel filled with burnt charcoal; the scent of frankincense and aloe, vervain and musk hung heavy in the air.

Sebastian felt a faint, inexplicable chill run up his spine.

Turning, he let his gaze rove over the objects laid out on the long, narrow table. Two knives, one with a white hilt, the other with a black hilt, lay beside a short lance. The tips of all three were stained dark with what looked like blood. Beside the blades rested a trumpet flanked by two white candles.

Frowning, Sebastian went to throw open the lid of the trunk and found himself staring at a white linen robe with a series of curious geometric symbols embroidered on the breast in red silk thread. Beneath the robe lay a pair of white leather slippers covered with more strange designs also in red, and a square package wrapped in black silk.

Opening it gingerly, he exposed a pile of snowy white,

newly made vellum sheets. Each sheet contained a single figure composed of circles, symbols, and geometric forms similar to that on the floor, but differing in subtle ways. Some were drawn in brilliant blues and reds, others in gold and green or black and silver. He flipped through them, pausing at one in particular that seemed to both repel and attract him at the same time.

At its center lay what looked like a spinning disk within a triangle. Around the triangle were drawn two circles, one within the other, between which was written what looked like a verse. He hesitated a moment, then rolled the parchment like a scroll and thrust it inside his coat. Replacing the remainder of the vellums and the white garments, he lowered the lid of the chest and went to close the curtains.

He found himself wondering what Samuel Perlman must have thought when he first unlocked the door to this room. Or had Perlman already known of his uncle's peculiar interests before he began searching the house on Fountain Lane?

Sebastian shut the door behind him, then went in search of the aged butler.

With a deliriously excited Campbell once more at his side, he examined the rest of the house, from the attics and dusty, crowded bedrooms down to the kitchen basement. But his search was perfunctory, for he had no real expectation of finding anything.

Men like Daniel Eisler did not give up their secrets easily.

Chapter 36

The little girl looked to be eight or nine years old, although she told Hero she would be twelve the week before Christmas. Hero was beginning to realize that she was hopeless when it came to estimating children's ages.

A plain child named Elsie, she had small, unremarkable features and a habit of frowning thoughtfully before she answered each of Hero's questions. Her nondescript hair was braided inexpertly into two plats that stuck out at odd angles from her head, while her faded navy frock was hopelessly tattered, with large, triangular rents that someone had tried to repair with big, crooked stitches. But her face was surprisingly clean, and she wore a cotton bonnet tied around her neck with ribbons. She'd pushed the bonnet off her head, so that it bounced about her shoulders every time she dropped a curtsy—which was often.

"I been sweepin' nine months now, m'lady," she told Hero with one of her bobbing curtsies. "Me mother died last year, you see. She used to bring in money making lace, and now she's gone, me da can't make enough to keep us." She nodded to the two small children, a boy of about three and a girl of perhaps five, who sat on the steps behind her playing with a pile of oyster shells. "I gots t' bring the little ones with me when I sweeps, which scares me, 'cause I'm always afraid they're gonna run out in front of a carriage when me back is turned."

Hero watched a stylish barouche drawn by a team of high-stepping bays dash up the street and knew an echo of the little girl's fear. Children were always being run over and killed in the streets of London. She cleared her throat. "What does your father do?"

Elsie dropped another of her little curtsies. "He's a cutler, m'lady. But the work's been slow lately. Real slow."

"And was it his idea that you take up sweeping?"

"Oh, no, m'lady. I got the idea all by meself. At first I tried singing songs. I could get four or five pence a day for singing—even more on Saturday nights at the market."

"So why did you give that up?"

"I only knows a few songs, and I guess people got tired of hearing 'em, because after a while, I wasn't makin' much at all. If I could read, I could buy some new ballads and sing 'em, but I ain't never been able t' go t' school on account of having to watch the children."

"Would you like to go to school?"

A wistful look came over the child's small, plain features. "Oh, yes, m'lady. Ever so much."

Hero blinked and looked down at her notebook. "And how much do you make sweeping at your crossing?"

"Usually I takes in between six and eight pence. But I can't come in really wet weather, on account o' the little ones." Another carriage was rumbling down the street toward them, and Elsie cast a quick, anxious glance at her siblings.

"How long do you find your broom lasts?"

"A week, usually. I don't sweep in dry weather. The take is always bad on those days, you know. So when it's dry, I go back to singing."

"That's very clever of you," said Hero, impressed. All the boys to whom she'd spoken had also complained about the poor "take" in dry weather. But Elsie was the first crossing sweep she'd found who thought to do something else on those days. "What time do you usually come to work?"

"Well, I try to get here before eight in the morning, so's I can sweep the crossing before the carriages and carts get thick. They scares me. I always try to stand back when I see one coming."

"And how late do you stay?"

Elsie frowned thoughtfully. "This time o' year, usually till four or five. Me da wants me home before it starts gettin' real dark. So I can't stay out late like the boys."

"Who gives you more money? The ladies or the gentlemen?"

"Oh, the gentlemen almost always gives me more than the ladies. But there's an old woman what keeps a beer shop, just over there." She nodded across the narrow street. "She gives me a hunk o' bread and cheese every day for tea, and I shares it with the children."

Hero checked her list of possible questions. "What do you see yourself doing in ten years' time? Do you think you'll always be a crossing sweeper?"

"I hope not." Elsie glanced back at the two children now following the progress of a bug along the steps. "Once Mick and Jessup gets big enough to look after themselves, maybe I could get a situation as a servant in a house. I'd work hard—truly, I would. Only, you can't get a situation without proper clothes, so I don't know how that'll ever come to pass." She smoothed one anxious hand down over her tattered skirt.

Hero smiled. "Did you mend your dress yourself?"

"No, m'lady. Me da did that. He braids me hair every morning too, b'fore he goes out lookin' for work."

Simple words, thought Hero. But they transformed the unknown father from some unfeeling monster who sent his little girl out to sweep the streets into an impoverished man doing the best he could to care for his young children without a wife. She pressed a guinea into the girl's small hand. "Here. Get yourself and the children something to eat, then go home for the day."

The little girl's nearly lashless eyes grew round with wonder, and she dropped another of her bobbing little curtsies. "Oh, thank you, m'lady."

Hero was watching the children run off, hand in hand, when a frisson of awareness passed over her.

She turned her head to find Devlin walking toward her, the fitful afternoon sun warm on his lean, handsome face, his movements languid and graceful and sensuously beautiful. And it struck her that there was something so deliciously wicked about a woman enjoying the mere sight of her husband in broad daylight that the Society for the Suppression of Vice would probably outlaw it, if they could.

"You can't save them all, you know," he said, coming to stand beside her, his gaze on the running children. "There's too many of them."

"How did you know what I was thinking?"

"I was watching you. It's written all over your face."

"Ah. I'm beginning to wonder if it's the baby that's turning me into such a maudlin sentimentalist. Whatever you do, don't tell Jarvis. He'd be scandalized."

Devlin laughed out loud. "Your secret is safe with me."

They turned to walk toward her waiting carriage. "Were you looking for me for some reason in particular?"

"I was. I've something I'd like to show your Miss Abigail McBean. Care to introduce me to her?"

"Of course. What is it? Another manuscript?"

He shook his head. "Something that I suspect is far more sinister."

⁂

"It's called a magic circle," said Abigail McBean, holding the unrolled vellum with hands that were not quite steady. Sebastian and Hero were seated in Abigail's crowded little morning room, with its towering shelves overflowing with manuscripts and learned texts on magic, alchemy, and witchcraft. "Where did you get this?"

Devlin said, "I found it along with a number of others in a chest in Daniel Eisler's house."

She looked up at him. "You say there were many?"

"Yes."

"So what made you choose this particular one to bring to me?"

Hero watched in bemusement as a faint hint of color touched her husband's high cheekbones. "That I'm afraid I can't fully explain. At the risk of sounding fanciful, this one seemed more powerful . . . almost menacing."

"That's because it is. In fact, I'd describe it as downright nasty." Rising to her feet, she went to select a volume from her shelves and brought it back to lay it open on the table before them. On the page was an almost identical figure. "This circle is known as the fourth pentacle of Saturn."

Devlin looked up at her and shook his head. "What does that mean?"

"In magic, there are seven heavenly bodies, each of which rules its own day and certain designated hours within the day. Operations—which is what 'magic spells' are called by those who practice them—are thought best performed on the hour and day ruled by their relevant planet. The sun is considered the realm of temporal wealth and the favor of princes; Venus governs friendship and love, while Mercury is devoted to eloquence and intelligence. The moon is the planet of voyages and messages. The hours and days of Jupiter are best for obtaining riches and all you can desire, while Mars is for ruin, slaughter, and death."

"And Saturn?"

She met his gaze squarely. "The hours and days of Saturn are for summoning souls and demons from hell."

"Nice," said Devlin.

Abigail pointed at the Hebrew words printed around the sides of the triangle. "This is from Deuteronomy, chapter six, fourth verse, and reads, 'Hear, oh Israel; the Lord our God is one Lord.'"

"The Bible?" said Hero in surprise. "Are you telling me this nasty old man was performing magic spells while quoting the Bible?"

Abigail nodded. "Most of the grimoires contain biblical verses. The Bible has long been considered a source of powerful magic." She traced the strange writing around the circle. "See this? It's from the Psalms. It reads, 'As he clothed himself with cursing like with a garment, so let it come into his bowels like water, like oil into his bones.'"

Devlin frowned. "What alphabet is that?"

"It's an alphabet of twenty-two letters called the *transitus fluvii*. It's found in Heinrich Cornelius Agrippa's sixteenth-century grimoire, *Third Book of Occult Philosophy*, although I don't know if it originated with him. Basically I guess you could call it an occult alphabet." She sank back into her chair. "The items on the table you described would be used for various magic rituals or operations. The short lance is supposed to be dipped in the blood of a magpie, while the knife with the white hilt is dipped in the blood of a gosling and the juice of the pimpernel."

"And the knife with the black hilt?" asked Hero.

Abigail glanced over at her. "A knife with a black hilt is only used to summon evil spirits. It's dipped in the juice of hemlock and the blood of a black cat."

"Oh, God," whispered Hero. "That's what the cat was for."

"And it explains why Eisler kept all those birds," said Devlin, picking up the vellum to study it again.

Abigail nodded. "They would also have been used for sacrifices. White animals and birds are typically sacrificed to good spirits, and black to evil spirits."

"He did seem to favor the black," said Devlin.

Abigail laced her hands together in her lap so tightly the knuckles showed white. She looked like a simple, red-haired spinster, prim and plain—until one remembered she was surrounded by texts on magic and the darkest secrets of the occult. "He was not a nice man," she said, her voice oddly strained, tight. "I'm glad he's dead."

"You sound like Hero," said Devlin, looking up.

"He caused great harm and unhappiness to many. True justice is rare in this world, but this time, at least, I think we have seen it in action."

"Unless an innocent man hangs for his murder."

Abigail's anger seemed to drain away, leaving her looking troubled. "You will be able to prove that this man Yates is innocent, won't you?"

"I don't know." Devlin carefully rolled the white sheet of vellum. "You said this is called the fourth pentacle of Saturn. What is it used for?"

"Operations of ruin, destruction, and death."

"I wonder whose death he was trying to cause," said Hero.

Devlin's gaze met hers. "If we knew that, we might know who killed him."

Chapter 37

"Ah, Lord Devlin," said Sir Henry Lovejoy when Sebastian stopped by Bow Street to see him later that afternoon. "I was just about to send a message round to Brook Street. I've discovered some interesting information about that fellow you asked me to look into."

"You mean Jud Foy?"

"That's the one, yes."

"You've found him?"

"Not yet, no. But I thought you might like to know that it seems he was once a rifleman."

"With what regiment?"

"The 114th Foot. He was invalided out in 1809."

"Good God, is he Sergeant Judah Foy?"

"He is, yes." Something of Sebastian's reaction must have shown on his face, because Lovejoy's eyes narrowed. "You know him?"

"You could say that."

※

Tyson was cupping wafers at Menton's Shooting Gallery when Sebastian came to stand off to one side and quietly watch. The man's movements were smooth and assured, his aim as flawless as one might expect of someone who'd purchased his first pair of colors at the age of sixteen.

He shot three more times before looking over at Sebastian and saying, "I take it you're not here for the entertainment value?"

Sebastian crossed his arms at his chest and smiled. "Don't mind me."

Tyson's handsome features remained impassive. But Sebastian saw his eyes darken. He handed his flintlock to the attendant and stripped off the leather guards he wore to protect his cuffs from the powder. "I've finished."

Sebastian watched him walk over to pour water into a basin and wash his hands. "Tell me about Jud Foy."

Tyson paused for a moment, then went back to soaping his hands. "Who?"

"You do remember Sergeant Judah Foy, don't you? He was a rifleman with your regiment. Not only that, but he's the sergeant who testified in your defense at your court-martial. If it hadn't been for him, you'd have hanged."

"I remember him."

"I must admit," said Sebastian, "his appearance has changed so radically that I didn't recognize him."

Tyson shook the water from his hands and reached for the towel offered by an attendant. "I'm not surprised. He got kicked in the head by one of the supply wagon's mules. He's never been right since then, which is a polite way of saying the man belongs in a madhouse."

"You wouldn't happen to know where I might find him?"

"Did you try Bedlam?"

Sebastian shook his head. "He's very much a free man. And he seems to be laboring under the opinion that he's suffered some sort of injustice. Do you know anything about that?"

Tyson tossed the towel aside. "As I recall, after the accident he had difficulty distinguishing between his own property and that of others. Why? What does any of this have to do with me?"

"I don't know that it does."

Tyson reached for his coat and shrugged into it. "I told you, the man is mad."

"Is he dangerous?"

"He may well be." Tyson adjusted his cuffs. "Do you think him involved in Eisler's murder in some way?"

"Was Foy acquainted with Eisler?"

"Now, how would I know? The man was a sergeant — not exactly one of my intimates."

"Unlike Beresford?"

Tyson looked over at him. "What's that supposed to mean?"

"Did you know Eisler was in the habit of acquiring information about people and then using it against them?"

Tyson turned to walk toward the entrance. "I can't say I'm surprised. Are you?"

Sebastian fell into step beside him. "It occurs to me that Eisler could have been playing his tricks on Blair Beresford — threatening to tell Hope about his gambling losses."

Tyson looked over at him. "What makes you think Beresford has gambling debts?"

"He told me himself."

"Beresford isn't exactly what you'd consider a ripe target for blackmail. He has no money — as Eisler himself obviously knew all too well."

"To my knowledge, Eisler's form of blackmail was more subtle than your normal variety of extortion."

Something flickered across Tyson's face, then was gone. "Perhaps. But I can't imagine what Beresford has that might have interested Eisler. He's the younger son of a small Irish landowner, in London for a few months."

"Seems an unusual friend for someone who spent ten years fighting from India to Spain."

Tyson drew up on the flagway before the shooting gallery. The golden September sunlight fell hard across his face, accentuating the harsh lines and deep grooves dug there by a decade of forced marches and indifferent rations and overexposure to a fierce tropical sun. "What are you suggesting? That I ought to be spending my days at the Fox and Hound, knocking back tankards of stout and reminiscing with my fellow officers about the good old days? I'm twenty-six, not seventy-six. Blair Beresford is quick-witted and endlessly amusing. He's also a brilliant poet. He took the Newdigate Prize at Oxford for one of his poems. Did you know?"

"No."

"There is much that you do not know." Tyson squinted up at the sun. "And now you really must excuse me. I've an appointment with my tailor."

Sebastian watched the lieutenant turn to saunter toward Bond Street, but stopped him by saying, "How did you happen to meet Beresford, anyway?"

Tyson pivoted slowly to face him again, his dark eyes narrowing with a tight smile that could have meant anything. "We met through Yates."

Then he touched his hand to his hat and walked on.

※

Since her marriage to Russell Yates, Kat Boleyn had lived in a sprawling town house on Cavendish Square. It was a fashionable address favored by the nobility and wealthy merchants and bankers, all of whom no doubt looked upon their notorious new neighbors with scandalized horror. Kat might have been the most acclaimed actress on the London stage, but she was still an actress. And although it was not well-known, she'd once survived as a homeless, abused child on the streets of London by selling the only thing of value she possessed: herself.

It was a time she rarely spoke of. But Sebastian had seen the way she looked at the young, ragged girls who haunted the back alleys of Covent Garden. He knew only too well the mark those days had left upon her. He'd tried to ease the damage done to her by that desperate time, by the English soldiers who'd raped and killed her mother, by her aunt's lecherous husband. But he knew he'd never really succeeded. And he found himself pondering why he was remembering these things now, as he mounted the steps to her front door. For Kat was a woman who asked for neither pity nor solace, but who forged her own victories. . . .

And her own revenge.

She was crossing the vast marbled entry hall when her staid butler opened the door to Sebastian. He saw the breath of surprise that shadowed her face at the sight of him, for she had been married a year and yet this was the first time he had ever come here, to the house she shared with Yates.

"Devlin," she said, taking both his hands to draw him into a nearby salon. "What is it? Have you discovered something?"

She wore a simple gown of white figured muslin sashed in primrose, with a delicate strand of pearls threaded through the dark, auburn-shot fall of her curls, and he held her fingers just a shade too long before squeezing them and letting her go. "Nothing that makes any sense yet. But I don't like the way Yates's name keeps coming up the more I look into things."

She held his gaze squarely, her eyes deep and vividly blue and so much like those of the man who was her father and not his that it still hurt, just to look at her.

She said, "He didn't do it, Sebastian."

"Maybe he didn't. But I'm beginning to suspect he knows far more about what is going on than he would have me believe." He drew her over to sit beside him on a sofa near the window. "Are you familiar with a man named Blair Beresford?"

Kat Boleyn might never receive invitations to London's most exclusive balls and parties, but she still socialized with Yates's easygoing male friends and acted as hostess at his dinners. She thought about it a moment, then shook her head. "I don't believe so. Why? Who is he?"

"A beautiful, curly-headed, blue-eyed Irish poet only lately down from Oxford."

She gave a soft laugh. "In general, Yates has very little patience with poets—especially those just down from Oxford."

"What about an army lieutenant named Matt Tyson? Mid-twenties. Dark. Also good-looking, although not in Beresford's boyish way. Has a rather rakish scar on his chin."

"Him I do know. Yates finds him amusing."

Amusing. It was the same word Tyson had used to describe Beresford. "But you don't like him?" said Sebastian.

Her smile faded. "He's never been anything except charming and gracious to me. But . . ."

"But?"

"Let's just say I wouldn't ever want to turn my back on him—metaphorically speaking, of course."

"Do you know if he"—Sebastian hesitated, struggling for a way to put his question into words—"has the same inclinations as Yates?"

She understood what he meant. "I don't know. But I can ask." She tipped her head to one side, her gaze on his face, and he wondered what she saw there. She was always far too good at knowing what he was thinking. "Why did you come here to me, Devlin? Why not ask Yates directly?"

"Because I'm not convinced he is being as honest with me as he could be."

She pushed up from the sofa and went to fiddle with the heavy satin drapes at the window overlooking the square.

"What?" he asked, watching her.

She exhaled a long breath. "To be frank, I'm not certain he's being exactly honest with me either."

"Why? Why would he lie?"

She shook her head. "I don't know." But her gaze slid from his in a way he did not like.

He said, "Do you know anything about a large blue diamond whose sale Eisler was handling? A diamond that may once have formed part of the French Crown Jewels?"

He watched her carefully and saw no trace of anything in her face other than puzzlement and surprise, followed swiftly by what looked very much like fear.

But then, he reminded himself, it would never do to forget that Kat was an actress. A very good one. And it struck him as ironic and troubling that he found himself doubting both of the women in his life—although for vastly different reasons.

She said, "What are you suggesting? That the French are somehow involved in Eisler's murder?"

"You know about Napoléon's quest to recover the French Crown Jewels?"

"Yes."

A simple answer that told him she probably knew more than he did. Once, she had worked for the French, passing secrets to Napoléon's agents in an effort to weaken England and free Ireland. She claimed she'd severed that relationship long ago. But Sebastian suspected she still had contacts with her old confederates—as did Yates.

He said, "Who would Napoléon task to secure the diamond? Would he send in someone new? Or would he use a contact already in place?"

"It's difficult to say. He's taken both approaches in the past."

"Would it be possible to find out?"

He half expected her to tell him no. Instead, she twitched the heavy drape in place and smoothed it down, although it already hung straight. "I can try."

He let his gaze drift over the familiar planes of her face: the thickly lashed, slightly tilted eyes; the small, childlike nose; the wide, sensual mouth. His love for her still coursed deep and strong, as he knew it always would. He had loved her since he was so very young, untested by battle and as yet untouched by the bitterest of disillusionments. Even when he'd believed she'd betrayed him—even when he had tried to forget her—he had loved her still. Their souls had touched in a way granted to few, and he knew that even if he never saw her again, his life would forever be entwined with hers.

But he also knew that with every passing day, the distance between them yawned subtly deeper and wider.

And it disturbed him to realize the extent to which he neither trusted nor believed her.

Chapter 38

After Devlin left, Kat sat down and composed a carefully worded note she dispatched to a certain Irish gentleman of her acquaintance. Then she ordered her carriage and set off for Newgate Prison.

She found Yates standing beside his cell's small, barred window overlooking the Press Yard. There was an uncharacteristic tension in the way he held himself, and she went to slide her arms around his waist and press her cheek against his taut back in a quiet gesture of friendship and comfort. They were two outcasts who'd made common cause together against both their enemies and the disapproving world. In many ways, he was like the brother she had never had. And she found she had to squeeze her eyes shut against a sudden upsurge of unexpected emotion at the thought of losing him.

"This is a pleasant surprise," he said, closing his hands over hers and tilting back his head until it rested against hers. "I didn't expect to see you again today. Shouldn't you be getting ready for the theater?"

"I've time yet."

Beneath her encircling arms, she felt his torso expand with his breath. He said, "Your dashing viscount came to see me this morning."

"Devlin isn't my viscount anymore."

"True. But then, he's not exactly your brother either,

is he?" When she remained silent, he said, "I'm sorry. That was totally uncalled for."

"It's all right," she said softly.

He nodded toward the window, where the ancient masonry that formed the prison's gatehouse was just visible. "Do you know what that chamber is over there, right above the entrance gate? They call it 'Jack Ketch's kitchen.' I'm told that's where they used to preserve the quartered bodies of those executed for treason, before putting them on display around the metropolis. They'd boil them in vast cauldrons full of pitch, tar, and oil. Must have smelled . . . ghastly. The heads were treated to a different process, of course; those were parboiled with bay, salt, and cumin. I suppose I should be thankful that in our own more enlightened era, I can look forward to merely dancing the hempen jig for the amusement of the populace, before being given over to the surgeons for the edification of their students."

"You're not going to hang."

A faint smile touched his lips. "The verdict of the coroner's inquest is in. My trial has been scheduled for Saturday; did you know?"

"Oh, God. So soon?" She was aware of a pressing sense of urgency that came close to panic. And she understood, then, why he had been standing here watching the last of the light fade from his prison's walls.

She said, "Is there anything you know about Eisler that you haven't told Devlin?"

"I don't think so." He turned to face her. "Do you think I *want* to hang?"

She studied his dark, handsome face, the gold pirate's hoop in his ear winking in the fading light. She said, "To be honest, I don't understand why you're still in prison. Jarvis could have had all charges against you dropped days ago, only he hasn't done it. He knows you have the power to destroy him; all you need do is release the evidence you have against him. Yet he's not afraid. Why not?"

He remained silent. But she read the answer in his face.

"It's because of me, isn't it?" she whispered. "That's what he told you when he came to see you the night of your arrest. He warned you that the documents you hold can protect you, or they can protect me, but they can't protect us both."

Yates held himself very still.

She said, "I'm right, aren't I? He told you that if you made any move against him, he'd have me killed."

Yates turned to where a bottle of his best brandy stood beside a glass. "Unfortunately, I've only the one glass. May I offer you something to drink?"

She shook her head.

"You don't mind if I do?" He poured himself a large measure. "So you see," he said, setting the bottle aside, "I have even more incentive to cooperate with your viscount than you previously thought."

He took a long, slow swallow of his brandy and looked over at her. "You came for a reason; what was it?"

"Devlin wanted me to ask you about Matt Tyson."

Yates frowned. "I already told him I know the man only slightly. What more is there?"

"Where did you meet him?"

"In a molly house on Pall Mall. Why?"

Kat sucked in a quick breath. "So he's a molly?"

"Of course he is. So is Beresford."

⁕

The last of the light was leaching rapidly from the sky.

Kat knew she should be at the theater, preparing for that evening's performance. Instead, she went for a stroll through the flower stalls of Covent Garden Market.

Already, the square lay in deep shadow, the few remaining vegetable and fruit sellers scrambling to hawk their fading produce, cheap, before closing for the night. Only the florists, nurserymen, and bouquet girls were still doing a brisk trade, selling flowers to the theater, music hall, and restaurant managers and to earnest beaux looking for posies to present to their lovers. The air was full of laughter and shouting and a sweet, familiar medley of floral scents that always took her back to another time, another place.

When she was a little girl growing up in a small white house overlooking the misty emerald swath of a Dublin green, Kat's mother and stepfather used to take her to the market that set up every Wednesday afternoon in the cobbled medieval square of their parish church. She could remember running excitedly from one stall to the next, exclaiming over the displays of satin hair ribbons and lace collars and carved wooden tops. But her mother's favorite stalls were always those selling bunches of yellow daffodils and rainbow-hued tulips, or pots of rue and pennyroyal, hollyhock seedlings and briar rose cuttings. She'd take them home and plant them in the narrow strip of garden beside their cottage's front stoop. Even now, all these years later, if Kat closed her eyes and breathed deeply, she could still see her mother's strong hands sinking into the rich dark earth, a faint faraway smile on her lips that told of a deep and rare contentment.

In some indefinable way, Kat knew that the child she'd once been had resented the joy and peace her mother found in her garden. But she'd never been able to decide if her selfishness came from the wish that her mother would find that deep, unalloyed joy in her daughter alone, or if she'd simply envied the tranquility she glimpsed in her mother's face. And it shamed Kat now to remember that she had begrudged her mother those brief interludes of peace and happiness.

There had been so little of either in Arabella Noland's short life.

Now, as she breathed in the heady scents from the banks of Michaelmas daisies, ferns, and chrysanthemums, Kat found herself wondering if it was her mother's spirit that had guided her here, to the peace of this place. Or was this love of growing things a trait passed down from mother to daughter, like dark hair and a talent for acting? A tendency that had always been there, nestled hidden within her, only waiting to be discovered.

She smiled at the thought. Then the smile faded as she became aware of a sudden charge of tension in the atmosphere, the rush of heavy feet. A trader's high-pitched voice whined, "'Ey! Wot the 'ell ye doin'?"

Kat's eyes flew open.

Rough hands seized her from behind. She lunged against the unseen man's fierce grip, tried to scream. A calloused palm slapped down across her mouth, grinding her lips against her teeth and flattening her nose so that she had to fight to draw air. She smelled dirt and onions and fetid breath as he pressed his beard-roughened cheek against hers and whispered, "Come wit' me quiet-like, an' I'll see ye don't get hurt."

Chapter 39

Kat heaved against the man's hold and felt his arms tighten around her in a fierce hug. He dragged her backward, toward the shadowy, narrow lane that ran along the old, soot-stained nave of the church. She tried to bite the thick, dirty fingers smothering her, but the pressure was so brutal she could get no purchase.

"I say, there," bleated one of the florists, stepping from behind his stall. "You can't do that!"

A second man—a wiry, black-haired brute with a pock-scarred face and small, sharp nose—turned to thrust a blunderbuss pistol into the trader's face. "Mind your own business or lose your head." His English diction was careful and precise, but Kat caught the faint, unmistakable traces of French inflection and knew a new leap of terror.

The florist backed off, hands splayed out at his sides, face slack.

Her heart was pounding, her mouth achingly dry, the shouts of the scattered costermongers and stall keepers echoing oddly in her head, as if she were at the base of a well. The market square spun around her in a blur of startled, frightened faces, wet paving, spilled chrysanthemums. A flock of pigeons whirled up from the church portico, pale outstretched wings beating the cool damp air. She tried to twist her body sideways, but her captor's fingers dug into her cruelly, his breath hot against her ear. "Ye want to live, don't give me trouble. Ye hear, girl? Because wot I do wit' ye afterward is up t' me. Ye got that?"

She made herself go utterly limp, as if fainting from fear, her hands dangling slack at her sides. She heard him give a grunt of satisfaction. "Have yer friend bring the bloody cart up, quick," he told his pockmarked companion. "Let's get out o' 'ere."

They were passing the last stall in the row, a rough shed given over to the sale of earthen crockery, the stall's seller cowering wide-eyed against the rickety frame, as if he could somehow make himself disappear into the weathered post behind him. Kat's captor was half dragging, half carrying her now, a drooping deadweight that sagged in his arms, so that his effort was more focused on keeping her upright than on restraining her.

Flinging out one hand, she grasped the lip of a stout pitcher from the edge of the stall's counter and swung it up and back to smash it against the side of her captor's head. He let out a rumbling roar, his grip on her slackening with surprise and pain.

She twisted sideways, ignoring the wrenching pain that shot from her wrist as he tried, too late, to tighten his hold on her. "You bloody son of a bitch!" she screamed, grabbing a platter off the stall and breaking it against his face. "I ought to cut out your bloody liver and feed it to the crows!"

He howled, blood spurting from his cut face, his arms flinging up to protect his head as she snatched up a bowl and hurled it at him.

"Oy, wot ye doin' to me crockery?" bleated the stall owner.

"Your bloody crockery?" shouted Kat, whirling to heave a plate at him. "You worthless, stinking coward! You would have just stood there and watched him kill me!"

"You fool," screamed the pockmarked man to his companion as a shouting, angry crowd of stall keepers and costermongers, bouquet girls and nurserymen bore down on them. "Don't just stand there. Grab her!"

"'Tain't no way to treat a lady!" hollered a big, black-haired porter.

"You mind your own business," growled the pock-marked man, flourishing his pistol.

A rotten tomato flew through the air to break in a red splat against his face.

The air filled with the day's unsold produce, spoiling turnips and overripe melons, moldy pears and putrid apples. For one moment, the two men held their ground. Then the plucked, gutted carcass of a chicken whacked against the side of the bigger ruffian's head. He turned and ran, feet slipping and sliding on a sea of rotten vegetables, splattered fruit, and smashed crockery. His companion hesitated a moment, then followed, swerving around the church steps to duck down the side street.

"Lay a hand on me again, and I'll kill you! You hear?" yelled Kat, hurling a last earthenware bowl after them as they pelted down the lane to their waiting cart. She was no longer Kat Boleyn, the toast of London's stage; she was Kat Noland, the scrappy, angry young orphan who'd struggled to survive in the fetid back alleys of a vast, unfriendly city. "I'll cut off your pathetic yards and feed them to the stray dogs in Moorefield. I'll decorate London Bridge with your entrails. I'll—"

But the men were already piling into their waiting cart, its driver whipping up his horses into a mad gallop that took them careening around the corner and out of sight.

Kat let her hand fall back to her side, her fingers clenched tight around the lip of the rough mug she still held, her heart thundering in her chest.

✢

"Do you know the story of the mice and the cat?" asked Emma Wilkinson, looking up at Sebastian with her father's big gray eyes.

They were seated before the feeble fire in Annie Wilkinson's tiny Kensington parlor. He had come here, as promised, to tell Emma a story before she went to bed. He'd expected the experience to be awkward, for he was a man with little exposure to children. But as Emma settled more comfortably against him and he felt her baby-soft curls brush his chin, he was surprised to find his thoughts drifting to the child that would be born to Hero in just a few short months.

"It's my favorite," said Emma.

"I might not tell it exactly the same as your papa."

"That's all right," said Emma. "Papa always tells it a little differently each time."

Sebastian glanced over to where Annie sat darning a sheet by the fading light of the rainy day. And he knew by the quick rise and fall of her chest that the child's use of the present tense was not lost on her either.

"Very well," he said. "Once upon a time, a colony of mice lived a happy, peaceful existence within the walls of a small village shop. The mice were well fed and content. But the man who owned the shop wasn't happy with all those mice stealing his grain and nibbling on his cheese. So he bought himself a cat, who patrolled his shop and quickly terrorized the poor mice to the point they were too afraid even to come out of their little holes in the wainscoting and eat."

"What color was the cat?" Emma asked.

"A big black cat with a bushy tail."

"Papa always says, 'a tabby.'"

"Sorry."

Emma giggled.

"Anyway," said Sebastian, "the mice quickly realized that if they didn't do something about the cat, they would either starve to death or get eaten themselves. So they all got together to try to come up with a solution. There was much arguing and shouting, but no one could think of anything that would work. Finally, a clever young mouse stood up and said, 'The problem is that the cat is so quiet we can't hear him when he's sneaking up on us. All we need to do is tie a bell around his neck, and that way we'll always know when he's coming.'

"Now, all the other mice thought this was a splendid idea. Everyone was cheering and clapping the young mouse on the shoulder and telling him how very clever he was and calling him a hero. All except for one old mouse, so aged his hair had turned as white as the frost. He cleared his throat and stood up to say"—Sebastian dropped his voice into a gravelly Glaswegian rasp—"'I'll not be denying that tying a bell about the cat's neck would surely warn us of his approach. There's only one wee problem.' The old man paused to let his gaze drift around the assembly of anxious mice and said—"

"'*Who bells the cat?*'" shouted Emma, jumping up to clap her hands before collapsing against him again in a fit of giggles.

"You've heard this before," said Sebastian in mock solemnity.

"Only about a hundred times," said Annie, setting aside her darning to come take the child into her arms. Her gaze met his over the little girl's dark head. "Thank you."

"It was my pleasure. Truly."

A faint smile touched her lips. "You'll make a wonderful father."

Afterward, he wondered whether it had been an idle remark, or if something of his own thoughts and emotions had shown on his face.

✢

Later that evening, Sebastian was looking over a history of the French Revolution while Hero sat reading Abigail McBean's English translation of *The Key of Solomon*. The black cat lay curled up on the hearth beside them.

"Listen to this," she said, reading aloud. "'I conjure you Spyritts by all the patryarchs, prophets, Apostles, evangelists, martyrs, confessors, vyrgyns, and wyddowes, and by Jerusalem, the holy cytty of godd, and by heaven and earth and all that therein is, and by all other vyrtues, and by the Elements of the worlde, and by St. Peter, apostle of Rome, and by the croune of thorne that was worne on godd's head.'" She looked up. "I thought this was supposed to have been written by Solomon."

"Details, details," said Sebastian, looking up as a distant knock sounded at the front door.

"Expecting anyone?" asked Hero.

Sebastian shook his head.

A moment later, Morey appeared in the doorway. "The Earl of Hendon to see you, my lord."

Sebastian was aware of Hero's silent gaze upon him. In all the weeks of their marriage, Hendon had never yet paid a call on Brook Street, nor had Sebastian taken his bride to Hendon's sprawling pile in Grosvenor Square. Yet she had never asked him that most obvious question: *Why?*

Morey cleared his throat. "His lordship says it is a matter of the utmost importance. I've taken the liberty of showing him to the library."

Sebastian was aware of a deep sense of disquiet. After all that had been said between them, he could think of few developments that would motivate Hendon to come here.

None of them were good.

"Excuse me," he said to Hero, and left the room.

He found the Earl standing before the library's empty hearth, his hands clasped behind his back, his heavily jowled features sagged with worry.

"What is it?" asked Sebastian without preamble. "What has happened?"

"Kat was attacked this evening in Covent Garden Market."

"Is she all right?" It came out sharper than he'd intended.

Hendon nodded. "Yes. Fortunately, the costermongers and stall keepers rallied and helped her drive the assailants away. She suffered a slight injury to her arm, but that is all."

Wordlessly, Sebastian walked over to pour two brandies. He handed one to the Earl.

Hendon took it without hesitation. "She says she doesn't know who the men were or why they attacked her."

Sebastian took a long, slow swallow of his own brandy and felt it burn all the way down. "You don't believe her?"

"I don't know what to believe—although frankly I'm inclined to suspect it has something to do with this damned business about Yates."

"If so, why wouldn't she tell you?"

"I don't know. I was hoping perhaps you knew the answer to that."

Sebastian shook his head. "I'm afraid there's far too much going on here that I don't understand yet."

Hendon stared down at his brandy. "She tells me you have undertaken to prove Yates's innocence."

When Sebastian remained silent, Hendon cleared his throat and said gruffly, "Thank you."

"I'm not doing it for you."

There was a long, pained pause. Then Hendon said, "No. Of course not." He set aside the brandy untasted and reached for his hat. "Give my regards to your wife." Then he bowed and left.

Sebastian sent at once for his carriage to be brought around. He was waiting with one arm propped against the mantel, his gaze on the cold hearth before him, his thoughts far away, when he felt the black cat brush against his leg and looked up to find Hero watching him.

"I beg your pardon," he said, straightening. "I didn't hear you come in."

"That's a first." She bent to scoop up the purring cat into her arms. "Has something happened?"

"Kat Boleyn was attacked this evening in Covent Garden. She's unhurt, but it's ... worrisome."

A frown line appeared between Hero's eyes. "You think it's connected in some way to Eisler's murder?"

"Yes."

She said, "Why would Hendon bring you word of Kat Boleyn?"

His gaze met hers. And he found himself thinking, *When enemies become friends and then lovers, at what point do the last barriers drop? When are the final secrets revealed?* She had been his wife for six weeks; she shared his bed every night and was carrying his child. Yet there was so much they did not know about each other, so many things he'd never told her, so much of which they'd never spoken.

And neither had ever uttered those three simple but powerful words, *I love you.*

He said bluntly, "Kat is Hendon's natural daughter. None of us knew it until last autumn. To say the discovery was distressing would be one of the year's great understatements."

He saw the shock of comprehension in her eyes, along with something else he hadn't expected.

"Oh, God," she whispered. "Sebastian. I'm so sorry."

He drained his brandy and set the empty glass aside. "If you're imagining our quaint family circle as some grand tragedy, don't. In the end, that discovery—as sordid and shocking as it was—turned out to be only the first act in what has since come to resemble nothing so much as a tawdry farce."

"You don't look to me as if you're laughing."

"Yes, well . . ." He would have said more, for there was so much else he needed to tell her. Only, at that moment Morey appeared in the doorway to say, "Your carriage is ready, my lord."

He hesitated.

She reached out to touch his arm lightly. "Go on, Sebastian. I understand."

And so he left her there, the black cat held cradled in her arms like a child.

Chapter 40

*H*e found Kat curled up on the sofa before a fire in her drawing room, her left arm resting in a sling.

"Please don't get up," Sebastian said, as she struggled to do so.

She sat up anyway, her small stockinged feet peeking out from beneath the hem of her muslin gown. "I asked Hendon not to carry this tale to you. But he obviously didn't listen."

Sebastian came to rest his hands on her shoulders and stare down into her upturned face. "How are you? Truly."

"Gibson says it's nothing serious—a sprain only. One of the men grabbed hold of my arm and I must have twisted it in my attempt to get away."

"What the bloody hell happened? And why the devil did you go to Hendon rather than to me?"

"Stop glowering, Sebastian. I didn't go to Hendon. He stopped by this evening by chance to see how I was doing, and I made the mistake of giving him an honest answer when he asked how I came to injure myself."

"*Did* you give him an honest answer?"

She smiled. "For the most part. I have no idea who those two men were. But I don't think their intent was to kill me—at least, not right away. They were trying to drag me to a cart they had waiting nearby."

Sebastian walked away to stand at the window overlooking the darkened square below. "Did you act on the question I asked you this afternoon?"

"I did, yes. But I only sent a vague message to someone requesting a meeting. I didn't go into detail on why."

He glanced over at her. "They might know why."

She shook her head. "I don't believe this individual would harm me."

"So certain?"

She smoothed her free hand down over her lap and did not answer him.

He said, "I think Napoléon's men are still looking for that diamond. If they didn't kill Eisler but believe that Yates did, they might think he has it."

"So why snatch me?"

"To use as a bargaining chip, perhaps?"

"As in, 'You give us the diamond and we will give you your wife'?" She considered it a moment, then said, "I believe one of the men who tried to grab me may have been French."

Sebastian frowned. "Thin? With a pockmarked face?"

"Yes. How did you know?"

"I tangled with him in Seven Dials last night." He paused. "Did you have a chance to speak to Yates?"

She nodded. "You were right about Beresford and Tyson. They are mollies." She kept her gaze on his face. "That's significant; why?"

"Eisler liked to collect information on people."

"You mean for blackmail?"

"I don't think he extorted actual cash payments in return for his silence. He used what he knew to influence people, to force them to do what he wanted them to do."

"I'd call that blackmail."

"In a sense, I suppose it is."

She frowned thoughtfully. "According to Yates, Blair Beresford is the younger son of a small Irish landowner. What could he possibly have that Eisler either wanted or could use?"

"I wasn't thinking about Beresford."

"You mean Tyson?" She was silent for a moment, as if considering this. Then she said, "He's also a younger son."

"He is. But he had gems he was selling to Eisler. Eisler may have tried to use the information he had to drive a hard bargain."

"You're suggesting this gives Tyson a motive for murder?"

"I'd say it does, yes. Although if Eisler tried to use threats to pressure Matt Tyson, he was a fool. Tyson is the kind of man who would as soon slit your throat as look at you."

"Where does he say he was last Sunday evening?"

"Beresford claims they spent the evening in Tyson's rooms in St. James's Street."

She raked the curls off her forehead with a hand Sebastian noticed was not quite steady. "We're running out of time, Devlin. Yates's trial has been scheduled for Saturday."

He wanted to go to her, to take her in his arms and hold her in comfort. It occurred to him that if she were, in truth, his sister, then he could have done so and no one would have thought twice about it.

And that suddenly struck him as the cruelest irony of all.

He said, "The person you sent your message to—who was it?"

"You know I can't tell you that."

"Even to save your own life?"

But she only shook her head, a sad smile playing about her full, beautiful lips.

※

Leaving the house in Cavendish Square, Sebastian walked into a crisp night scented by a pungent mixture of coal smoke and damp stone and the hot oil from the street lamps that flickered faintly, as if stirred by an unseen hand. He started to leap up into his waiting carriage, then changed his mind and sent his coachman home.

Turning toward Regents Park, he walked down wide, paved streets lined with stately brick and stucco houses that stood where just twenty-five years before he and his brothers had run through meadows golden with ripening hay. In those days, there'd been a small pond shaded by chestnuts—just about there, he decided, where that livery stable now stood. He remembered one time when his brother Cecil had found an old Roman coin buried in the mud while they were collecting tadpoles, and Richard, the eldest and therefore their father's heir, had tried to claim it as his own in some twisted interpretation of the rules of primogeniture. Their mother had been there too, the sun warm on her fair hair, her voice gay with laughter as she separated the squabbling boys. And none of it—*none of it*—had really been as he'd thought it to be.

At what point? he thought again. *At what point do the last barriers drop? When are the final secrets revealed?*

But when he arrived back at Brook Street, it was to find Hero's bedroom in darkness. He stood for a moment in the doorway and watched the gentle rise and fall of her breathing. Then he turned away.

By the time he awoke the next morning, she had already left for more of her interviews.

❧

Thursday, 24 September

At precisely five minutes to eleven the next morning, Sebastian walked into the Lambeth Street Public Office to find Bertram Leigh-Jones bustling about with flapping robes, his wig askew as he sorted through a stack of files.

"We don't open until eleven," snapped the magistrate. "What do you want?"

"I'm wondering if you have a list of the people who owed Daniel Eisler money."

Leigh-Jones grunted, his attention all for his files. "Now, why would I want something like that?"

"From what I'm hearing, Eisler dabbled in everything from blackmail to magic to sexual exploitation. A man like that accumulates a lot of enemies."

The magistrate looked up. "Maybe. But that doesn't alter the fact that Russell Yates is the one who actually killed him. He'll be standing trial this Saturday."

"Rather hasty, don't you think?"

"As it happens, no, I don't. The man is clearly guilty. Why keep him locked up at His Majesty's expense when he could provide a spot of sport for the populace by dancing at the end of a rope?"

Sebastian studied the man's overfed, self-confident face. "I've heard it said that when King George was still in his right mind, it was his habit to personally examine the cases of each and every prisoner condemned to death in London. They say he could frequently be found weighing the evidence against them in the small hours of the night, and that he would closet himself with his chaplain to pray at the time of their deaths."

"Did he, now?" Leigh-Jones banged his files together and gathered them under one beefy arm. "Well, it's no wonder he went mad, then, now, isn't it? If you ask me, a morning spent watching a half dozen rascals hang is nearly as good a sport as a foxhunt." He gave Sebastian a broad wink. "You could join us afterward at the keeper's house for a breakfast of deviled kidneys. It's quite the tradition, you know. Now, you'll have to excuse me; I've a hearing to attend." He put up a hand to straighten his wig. "Good day to you, m'lord."

Chapter 41

Hero spent much of the morning in the shadow of Northumberland House, interviewing the gang of young sweepers who worked Charing Cross. An irregular open space at the end of the Strand where Whitechapel, Cockspur, and St. Martin's Lane all came together, the intersection was heavily traveled. All agreed it was a "capital spot" with lots of "gentlefolk" passing to and fro. The problem was, there were simply too many of the lads for any of them to do well.

She was talking to a tall, gangly redhead named Murphy when she became aware of the sensation of being watched. She glanced around, her gaze assessing the intersection's fenced-in bronze equestrian statue, the classical facade of the Royal Mews, the flock of ragged, barefoot boys clutching brooms. She had never considered herself a fanciful woman. But the unsettling conviction remained.

"It's that feller over there," said Murphy when she glanced around for the third or fourth time. "Be'ind the dustman's cart just outside the coaching 'otel there. 'E's been staring at ye fer a good long while."

The dustman's cart rolled forward, and she could see him now, an unkempt scarecrow of a man with sunken eyes and a scarred cheek and a madman's fatuous grin.

Hero thrust her notebook into her reticule and paid the boy generously for his time. "Thank you."

With one hand still in her reticule, she strode purpose-fully across the street toward Jud Foy. She half expected him to bolt. But he just stood there, grinning, while she walked up to him.

"Why are you watching me?" she demanded.

His mouth opened and his chest jerked as if he were laughing, only he made no sound. "Been watching you for days, I have. You only just now noticed it? Saw you talking t' the little girl in Holburn."

"Why?"

"Why?" he repeated, his eyes clouding as if the ques-tion confused him.

"Why are you watching me?"

"You can learn all kinds of int'resting things about a person by watching them."

"Follow me again," said Hero, "and I'll have you taken up by the constables."

He gave another of those strange, soundless laughs. "If you see me."

She started to turn away but stopped when he added, "I noticed you got yourself a cat. Black cats are unlucky, you know."

She pivoted slowly to face him again. "What is that supposed to mean?"

"Time was, people'd drown a black cat. Or maybe—"

She drew the brass-mounted muff pistol from her reticule and pointed it squarely between his eyes. "You'd best hope my cat is very long-lived, because if anything happens to him—*anything*—you're going to wish you died a hero's death on the battlefields of Europe. Do I make myself clear?"

She was dimly aware of a whiskered man in an old-fashioned frock coat who turned to stare at her open-mouthed; a dowager in a sedan chair let out a startled shriek. Foy held himself painfully still, his idiot's grin wiped from his vapid face.

"You'd shoot a man over a *cat*?"

"Without compunction."

"Mother of God. You're as mad as your husband."

She shook her head. "The difference between Devlin and me is that he probably wouldn't actually shoot you. I would." She pointed the pistol's nozzle toward the sky and took a step back. "Stay away from my cat."

❧

Sebastian arrived back at Brook Street to find Hero seated on the steps of the terrace overlooking the parterred garden. She still wore her dove gray carriage dress trimmed in the palest pink. But she'd taken off her plumed pink velvet hat and kid gloves and laid them with her reticule on the paving stones beside her. She held the black cat in her lap and was stroking him under the chin when Sebastian walked up to her.

"The Member of Parliament from South Whitecliff tells me that my wife shot three men at Charing Cross this morning. But the baker's boy swears it was only one."

She buried her face in the cat's soft black fur. "You should know better than to believe everything you hear. I found Jud Foy watching me again. He threatened the cat. I suggested that neither activity was a good idea. But with great restraint, I did not shoot him."

Sebastian moved her reticule so that he could sit beside her and heard the heavy *chink* of her flintlock. "Was he impressed with your sincerity?"

"I believe he was."

He reached out to caress her cheek with the backs of his fingers. "I'm sorry."

She raised her head and looked at him. "I may perhaps have overreacted."

"I don't think so."

She gave a soft chuckle. But her smile faded quickly. "I don't understand why he's doing this—what he wants."

"Matt Tyson says he was kicked in the head by a mule."

"Tyson? Tyson knows him?"

"Foy testified for the defense at Tyson's court-martial—
he was a sergeant with Tyson's regiment. A rifleman."

She flipped the cat onto his back so that she could rub
his belly. "Jamie Knox was a rifleman, wasn't he?"

"Different regiment."

She looked up then, her gaze meeting his. "You think
there are so many ex-riflemen in London that they don't
know each other?"

❧

Jamie Knox was seated at a rear table in an eating house
off Houndsditch when Sebastian drew out the chair opposite him and sat down.

"Please, do have a seat," said the tavern owner, cutting a slice of roast mutton.

"I'm looking for an ex-rifleman named Jud Foy."

Knox waved his fork in an expansive gesture that
took in the simple wainscoted room with its closely
crowded tables and chairs, its cheerfully glowing fire.
"Don't see him here, do you?"

"But you do know him."

"I know lots of people. It's one of the hazards of running a tavern."

Sebastian studied Knox's lean, high-boned face. The
likeness between Sebastian and this man was startling.
Both had the same deep-set golden eyes beneath straight
dark brows, and similarly molded lips. But it was the differences that intrigued Sebastian the most. In Knox's
case, the nose inclined more toward the aquiline, and
there was a faint cleft in his chin. Characteristics he inherited from his barmaid mother? Sebastian wondered.
Or from the unknown father both men probably shared?

"You still all fired up about Eisler?" asked Knox,
stabbing his fork into a potato.

"I'm still looking into his death, yes."

Knox chewed slowly, then swallowed. "What's it got
to do with Foy?"

"I don't know that it has anything to do with him. But the man has been menacing my wife."

A faint gleam of amusement deepened the gold in the other man's eyes. "I heard about this morning's incident at Charing Cross."

"Did you, now?"

Knox reached for his ale. "Foy's not right in his head."

"I heard he was kicked by a mule."

"That's the official story."

Sebastian laid his forearms on the tabletop and leaned into them. "Care to elaborate?"

Knox shrugged. "I heard he was found near the stables with his head bashed in. Could've been a mule. Could also have been a rifle butt."

"Why would someone want to cave the man's head in?"

"They say Foy had just testified at some officer's court-martial."

"This was after Talavera?"

Knox shrugged. "Could be. I've forgotten the details. The man isn't exactly one of my boon intimates. You did catch the part about him not being right in the head, didn't you?"

"Do you know where I could find him?"

Knox cut another slice of mutton, chewed, and swallowed.

Sebastian said, "You do know, don't you?"

"If I did, why would I tell you?"

"I think Foy might be in danger."

Knox huffed a soft laugh. "From Lord and Lady Devlin?"

"No. From the man—or men—who killed Daniel Eisler."

Knox pushed his plate away and reached for his ale. He wrapped both hands around the tankard, then simply sat silently staring at it.

Sebastian waited.

"I've heard he keeps a room at the Three Moons, near St. Sepulchre, in Holburn." Knox drained his tankard and pushed to his feet. "Don't make me regret telling you."

Chapter 42

$\mathcal{J}$ud Foy was coming down the inn's rickety back steps, his lips pursed in a tuneless whistle, when Sebastian reached out to clench his fist in the man's foul, tattered coat front and swing him around to slam his back against the near wall.

"Here, here," bleated Foy, his hat tipping sideways, his watery eyes going wide. "What'd you want to go and do that to me for?"

Sebastian searched the man's mad, gaunt features for some ghost of the stout, brash sergeant who'd testified for the defense at Matt Tyson's court-martial three years before. But the man was so changed as to be virtually unrecognizable. "I have a problem with people menacing my wife."

"Me? I didn't menace her. If anything, she menaced me. Shoved her little muff gun in my face, she did, and threatened to blow my head off."

"You were following her. Watching her."

"I wouldn't hurt her. I swear I wouldn't."

"You threatened her cat."

"I don't like black cats. Ask anybody. They're bad luck."

"Harm a hair on that cat's body, and I'll kill you."

"Over a *cat*?"

"Yes."

"And they say I'm touched in the head."

"Tell me what happened to you after Talavera."

Foy's face went slack with confusion. "What you mean?"

"How did you get hurt?"

"Don't rightly know. They found me near the stables with my head stove in and bits of my skull poking out. Thought I was a goner, they did. But I fooled 'em, didn't I?" He closed his eyes and huffed his eerie, soundless laugh.

"You don't remember what happened to you?"

"I don't remember much of anything from before then."

"You'd recently testified at a court-martial. Do you remember the name of the man on trial?"

"Aye. That I do remember. It was Tyson. Lieutenant Matt Tyson."

Sebastian released his hold on the man's ragged coat and took a step back. "When you told me you saw me coming out of 'his house,' whose house did you mean?"

Foy grabbed his battered hat as it started to slide down the wall. "That diamond merchant what lived in Fountain Lane. Can't remember his name now."

"Eisler?"

Foy carefully replaced the hat on his head. "Aye, that was it. Daniel Eisler."

"Why were you watching his house?"

"He had something that belonged to me."

"What?"

The man's thin chest shuddered with his silent laughter. "What you think?" He leaned forward as if whispering a secret, his breath foul. "Diamonds."

"Eisler had your diamonds?"

"He did."

"How did he get them?"

"Somebody sold them to him."

"Define 'somebody.'"

"Never give me my share, he didn't."

"Who? Who never gave you your share?"

"I can't remember."

Sebastian studied the man's skeletally thin face, the gaunt, beard-stubbled cheeks, and rainwater gray eyes lit by an unearthly gleam. And he found himself wondering not for the first time just how much of the man's madness was real and how much was put on for effect. "You say you were watching Eisler's house on Monday?"

"I was."

"Eisler was dead by then."

"I know that."

"Were you watching the house the evening before?"

"I was."

"Did you see who came in and out that evening?"

"I did."

"Tell me what you saw."

"Why should I?"

Sebastian took a menacing step toward him again.

Foy threw up his hands and skittered sideways along the wall. "All right, all right!"

"Who did you see?" Sebastian demanded.

Foy's tongue flicked out to wet his dry, cracked lips. "Well, first there was this gentleman."

"Who?"

"How would I know? Never seen him before."

"How old?"

Foy shrugged. "Forty? Fifty? Hard to tell sometimes, ain't it?"

"What did he look like?"

"You think I can remember?"

"Tall? Thin? Short? Fat?"

A frown contorted the man's face. "Tallish. I think. Dressed dapper. I told you—I don't exactly remember. I didn't pay him no mind. Why would I?"

"How long did he stay?"

"Not long. Ten minutes. Maybe less."

"What time was this?"

"'Bout the time it was gettin' dark, I reckon. I didn't see him too good."

Sebastian tamped down a welling of frustration. "Who else did you see?"

Foy screwed up his face again in thought. "I think the doxy came next."

"A woman? When did she come?"

"Maybe an hour later."

"Do you remember what she looked like?"

Foy shook his head. "It were dark by then. Can't nobody see in the dark."

"How did she arrive?"

"Some gentleman brung her in a hackney. He waited in the carriage while she got down and went into the house. Then he drove off. And I didn't see him, so there ain't no use in asking me what *he* looked like."

"If you didn't see him, then how did you know he was a gentleman?"

"Because I seen his outline in the window when he leaned forward. He had a dapper hat on."

"His hat? You know he was a gentleman by the silhouette of his hat?"

"Aye. He had one of them folding, two-corner jobs, like what the gentry wears to the opera."

"You mean, a chapeau bras?"

"You think I know what they're called?"

"And then what happened?"

Foy twitched one thin, ragged shoulder. "I dunno. I left not too long after that."

"You didn't see the woman come out again?"

"No."

"Did you see anyone else hanging around while you were watching the house?"

"No. It's nearly all warehouses and storerooms down there now; have you noticed?" A tic had started up to the left of the man's mouth, the grainy, filth-encrusted skin twitching in tiny, uncontrollable spasms.

Sebastian said, "I think you're holding back on me, Foy. There's something you're not telling me."

Foy stared at him with vacant, rheumy eyes.

It might have been impossible to tell how much of the man's madness was feigned, how much was acquired, and how much had always been there, but Sebastian did not make the mistake of believing the ex-soldier harmless. Madness was always dangerous, especially when coupled with brutal self-interest. Yet he suspected that Foy was outclassed in perhaps all but evil by those into whose orbit he had now drifted.

Sebastian said, "I don't know how much of what you're telling me is true, and how much is sheer, unadulterated balderdash—"

"That's a right hurtful thing to say, it is."

"—but I think you've stumbled into something you don't understand here. Something that could get you killed."

Foy grinned, opened his eyes wide, and pursed his lips to push his breath out in a mocking sound. "Ooo-ooo. Think I should be scared, do you? I'm missing a chunk of my skull and a part of my brain, and I'm still here, ain't I? I reckon I'm a pretty hard fellow to kill."

"No one's hard to kill," said Sebastian, and left him standing at the base of the stairs, a skeletal figure clothed in tattered rags that hung like a shroud about the frame of a man long dead.

※

Charles, Lord Jarvis, leaned back in his chair, his feet stretched out toward the hearth in his Carlton House chambers as he studied the man who stood before him. He found Bertram Leigh-Jones a slob of a man, big and unkempt but full of bluster and self-importance tinged, Jarvis suspected, with no small portion of vice.

Jarvis lifted a pinch of snuff to one nostril and sniffed. "I trust you understand your instructions?"

"I do, my lord. But—"

"Good." Jarvis closed his snuffbox with a snap. "That will be all."

"But—"

Jarvis raised one eyebrow.

Mr. Leigh-Jones's full cheeks darkened. He set his jaw, said, "As you wish, my lord," and bowed himself out.

Jarvis was gazing after him, a thoughtful frown on his face, when one of the ex-military men in Jarvis's employ appeared at the entrance, his dark, rain-splattered cloak swirling as he swung it from his shoulders.

Jarvis smiled. "Ah, Archer. Come in and close the door. I have an assignment for you."

Chapter 43

*A*lthough both men had already denied it, Sebastian suspected that the shadowy chapeau bras glimpsed by Foy through the windows of a hackney the night of the murder in all likelihood belonged to either Blair Beresford or Samuel Perlman.

He decided to start with the young Irish poet.

It took a while, but Sebastian finally traced Beresford to the churchyard of a small eighteenth-century chapel that lay just to the northeast of Cavendish Square, where the younger man was winding his way among the tombstones. Pausing beneath the arched lych-gate, Sebastian watched as Beresford stood beside one of the newer monuments, removed his hat, and bowed his head in prayer.

Beresford prayed silently for some minutes before replacing his hat and turning toward the street. Then he saw Sebastian and drew up, an angry flush mottling his cheeks. "What? A man can't even pray over his own dead sister without being spied on?"

"You have a sister buried here?" said Sebastian in surprise.

"My younger sister, Elizabeth. Louisa invited her to London two years ago, for the Season. It was a dream come true for her. I'd never seen her so excited."

A breeze rattled the yellowing leaves of the hawthorns in the churchyard and brought them the scent of damp earth and dying grass. "What happened?"

"She died of fever just five weeks after she arrived."

"I'm sorry."

A muscle jumped along the younger man's jaw, but he said nothing.

Sebastian turned to leave.

Beresford stopped him by saying, "I take it you wanted to speak to me about something?"

Sebastian shook his head. "It can wait for a more appropriate time."

"Why? Out of respect for my sister? She's dead. If you've something to say to me, just say it."

Sebastian squinted up at the chapel's awkward, neoclassical facade. "I have a witness who says he saw a man in a hackney carriage drop a woman of the street at Eisler's house an hour or so after sunset the night of the murder. A man wearing a chapeau bras."

Beresford's face hardened in a way that made him look considerably older—and less gentle. "If you're asking if that man was I, the answer is no. I already told you that."

"So you did. Then tell me this: When was the last time you saw Eisler?"

"The Saturday before he died."

The readiness of the man's answer took Sebastian by surprise. "Was that the last time you provided him with a woman?"

"As a matter of fact, no. I saw him here."

"Here?" Sebastian wasn't certain he'd understood right. "At Portland Chapel?"

"That's right."

Sebastian stared out over the rows of graying, moss-covered tombstones. The chapel was less than a century old, and already the churchyard was filled to overflowing. He said, "When was this?"

"Late Saturday afternoon."

"What was he doing here?"

"I didn't ask."

"Did you speak to him?"

"I did. I hadn't intended to, but he approached me. Accused me of following him. If you ask me, he'd been drinking. He was talking wild—said he knew 'they' were watching him. He even accused me of working for 'them.' But when I asked who 'they' were, he just started ranting about some Frenchman named Collot."

"Jacques Collot?" asked Sebastian sharply. "What about Collot?"

"I told you, the old goat was obviously foxed. He was practically raving. Nothing he said made much sense. He said it was all Collot's fault."

"What was Collot's fault?"

Beresford shrugged. "I assumed he meant the fact that someone was watching him. I don't really know—I tell you, he was as drunk as a wheelbarrow."

The wind gusted up again, scuttling dead leaves across the overgrown path and ruffling the younger man's soft golden curls. After a moment, Beresford said, "Look . . . I know you think I killed him, but I didn't. I'm not saying I didn't want to. To be frank, I even thought about it a few times—about how I could maybe do it. But I'm too much of a coward to ever go through with something like that." His features twisted with what looked very much like self-loathing. "I let that little piece of human excrement use me as a tool to satisfy his sick carnal urgings. He talked to me like I was filth. Threatened me. And I took it. Because I was too weak and afraid to do anything about it."

"Sometimes admitting that you've been weak takes more courage than walking into a man's house and putting a bullet in his chest."

Beresford gave a mirthless laugh and shook his head. "No." Then his features sharpened.

"What?" asked Sebastian, watching him.

"I was just remembering something else Eisler said— about that Frenchman, Collot."

"What about him?"

"He said he had a big mouth."

⁂

Darkness was just beginning to fall, the last of the light leaching from the sky as Sebastian walked the narrow streets and alleys of St. Giles looking for Jacques Collot. The reek of newly lit tallow candles and torches filled the air, mingling with the smell of roasting mutton and spilled ale and cheap gin.

He tried the Pilgrim first, then a string of ale shops along Queen Street, then the tavern where he'd spotted the Frenchman in consultation with his three confederates.

Nothing.

He was passing the smoke-blackened ruins of what looked like an old coaching inn when a low, anxious voice hissed at him from out of the darkness.

"Pssst."

Sebastian turned to find Collot hovering in the shadows of the burned inn's scorched, refuse-filled arch. He had his hat brim pulled low over his forehead and the collar of his greatcoat turned up, although it was not cold.

"Why are you hiding in the shadows?" asked Sebastian, walking up to him—but not too close.

"Why? Because I am nervous! Why do you think?" He cast a quick, harried glance around. "Many people are looking for me, asking about me. Why are you stirring up trouble by looking for me again?"

Sebastian stared through the arch at the abandoned yard beyond. It appeared deserted, its piles of blackened timbers and rubble standing quiet and still in the deepening darkness. "I wanted to talk to you."

"The last time you talked to me, you ripped my coat. See? Look here." He turned sideways to display a large rent down one shoulder.

"My apologies," said Sebastian. "I want to know how

you discovered that Eisler had in his possession a certain big blue diamond."

"Why should I tell you? Hmm? Give me one reason why I should tell you."

"To save your coat?"

Collot's wayward eye rolled sideways. "I am a man with many contacts. I hear many things. Who can say where I learn things?"

"I suspect you could say where." Sebastian showed his teeth in a smile. "If the alternative becomes unpleasant enough."

"Monsieur." Collot threw up his hands like a man warding off evil. "Surely this is unnecessary."

"How did you discover Eisler had the diamond?"

"He showed it to a woman I know. A *putain*. She told me."

"A whore? Why would Eisler show a priceless gem to a woman off the streets?"

"Why? Because he was a sick *salaud*; that is why." Collot hawked up a mouthful of phlegm and turned his head to spit. "You would not believe some of the things I could tell you."

"Try me."

But Collot only shook his head.

Sebastian said, "How did Eisler find out you knew about the diamond?"

"What makes you think that he did?"

Sebastian smiled. "You're not the only one who hears things."

Collot sniffed. "He knew because I wanted him to know. He cheated me, you see—in Amsterdam. It might have been twenty years ago, but Collot does not forget these things. I brought him my share of the gems from the Garde-Meuble. We agreed on a price. Then, after I handed them over, he paid me a third of what he had promised. Said if I set up a squawk, he would tell the authorities I had tried to rob him. He was a respected merchant; I was a known thief. What could I do? He said

I was lucky he had given me anything at all for the jewels. I should have killed him right there."

"Why didn't you?"

Collot squared his shoulders with a strange kind of pride. "I am a thief, not a murderer."

"So what did you hope to accomplish by going to him now, after all these years?"

"I told him I wanted the rest of the money he owed me, and that if he did not give it to me, I would tell the French he had the *diamant bleu de la Couronne*."

Sebastian was aware of a burst of laughter from the throng of drunken men in the street behind him. The last of the light had vanished from the evening sky, leaving the narrow lane dark and windswept. "And? What did he say?"

"The old bastard laughed at me. He laughed! Then his face changed, and suddenly he was shaking with rage. It was as if he had been possessed by a demon. He said if I ever thought of breathing a word to Napoléon's agents, he would see me buried alive in an unmarked grave. Who talks like that? Hmm?"

"When was this?"

"Friday."

"So what did you do?"

Collot rolled his shoulders in an expansive Gallic shrug. "I told."

"Who? Who did you tell?"

"Why, the agent of Napoléon, of course. Who else? Eisler did not think I would do it. He did not believe I would have the courage. But I did. He should never have said those things to me."

Sebastian studied the Parisian thief's mobile, beard-shadowed face. "Are you telling me that you know the identity of one of Napoléon's agents in London?"

Collot's elastic mouth curved into a grin. "Like I said, I know things."

"So who is it?"

The old thief gave a deep, husky laugh. "Believe me, you do not want to know."

"But I do."

Collot shook his head, his smile still wide, his eyes sparkling with amusement. "I could tell you it is someone you know. More than that: It is someone you trust." He laughed out loud. "But I won't."

Sebastian resisted the urge to grab the man and shake him. "Tell me this: Were you handsomely compensated for your information?"

Collot's face fell.

"No?" said Sebastian, watching him. "Why not?"

"They said they already knew. They said they had known for weeks."

Sebastian was aware of a dark carriage being driven slowly up the street. He said, "You do realize that they are probably the ones watching you? They killed Eisler, and now they're going to kill you."

"Non."

"Yes. Tell me who they are."

"Non." Collot started to back away, his head shaking from side to side, his wayward eye going wild. "You are trying to get me killed! What do you take me for? A f—" He broke off, his expressive face going slack with shock as the explosive crack of a rifle echoed in the narrow street and the front of his coat dissolved into a pulpy sheen.

"God damn it!" swore Sebastian, barreling the crumpling Frenchman deep into the fetid, protective darkness of the old archway. He caught the man's falling body beneath the arms, propping him upright so he wouldn't choke on his own blood. But it was already too late.

He saw Collot's eyes roll back into his head, heard the rattle in his throat, felt the essence of his life ease away, leaving Sebastian holding a silent, empty husk that seemed to collapse and diminish before his eyes.

Chapter 44

*S*ome hours later, after a tense and unpleasant inter-
lude with the local constabulary, Sebastian walked into
Kat's dressing room at the Covent Garden Theater. The
curtain had just fallen. He was still covered in blood, and
he wasn't in the best of moods.

"Devlin," said Kat, starting up from her dressing table. "You're hurt!"

She still wore the elaborate stomacher and velvet
gown of her character, and he stopped her before she
could get too close to him. "Careful. You'll ruin your cos-
tume. And I'm fine. It's not my blood."

She drew back, her gaze on his face. "Whose is it?"

"An old Parisian thief named Jacques Collot. He was
one of the original gang who stole the French Crown
Jewels from the Garde-Meuble. He found out Daniel
Eisler was handling the sale of Hope's diamond and
tried to use his knowledge of the stone's origins to wea-
sel money out of Eisler."

"How?"

"By threatening to tell Napoléon's agent where to
find the French Blue. Eisler made the mistake of laughing at him."

"Collot went to the French?"

"He did."

She turned away to fiddle with the hairpins and combs

scattered across the surface of her table, her heavy dark hair falling forward across her face as she asked with what struck him as studied casualness, "And was he able to tell you the name of the person Napoléon has charged with the stone's recovery?"

He kept his gaze on her half-averted profile. "No. He was killed before I could get it out of him. Shot, probably by the same person who killed the young thief in the alley behind Eisler's house Monday night."

He waited for her to make some response. When she didn't, he said quietly, "Is it you, Kat? Are you working for the French in this?"

She'd sworn she'd severed her association with the French well over a year ago now. But that had been before. Before their lives and their future together had unraveled in a morass of long-buried secrets and Hendon's self-serving lies. Before she married Russell Yates, and Sebastian married the daughter of Charles, Lord Jarvis, the man who'd sworn to see her die an ugly, painful death.

She looked up, her eyes going wide, her mouth forming an O of surprise and hurt as she drew in a quick breath. "I can't believe you just asked me that."

He looked into her beautiful, beloved face, saw the hurt that pinched her features, saw her eyes film. He said, "I'm sorry."

She shook her head, blinking rapidly as if she were fighting back tears. "I suppose I should be flattered that you still trust me enough to believe I'd give you an honest answer."

"Kat—"

He reached for her, but she pulled away. "No. Let me finish. My love of Ireland is unchanged. I would do anything to see her free of this murderous occupation— anything, that is, except go back on the pledge I made to you."

He felt as if he'd just sliced open his own chest and torn out his heart. "I should never have doubted you."

"No." To his surprise, she reached up to press her fingertips to his lips. "People are dying. I can understand why you felt you needed to ask. I kept the truth of my association with the French a secret from you when I should not have, and that will always be between us. It's not good for a man and woman to keep things from each other. Secrets destroy trust. And without honesty and trust, love is just . . . a shifting mirage."

He took her hand in his, pressed his lips to her palm, then curled his fingers around hers. "My love for you was never a mirage."

They stood face-to-face, nothing touching except their hands. He could feel the tiny shudders trembling through her, breathed in the familiar theater scents of greasepaint and oranges, looked into the deep blue eyes that were so much like those of her father. He said, "Do you ever think what would have happened to us if you hadn't listened to Hendon all those years ago? If you had listened instead to your heart and married me when you were seventeen and I was twenty-one?"

"I think of it all the time."

He leaned his forehead against hers, drew in a deep breath.

She said, "I did the right thing, Sebastian. For you and for me."

"You can still say that? Despite all that's happened?"

"Yes. We would have destroyed each other had we wed. I couldn't have continued on the stage as Lady Devlin, yet I would never have been accepted into society. So what would I have done instead? Sit home and embroider seat cushions? I'd have been miserable, and in the end I'd have made you miserable too."

"We could have found a way," he insisted.

Although for the first time, he was aware of a whisper of doubt.

Faint, but there.

❧

That night, a new storm swept in from the north. A fierce wind rattled the limbs of the elms in the garden and sent dead leaves scuttling down the street. Hero could see streaks of lightning rending the sky, hear the patter of wind-driven rain against the window. She lay alone in her bed, her eyes on the tucked blue silk of the canopy overhead, her hands resting low on her belly, on the swelling of the child she had made with a man she'd barely known but who was now her husband.

She heard him come in when the storm was at its fiercest. But though she listened carefully, she didn't hear him mount the steps to the second floor. And so, after a time, she drew on her dressing gown and went in search of him.

She found him in the dining room, beside the long windows overlooking the wind-savaged garden. He had his back to her and did not turn when she paused in the doorway. He'd stripped off his wet coat and waistcoat, and she could see the tense set of his shoulders through the fine cloth of his shirt. The air was damp and close with the smell of the rain and the tang of blood and an elusive scent she realized suddenly was peeled oranges. And she knew the pain of a woman who has given her heart to a man who lost his own heart long ago to some-one else.

But all she said was, "I hope that's not your blood I smell."

He turned his head to look at her over his shoulder. "It's not. Jacques Collot is dead. He was telling me about how he came to know Eisler had the blue diamond in his possession when someone put a bullet in his chest with a rifle."

"You didn't see who did it?"

"I was too busy trying not to get shot myself."

Crossing to the table beside the dying fire, she poured a glass of brandy and went to hold it out to him. "Here."

He took the glass from her hand, his fingers covering

hers for a moment. He said, "There's something I must tell you."

"Tell me later. You should come to bed. You're wet and cold."

"No." He set the brandy aside and reached to draw her into his arms. "I've put it off too long already."

She felt his hands slide down her back to rest on her hips, holding her—but not too close.

He said, "I first fell in love with Kat Boleyn when she was sixteen and I was just down from Oxford. Hendon grumbled about it, although if truth be told, I think he expected some such thing. It's not exactly unusual for a young man to have an opera dancer or an actress in keeping. What he didn't expect was that I'd want to spend the rest of my life with her."

"You don't need to tell me—"

"No, please, hear me out. When I told him I'd asked Kat to marry me, he flew into a rage and swore I wouldn't see another penny from the estates until he was dead. I told him I didn't care." A sad smile touched his lips. "The world well lost for love and all that."

A flash of lightning lit up the room with a throbbing blue glow chased by a rumble of thunder. She waited.

After a moment, he said, "What I didn't know was that Hendon went behind my back and saw Kat. He told her that such a marriage would ruin my life and offered her twenty thousand pounds if she would leave me. She threw him out of her rooms. But his words had had their effect. She decided that he was right—that if she truly loved me, then she'd let me go—for my sake. So she told me she had no intention of marrying a pauper, and since my father was standing firm on his threat to cut me off, she wanted nothing more to do with me."

"Oh, Sebastian," Hero whispered. "How . . . fiercely noble of her."

He sucked in a deep breath that flared his nostrils. "That's when I bought my commission and left England. I wasn't exactly trying to get myself killed, but I wouldn't have minded terribly if it had happened. When I came back to London some six years later, I thought I'd managed to put it all behind me."

"Until you saw her again," said Hero softly, although what she really wanted to say was, *Why? Why are you telling me this now?*

He nodded. "Eventually I found out the truth about what had happened all those years ago—that she had lied to drive me away from her. I asked her again to marry me, but she still refused. She said nothing had really changed, that she loved me too much to allow me to ruin myself by marrying a woman off the stage. In my arrogance, I was convinced I could change her mind, eventually. Only . . ."

"Then you discovered she was Hendon's daughter."

She watched him reach for his drink and down half the glass in one long pull. The tension in the air was like an unnatural hum that had nothing to do with the storm.

He said, "I knew that in all fairness, I couldn't blame Hendon for the blood relationship between them—after all, he was the one who'd been trying to drive Kat and me apart for years. But it took me a long time to forgive him for the undisguised satisfaction he showed at finally achieving what he had worked so hard to accomplish."

She started to say, *But if you have forgiven him, then why are you still estranged from him?* Only, something in his face made her hold her peace.

He drained his glass and went to pour himself another brandy, as if he felt the need to put some distance between them. He said, "And then, last May, I discovered that in December of 1781, Hendon sailed for America on a secret mission for the King."

Hero stared at him. Jarvis had sailed on that mission too. She tried to recall if she'd known the date of their sailing, if she knew when—

He said, "I will turn thirty next month. I assume you can do the sums?"

She watched him set aside the brandy decanter,

watched him carefully replace the stopper, and understood finally what he was trying to tell her. "Are you certain Hendon's not—"

"Yes. He tried to deny it at first, but in the end he was forced to admit the truth."

"Do you know who—"

"No. My mother never said." He stared at her from across the length of the room.

His mother, Hero knew, had disappeared at sea years ago, when Devlin was still a child.

Hero was suddenly aware of the fury of the storm, of the wind rattling the windowpanes in their frames and the rain pounding on the terrace paving. He said, "I would have told you before we married, had the circumstances been different. But as it was . . ."

She said, "Jarvis knew. He was on that ship with your father. So he's always known."

"Yes."

Yet he hadn't told her. *Why?* she wondered. Aloud, she said, "And the Bishopsgate tavern owner? Jamie Knox? Where does he fit in all this?"

"I honestly don't know. He could conceivably be my half brother. Or a cousin, perhaps. I find it difficult to believe the resemblance between us is nothing more than a coincidence. Unfortunately, his own paternity is . . . cloudy."

When she remained silent, he said, "I will understand if this knowledge alters your opinion of me."

"It hasn't lowered it, if that's what you mean." She drew a deep breath that shuddered her chest. "Why now? Why did you decide to tell me this now?"

"Because I realized I don't want this secret between us anymore."

She suddenly felt both humbled and oddly, buoyantly hopeful. "I've kept secrets from you," she said quietly.

"You've kept your father's secrets. There is a difference."

Then the full implications of what he'd told her struck her. "So Kat Boleyn is not your half sister?"

"No. And Hendon knew it all along, damn his hide. He knew it, and he kept it to himself because he realized he'd finally hit upon the one sure thing that would keep us apart."

And that, Hero now realized, was what had caused this new, intractable estrangement between the two men.

She said, "Hendon could have repudiated you years ago, but he didn't. It could only be because he cares for you—*loves* you—as a father. He did what he thought was right for you."

"Hendon did what he thought was right for the St. Cyr name and the St. Cyr bloodline. Nothing is more important to Hendon than fulfilling what he believes is owed to his heritage. Nothing."

"But the cousin who stands behind you in succession—"

"The distant cousin who would become Viscount Devlin in my stead is in reality a vicar's by-blow, whereas my mother was herself a St. Cyr, through her grandmother. So you see, St. Cyr blood does flow in my veins, even if it didn't come from Hendon himself."

"I think you do Hendon an injustice. Kat Boleyn is his daughter. If you had married her, then your child—your *heir*—would have been his own grandson."

Devlin gave a soft, humorless laugh. "An actress's son as the future Earl of Hendon? Hendon would stop at little short of murder to prevent such an abomination from ever coming to pass."

She turned to stare out the window at the storm-thrashed garden. "Yet if Yates hangs for this murder, you could now marry Kat . . . if you weren't married to me."

"Hero . . ." He came to stand behind her. She was aware of his hands hovering for a moment over her shoulders without touching her. Then he turned her in his arms and drew her close. She felt his breath warm against her cheek, the beating of his heart against hers. He said, "I've loved Kat since I was twenty-one. There was a time I'd have sworn I could never learn to love anyone again. But . . . I was wrong."

She touched her fingertips to his lips. "You don't need to tell me what you think I want to hear."

He gave her a strange, crooked smile. "I hope it is what you want to hear, because I'm telling you how I feel."

She said, "It's what I want to hear."

He took her hand in his and pressed a kiss against her palm. "'Rise up, my love, my fair one,'" he quoted softly, his features growing taut, his eyes half-lidded, intense, "'and come away. For, lo, the winter is past, the rain is over and gone.'"

A loud clap of thunder shook the room, and they laughed together.

She wrapped her other hand around his, their fingers entwining. "'The flowers appear on the earth,'" she whispered. "'The time of the singing of birds is come, and the vines with the tender grape give good smell. Arise, my love, my fair one, and come away.'"

"I think you left out a couple of lines," he said, pressing her back against the wall so that he could get at the ties of her dressing gown.

She brought up one bare leg to wrap around his hip and let it slide slowly, provocatively down the hard length of his thigh. "I was in a hurry," she said, and caught his laugh with her kiss.

Chapter 45

*E*arly the next morning, Hero walked into the dining room of Jarvis House in Berkeley Square to find her father looking over a stack of reports while consuming a solitary breakfast. Wordlessly, she closed the door in the footman's face and leaned back against it.

"This is ominous," said Jarvis, his gaze still fixed on the papers in his hand.

She pushed away from the door and came to stand in front of him. "You knew Devlin was not Hendon's son, yet you chose not to tell me. Why?"

He looked up, his face—as always—inscrutable. "Under the circumstances, I saw no point. Are you suggesting it would have altered your decision to marry, had you known the details surrounding his birth?"

"No."

"I didn't think so."

He dropped the report he held beside his plate and leaned back in his chair. "So Devlin finally told you himself, did he?"

"Yes." She pulled out the chair beside him and sat. "Devlin says he doesn't know who his father is. Do you?"

"Unfortunately, no. Believe me, I have tried over the

years to discover the man's identity. One never knows when such information might prove useful. But none of my attempts have thus far met with success." He templed his hands before him. "Did Devlin also tell you that his mother still lives?"

"She what?"

"Omitted that little detail, did he?" Jarvis reached for his snuffbox and calmly opened it with the flick of a finger. "Oh, yes. She's still quite alive. Although as it happens, he does not know where she is."

Hero watched him lift a delicate pinch to one nostril. "But you do, don't you?"

He inhaled sharply and smiled. "I think perhaps I shouldn't answer that question."

Her gaze met his. "You just did."

❧

It occurred to Sebastian that the more he learned about Daniel Eisler, the more he found it a wonder that someone hadn't killed the nasty bastard years before.

Eisler's life had been populated by an endless stream of desperate men and women upon whom he inflicted financial ruin, sexual degradation, and burning humiliation. Sebastian knew the names of some of his victims—but only some. The number of people who'd wished the man dead must have been beyond counting. And Sebastian had less than twenty-four hours to find the one who'd finally given in to his—or her—lethal urges.

Both Blair Beresford and Jacques Collot had admitted wanting to kill the diamond merchant. Would someone who actually followed through on his murderous impulses admit to them? Sebastian didn't think so. But then, he'd learned long ago the fallacy of assuming others shared his own nature.

Yet he also found himself wondering, *Why now?* After decades of successfully cheating, blackmailing, and exploiting those unfortunate enough to stumble into his web, why had Eisler finally paid the ultimate price for his greedy machinations? Had he simply misjudged the wrong man? Or had he fallen afoul of forces too powerful for him to control?

Sebastian was seated at his breakfast table pondering these questions when a distant peal sounded at the front door. A moment later, Morey appeared to clear his throat and bow.

"A gentleman to see you, my lord. Colonel Otto von Riedesel apologizes for the incivility of calling upon your lordship at this hour but wishes to stress the importance of his errand."

"Show him in—and bring him a tankard of ale." Sebastian glanced down at the black cat seated on the rug at his feet. "And you behave."

Green eyes gleaming, the cat flicked its tail and looked vaguely evil.

The colonel came in with a quick step that jangled the spurs at his boots and swirled the black cape he wore thrown over his shoulders. "Please, do not get up," he said. "My apologies for interrupting your repast."

"May I offer you something, Colonel?"

"Thank you, but no." He held his black shako beneath one arm; raindrops quivered on the ends of his mustache and on the high blue collar of his black dolman. "I require only a moment of your time."

"Please, sit down."

"Thank you."

Von Riedesel sat, bringing with him all the scents of a rainy morning mingled with the odor of warm horseflesh, as if he had only just come in from exercising his hack in the park. He smoothed the splayed fingers of one hand down over his face, wiping the moisture from his mustache. Then he hesitated, evidently at a loss as to how to begin.

Sebastian said, "I take it you've heard of the death of Jacques Collot?"

Von Riedesel nodded, his normally ruddy cheeks pale. "You knew him?"

"Me? No. But I knew of him—of his involvement in

the theft at the Garde-Meuble." The man's voice was strained, his accent more pronounced than usual. "Vhy vas he killed? Do you know?"

"Presumably because someone was afraid that he might talk."

The Brunswicker rested his forearms on the tabletop and leaned into them. "But vhat could he know?"

"Well, he knew the late Duke once possessed a certain large blue diamond."

"Sir!" Von Riedesel sat back sharply. "If you mean to suggest—"

"That you had a reason to kill him? Well, you did, didn't you?"

The Brunswicker surged to his feet. "I refuse to stay here and—"

"Sit down," said Sebastian. "Since you're here, you might as well answer some of my questions. Unless, of course, you prefer that I address them to the Princess?"

"I ought to call you out for this!"

Sebastian chewed and swallowed. "But you won't, because that would draw the attention of the public—not to mention the Prince Regent—precisely where you don't want it. Sit."

The colonel sat.

Sebastian cut another slice of ham. "Daniel Eisler had a nasty habit of collecting damaging information about people—especially important, vulnerable people." He paused to glance over at the colonel, who sat staring rigidly ahead. "It occurs to me that he could have discovered something Princess Caroline did not want publicly known. Something such as the details of the sale of her father's jewels, perhaps? Or was it proof of her extramarital dalliances?"

"Whoever told you Eisler had damaging information about the Princess was lying."

"Actually, you told me."

"Me? But I never—"

"Otherwise, why are you here?"

New beads of moisture had appeared on the Brunswicker's full cheeks. Only, this time it was sweat, not rain.

Sebastian said, "Eisler wasn't your typical blackmailer. He liked to use his information to torment people, or to bend them to his will. So what did he want from the Princess?"

"I can't tell you that!"

"Did she give him what he wanted?"

Von Riedesel pressed his lips into a thin, flat line, then nodded curtly. "Yes."

Sebastian gave up on his breakfast and leaned back in his chair. "You've served and protected the Duke's daughter for more than a decade. I can't see you standing idly by while a nasty little diamond merchant threatened her."

"You are suggesting—vhat? That I vent to his home Sunday night and put a bullet through him?" If the Brunswicker's face had been pale before, it was now suffused with color. "As it happens, I spent last Sunday evening in the company of a voman of my acquaintance—and no, I have no intention of telling you her name." He pushed to his feet, the movement so violent the chair toppled over, startling the cat. "Good day to you, sir!"

He had almost reached the door when Sebastian said, "Tell me this: Did the Prince know about Eisler's interest in his wife's affairs?"

Von Riedesel paused at the door to look back at him. "No. But I'll tell you who did know."

"Who?"

A gleam of malicious triumph flashed in the Brunswicker's small brown eyes. "Jarvis. Jarvis knew."

❧

Half an hour later, Sebastian was on the verge of leaving to make a formal call on his father-in-law when he received a message from Sir Henry Lovejoy. Jud Foy had been discovered sprawled against one of the tombstones in St. Anne's churchyard.

Dead.

Chapter 46

Sebastian found Sir Henry standing in the lee of the church's soot-stained, redbrick walls, his shoulders hunched and the collar of his greatcoat turned up against the morning drizzle.

Jud Foy still lay sprawled where he had been discovered, half-propped against a mossy tombstone like a man who'd stretched out for a nap. Except that his eyes were wide and staring, and someone had bashed the side of his head into a bloody pulp.

"Given your interest in the fellow, I thought you'd want to know," said Sir Henry when Sebastian walked up to him.

"Who found him?"

"The sexton. He tells us he heard a commotion late last night but saw nothing when he went to investigate. It was only this morning he noticed the corpse."

Sebastian went to hunker down beside the body. In death, Foy seemed to have shriveled to little more than a loose collection of rags drummed into the mud by the previous night's rain. After a moment's hesitation, he reached out to touch the dead man's sunken cheek.

He was cold.

Looking up, Sebastian squinted through the drizzle to where a couple of constables were working their way across the overgrown churchyard. "Have they found anything?"

"Nothing, I'm afraid." Sir Henry paused. "I heard about last night's shooting in St. Giles. You weren't hurt?"

Sebastian shook his head. "They weren't shooting at me."

Sir Henry nodded to the dead man beside them. "Does this make any sense to you?"

"None of it makes any sense to me."

The magistrate frowned. "One wonders what he was doing in a churchyard."

"Meeting someone, perhaps?"

"Surely a tavern would have been more suitable . . . not to mention warmer and dryer?"

"It would also have been more public."

"There is that." Sir Henry reached for his handkerchief and wiped his nose with a sniff.

Sebastian said, "You'll be sending the body to Gibson?"

The magistrate's eyes narrowed in a thoughtful frown. But all he said was, "Indeed. I've just dispatched one of the lads to the Mount Street dead house for a shell."

Sebastian was pushing to his feet when something half-hidden beneath the dead man's greasy, ragged coat caught his eye. He reached for it and found himself holding a small leather pouch embossed with the stylized initials DE. He'd seen the device before; it was Daniel Eisler's.

Loosening the pouch's rawhide tie, he shook some half a dozen small stones into the palm of one hand. They winked up at him, somehow snatching a measure of light from the dreary, overcast day and turning it into a brilliant rainbow of fire.

"What is it?" Lovejoy asked, leaning forward to see.

"Diamonds," said Sebastian. "I think they're diamonds."

※

After the men from the dead house had carried off what was left of Jud Foy toward Tower Hill, Sebastian bought

Sir Henry a cup of hot chocolate from a coffeehouse on Leicester Square.

"Is Foy the ruffian I hear accosted Lady Devlin in Charing Cross yesterday?" asked Sir Henry, his hands wrapped around his steaming mug. His nose was red, and Sebastian noticed he kept sniffing.

"Yes."

The magistrate reached for his handkerchief. "Remarkable woman, her ladyship. Quite remarkable. Not to mention formidable."

"She didn't bash in Foy's head."

Sir Henry's eyes widened above his handkerchief. "Good heavens. I hope you don't think I was suggesting any such thing?"

Sebastian smiled and shook his head. Then his smile faded. "I hear Yates is scheduled to stand trial tomorrow morning."

"He is, yes. I'm told they're so confident of conviction that the keeper has already ordered the construction of the gallows for Monday morning."

Sebastian took a sip of his coffee and practically scalded his tongue. "Perhaps the deaths of two men linked to the case will lead the authorities to reconsider."

"It might if we were dealing with anyone other than Bertram Leigh-Jones." Lovejoy touched his handkerchief to his nose again. "Although there's no denying Foy's possession of that pouch of diamonds is certainly suggestive."

"I don't think Foy is our killer. But he might well have known who the killer was."

"The man was a pauper. How else could he have acquired those stones?"

"I don't know," said Sebastian. But it was only a half-truth. Because Sebastian could think of at least two plausible scenarios. One involved Napoléon's unknown agent.

The other implicated Matt Tyson.

❧

Sebastian spent the next couple of hours talking to several veterans of the Peninsular War, including an organ-grinder in Russell Square who'd lost a leg at Barossa and a sergeant who lived in one of the almshouses funded by Benjamin Bloomsfield.

By the time he reached Matt Tyson's lodgings in St. James's Street, the morning's rain had ended and the low, heavy clouds were beginning to break up. A ragged, barefoot boy in a cut-down man's coat held together with string was busy sweeping the mud and manure from the crossing with a worn broom of bundled twigs lashed to a stick. Sebastian tipped him tuppence as he crossed the street and watched the boy's eyes go wide. It shamed him to realize that before Hero had embarked on the research for her article, the army of half-starved urchins who eked out miserable livings as crossing sweeps had been largely invisible to him, a necessary nuisance whose existence he acknowledged without really questioning it.

He was just reaching the far flagway when Tyson exited his lodging and paused to close the door behind him. He was as impeccably dressed as always, in buff-colored breeches and a military-styled dark blue coat, his handsome face hardening as his gaze clashed with Sebastian's.

"We need to talk," said Sebastian.

"I have nothing further to say to you."

"Actually, I rather think you do. You see, I've just had an interesting conversation with several veterans of the 114th Foot."

Tyson ran his tongue across his perfect top teeth. "Very well. Do come in."

His rooms on the first floor were spacious and elegantly furnished with the same exquisite taste—and expense—he lavished on the raiment of his person. The hangings were of figured burgundy satin, the furniture of the finest gleaming rosewood. He did not invite Sebastian to sit, but simply stood with his back to the closed door, his arms crossed at his chest. "Say what you have to say and then get out."

Sebastian let his gaze rove over the shelves of leatherbound books, the gilt-framed oils, the marble bust of a Roman boy. Tyson appeared to be doing quite well for a younger son who'd just sold his commission.

As if aware of the drift of Sebastian's thoughts, Tyson said, "One of my maiden aunts recently died, leaving me her portion."

"And then of course there's whatever you cleared from the sale of the spoils of Badajoz."

Tyson tightened his jaw and said nothing.

Sebastian went to stand before a tasteful oil depicting a foxhunt. "You told me Jud Foy's injuries came from a mule. Only, that was never actually established, was it? In fact, there's a good possibility someone tried to cave in his head with the butt of a rifle."

"Now, why would anyone want to do that?"

Sebastian continued his study of the room. "I think you paid Foy to perjure himself. Then you tried to kill him in order to eliminate the possibility that he might be inspired to tell the truth at some point in the future— and maybe even so that you could take back whatever you'd used to bribe him."

"Believe me, if I'd wanted to kill him, he'd be dead."

"Actually, he is dead. Someone bashed in his head last night in St. Anne's churchyard—fatally this time."

Sebastian watched the other man's face carefully.

But Tyson remained impassive, his only reaction a faint tightening of his lips into the suggestion of a smile. "I'd be tempted to say, 'How tragic.' Except that, given the fact the poor sot's life was hardly worth much at this point, 'How ironic' might be more appropriate. Or perhaps, 'How poetic'?"

Sebastian felt no inclination to return the man's smile. "Interestingly enough, he had a small pouch of loose diamonds in his pocket when he was found."

"Am I to take it you're suggesting the gems implicate me in some way? And here I thought you believed me addicted to stealing jewels as opposed to using them to decorate the bodies of my alleged victims."

"I think you failed the first time you tried to kill Foy, after Talavera. But since he couldn't recall anything, it served your purpose just as well. Only, then he started remembering things, didn't he? Not everything, perhaps, but enough to realize that you owed him. So he came looking for you, and you decided to shut him up permanently. You lured him into the churchyard on the pretext of paying him off with a pouch of small diamonds, and then you bashed in his head while he was distracted by the gems."

Tyson's smile hardened. "And then left them? What a curious thing to have done."

"I can think of two logical explanations. It's possible Foy had the diamonds in his hand when he fell, and in the darkness you couldn't immediately find them. Then the sexton came to investigate the racket he'd heard, and you had to abandon the search and simply run."

"And the second explanation?"

"You deliberately planted the diamonds on Foy to make it look as if he murdered Eisler."

"So you're suggesting—what? That I also killed Eisler? You can't be serious."

"I am, actually. You see, Eisler liked collecting damaging information about people, and you have a dangerous secret. One you share with Beresford. And Yates."

Tyson laughed out loud.

Sebastian said, "You're the only person I know with a motive to kill both men."

Tyson was no longer laughing. "That doesn't mean that I did it. Foy was mad. He'd discovered I recently sold a number of gems to Eisler, and he somehow convinced himself they were rightfully his. Eisler told me the fool accosted him one night, demanded Eisler turn over what he considered 'his' property. Threatened to kill him if he didn't."

"What would you have me believe? That Foy killed Eisler and stole the pouch of diamonds from him? And then . . . what? Fell victim to footpads?"

"It's possible."

Yes, it was possible, Sebastian thought. Foy himself had admitted to watching Eisler's house, and he was just crazy enough to kill Eisler and take the jewels he considered rightfully his. But Sebastian didn't think so.

He kept his gaze on the former lieutenant's hard, even-featured face. "We both know you're capable of murder."

Tyson smiled. "That's something we have in common, isn't it? *Captain.*"

Chapter 47

That afternoon, Kat Boleyn drove her high-perch phaeton to the Physic Garden in Chelsea. Leaving her horse in the care of her groom, she walked briskly down a dripping, mist-shrouded path to a secluded pond. When the days were fine, Kat could lose herself for hours in the old apothecary garden's lush border beds and vast plantings. But on this day, she was in no mood to linger.

The man she had come to meet was already waiting for her at the water's edge. He turned as she approached, a tall, powerful figure in shiny Hessians, fawn-colored breeches, and a well-tailored dark coat.

"Top o' the mornin' to you," he said, exaggerating his brogue. His name was Aiden O'Connell, and he was the younger son of the Earl of Rathkeale, an ancient Irish family long infamous for their enthusiastic cooperation with the invading English. Kat still found it difficult to believe that this man—young, handsome, rich—had chosen to risk everything by quietly working for Irish independence. Like Kat before him, he had decided that one of the best ways to help the Irish and weaken the English was to assist their enemies, the French.

He tipped his hat, a lazy smile deepening the two improbable dimples in his lean cheeks. "Is it too much to be hoping that you've had a change of heart and are willing to work with us again?"

"You know me better than that," she said as they turned to walk along the banks of the pond, the mist wafting cold and damp against their faces.

"Ah, so I feared," he said with a mournful sigh. "Then why, pray tell, are we braving one of the coldest September mornings I can remember to meet?"

"Because Russell Yates is about to hang for a murder he didn't commit, and more people are dying every day."

When the man beside her remained silent, she said, "You know about the French Blue?"

He squinted at the ghostly shapes of the chestnut trees on the far side of the pond. "I do, yes."

"I need to find out who Napoléon has tasked with its recovery."

"That I don't know."

She swung to face him, the heavy woolen skirts of her carriage dress swirling around their ankles. "Don't know—or won't tell?"

A soft light of amusement gleamed in the depths of his hooded green eyes. "Don't know . . . but wouldn't tell if I did."

"Then at least tell me this: Is he English?"

"In truth, I don't know. It may even be a woman, for all I've been told. But I do know this: Napoléon is not happy with his agent's performance. He's dispatched someone else—someone from Paris—to assist in the gem's recovery. Someone who's said to be quick and clever and very dangerous."

"A man with a pockmarked face?"

"I don't know; I haven't seen him."

"I have. He tried to kidnap me from Covent Garden Market."

O'Connell's lips tightened into a thin line. "I heard about that."

"From your French masters?"

His nostrils flared, his head rearing back. "*Bloody hell.* Is that what you think? That I had a hand in that?"

"What else am I to think?"

"I heard about what happened the same way everyone else in London heard of it—it's all over town! Besides which, why the devil would Napoléon's agents want to get their hands on you anyway?"

"It makes sense if they think Yates killed Eisler and took the French Blue. Steal Yates's wife, and offer to make a trade."

O'Connell was silent.

"Well, doesn't it?" she said.

The Irishman drew in a long, ragged breath. "I suppose it's possible. But if it is true, I know nothing about it." He reached to gently touch the back of one hand ever so briefly to her cheek. "And remember this: The French are no more my masters than they were yours. I work with them—not for them."

She searched his deceptively open, handsome face. But he was a man who, like Kat herself, played a dangerous game and had learned long ago to give nothing away. She said, "Is there anything you can tell me that I might be able to use?"

O'Connell shook his head. "Only this: I don't envy whoever has been set to this task. The potential rewards are undoubtedly great. But should they fail to recover the diamond, Napoléon is bound to suspect he's been betrayed—that his agents have simply decided to keep the gem for themselves."

"In other words, if they fail, they'll be killed," said Kat.

"More than likely, yes. And they know it. Which means that whoever you're dealing with is doubly dangerous, because their very survival depends on the successful completion of their mission. Get in their way, and you're liable to end up dead."

He hesitated a moment, then added, "You might consider giving the same warning to Lord Devlin."

Chapter 48

This was the part of a murder investigation that Sebastian always dreaded, when the bodies of witnesses and potential suspects started piling up, and for every question answered, two more arose. With a growing sense of urgency, he left St. James's Street and headed toward Tower Hill.

The rain might have ended, but the wind blowing off the river was bitter cold and felt more like December than the end of September. He found the surgeon whistling an old Irish drinking ditty as he bent over the granite slab in the center of his small outbuilding. Naked and half-eviscerated, the shrunken corpse of Jud Foy looked faintly blue in the thin morning light.

"Ah, there you are," said Gibson, looking up. He set aside his scalpel with a clatter and reached for a rag to wipe his gory hands. "Thought I might be seeing you, then."

Sebastian nodded to the cadaver's ruined head. "I take it that's what killed him?"

"It did, indeed. Most effectively."

"What can you tell me about it?"

"Well . . . The blow appears to have come from his left, which would be consistent with an attacker who is right-handed."

"Unless he was struck from behind."

Gibson shook his head. "Judging from the angle, I'd say he was facing his killer."

Sebastian hunkered down to study the pulpy mess. "Any idea what he was hit with?"

"Something long and heavy, and wielded with powerful force. I'd say whoever hit him was aiming to kill, not incapacitate."

"Seems a curious choice of weapon. I mean, why bludgeon him? Much easier—and surer—to simply stick a knife between his ribs."

"The bludgeon is a common weapon amongst footpads."

"There is that. The intent could have been to make it look as if he'd been set upon by common thieves."

Gibson tossed his rag onto a nearby shelf. "You do know this wasn't the first time someone tried to cave in his head, don't you? From what I can see, it's a miracle the man was alive."

Sebastian straightened. "I heard he was kicked in the head by a mule in Spain."

"A mule?" Gibson shook his head. "That was no mule."

"Oh?"

"I've seen men kicked in the head by mules, and I've seen what a rifle butt can do to a human skull when swung with a measure of force and skill."

Sebastian nodded to the gaping wound. "Could this have been done by a rifle butt?"

"No. More likely a length of lead pipe."

"Lovely." He went to stand in the open doorway and draw the cold, damp air into his lungs.

"I heard some interesting talk down at the pub a while ago when I popped in for a bite to eat," said Gibson, limping over to join him. "They're saying the authorities have decided to set Russell Yates free."

Sebastian stared at him. *"What?"*

"Mmm. Something about a pouch of Eisler's jewels found on our friend here. They're saying it's more than likely that he's the killer."

"But . . . I don't think he is."

Gibson studied Sebastian's face through narrowed eyes. "And here I was thinking you'd be over the moon, hearing that Yates might be freed."

Sebastian shook his head. He was remembering what Kat had told him, about the visit Jarvis had paid to Yates's cell that first night—and the worry in her eyes when she said it. "Nothing about Yates's incarceration has felt right from the very beginning," he said. "Somehow this just seems all a piece with the rest of it."

"Could be just a rumor."

Sebastian pushed away from the doorframe. "Only one sure way to find out."

❧

A supercilious clerk at the Lambeth Street Public Office informed Sebastian that Fridays were not one of Bertram Leigh-Jones's days of attendance.

"He attends Tuesdays, Wednesdays, Thursdays, and Saturdays," said the clerk, casting a sour glance toward the rear of the hall, where a blowsy doxy in a tattered purple satin gown and improbably red hair was haranguing a constable in a high-pitched cockney whine.

"*I didn't do nothin' o' the sort,*" she screeched. "*I'm a good girl, I am.*"

Sebastian kept his gaze on the clerk's thin, bony face. "So you're saying he was not in attendance last Monday?"

"He was not."

"Then how did he come to be involved in the committal of Russell Yates?"

"As it happens, Mr. Leigh-Jones was in the vicinity of Fountain Lane when the hue and cry was raised. As such, he took charge of the pursuit and capture of the suspect and the interrogation of the witnesses before formally committing the villain to Newgate. He was here until dawn."

"Commendable."

The clerk sniffed. He appeared to be in his late thirties or early forties, with greasy dark hair plastered to a prominent skull and a nose to rival that of Wellington himself. "Mr. Leigh-Jones is a most conscientious magistrate."

"And where might I find him?"

From the depths of the hall came the doxy's loud, strident complaint: *"I tell ye, I never! 'Tis nothin' but a Banbury Tale, the lot o' it!"*

The clerk was forced to raise his own voice to compete. "Mr. Leigh-Jones does not like to be disturbed on his off days. You may come back on Saturday, if you wish. We open at eleven."

"I'm afraid this won't wait."

The clerk went back to writing in his ledger. "Unfortunate, under the circumstances. You could see Mr. Dixon, the magistrate currently in attendance. Or you can return on Saturday. The choice is yours."

"And here I thought you just said Mr. Leigh-Jones was a most conscientious magistrate. I don't think you'll find him inclined to reward you for your zeal in protecting him from the Palace."

"The Palace?" The clerk looked up, a wave of conflicting emotions passing over his face, doubt followed by indecision chased by annoyance and chagrin.

Sebastian started to push away from the desk. "I'll tell His Highness—"

"No! One moment, please."

Sebastian paused.

The clerk threw a quick look around, then leaned forward to lick his thin lips and whisper, "His house is in the Crescent, off the Minories. Number four."

"Thank you," said Sebastian, just as the doxy let out a high-pitched, ear-shattering squeal.

"Oooo. Say that again, ye whore's son, an' I'll scratch yer bloomin' eyes from yer 'ead and feed 'em to the bleedin' chooks!"

※

Bertram Leigh-Jones lived in a comfortable eighteenth-century town house built of good sturdy brown brick with white-painted window frames and a shiny green door. Sebastian half expected the magistrate to refuse to see him. But a few minutes after he sent up his card with the thin, mousy-haired young housemaid who'd answered his knock, she reappeared to say meekly, "This way, my lord."

He found Leigh-Jones in a small chamber overlooking the Crescent. The room had been fitted up as a work-space, with a large, sturdy table in the center and an array of shelves piled high with a jumble of paints, pots, tools, and bins filled with pieces of fine wood; the air was thick with the smell of linseed oil and a pot of hot hide glue. The magistrate himself sat perched on a high stool, a pair of spectacles on the end of his nose as he focused on fitting a minute piece of rigging to a partially con-structed model of a Spanish galleon.

He cast a quick glance at Sebastian before returning his gaze to the model. "You have some nerve, coming here," he said, his big, blunt figures surprisingly nimble at their task.

"I'm told you believe the pouch of diamonds found on Jud Foy's body came from Daniel Eisler."

"Oh? Who told you that?"

"Is it true?"

"As it happens, it is, yes."

"How can you be so certain?"

"The initials, of course. You did notice them, didn't you? Not only that, but a woman at the greengrocer's on the corner remembers seeing Foy watching Eisler's house." Leigh-Jones sighed and straightened, his hands coming to rest at the edge of his worktable. "One would think you'd be pleased to hear that evidence has come to light suggesting your friend Yates is not, in fact, the mur-derer of Mr. Eisler."

"You're saying that Jud Foy is?"

"Was," corrected Leigh-Jones, pushing to his feet to

putter around to the other side of his worktable. "In Foy's case, the verb is most definitely 'was.'"

"You'll be releasing Yates?"

The magistrate's focus was all for his model. "I believe so, yes. We're simply waiting on a few more pieces of information."

"Such as?"

Leigh-Jones looked at him over the rims of his glasses. "You can read about it in the papers along with everyone else."

"So who are you suggesting killed Foy?"

"Footpads, most likely. Fortunately, the sexton frightened them off before they were able to relieve the scoundrel of his ill-gotten gains."

"And Collot? Who killed him?"

"Who?"

"Jacques Collot. He was shot by a rifleman near Seven Dials last night."

"Ah, you mean the French thief. What has he to do with anything?"

"Quite a lot, actually."

"I rather think not." The magistrate's protruding belly shook with his breathy laughter, although Sebastian could see little real humor in the man's face. "I've no doubt it's a blow to your pride, having some common East End magistrate solve a murder that stumped you. But if it's any consolation, I myself was wrong about Yates, now, wasn't I? The important thing is that Eisler's murder has been solved, the man responsible is dead, and the good people of London can go to sleep in their beds at night without needing to worry there's some madman wandering in their midst."

Sebastian studied Leigh-Jones's fleshy, florid face: the watery, blinking hazel eyes; the small mouth pulled back into a self-satisfied grin. He'd learned long ago that for far too many people, it wasn't really important that justice be done. Unless they were personally involved in some way, most cared little if an innocent man was hanged. What mattered was that those in authority be seen as having successfully fulfilled their duty to keep the people safe from fear or any perceived threat that might disrupt the tranquility of their lives. In that sense, Jud Foy dead was far more useful than Jud Foy alive. Dead men told no tales and answered no questions.

Sebastian said, "And if Foy wasn't actually responsible?"

The magistrate's cheeks darkened suddenly to an angry hue as he punched the air between them with one glue-smudged finger. He was no longer smiling. "No one will thank you for that kind of talk. You hear me? No one."

"I'm afraid I can't agree that should be a factor here," said Sebastian, and left him there with his bits of wood and hemp and his pot of simmering glue.

Chapter 49

*S*ebastian was crossing Pall Mall, headed toward Carlton House, when he heard himself hailed by Mr. Thomas Hope.

"My lord," said Hope, panting slightly from the unaccustomed exertion of hurrying up the street. "This is fortuitous indeed. If I might have a word with you for a moment?"

"Of course," said Sebastian, moderating his pace to the other man's slower gait. "Is something wrong?"

The banker's mouth worked furiously back and forth. "You've heard, I assume, that Yates is to be released from prison?"

"I had heard, yes. Do I take it you find that troubling?"

"What? Oh, no. It's not Yates's release that worries me, per se. It's what we're hearing about the death of this fellow Jud Foy. All these deaths associated with the diamond! It's as if it's cursed or something. First King Louis and Marie Antoinette, then the Duke of Brunswick. And now Eisler and Foy and that French thief whose name for the moment escapes me. To be frank, I'm worried about Louisa."

Sebastian studied the banker's homely, haggard face. He wondered if Hope realized he'd just admitted to knowing the true origins of his rare blue diamond. "You don't still have the diamond, do you?"

"No. But then, neither did the King and Queen of France when they lost their heads. Or Brunswick when he was killed in battle. Or—"

"People die all the time. I've no doubt if you knew the entire history of any large gem, you'd find many people associated with it who died violently. Apart from which, I don't believe Jud Foy actually had anything to do with the diamond."

"You don't? But . . . They're saying he's the one who killed Eisler! Are you suggesting you now believe *Yates*—"

"No. To be frank, I still don't know who killed Eisler. Or why."

Hope sank his upper teeth into his lip and worried it back and forth, as if summoning the courage to speak. "I fear I've not been entirely honest with you."

"Oh?"

"I told you I didn't know if Eisler had a buyer interested in my diamond. That was not strictly true."

Sebastian waited.

Hope sucked in a deep breath, then blurted out, "Prinny. Prinny was interested. Most definitely interested."

Sebastian said, "I had rather suspected that."

"You did?"

"I don't imagine there can be many potential buyers for a stone of that caliber."

"True, true. But there is one thing you may not know: The Prince's representative was scheduled to meet with Eisler in Fountain Lane the very night he was killed."

"Do you know the identity of that individual?"

Hope shook his head. "Unfortunately, no. But I should think it would not be all that difficult to discover. I believe Lord Jarvis was also involved in the negotiations."

"*Jarvis?*"

Hope blinked rapidly several times, so that Sebastian wondered what the man saw in his face. "Yes, my lord."

⁂

Sebastian's history with his father-in-law was defined by a level of antagonism that had included—but was not limited to—physical assault, larceny, attempted murder, and a certain memorable kidnapping incident.

In one sense, Sebastian could not help but admire the big man's dedication to the preservation of England and her monarchy. But he had no illusions about the level of Jarvis's ruthlessness. The King's powerful cousin could have taught Machiavelli a thing or two about duplicity, cunning, and the unswerving elevation of expediency over such maudlin notions as sentiment, principle, and morality.

To Sebastian's knowledge, Jarvis possessed only one humanizing trait, and that was his affection for his sole surviving child, Hero. The man despised his aged, grasping mother and his two foolish sisters and would probably have consigned his addlebrained wife to Bedlam had it not been for Hero.

But when Sebastian reached Carlton House, it was to discover that Lord Jarvis was not there.

Swearing softly to himself, Sebastian turned toward his father-in-law's Berkeley Square town house.

His peal at the door was answered by a trim, wooden-faced butler named Grisham whom Sebastian suspected had not yet forgiven him for a certain incident a few weeks before, when Sebastian had hauled a dead body up the curving staircase to dump it on Lord Jarvis's drawing room carpet.

"My lord," said Grisham, his professional mask firmly in place. "I am afraid Lady Devlin is no longer here, having left shortly after her conversation with his lordship this morning."

"Actually, it's Lord Jarvis I was interested in seeing."

A breath of wariness clouded the butler's normally impassive features. "Unfortunately, his lordship is unavailable at the moment, as he has retired to his dressing room in preparation for an important audience with—"

"That's quite all right," said Sebastian, brushing past the butler and heading for the stairs. "I won't be but a moment."

There was a time when such an intrusion would have motivated Grisham to call the constables. Now he had to content himself with closing the front door with unusual force.

Sebastian took the stairs two at a time and entered the dressing room without knocking.

Jarvis was standing before his dressing table, his back to the door. Pausing in the act of fastening his cuffs, he looked up, his gaze meeting Sebastian's in the mirror. He calmly straightened his cuffs and glanced over at his valet.

"Leave us."

The man bowed and carefully laid the neckcloths he'd been holding over the nearby daybed. "Yes, my lord."

Jarvis waited until the man had closed the door. Then he turned to select one of the cravats. "Well?"

"The Prince's representative who was to meet with Eisler the night he was killed—who was it?"

Jarvis carefully eased the length of starched linen around his neck. "Heard about that, did you?"

"Yes."

"To be frank, I'm somewhat surprised you didn't make this discovery days ago."

Sebastian gave his father-in-law a hard, gritty smile. "His name?"

"The gentleman's identity is immaterial—an amateur although highly knowledgeable lapidary who had agreed to inspect the gem prior to its formal presentation to the Prince by Eisler at the Palace."

"Which was scheduled for when?"

"Tuesday."

"When one is dealing with murder, no potential witness—or suspect—is 'immaterial.'"

Jarvis smoothed the folds of his cravat, his gaze on his reflection in the mirror. "The gentleman in question arrived at the scene nearly an hour after the shooting occurred and, upon observing the commotion, quietly left. He declined to step forward because he has no information of merit to add and because it is of the utmost importance that the Prince not be seen to be involved in anything of this nature."

"And does the Prince know, I wonder, that the gem in question was once the French Blue?"

"As it happens, he does. Indeed, the item he ordered designed for it was to be an emblem of the Golden Fleece."

"But he isn't a member of any of the Orders of the Golden Fleece."

"He is confident that he soon shall be." Jarvis turned from the mirror. "I fail to understand your continuing interest in this affair. The authorities have determined some deranged ex-soldier murdered Daniel Eisler. I understand he was seen actually watching the house."

"Jud Foy was watching the house, yes. But I don't think he killed Eisler."

A faint smile curled Jarvis's full lips. "So certain?"

Sebastian studied the big man's half-averted profile. He could not shake the suspicion that behind this subtle play and counterplay of arrest, imminent hanging, and sudden release lurked Jarvis's long vendetta against Russell Yates and Kat Boleyn. He said, "And does the Prince know that the diamond he covets was once in the possession of his own wife?"

"That he does not know."

"Yet you do?"

Jarvis turned, his face set in bland lines. "Seventeen years ago, His Royal Highness took an unfortunate, instant dislike to his bride. That dislike has since solidified into an aversion—"

"Actually, I think I'd be more inclined to call it an irrational but powerful loathing colored by a petty lust for revenge."

"—and a determination," continued Jarvis, ignoring

the interjection, "to be rid of his wife. Such a step would, however, be disastrous for the stability of the realm and the future of the monarchy."

"Hence the need to conceal from the Prince the entire history of the stone?" said Sebastian. "If my memory serves me correctly, the Prince Regent was named executor of Brunswick's estate, which means that Princess Caroline technically should have handed over to her husband's keeping any of the old Duke's jewels in her possession. Obviously she did not do so."

"Caroline may be stupid, but she's not that stupid," said Jarvis. "Fortunately, she at least stopped short of publicly accusing Prinny of playing fast and loose with her father's estate."

"Unlike her brother, the current Duke."

"Just so."

Sebastian said, "I think Daniel Eisler knew the circuitous route the stone had taken to come into Hope's possession and was using that knowledge to apply pressure on the Princess in order to obtain something from her that he wanted. You wouldn't happen to know what that was, would you?"

"No."

Sebastian studied the big man's complacent, aquiline countenance. "I don't believe you."

Jarvis possessed a startlingly winsome smile he could use with devastating effect to charm and cajole the unwary and the credulous. He flashed that smile now, a sparkle of genuine amusement lighting his steel gray eyes. "Would I lie to you?"

"Yes."

The sound of Jarvis's laughter followed Sebastian down the stairs and out of the house.

Chapter 50

"*I* don't know how I can ever properly thank you," said Yates.

The two men were walking along the Serpentine in Hyde Park, the evening sun glittering on the breeze-ruffled expanse of water, the long grass and frost-nipped leaves of the nearby stand of oaks and walnuts drenched with a rich golden light. Sebastian noticed Yates kept lifting his face to the setting sun and breathing deeply of the crisp fresh air, as if savoring every subtle nuance of his new freedom.

Sebastian said, "You actually don't have much to thank me for, as it turns out. I had nothing to do with the authorities' decision to set you free. That was all Jud Foy's doing—however inadvertent that may have been."

"They're saying he killed Daniel Eisler."

"It's always possible."

Yates glanced over at him. "But you don't believe it?"

"No, I don't."

"So how do you explain the pouch of diamonds they're saying was found in his possession?"

"Easy enough to plant evidence on a man's dead body, thus casting suspicion in his direction. He's not exactly able to defend himself against the accusation, now, is he?"

"No. But . . . why bother? The authorities were already convinced they had the killer—me—in custody."

"You don't find his death rather convenient, given the timing of the decision to set you free?"

Yates glanced over at him, a troubled expression drawing his brows together. "And will you still continue looking for the killer?"

Sebastian paused to watch a duck lift off the surface of the canal, wings beating the soft evening air, its quack echoing across the water. After a moment, he said, "I wish I could believe it's all over. But I don't."

Yates drew up beside him, his gaze, like Sebastian's, on the duck's awkward flight. He said, "Kat doesn't trust Jarvis."

Sebastian shook his head and blew out a long, heavy breath. "Neither do I."

❧

Sebastian was walking up Brook Street when he noticed a tall, dark-haired man striding toward him with the long-legged gait of a soldier who has covered many, many miles.

One hand in his coat pocket, Sebastian paused and let Jamie Knox come up to him.

"Looking for me?" Sebastian asked quietly.

Knox drew up, his yellow eyes narrowed to thin slits, his jaw set hard. "Jud Foy is dead."

"I know."

"Did you kill him?"

"I did not."

Knox chewed the inside of one cheek. "I'm thinking he's dead because I told you where to find him."

"I don't think so. But I could be wrong."

Knox nodded. "You remember when you promised that if you ever discovered I shot that French lieutenant, you'd see me hang?"

"Yes."

"So you'll understand when I say that if I find out you did kill Foy, you're a dead man."

Knox started to turn away.

Sebastian said, "I didn't realize Foy was a friend of yours."

Knox paused to look back at him. "He wasn't. Bloody hell, the man was crazy."

Sebastian started to laugh. And after a moment, Knox joined him.

❧

Sebastian walked into the house, poured himself a glass of burgundy, and went to stand staring thoughtfully out the dining room window at the black cat, who was lying on the top step of the terrace, fastidiously engaged in the never-ending task of bathing its long, silky fur. An idea was forming in his mind, a suspicion borne of a series of subtle inconsistencies and improbabilities almost too amorphous to name.

He drained his wine and sent for Jules Calhoun.

"What can you tell me about Bertram Leigh-Jones?" he asked when the valet appeared.

The valet looked vaguely surprised. "You mean the chief magistrate at Lambeth Street Public Office?"

"I do, yes."

Calhoun opened his eyes wide and blew out a long breath. "Well, he's a piece of work, no doubt about that."

"Meaning?"

"He runs that district like it's his own private fiefdom. Makes the publicans give him a cut if they want to be certain he'll renew their licenses. And I suspect his handling of the vestry's poor fund wouldn't bear too close an inspection either."

"In other words, he's not exactly what one might call an honest man."

"Actually, I'd say he's fairly typical of East End magistrates."

"Someone from Lambeth Street seems suddenly to have been moved to interview the woman at the greengrocer's on the corner of Fountain Lane. I'd be interested to know when that conversation took place."

"I'll see what I can discover, my lord."

Sebastian nodded. "Just be careful. This is a magistrate who thinks hanging half a dozen men before breakfast is good sport."

Chapter 51

That night, as Kat prepared to leave for the theater, a heavy fog rolled up from the river, swallowing the city in a thick white mist.

She was in the hall, easing the hood of her cloak up over her hair, when Yates appeared in the doorway from the library, a glass of brandy held in one hand. He'd been drinking steadily since his release from Newgate, although Kat couldn't say she blamed him.

"I think perhaps it would be best if I were to ride with you in the carriage tonight," he said.

"Good heavens, why?"

He met her gaze and held it. "You know why."

She gave a soft laugh that sounded forced even to her own ears. "I've never heard of anyone holding up a carriage on the streets of London, if that's what concerns you."

"There's always a first time."

"If it comes to that, I've a footman and a coachman to protect me."

He drained his glass and set it aside. "Humor me?"

She smiled, a genuine smile this time. "All right."

They drove through streets shrouded in white and unusually light in traffic. Yates said, "Devlin tells me he intends to continue his pursuit of Eisler's killer."

"Does that surprise you?"

"In a way it does, yes. Eisler was a vile excuse for a human being. What does it matter who killed him? The world is well rid of him."

"Perhaps. Yet more people are now dying."

"An aging Parisian jewel thief and a half-mad ex-soldier?"

"Do you consider the world well rid of them too? I suspect there are many who would say the same of a Covent Garden actress—or an ex-pirate with a tendency to frequent the city's most notorious molly houses."

His lips quirked into a crooked smile. "I suppose you do have a point. Still—" He broke off, sitting forward suddenly.

They were rounding the long, sweeping curve from Oxford Street to Broad. The fog was thicker here nearer the river, the dark trees and squat bell tower of St. Giles looming ghostlike out of the mist.

"What is it?" she asked, just as a team of black horses erupted from a narrow lane to their left, eyes wild, hooves flashing, nostrils flaring wide in the cold night. In the horses' wake, a heavy, old-fashioned traveling coach careened from side to side, its coachman driving straight toward Kat's delicate town carriage.

"What the hell?" swore Yates as their own coachman shouted in alarm. Horses squealed, the carriage lurching sharply as their driver hauled his team hard to the right. Kat had a tilted vision of tumbled gray tombstones and the rusty spikes topping the churchyard wall.

The carriage shuddered to a standstill.

"Are you all right?" asked Yates.

"Yes. But—"

The coachman's startled cry cut through the night, followed by an ugly thump.

She said in a low, urgent voice, "Yates," just as a man dressed in footmen's livery and a powdered wig jerked open the carriage door, a blunderbuss pistol in one hand.

"What the devil?" thundered Yates.

The man grabbed Kat's wrist and hauled her forward.

"If you're smart, you'll stay out of this," he warned Yates in an unexpectedly cultured voice.

"This is madness," said Kat, falling heavily against him as he dragged her through the doorway to the pavement. The air was cold and damp against her face, the churchyard's earthy scent of decay thick in her nostrils. "We have nothing of value for you to steal!"

He pressed the cold steel of his pistol's muzzle against her temple and gave her a tight smile. "There's only one thing I need from you."

Panic thundered her heart, caught her breath in her tight throat as she heard the soft *snick* of the pistol's hammer being pulled back. She lunged wildly against the hand on her arm, but his grip tightened cruelly, holding her fast.

She saw Yates rear up in the open carriage doorway, a small pistol in one hand. The night filled with the roar of flames and the acrid stench of burnt powder, and the chest of the man holding her dissolved in a warm, wet spray of blood.

He went down, hard.

"Mason!" shouted a second assailant, who'd been holding a gun to the head of Kat's own wide-eyed footman.

"Yates! Look out!" cried Kat as the second assailant turned, leveled his double-barreled pistol on Yates, and fired.

"Yates!" she screamed.

Yates tumbled face-first to the pavement.

Arm outstretched, the assailant calmly cocked his pistol's second barrel and turned the muzzle toward Kat.

Kat froze.

"No! Leave her," shouted the heavy coach's tall, dark-caped driver. "That's Russell Yates you've just killed, you fool. You know our orders. Grab Mason and let's get out of here."

"Yates?" Kat went to crouch beside him. She was only dimly aware of the dark coachman whipping his horses, the old coach pulling away.

"Oh, *Yates*," she whispered, and gathered his bloody, broken body into her trembling arms.

❧

An hour later, Kat was crossing the entry hall of her Cavendish Square house when a preemptory peal sounded at the front door.

She was expecting Paul Gibson, for she'd asked the surgeon to come examine her injured coachman. Instead, her butler opened the door to Charles, Lord Jarvis.

She froze, one hand on the newel post, her husband's blood still soaking the bodice and skirt of her silk evening gown.

Jarvis carefully removed his mist-dampened hat, a faint smile touching his lips as he met her furious gaze. "I believe we need to talk. Don't you agree?"

Chapter 52

*T*hat evening, Hero attended a concert with her mother while Sebastian settled in the library with a glass of brandy and the English translation of *The Key of Solomon.* He was still at it some hours later when Jules Calhoun returned from St. Botolph-Aldgate.

"Discover anything?" Sebastian asked, thankfully setting aside the ancient grimoire.

"I did, actually," said Calhoun. "It seems that in the immediate aftermath of the murder, Lambeth Street showed little interest in interviewing the residents of the area."

"When Yates was in custody."

"Yes. But constables began canvassing the neighborhood on Wednesday, asking all sorts of questions."

"Interesting, given that Leigh-Jones was at the time still confidently insisting on Yates's guilt."

"Indeed, my lord. Yet it was Mr. Leigh-Jones himself who spoke to the corner greengrocer yesterday morning."

"Not today?"

"No, my lord. Definitely yesterday."

"So *before* Foy's death. I wonder what—"

"Gov'nor!"

Sebastian broke off as Tom's voice echoed through the house. They could hear the boy's footsteps pounding across the entry's marble floor. "Gov'nor!" The tiger burst into the room, eyes wide, chest heaving, mouth agape as he sucked in air.

"Well, what is it?" asked Sebastian.

"It's Russell Yates! 'E's *dead*."

❧

The ex-pirate lay beneath a sheet on a bed in his Cavendish Square house, his dark, too-long hair a stark contrast to the white linen pillow cover, his hands folded at his chest, his eyes closed, his features so serene that he might have been sleeping. But Sebastian knew death when he saw it.

Kat knelt beside the bed, her head bowed in prayer, the beads of a rosary slipping through her fingers. Sebastian paused in the doorway, aware of a flicker of surprise. He'd always known Kat was raised Catholic, but somehow he'd assumed she no longer practiced her faith. In that, he realized, he had erred.

She looked up then, made the sign of the cross, and rose to her feet.

He went to enfold her in his arms, and she came to him without hesitation and trembling with need. Her cheeks were stained with tears, and as she rested her head on his shoulder, a faint sob racked her body. For one long, suspended moment, he simply held her. Then she drew back, putting space between them.

He said, "Tell me what happened."

She swiped a palm across one wet cheek. "We were on our way to the theater. Yates had insisted on riding with me. He never does that, but he was worried because of the attack in the market. We were just making the curve near St. Giles when an old traveling coach came charging out of an alley and forced my own carriage into the churchyard wall. There were two men dressed in livery, as well as the driver. But I could tell by their voices that none of them were what they seemed. The driver struck my coachman with a long staff, knocking him from the seat. Gibson says he's concussed, but he should be all right."

Sebastian knew a deep sense of disquiet. While some of the heaths surrounding the city could still be dangerous, it was unheard of for a carriage to be held up on the streets of London itself.

She drew a shaky breath. "One of the men dragged me out of the carriage. He was going to kill me. Only, Yates shot him. And so . . ." Her voice cracked. She swallowed, but it was still a moment before she could continue. "And so one of the other men killed him. And then . . . It was the strangest thing. Once Yates was dead, they let me go and drove away."

"You think they were the same men who attacked you in Covent Garden Market?"

She shook her head. "No. These men might have been dressed as servants, but their voices were educated." Her jaw hardened, her nostrils flaring with a quickly indrawn breath. "I think they were Jarvis's men."

"You recognized them?"

"No. But he came to see me. Here. Tonight."

"Jarvis came here?"

She nodded. "Less than two hours after Yates was killed. He wanted to make certain that I had a perfect understanding of the situation that now exists between us."

"Namely?"

"I keep his secret, I keep my life. I choose to destroy him . . . I destroy myself."

Sebastian searched her strained face, noting the new lines of anger and determination that bracketed her mouth. He had never discovered the nature of the documents Yates held, but there was no doubt in his mind that they were powerful indeed.

He said, "Did Jarvis tell you he was behind tonight's attack?"

"No. But what other explanation is there? Those men made it obvious their purpose was to kill me. Not Yates. Me. But once they'd shot Yates, they let me live. 'You know our orders,' I heard one of them say. I think Jarvis gave strict instructions that they were to kill either me or Yates—but not both of us."

"If the French are still convinced that Yates killed Eisler and stole the blue diamond, they would be very careful not to kill the only two people who might know the current location of the stone."

"True. But then, why not kidnap me, the way the men at Covent Garden sought to do? Why not take me, force me to hand over the diamond, and then kill me?"

He studied her pale, beautiful face. "I don't know. Have you managed to learn anything about the agent tasked by Napoléon to recover the French Blue?"

She shook her head. "My friend claims not to have been told. From what he said, I suspect the individual involved is English, although a second person was recently dispatched from Paris to assist him."

"Him?"

"Or her. My contact did not specify which."

She fell silent, her gaze drifting back to Yates's pallid face.

Sebastian reached out to take her hand in his. "I'm so sorry, Kat," he said. "I know how much Yates had come to mean to you."

She drew in a deep breath that shuddered her chest. "In the past, I never allowed myself to be frightened. But . . . I'm frightened now."

He tightened his grip on her hand. "I will always stand your friend, Kat. Always. No matter what happens."

Her gaze met his. "Will you, Sebastian? And if Jarvis was behind this?"

"I told Jarvis a year ago that if he harms a hair on your head, I'll kill him. That hasn't changed."

"And what will it do to your marriage, do you think, if you kill your wife's father?"

He said nothing, but there was no need. For they both knew the answer to her question.

Chapter 53

Charles, Lord Jarvis, was with the Regent in a gaming hell near Portland Place, his bored gaze fixed on a spinning roulette wheel, when Sebastian walked up to him and leaned in close to say, "I understand you made a visit to Cavendish Square this evening."

Jarvis shifted his gaze to the Prince. "You refer, I take it, to my condolence call on Yates's devastated young widow?"

"A condolence call? Is that how you would describe it?"

"You would describe it differently?"

Sebastian studied the big man's full, arrogant face. "A year ago, I warned you that if you made a move to harm Kat Boleyn, I would kill you. Understand this: My marriage to your daughter changes nothing. If I discover that you were behind tonight's attack, you're a dead man."

Jarvis turned to look directly at him, the gray eyes that were so much like his daughter's narrowed and hard. "Likewise, I presume you understand that your marriage to Hero in no way protects you. You interfere in any way with what I deem necessary for the preservation and prosperity of the realm, and I will eliminate you. Without hesitation or regret."

The two men's gazes met, clashed.

Sebastian gave a slow, measured bow and walked away.

❧

Hero returned to Brook Street to find Devlin sprawled in a worn leather armchair beside the library fire, his gaze on the glowing embers, the black cat stretched out on the hearthrug beside him.

He looked up when she paused in the doorway. A nearby brace of candles cast a harsh pattern of light and shadow across his lean features. "Have you seen your father?" he asked.

"No; why? Have you two been at swords and daggers again?"

"Something like that."

She went to rest one hand on his shoulder in an awkward gesture of comfort. "I heard about Yates. I'm sorry; I know you liked him."

He covered her hand with his own. "He was an interesting man. I'd like to have known him better. And now . . . he's dead."

"Kat Boleyn was unharmed in the attack?"

"Yes."

"Thank goodness for that, at least." She hesitated. "Surely you don't think Jarvis had something to do with what happened tonight?"

"Honestly?" His head fell back, his gaze meeting hers. "I don't know."

She could feel the anger and determination that twanged through him. And she knew the heartache and deep disquiet of a woman who loved two men — a father and a husband — who hated each other.

She said, her voice quiet but steady, "He's my father, Devlin. I cherish no illusions as to what manner of man he is. But I still love him dearly."

"I know."

"And it doesn't make any difference, does it?"

"It does. But . . ."

"But not enough." She moved to scoop up the black cat and cradle him against her for a long, silent moment.

Then she looked up. "I'm going to bed. Are you coming?"

A soft whisper of ash falling on the grate filled the sudden hush in the room.

He said, "Do you want me?"

"Yes."

※

Their lovemaking that night had an edge to it, a raw desperation that hadn't been there before.

Neither spoke again of that day's events, or of the shadow it had cast between them. But the awareness of it was there, as was the knowledge that the woman to whom Sebastian had lost his heart so long ago was now free.

※

Saturday, 26 September

Sebastian's dreams took him many places. To a wild, windswept Cornish hillside overlooking a rocky cove; to hot, fever-racked nights beneath a West Indian sky aglitter with a universe of unfamiliar stars; to a dry, sun-blasted land of smoke-blackened walls and vacant-eyed women and the desiccated, bleached bones of long-dead men.

But that night, Sebastian dreamed of demure ladies in gowns of heavy velvet and brocade, their wimples white in the spring sunshine. He wandered crushed-gravel paths shaded by leafy chestnut trees; breathed in the scents of lavender and apothecary roses, vervain and lemon balm. Climbing the steps to a broad, freshly swept terrace, he entered a graceful sandstone house, its leaded windows unshrouded by ivy or cobwebs or the grime of ages.

The flagstones beneath his feet were well scrubbed and unbroken, the newly whitewashed walls hung with rich tapestries and crossed swords. As he moved down the passage, he heard the distant lilting notes of a pipe, a child's laughter, a man's chanting voice suddenly hushed. And he awoke with a start, legs swinging over the edge of the bed as he sat up, the icy air of the pale morning biting his naked flesh.

"What's wrong?" asked Hero sleepily, rolling over to lay a hand on his arm.

"There's something about Eisler's house that has been bothering me for days now."

She sat up, her dark hair tumbling about her bare shoulders as she hugged the quilt to her against the cold. "What about the house?"

He pushed to his feet. "Something in the proportions of the rooms is off. I can't quite put my finger on it. But I want to take another look at it." He glanced back at her. "Care to come?"

"Do you think Perlman will agree to let us search the house again?"

Sebastian smiled. "I don't intend to ask him."

※

The door to the crumbling old Tudor house in Fountain Lane was opened by a sour-faced woman in black bombazine and a yellowing cap. She was as stout as her husband was lean and a good fifteen to twenty years younger, with thick, bushy gray brows, a bulbous nose, and small dark eyes half-hidden by fat, puffy lids.

"Good morning," Sebastian said cheerfully. "I'm—"

"I know who you are." She sniffed. "Campbell's off to market this morning—thanks be to God. Ever since you come here the other day, he's done nothing but crow about how he 'helped' the great Lord Devlin with one of his 'investigations.' *Humph.*"

Sebastian and Hero exchanged glances.

Hero said, "We're here to look at the house again," and brushed past the housekeeper without giving her a chance to object. Just inside the entrance, Hero drew up in undisguised astonishment. "Good heavens."

"Sure, then, the place ain't as clean and tidy as it could be," bleated Mrs. Campbell, her manner changing instantly from challenging to wheedling. "But then, Mr. Eisler was ever so particular about his things, preferring to see them disappear beneath dust and cobwebs rather than have me lay a hand on them."

"And did he take the same attitude toward the floor?" asked Hero, her gaze focused on the ancient flagstones half-buried beneath decades' accumulation of dried leaves, dirt, and debris.

"It's only me now, you know. And I'm not as young as—"

Sebastian said, "Thank you, Mrs. Campbell. That will be all for now."

The housekeeper sniffed and disappeared toward the kitchen, muttering beneath her breath.

Hero turned in a slow circle, her eyes widening as she took in the jumble of exquisite, dust-shrouded furniture, the row after row of grand old masters, their heavy gilded frames mildewed and flyspecked.

"The entire house looks like this," said Sebastian.

"And you think the proportions of the rooms are off? How can you even see the proportions through this mess?"

Sebastian led the way through the stone-cased archway to the corridor. "First, look at the size of the chamber Eisler used as his office."

She peered through the door at the chaos wrought by Samuel Perlman's determined search for his uncle's account books.

Sebastian said, "Now come back through here"—he strode to the long parlor and pushed aside the curtain that covered the second door—"and look at where this room ends."

Frowning, she went back and forth between the two rooms several times, then came to stare thoughtfully at the parlor's back wall. "I see what you mean. It's as if there should be another small room between the two chambers. Part of the space is obviously occupied by the chimney for this massive old fireplace. But it's off-center, and there isn't a hearth on the other side, as you would expect." She glanced over at him. "What are you suggesting?"

Sebastian moved to the fancifully carved mantelpiece and began methodically pushing, pulling, and twisting the various intricately depicted beasts and fruit-laden garlands. "My brother Richard noticed something similar in our house in Cornwall. We eventually realized there was an old priest's hole everyone had long ago forgotten."

Hero came to help, focusing her attention on the muntins, styles, and rails of the paneled wall to the left of the hearth. But after a moment, she paused and sniffed.

"What is it?" he asked, watching her.

"Don't you smell it?"

He shook his head. "Mold? Dry rot? Dead men's bones? What?"

"And here I thought all your senses were unnaturally acute."

"Not my sense of smell. It's actually rather poor."

She turned to look at him. "Really? I can think of any number of situations in which that would be a definite advantage."

"This obviously isn't one of them. What do you smell?"

"Urine. It's very strong—and the smell is coming from behind this section here." She tapped on it experimentally. "Does that sound hollow to you?"

"Yes." He stood back, his gaze assessing the joints of the age-darkened paneling. Now that he knew where to look, the subtle outline of one section was vaguely discernable. He reached for the dagger in his boot.

"Your knife?" she said, watching him. "You're going to use your *knife*? For what?"

He eased the tip of his blade into the joint nearest the hearth. "If I can find the catch—" He paused as he felt the edge of the dagger hit metal. He worked slowly and carefully, manipulating the catch in first one direction, then the other. Shifting the blade to beneath the latch, he pressed upward and heard a faint *snick*.

The panel slid to one side.

"I suspect that's cheating, but it's still impressive," said Hero.

"Thank you."

Thrusting his dagger back into its sheath, he pushed the panel open wider.

The space beyond was perhaps six by eight feet, dusty and empty except for two ironbound wooden trunks, a basket of small glass containers stoppered with cork, and a faint damp stain still visible on the paving stones just inside the opening. In the stale air of the ancient enclosed space, the odor of urine was pungent.

Hero wrinkled her nose. "Do you think someone was shut up in here so long they couldn't hold it?"

A crumpled cloth lying to one side of the entrance caught Sebastian's attention. Reaching down, he found himself holding a cheap configuration of yellowed muslin reinforced by whalebone, its tapes badly frayed with wear.

"Good heavens," said Hero. "It's a woman's stays."

Sebastian passed it to her.

"They're so tiny." She looked up to meet his gaze. "You think these stays belonged to the owner of the blue satin slippers?"

Sebastian swung around to look back at the long, old-fashioned parlor. Anyone shut up in the priest's hole would have had an excellent view of whatever transpired in the room . . . if there was a peephole.

It took him only a moment to find it, cleverly worked into the pattern of the wainscoting.

He said, "I suspect Eisler shoved his bit o' muslin— and most of her clothes—in here when they were interrupted by someone coming to the front door. She was probably watching through the keyhole when the visitor shot Eisler and was so frightened she wet herself. Yates said he burst into the house as soon as he heard the shot fired, followed almost immediately by Perlman."

"So where was the killer?"

"He could have bolted immediately for the rear entrance. Or he might have hidden behind a curtain until both Yates and Perlman were gone, and then run."

"Followed by your Blue Satin Cinderella, who dropped her stays and didn't dare stop long enough to retrieve her slippers. She must have been very frightened."

"Well, she would be, wouldn't she?"

Hero nodded. She folded the small, tattered garment as carefully as if it were something fine and precious. "So she knows who the murderer is."

"She may not know who he is, but she could probably identify him."

Hero looked up, her face solemn. "The question is, Does *he* know about *her*?"

"I hope not."

Chapter 54

The largest of the two trunks opened to reveal stacks of worn leather-bound ledgers.

"The missing account books?" asked Hero, peering over Sebastian's shoulder as he leafed through the top volume.

He nodded. "Telling, isn't it? He leaves everything from priceless fifteenth-century Italian canvases to exquisite Greek marbles lying about the house gathering dust, yet he hides these away."

He moved on to the next, smaller chest. This one contained a curious assortment of objects, each carefully wrapped in squares of white or black silk and bound up with cord. He unwrapped a snuffbox, a vinaigrette, a gold chain with a locket such as a man might present to his bride as a wedding gift. Only, in this instance, the enameled pattern on the face of the locket was worked into the golden crown and three white feathers of the Prince of Wales.

He held it up. "Look at this."

"Prinny?" said Hero reaching to open the locket. Inside lay a curled lock of golden-red hair.

"I think we now know what Eisler wanted from Princess Caroline."

"A locket with the Prince Regent's hair? But . . . why? It can't be worth much."

"It is to someone interested in magic 'operations' aimed at increasing their wealth and attracting the favor of princes."

Hero peered into the chest. "Is that what all these items are? The personal possessions of powerful people he wished to influence by casting spells over them?"

"Influence or destroy."

Hero went to hunker down beside the basket.

"What are they?" he asked, watching her lift one of the small glass containers.

"They look like vials filled with . . ." She eased open the cork and sniffed. "Dirt." She turned it toward the light. "How very curious. Each is labeled with a name. This one says, 'Alfred Dauncey.'"

"I knew Dauncey. He blew out his brains last year. They say he was deeply in debt—all rolled up."

She picked up another vial. "This says, 'Stanley Benson.' Isn't he the baronet's son who slit his own throat last winter?"

Sebastian nodded. "Rumor has it he was also in the clutches of some moneylender."

She stared down at the mound of glass vials. "Good heavens. Do you think *all* these people killed themselves because of Eisler?"

"I suspect so."

She reached for another vial. "This one says . . ."

"What?" he prompted when her voice trailed off.

Her gaze met his. "This one says, 'Rebecca Ridgeway.'"

Sebastian studied her strained, suddenly pale face. "That's significant; why?"

"Rebecca Ridgeway was Abigail McBean's sister. The one who died last spring."

❧

Miss Abigail McBean sat on the comfortably worn sofa in her cozy little drawing room, her head bowed, the small, dirt-filled vial in her hand. On the cushion beside her lay one of Daniel Eisler's leather-bound account books opened to a page where the third name from the bottom read *Marcus Ridgeway, 2000 pounds*. Beside that, Eisler had scrawled, *Paid in full, 2 April 1812*.

Hero sat in an armchair near the fire; Sebastian stood on the far side of the room.

After a moment, Abigail cleared her throat painfully and said, "Rebecca was my younger sister. She was ... quite different from me. Pretty. Delightfully vivacious. Always far more interested in parties than books. She married Marcus when she was just nineteen. Unfortunately, my late brother-in-law was a handsome and charming but sadly flawed man: weak, irresponsible, and capable of breathtaking selfishness. He was constantly in debt, but somehow he always found a way to right himself again."

"What happened last spring?" asked Hero gently.

"Rebecca came to me in tears, just before Easter. She said Marcus had fallen deep into the clutches of some St. Botolph-Aldgate moneylender and was on the verge of ruin. I'd helped Marcus in the past, but he never paid me back, and I ... I live on a very limited income."

"You told her you couldn't help her?"

Abigail nodded without looking up. "Yes. A week later, they were both dead."

"How?"

She traced her sister's name on the vial's label with trembling fingertips. "Marcus was found floating in the Thames near the Wapping Stairs."

"Do you think he killed himself?"

"Marcus?" She shook her head. "In my experience, suicide generally requires a measure of either guilt or despair. But Marcus had a gift for convincing himself that nothing was ever his fault. And no matter how desperate his situation, he was always certain he'd somehow come about."

Hero nodded to the open ledger. "He obviously did. Somehow."

Abigail's brows drew together in a crinkling frown.

"And your sister?" Sebastian asked quietly.

"They pulled Rebecca's body out of the river the next day."

A heavy silence settled on the room, broken only by the distant sound of a child's voice, chanting, *"Oranges and lemons, say the bells of St. Clement's. . . ."*

Hero said, "What do you think happened to them?"

"In truth?" Abigail looked up, her face mottled and puffy with unshed tears. "I think Rebecca killed him. And then she killed herself. Although I could be wrong. It could have been an accident. The coroner's court returned a verdict of death by misadventure."

"Why did Eisler have a glass vial of dirt with your sister's name on it?"

"I don't believe he knew Rebecca was my sister," she said quietly.

"'When will you pay me?' say the bells of Old Bailey," chanted the child in the garden below.

Sebastian said, "How long before he died had Eisler been coming to you for consultation on his work with the grimoires?"

"Several years."

"So when your sister told you about her husband's St. Botolph-Aldgate moneylender, you must have suspected who she was talking about?"

"Yes."

Sebastian was aware of Hero's hard gray eyes upon him. But all he said was, "Eisler had a collection of these vials. I recognized several of the names of young men who recently committed suicide."

Abigail's hand closed around the vial. "Some people believe that those who take their own lives will haunt anyone they blame for driving them to it. There are numerous operations in the various grimoires for binding the souls of suicides. Most are best performed with earth from the graves of the dead."

"Chip-chop, chip-chop, the last man's dead!"

An outburst of children's laughter drew Sebastian's attention again to the window overlooking the garden, where a fair-haired little girl had collapsed with her brother in a fit of giggles. He was remembering what John Francillon had told him, that Eisler feared dead men. He now understood what the lapidary had meant.

Abigail said, "Did you find a vial for Marcus?"

Sebastian shook his head. They had written down all the names on the vials and brought away with them Eisler's account books. The rest they left as they had found it, carefully closing the section of paneling behind them. "No."

Abigail pushed out her breath in a strange sound. "Eisler obviously realized Marcus wasn't the type to do away with himself." Her gaze returned to her brother-in-law's name in the account book beside her, her brows twitching together in a troubled frown. "I wonder how Marcus managed to repay his debt."

Sebastian and Hero exchanged silent glances.

But if Abigail McBean did not know the truth, Sebastian had no intention of telling her.

※

"Admit it," Hero said to him later, as they drove away from Abigail McBean's modest Camden Place house. "You think Abigail killed him."

Sebastian looked over at her. "Don't you?"

He expected her to leap to her friend's defense and insist Abigail McBean was incapable of murder. Instead, she said, "Do you think Abigail knows that Marcus Ridgeway forced his wife to prostitute herself to Eisler in order to pay off his debt?"

"I suspect she does—if she killed Eisler. Otherwise . . . I hope not. She doesn't need to live with that knowledge on top of everything else."

Hero said, "I keep thinking about all those glass vials. So many men and women, driven to death by that loathsome man."

"And by their own weaknesses."

When Hero remained silent, Sebastian said, "Think about this: Abigail McBean has known for the last five months that Eisler was implicated in the death of her sister and brother-in-law. Yet she continued to assist him with his interpretation of the ancient grimoires and their magic operations. Why?"

Hero shook her head. "I don't know. It doesn't make sense."

"It does if you understand just how frightened of the souls of dead men Eisler was."

"You think Abigail was deliberately feeding that fear? To torment him?"

"Yes."

"So why kill him? Why not simply continue to torment him, if she'd chosen that as her means of revenge?"

Sebastian stared out the window at the rolling, misty undulations of Green Park, deserted now in the cold and damp. "Perhaps she learned of another victim, someone she knew and also cared about. Someone who made her decide Eisler needed to be stopped—permanently."

"What other victim?"

But Sebastian only shook his head, his gaze on a fog-shrouded copse of oaks.

⁂

While Devlin settled down in his library with Eisler's account books, Hero changed into a warmer carriage gown of soft pink wool and went in search of the crossing sweep named Drummer.

She found the boy working to clear a pile of fresh manure from his corner. He was reluctant to pause in his labors, but the promise of a silver coin lured him to the steps of St. Giles, where he sat with his bare hands tucked up beneath his armpits as he rocked back and forth for warmth. Hero noticed he had acquired a sturdy pair of leather boots, only gently worn by their previous owner.

"Ye want to know more about the crossin' sweeps?" he asked, looking up at her.

"Not today. I was thinking about how you told me that you and your friends often go to the Haymarket in the evening."

"Y-yes," he said slowly, obviously confused by this new line of inquiry.

"Have you ever found girls for a gentleman who takes them to an old man living in a ramshackle house just off the Minories in St. Botolph-Aldgate?"

Drummer froze, his skinny little body tense, as if he were about to bolt.

"Don't worry," said Hero gently. "You won't get into trouble for it. I'm trying to find a girl who was taken there last Sunday night. Do you know who she is?"

Drummer cast a quick glance around, as if to reassure himself that no one had overheard her question.

Then he nodded solemnly, his eyes wide and afraid.

Chapter 55

Sebastian found the name he was looking for entered under the heading for June 1812.

Major Rhys Wilkinson's debt was for five hundred pounds and had been partially repaid.

He set aside the ledger and rose to go stand with his palms resting on the windowsill, his gaze fixed unseeingly on the misty street before him. He tried to tell himself that the death of both men on the same night could be a coincidence. That Rhys was not the kind of man to commit cold-blooded murder over a debt of five hundred pounds. But he was haunted by the memory of a young girl with a dusting of cinnamon-colored freckles across her sunburned nose, who'd once shot a Spanish guerrilla point-blank in the face.

He was still standing at the window some minutes later when Hero's stylish yellow-bodied town carriage drew up before the house. He watched her descend the carriage steps, a ragged, incredibly dirty, gape-mouthed child clasped firmly by one hand.

"We'll have sandwiches, cakes, and hot chocolate in the library, as soon as possible," he heard her tell Morey, her footsteps brisk as she crossed the black-and-white-marbled entry hall. The room filled with the scent of coal smoke and fresh manure and grimy boy.

"This is Drummer," she said, releasing the child's

hand so that she could loosen the ribbons of her bonnet and yank off her gloves. "He's a crossing sweep at St. Giles, but he also works in the Haymarket in the evenings, helping gentlemen too shy to descend from their carriages to find girls." She gave the boy a nudge forward. "Make your bow and tell his lordship about Jenny."

The boy stumbled forward, a grubby wideawake cap clutched in both hands, his skinny chest jerking with his agitated breathing.

"Jenny?" prompted Sebastian when the lad remained mute.

"Jenny Davie," supplied Hero. "She's seventeen, and last Sunday evening she was hired by a gentleman in a hackney who was known to procure girls for a nasty old goat living in St. Botolph-Aldgate."

Sebastian led the boy closer to the fire, where the black cat looked up in slit-eyed annoyance at their intrusion. "What did this gentleman look like?"

Drummer raised a shoulder in the offhand shrug of a lad to whom one member of the nobility was pretty much like the next. "I reckon 'e looks like a nob."

"My age? Younger? Or older?"

Drummer frowned with the effort of thought. "Younger, I'd say—by a fair bit."

Sebastian and Hero exchanged glances. So Jenny Davie's procurer had not been Samuel Perlman.

"Fair?" asked Sebastian. "Or dark haired?"

"'E's got a mess o' curls as gold as a guinea. The girls always go with 'im real quick, because 'e's so good-lookin'. But 'e ain't never 'ad nothin' to do with any of 'em. Jist takes 'em to that old codger."

Blair Beresford, thought Sebastian. Aloud, he said, "Tell me about Jenny Davie."

Again that twitch of the shoulder. Circumstances had obviously taught Drummer long ago to take life—and people—as he met them, with little time for analysis or criticism. "Wot's there t' tell? She's a doxy."

"Where does she live?"

The boy's gaze slid away. "She used t' keep a room at a lodgin' 'ouse in Rose Court."

"But she's not there anymore?"

Drummer shook his head. "There's been a mess o' people lookin' for 'er."

"Oh? Such as?"

"Well, the curly-'eaded cove what 'ired 'er, fer one."

Interesting, thought Sebastian. "Who else?"

The boy's shoulder twitched. "Some Frenchman. 'E's been lookin' fer 'er real 'ard. He's even offered blunt to any o' the lads what could tell 'im where she's gone."

Sebastian saw Hero's eyes narrow and knew that the boy had not yet told her this part of his tale. "What does he look like?"

"'E looks like a Frenchman."

"Tall? Short? Old? Young? Dark? Fair?"

Drummer frowned. "Older than you, and shorter— but not real old or real short. I reckon 'e 'as a real bad pockmarked face, but I didn't pay him a whole lot o' mind. I mean, I ain't about to bubble on Jenny, so why would I? She said if anyone was to come lookin' fer 'er, we was t' keep mum."

"So you do know where she is."

The boy sucked in a quick breath as he realized his mistake. He edged toward the door but was stopped by the entrance of Morey, who came in bearing a heavy tray loaded down with sandwiches, small cakes, and a pitcher of steaming hot chocolate.

Hero said, "Here, let me fix you a plate of sandwiches. Do you prefer ham or roast beef?"

The boy swallowed hard. "Can I 'ave some o' both?" he asked in a small, hopeful voice.

"You certainly may." She heaped the plate with a generous selection of dainty sandwiches. "Is Jenny a London girl, born and bred?"

Drummer shoved a sandwich in his mouth and shook his head. "She and Jeremy—that's 'er brother—grew up in Bermondsey, down in Southwark. I remember 'im tellin' me their family 'ad a room over the gatehouse o' some old abbey down there. But their folks died o' the flux some years ago, and they didn't 'ave no kin, so they come up to the city lookin' for work."

"Is that where she's gone now?" asked Sebastian. "To Southwark?"

Drummer swallowed another bite of sandwich. "Nah. I wouldn't a told you if it was."

Hero poured the boy a mug of hot chocolate. "We want to help Jenny, not harm her. She needs help, Drummer. I'm afraid those other men you mentioned who are looking for her might kill her if they find her. And they are determined to find her. You must tell us where she is."

The boy paused in midchew, his gaze going from Hero to Sebastian and back.

Hero said, "I understand it's difficult to know whom to trust."

Drummer swallowed, hard.

"Tell us," said Sebastian, his voice quiet but implacable.

"White 'Orse Yard," Drummer blurted out, his chest jerking with the agitation of his breathing. "She's got a room at the Pope's 'Ead in White 'Orse Yard, jist off Drury Lane."

※

Sebastian took the boy with him, along with a hamper packed with more sandwiches and cakes, and a warm coat that had recently grown too snug for Tom. Hero was cross about her inability to accompany them, but even she had to admit that the uproar provoked by the appearance of a gentlewoman in a Drury Lane tavern was unlikely to be helpful.

The warren of narrow, crooked alleys and foul, dark courts around the Drury Lane and Covent Garden theaters had long ago degenerated into a precinct of flash houses, low taverns, and rat-infested accommodation houses where families of ten or more could be found crammed into a single small, airless room. Sebastian made certain both his coachman and the footman were armed, and slipped a small double-barreled flintlock into his own pocket.

It was still several hours before nightfall, yet already the narrow cobbled lane leading to White Horse Yard was filling with a rough, half-drunken crowd and a thick mist that drifted in a dense, wind-swirled, suffocating cloak between the tightly packed houses.

"Why did she take refuge here? Do you know?" Sebastian asked as the carriage drew up at the end of the lane.

Drummer shook his head, his mouth full of cake. "I think maybe she used to work round about 'ere, when she first come up to London."

"How do you know she's here? Did she tell you?"

"Her brother, Jeremy, tumbles with us. She wanted 'im to bring 'er some o' 'er stuff a couple days ago and 'e asked fer me 'elp. Only, she were right cross when she see'd me. That's when she made me promise not to tell where she is."

"She's right to be cautious."

The boy looked doubtful but paused to grab a couple more sandwiches and thrust them into his pockets before tripping down the carriage steps in Sebastian's wake.

Sebastian grasped the lad firmly by the arm and held on to him as they worked their way through the surging, boisterous crowd. The damp, smoky air was thick with the smell of broiling meat and unwashed bodies and the pervasive, inescapable stench of rot.

The Pope's Head in White Horse Yard occupied what looked as if it had once been the carriage house of a long-vanished grand residence, its redbrick facade now worn and blackened by grime, a broken gutter dripping a line of green slime down one side. As they approached the inn, the door flew open and two drunken soldiers staggered out, arms linked around each other's shoulders and heads tipped back as they sang, "King George commands and we obey, o'er the hills and far away...."

Drummer hung back, eyes wide, lips parted, chest jerking with his agitated breathing. "Do I gotta go in wit' ye? I mean, ye know—"

"Yes," said Sebastian, hauling the boy across the entrance passage to the inn's dark, narrow staircase. "I need you to convince Jenny that I'm here to help her."

"She ain't gonna be happy I brung ye."

Lit only by a single smoking oil lamp, the stairs creaked and groaned beneath their weight. But the telltale sounds of their approach were lost in the convivial roar from the taproom and the raucous laughter from a chamber at the end of the hall and a man's well-bred voice raised in anger on the far side of the door nearest the top of the steps.

"Where is it, damn you? I know you took it. Where is the diamond? Did you—"

The rest of his words were swallowed by a woman's terrified scream.

Chapter 56

"'*E*lp!" she shouted. "'*E's killin' me*. Somebody 'elp!"

Sebastian kicked in the door hard enough to splinter the thin wooden panels and slam it back against the wall.

The room beyond was small and dingy, the air close and foul. A single tallow candle on a battered table near the narrow bed flared in the sudden draft, casting long shadows across the bare floorboards and ancient paneled walls. Blair Beresford, his hat gone, his handsome features twisted with determination, had pinned a tiny slip of a girl against a tall, battered wardrobe, her birdlike wrists clasped in one hand and wrenched over her head.

"You son of a bitch," swore Sebastian, tackling him in a rush.

The two men went down together, hard. Jenny Davie, finding herself unexpectedly free, broke for the door.

"A guinea if you grab her and hold on to her!" Sebastian shouted at Drummer, then ducked his head as Beresford swung a fist at his face.

Sebastian scrambled to grab the man's wrists, grunting as Beresford jabbed his knee into Sebastian's groin and tried to scoot backward on his elbows. He was dimly aware of Jenny Davie shouting, "Ow, let me go, ye little shabba-roon!" as Drummer snagged her skirts and held on.

Beresford threw another wild punch that grazed the side of Sebastian's jaw. Grunting, Sebastian fisted his hand in the front of Beresford's waistcoat and hauled him up to slam his back against the near wall. "God damn it," swore Sebastian, breathing hard. "Somehow, I never pegged you for a killer."

Beresford bucked against Sebastian's hold, then subsided in resignation, a trickle of blood leaking from the corner of his mouth. "What the devil are you talking about? I didn't kill anyone."

"Then why the hell are you here?"

"The diamond." He jerked his head toward the girl. "She must have taken it! I was thinking that if I could recover it, it would be a way to pay Hope back for all he's done for me."

Sebastian swung his head to look over his shoulder at the girl, who had suddenly gone utterly still. "What makes you think she has it?"

"Because no one else does, and she was there. I dropped her in Fountain Lane less than half an hour before Eisler was killed. Look — I know I lied to you when I said I didn't take Eisler a girl that night. But everything else I told you was the truth. I swear!"

Sebastian tightened his hold on the younger man, his lips curling away from his teeth in a hard smile. "Why the bloody hell should I believe you? I think you shot Eisler, and now you're here to get rid of your last witness."

"Oy, what ye talkin' about, then?" scoffed Jenny Davie, her voice sharp. "'E ain't the cove what shot that old goat." Then, as if suddenly aware that she had captured the interested attention of everyone in the room, she looked quickly from one to the next and tried to take a step back. "What? What's everybody starin' at me for?"

For the first time, Sebastian took a good, long look at the girl Hero called the Blue Satin Cinderella. She looked more like fifteen than seventeen, with an incredibly tiny, small-boned frame and hair that might have been honey colored if it were cleaner. Her face was thin and delicately featured, her eyes a soft, luminous gray, her chin small and pointed.

"You saw who did it?" said Sebastian, releasing his hold on Blair Beresford. The younger man slid down the wall and just sat there, back pressed to the panels, legs outstretched.

"Course I did," she said. "That old goat took and shoved me in a nasty little cupboard when someone come a-knockin' at the door afore 'e was done wit' me. I saw the 'ole thing, and this cove"—she jerked her chin dismissively toward Beresford—"weren't even there."

"So who *did* shoot him?" Sebastian demanded.

"'Ow the bloody 'ell should I know?"

"You just said you saw him."

"That don't mean I know who 'e was!"

Sebastian tamped down a spurt of impatience. "But you can tell me what he looked like."

Jenny shook her matted hair out of her face. "Course I can. A death's-'ead on a mopstick, 'e was."

Sebastian stared at her, not understanding. "A what?"

She huffed her breath and rolled her eyes. "Ye know, a tall, skinny cove what looks like 'e ain't long for this world. An' 'e 'ad one of them cavalry mustaches."

Sebastian stared at her with the heavy heart of a man who has just had one of his worst fears confirmed.

"If ye ask me," Jenny was saying, "'e weren't right in the 'ead. 'E come in wavin' that gun around and sayin' 'e were there t' bell the cat."

"And then what happened?" asked Sebastian, keeping his voice even with difficulty.

"That old goat, 'e laughed at the cove, wanted to know 'ow exactly did 'e propose t' do *that*? Only, just then someone *else* come poundin' on the front door real hard. The skinny cove got spooked and looked around, and the old goat pounced on him. That's when the gun went off."

"And what did the, er, skinny cove do then?"

"Why, 'e bolted out the back door, just afore these other two coves come in, one after the other, with the chinless, curly-'eaded one hollerin' 'murder.'"

"And the diamond?" asked Blair Beresford from where he sat on the floor, a lock of golden hair tumbled across his dusty forehead. "What happened to the diamond?"

Jenny Davie pushed out her lips, opened her eyes wide, and shook her head. "I keep tellin' ye, I don't know nothin' about no diamond."

"Then why are you hiding here, in Covent Garden?" asked Sebastian. "Why didn't you go to the magistrates and tell them what you know?"

He saw the leap of fear in her wide gray eyes, saw her small pointed chin jut forward in determination, and knew his mistake an instant too late.

"Hold on to her!" he shouted at Drummer, just as Jenny hauled back her fist and punched the boy in the nose.

"Ow," he cried, tears starting in his eyes, blood spurting as he let go of the girl to cup both hands over his face.

"Stop her!" Sebastian yelled as Jenny bolted for the stairs. *"Bloody hell."*

Sebastian pelted after her, half running, half falling down the steep, narrow staircase. He reached the entrance passage just in time to see the girl squeeze through a boisterous knot of drovers trying to shove into the taproom.

By the time Sebastian pushed his way into the street, Jenny Davie had disappeared, swallowed up by the fog.

Chapter 57

Sebastian returned to the Pope's Head to find both Drummer and Blair Beresford long gone.

But the crossing sweep had simply returned to the carriage at the end of the lane and was waiting there for Sebastian. He had his head tipped back, the bridge of his nose pinched between one thumb and forefinger as he sought to stem the blood that still trickled from his nostrils. "Do I get my guinea?" he asked, his voice muffled by his oversized sleeve. "Even though she got away from me in the end?"

Sebastian handed the boy his handkerchief and steered him toward the carriage steps. "Considering your battle wounds, I'd say you earned yourself two guineas for this night's work."

The boy's eyes grew round above the voluminous folds of Sebastian's handkerchief. "Cor."

Sebastian pressed the coins into the boy's hand and turned to his coachman. "Take the lad back to Brook Street and ask Lady Devlin to see that he is attended to."

Drummer stuck his head back out the open door. "Ye ain't comin'?"

"I shall be along directly," said Sebastian, closing the door on him.

He nodded to the coachman, then went in search of a hackney to take him to Kensington.

⁂

The curtains were not yet drawn at the Yeoman's Row lodgings of Annie and Emma Wilkinson, allowing a warm, golden glow to spill from the parlor and light up the cool, misty night. Sebastian paused for a moment on the footpath outside. At the end of the street, the fenced gardens of Kensington Square lay dark and silent. But for a moment, he thought he could hear the echo of a child's chant, *"'When will you pay me?' say the bells of Old Bailey."*

"Wait here for me," Sebastian told the hackney driver and moved with an aching sadness to ring his old friend's bell.

⁂

"Devlin!" A delighted smile lit up Annie Wilkinson's features as she came toward him. "What a pleasant surprise. Julie"—she turned to the housemaid who had escorted him up the stairs—"put the kettle on and bring his lordship some of that cake we—"

Sebastian squeezed her hands, then let her go. "Thank you, but I don't need anything."

She turned to the wine carafe that stood with a tray of glasses on a table near the front windows. "At least let me get you a glass of burgundy."

"Annie . . . We need to talk."

She looked up from pouring the wine. Something in his tone must have alerted her, because she set the carafe aside and said with a forced smile, "You're sounding very serious, Devlin."

He went to stand with his back to the small fire burning on the hearth. "I had an interesting conversation this evening with a young girl named Jenny Davie."

Annie looked puzzled. "I don't believe I recognize the name. Should I?"

"I wouldn't think so. She is what's popularly dismissed by polite society as 'Haymarket ware.' A week ago, her services were engaged by a rather nasty old St. Botolph-Aldgate diamond merchant named Daniel Eisler." He paused. "You do recognize that name, don't you?"

She held herself very still. "What are you trying to say, Devlin?"

"Last Sunday evening at approximately half past eight, Daniel Eisler was shot to death by a tall, ill-looking man with a cavalry mustache. Now, I suppose there could be any number of men in London who fit that description. But this particular man seems to have had a fondness for old fables. He told Eisler that he'd come to bell the cat."

She forced a husky laugh. "It's a common enough tale."

"True. But I've seen Eisler's account books, Annie."

She went to stand beside the window, one hand raised to clutch the worn cloth as if she were about to close it, her back held painfully straight.

Sebastian said, "You knew, didn't you? You knew Rhys had killed him."

She shook her head back and forth, her throat working as she swallowed. "No."

"Annie, you said Rhys went out for a walk that night at half past eight and never came back. But Emma told me that her papa didn't get home in time to tell her a story that night. What's Emma's bedtime, Annie? Seven? Eight? She's in bed now, isn't she?"

"Seven." Annie turned toward him, her face haggard. "I didn't know what he'd done. I swear I didn't. I'll admit I suspected, but I didn't *know*. Not until today."

"Why today?"

"I'll show you," she said, and strode quickly from the room.

She was back in a moment, carrying a flintlock pistol loosely wrapped in a square of old flannel. When she held it out to him, he caught the sulfuric stench of burnt powder.

"You know what Rhys was like," she said. "He'd spent

half his life in the army. He knew the importance of taking care of his gun. He never fired it without cleaning it before he put it away. So as soon as I saw it like this, I knew ..."

Sebastian carefully folded back the cloth. It was an old Elliot pattern flintlock pistol with a nine-inch barrel and the gently curving grip favored by the Light Dragoons.

She said, "I didn't even know Rhys had borrowed money until he was already behind on the interest. That's when Eisler said he'd heard Rhys had a pretty wife, and that he was willing to forgive the interest on the debt if I ... if Rhys would agree ..."

"I know all about the way Eisler abused the women who found themselves in his debt," Sebastian said softly. "Did you do it, Annie?"

She drew back as if he had slapped her. "No!"

"But you were tempted?"

She pressed her fist to her lips, her eyes squeezing shut as she nodded. "We were so desperate."

"Annie ... You could have come to me at any time. I would have been more than happy to help. I told you that."

She dropped her hand to her side and sniffed, her lips pressing into a thin line. "I would never do that, and neither would Rhys."

Sebastian searched her tightly held face. "So what happened?"

"Rhys was so appalled by the proposal that he started looking into Eisler. You say you know about the way he used people, but we'd had no idea. One night, when Rhys was telling me of the things he'd learned, I said, 'Something needs to be done about that bastard. There must be some way to warn other people to steer clear of his traps.' I didn't mean anything by it—I was just thinking out loud. Only, Rhys said there was no way for the mice to bell the cat. That the only way to stop a man like Eisler was to kill him."

Her gaze dropped to the gun in Sebastian's hands, her breath backing up in her throat. "He'd been talking a lot lately about how much better it would be for Emma and me if he were dead—that Eisler wouldn't be able to pursue the debt, that Emma and I could go live with my grandmother, that I'd be free to remarry." She swallowed. "I always begged him not to talk like that, but . . ."

"When was the last time you saw Rhys, Annie?"

She blinked, and the tears swimming in her eyes spilled over to stream unchecked down her face. "It must have been half past nine. He . . . he came home, shut himself in the bedroom for a few minutes, then left, saying he was going for a walk. I knew he had a bottle of laudanum he kept in a drawer beside the bed. After he left, I went and checked. It was a new bottle—he'd found an apothecary willing to mix it especially strong, just for him. It was gone."

"That's when you contacted me and asked for my help in finding him?"

She nodded silently.

"Annie, Annie . . . Why didn't you tell me all this before?"

"I was afraid . . . and ashamed. Perhaps more ashamed than afraid."

"And when you saw in Monday's papers that Eisler had been killed?"

"I don't know. . . . I—I hoped it was just a coincidence. I mean, everyone was saying Russell Yates was found standing over the man's dead body. I didn't know then about the pistol. Not until today."

"What made you decide to look for it today?"

She scrubbed the heel of her hand across one wet cheek. "The chief magistrate from Lambeth Street Public Office came to see me."

"Bertram Leigh-Jones?" Sebastian felt his heart begin to beat faster. "What did he want?"

"He wanted to know when I'd last seen Rhys. I lied. I told him the same thing I've told everyone else—that

Rhys went out for a walk at half past eight and never came back. But as soon as he left, I went to the bedroom and looked in the drawer where I knew Rhys kept his pistol. When I saw it, I knew."

She turned away, her arms wrapping across her chest to hug herself. "At the time, I couldn't understand what had made Leigh-Jones suspect Rhys. But I suppose this girl you were talking about—this Jenny Davie—must have told him what she told you."

Sebastian shook his head. "No. I think Leigh-Jones got the information out of Jud Foy. Right before he killed him."

Annie shook her head, not understanding. "Who is Foy?"

"A half-mad ex-rifleman who was watching Eisler's house the night he died."

"But . . . why would Leigh-Jones kill him?"

"For the same reason he killed an old French jewel thief named Jacques Collot: because the chief magistrate at Lambeth Street has a dangerous secret he'll do anything to protect."

She looked at him blankly.

Sebastian said, "I think Bertram Leigh-Jones is working for Napoléon to recover a gem Eisler had in his possession—a rare blue diamond that once formed part of the French Crown Jewels and is now missing. The assumption has always been that whoever killed Eisler stole the diamond. At first, Leigh-Jones thought he had Eisler's killer—Yates—in prison. But something seems to have convinced Leigh-Jones that he had the wrong man. He started asking questions, and that led him to Foy. I think Foy told Leigh-Jones about Rhys, and that's why he came to see you today."

"You're saying that *Rhys* stole some diamond? But Rhys would never do anything like that! You know Rhys."

"I know. I think Jenny Davie has it. And unless I can stop him, she's liable to be Leigh-Jones's next victim."

⁂

It took what felt like an age for Sebastian's hackney driver to battle through the city's Saturday night traffic to the St. Botolph-Aldgate home of Bertram Leigh-Jones. Then the housemaid who opened the door to Sebastian's curt knock dropped an apologetic curtsy and said, "Begging your lordship's pardon, but Mr. Leigh-Jones isn't here."

"This is rather important," said Sebastian, aware of a rising sense of urgency. "Would you happen to know where he's gone?"

"I'm afraid he didn't say, my lord. Some Frenchman come to see him maybe half an hour ago, and they all went off in his gig."

"'All'? Was someone else with them?"

The housemaid nodded. "Oh, yes, my lord. The Frenchman brung a girl with him. A tiny slip of a thing, she was, and so scared."

Jenny, thought Sebastian. *Damn, damn, damn.*

Aloud, he said, "You have no idea where they might have gone?"

The housemaid screwed up her face with the effort of thought. "I think they might have said something about Southwark, but I couldn't tell you more than that."

"Southwark?"

"Yes, my lord," she said.

But Sebastian was already running to his hackney.

Chapter 58

The ancient abbey of St. Saviour in Bermondsey, on the southern bank of the Thames, had once ranked amongst the proudest religious houses in England, patronized by kings and favored by widowed queens in need of a place of refuge. Now only the lay church, a crumbling gatehouse, and a row of abandoned, half-demolished dwellings survived, their age-battered stone walls and broken slate roofs gleaming wet in the fitful, misty moonlight.

Why Leigh-Jones and his pockmarked French cohort would bring Jenny Davie here, to her old childhood home, Sebastian could only guess. But as his hackney swept around the curve of the ancient elevated causeway that once led to the priory, he caught sight of a gig drawn up beside what was now the parish church of St. Mary Magdalen. The gig was empty, the bay between the shafts grazing contentedly in the rank grass that grew along the wayside. Sebastian could see a narrow beam of light, as if from a shuttered lantern, weaving amongst the mossy gray tombs and tumbled headstones of the dark, fog-shrouded churchyard beyond.

"Pull up here," Sebastian ordered.

The hackney driver obliged. "Ye want I should wait fer ye again, yer lordship?" he asked hopefully. He obviously considered a night of dozing on the box far preferable to one spent constantly hustling new fares.

"Just take care to keep out of sight." Sebastian dropped quietly to the ground, then handed up his card to the jarvey. "And if anything should happen to me, take this to Sir Henry Lovejoy in Bow Street and tell him what you know of this night's work."

"Aye, my lord."

Leaving the hackney in the shadows of a line of darkened, dilapidated shops, Sebastian slipped down the street. The air here was heavy and wet, and thick with the pungent odors of the nearby tan yards and glue manufactories and breweries. On the flagway beside the church's ancient medieval tower, he paused, a cold wind billowing the mist around him.

He could see them now, three mist-shrouded figures: the magistrate's form tall and bulky; the Frenchman small, agile; the girl dragged along with one frail arm gripped in Leigh-Jones's meaty fist as they worked their way through the sunken, crowded graves. The moon had utterly disappeared behind the thick, bunching clouds.

The wall surrounding the churchyard was built of stone and low and crumbling; Sebastian climbed it easily. Hunkering down, he was slipping cautiously from one tomb to the next when the girl's voice, sounding surprisingly strong, stopped him.

"This is it," she said.

"You're certain this time?" snapped Leigh-Jones, raising his lantern to peer at the tomb before them.

"I *think* so."

The Frenchman gave a scornful laugh. "That's what she said before she wasted ten minutes digging around the foundations of the last tomb where she insisted she'd hid it."

"It ain't easy to see in the dark! Maybe if we could come back tomorrow when it's light, I could—"

Leigh-Jones said, "Just shut up and dig."

The Frenchman pulled a pistol from his waistband and pressed the muzzle against the girl's temple. "Only, make certain you have the right tomb this time, *ma petite*. No more games, hmm?"

Jenny Davie froze, the moist wind curling the honey-colored hair around her fine-boned face and flattening the skirts of her ragged dress against her legs. Unlike the two men, who were muffled in greatcoats and hats, she was bareheaded, her arms covered only by the thin stuff of her dress and wrapped across her chest for warmth. She stared back at the Frenchman, as if evaluating the seriousness of his threat. She must have decided he meant it, because she jerked her head toward a tomb that lay closer to the long wall of the church's nave. "I think maybe I made a mistake and it's over there."

The Frenchman grunted.

She led them to a tomb so old the weathered, moss-covered stones were cracked and crumbling, the top tilted at a forty-five degree angle. Crouching down near one end, she began to dig at the base, the rush of the disturbed, falling rubble sounding unnaturally loud in the fog-shrouded night.

At some point, she'd obviously brought the diamond here, to the place where she'd played as a child, and hidden it. As Sebastian watched, she hesitated in her digging. Then her left hand swooped into the rubble to close over something just as her right seized a chunk of stone the size of her fist. He could see the tension in every line of her body, see her gathering herself like a sprinter ready to run.

Leigh-Jones had set the lantern atop the tomb and now stood slightly off to one side, while the Frenchman had positioned himself nearby, his pistol held in a slackened grip. As Sebastian watched, Jenny drew back her hand and chucked the jagged rock at the Frenchman's head.

"*Mon Dieu,*" he swore. He tried to duck, lost his footing, and went down with a grunt.

Darting up, Jenny took off running across the darkened churchyard, toward the ancient ruined gatehouse shrouded by mist in the distance.

"Don't just stand there, you fool," shouted the Frenchman, scrambling to his feet. "After her! She's got the diamond!"

Leigh-Jones started off down the slope in a lumbering trot. "For God's sake, just shoot her!"

Taking careful aim on the girl's running figure, the Frenchman was tightening his finger on the trigger when Sebastian barreled into him.

The impact knocked the Frenchman flat on his back, the pistol exploding harmlessly into the air as it flew from his hand and spun out of sight into the high grass.

Rolling nimbly away from Sebastian's grasp, he reared up into a crouch, a knife gleaming in his fist. "You again," he spat.

Leaping to his feet, Sebastian snatched the horn lantern from the tomb's cracked surface just as the Frenchman lunged, blade flashing.

Pivoting, Sebastian smashed the lantern down on the Frenchman's hand, plunging them into darkness and sending the knife clattering against the side of the tomb. As the Frenchman staggered back, Sebastian swung the lantern again, this time at the man's head.

The Frenchman ducked, then came up with an explosive kick that drove the heel of his boot into Sebastian's right knee.

Sebastian's leg collapsed beneath him in a fireball of pain. As he fell, the Frenchman kicked at him again, aiming this time for Sebastian's head.

Hands flashing up, Sebastian grabbed the French agent's boot with both hands and twisted.

Caught off balance, the Frenchman fell back, his head making an ugly *thwunking* sound as it struck the edge of the tomb. He slithered down the side of the moss-covered monument in a disjointed sprawl, then lay still, an ugly sheen of dark wetness staining the weathered stone behind him.

Staggering to his feet, Sebastian gritted his teeth and set off in an ungainly lope toward the ancient abbey gatehouse at the base of the churchyard. Every step sent an excruciating jolt of agony radiating up from his injured knee, so that by the time he reached the rubbish-strewn cobbled court before the ruined gatehouse, a cold sweat filmed his body and his breath was coming ragged and fast.

Built of coursed rough stone, the gatehouse rose a story and a half above its central vaulted archway. Once, the recessed arch had been richly ornamented with carvings, the mullioned windows above embellished with a vinelike tracery. But the passing centuries had battered and crumbled the stone, while the smoke and grime of generations had blurred and obliterated the details of what remained.

To the west of the gatehouse ranged a long, two-story stone building that might once have been an attached guesthouse or almonry but had long since degenerated into mean lodgings. Now the buildings stood vacant, windows and doorways gaping, roof tiles broken and missing, their supporting timbers collapsing. All other traces of the abbey had vanished long ago; beyond these few ruined fragments stretched only market gardens and open fields, empty beneath the wind-bunched clouds scuttling and thickening across the black sky.

Jenny Davie and Bertram Leigh-Jones had disappeared.

Pausing in the shadows of the gatehouse's arched passageway, Sebastian stood still, listening. He heard the scuff of a heavy tread overhead, a girl's frightened gasp. Then came Leigh-Jones's voice, pitched to a coaxing croon that did little to disguise the gruff anger roiling beneath. "I'm not going to hurt you, girl. All I want is the diamond. Just give me the diamond and I'll let you go."

"Ye take me fer a flat?" yelled Jenny, her voice high-pitched with fear and defiance. "Don't ye come near me!"

Moving quietly, Sebastian crept up the tightly wound medieval staircase that opened to one side of the vaulted passage. The old stone treads were worn into such deeply sunken grooves in the center that the awkwardness of each step twisted his injured knee and stole his breath. By the time he reached the single chamber above, it was empty.

At one time, this had been a grand space, with oak-paneled walls and a sandstone fireplace built into the opposite wall. But much of the paneling had been torn down and burned for firewood, while part of the chimney had collapsed into a cascade of rubble strewn across the room's scarred wooden floor. At the far end of the chamber, a crude ladder led to the loft above. Sebastian had one foot on the first rung when Jenny screamed again.

"Get back," she cried. "I'm telling ye!"

"What are you doing, you fool girl?" growled Leigh-Jones. "Don't go out there! Are you mad? You'll slip and fall to your death."

"I told ye! Stay away from me!"

"You stupid strumpet! Get back in here. I get my hands on you, I swear to God, I'm going to kill you!"

Sebastian scrambled up the ladder to find himself in a low-pitched garret musty with age and damp and rot. Patches of black sky showed through a jagged hole in the roof; most of the row of casement windows built into the gabled end were gone, their casings gaping vacant to the wet, windy night.

Crossing swiftly to the opening, Sebastian found himself staring out over the roof of the adjoining structure. Straddling the ridge beam the way a man would ride a horse, the magistrate had stripped off his cumbersome greatcoat and was carefully scooting his way forward on his rump. Jenny Davie was already some ten to fifteen feet ahead of him. She was small and light enough to scramble over the tiles on her feet, although she was bent over nearly double, using her hands to help steady her balance on the wet, mossy slates.

"Come back here, you bloody doxy," Leigh-Jones roared.

"Leave me alone!" she screamed, her step faltering as she reached the gable end.

There was another, smaller building that abutted this

one, but its roof was some three or four feet below where she stood and of a steeper pitch. Sebastian saw her creep closer to the edge, then waver.

"Jenny, *don't jump!*" Sebastian shouted. "Stay where you are!"

Leigh-Jones jerked around to stare at him, his jaw thrusting out in annoyed fury, while Jenny screamed, "Go away and leave me alone! All of you!"

If she had turned onto her stomach and eased herself carefully over the gabled point, she might have made it. Instead, she rose and jumped.

Sebastian heard the clatter of breaking, falling tiles as she landed, lost her footing, and went down, vanishing from his sight. She let out a sharp scream, and Sebastian's breath caught in his throat. But she must somehow have managed to grab a handhold and stop her descent, because he heard her gasp, then fall utterly silent.

"Jenny!" Sebastian shouted, swinging his legs over the broken sill to the slates below. "Hang on!"

"You bloody interfering bastard," growled the magistrate. Grasping the roof's peak, he managed with surprising agility to swing his legs up and around, reversing his position so that he now faced Sebastian. "I should have had you killed when I had the chance."

"Give it up, Leigh-Jones," said Sebastian, hunkering down to lower his center of gravity. "You've had a good run, but the game's up now."

Leigh-Jones picked up a broken slate and chucked it at Sebastian's head. *"I'll see you in hell."*

Sebastian managed to duck the first two broken tiles; the edge of the third sliced open a long cut across his forehead. "God damn it," he swore. He took another step forward.

And felt his right foot punch through the rotten roof.

Chapter 59

The collapsing roof pitched Sebastian sideways. He grabbed the ridge of slate at the peak with his left hand, stopping his fall. But he was now pinned by his injured right leg, with his other leg splayed out awkwardly to the side and only one hand free.

"Looks like you're in trouble, don't it?" said the magistrate. Breaking off a long, jagged piece from the tile at his side, Leigh-Jones inched himself forward, the pointed slate clutched in his right fist like a knife.

The wind gusted up, carrying a splattering of raindrops that pattered on the mossy slate and stung Sebastian's face. Smiling, Leigh-Jones slashed downward with his blade, aiming straight for Sebastian's heart.

Sebastian clamped his free hand around the magistrate's wrist, stopping the slate's descent.

Still grinning, Leigh-Jones wrapped his other fist around his right wrist and leaned his considerable weight into his hands. The improvised blade inched lower.

Sebastian could feel the blood pounding in his head, hear his breath coming in ragged gasps. A warm wetness coursed from his cut forehead to sting his eyes. He scraped his left bootheel over the slates, desperate to find some purchase. Then the roofing under his left boot gave way, plunging his leg down into the emptiness beneath.

For a moment, he thought the entire roof was collapsing beneath their combined weights. Then he realized the ridge beam still held and that he was now effectively straddling it.

Shifting his weight, he locked his ankles together beneath him. "You greedy, traitorous son of a bitch," he snarled, freeing his left hand to slam a punch up into the magistrate's plump face.

The magistrate reeled back, his massive bulk no longer pressing the jagged slate toward Sebastian's heart. Gritting his teeth, Sebastian grasped the magistrate's wrists with both hands and drove the deadly point straight down into Leigh-Jones's own gut.

He saw the magistrate's eyes widen, saw his full cheeks expand with a mingling of shock and fury. Then he slipped sideways, shattering slates and smashing fragile timbers as his heavy body picked up speed. He flung his arms out, fingers scrabbling, frantic for a handhold. But his momentum was too great. He slid to the roof's edge and shot off it into the void.

He gave one high-pitched scream that was cut off by the thump of his body hitting the cobbles far below.

His breath still coming in harsh gasps, Sebastian wiped the mingling sweat and blood from his face with his forearm. Then, unlocking his ankles and carefully balancing his weight on both hands, he levered himself up out of the twin holes he'd punched through the roof's rotten fabric.

"Jenny!" he called, cautiously inching his way to the end of the building.

He could see her now. She lay facedown at the edge of the lower roof, her skirts and petticoats a torn, rucked-up froth around her.

"Hold on," he said, easing himself down to the smaller, steeper roof. "I'm here to help you."

Clamping one arm around the rough brickwork of the chimney that thrust up at the juncture of the two buildings, he leaned forward as far as he dared to where the girl clung to the edge. But he still couldn't quite reach her.

"Grab my hand," he told her, and prayed the damned chimney would take their combined weights.

"Why should I trust you?" she shouted, her voice snatched away by the buffeting wind.

"Because if all I wanted was the diamond, damn it, I'd let you fall off this damned roof and simply take the bloody stone from your dead body. That's why."

She lay still, her face a white mask of terror and indecision. Then, very slowly, she reached out a trembling hand toward him.

Tiny, clawlike fingers clamped around his arm. Sebastian clasped his own hand around her wrist, then said gently, "I've got you. All you need to do now is climb toward me, slowly."

She inched her way up the steep, mossy slope. The wind snatched at her skirts; the rain poured. Once, a fragment of slate broke beneath her foot and spun away into the darkness below. She let out a soft whimper but kept climbing.

When she was close enough, he shifted his grip on the chimney and hauled her up to him. They sat side by side, their backs pressed to the chimney's rough brick, their breath sawing in their chests, the wind driving the cold rain in their faces.

After a moment, she swallowed hard and said, "How do we get down from here?"

Sebastian looked over at her and grinned. "Very carefully."

Chapter 60

*B*rilliant and breathtakingly beautiful, the sapphire blue diamond lay nestled in a velvet-lined box on Sir Henry Lovejoy's desk.

Sir Henry frowned down at it a moment, then raised his gaze to Sebastian. "You're certain you wouldn't rather return the gem to Mr. Hope yourself?"

"I think not."

Sir Henry cleared his throat. "And this girl you were telling me about, the one who took the diamond from Eisler's house—what was her name again?"

Sebastian kept his features carefully composed. "Jenny."

"Just—Jenny?"

"I'm afraid so."

"I see. And she slipped away into the night before you could secure her so that she might face charges for the theft?"

"Just so."

Sir Henry went to stand at the window overlooking the morning bustle of Bow Street. "So you're saying Major Wilkinson shot Eisler, but Bertram Leigh-Jones killed Jacques Collot because the Frenchman found out Leigh-Jones was working for Napoléon?"

"Yes."

"And Leigh-Jones killed Jud Foy for essentially the same reason—so that his surreptitious interest in the diamond's whereabouts would remain unknown?"

"That, and so that he could plant the evidence on Foy's body to make it look as if the rifleman had killed Eisler."

"But Leigh-Jones already had a strong case against Yates."

Sebastian shrugged. "Given that Leigh-Jones had figured out that Yates wasn't the killer, he probably worried that the case against Yates might crumble. And the last thing Leigh-Jones wanted was renewed public interest in the murder." Sebastian also had a sneaking suspicion Leigh-Jones was under pressure from Jarvis to release Yates, but he kept that possibility to himself.

"Yes, it all makes sense," said Sir Henry after a moment. "But without the girl's testimony, your explanation of the events that likely transpired the night of Eisler's murder—while certainly plausible—must of necessity remain unproven. I therefore see no purpose in reopening an investigation that has already been officially closed." He paused to look around, one eyebrow raised. "Unless, of course, you know where the girl might be found."

Sebastian shook his head. "Sorry. No."

That, at least, was the truth. He saw no reason to add that his ignorance was deliberate, or that Hero knew exactly where Jenny Davie had found refuge.

"Unfortunate." Sir Henry ran the thumb and forefinger of one hand up and down his watch chain while he chewed his inner lip. "I've been contacted by the Palace. It seems the Prince's advisers have decided that the populace would be better off without the knowledge that a prominent London magistrate was actually working for the Emperor Napoléon. The people will therefore be told that Leigh-Jones was killed in the process of apprehending a dangerous French agent."

"How is the dangerous French agent doing, by the way?"

"He's still alive, but I'm told he won't be for much longer. He's never regained consciousness." Sir Henry hesitated, then added, "Leigh-Jones is to be given a hero's funeral. There's even talk of the Prince himself attending."

"How . . . ironic."

"It is, yes. But necessary."

"I wonder how long he'd been working for the French."

"If his bank account is anything to go by, I'd say quite some time. Makes you wonder, doesn't it, how many others like him are out there? People who are both known and respected, yet whose allegiance is elsewhere."

"I suppose we'll never know," said Sebastian, limping slightly as he turned toward the door.

"Lord Devlin—"

Sebastian paused to look back at him.

"I'm sorry about your friend."

Sebastian nodded. But he did not trust himself to speak.

Leaving Bow Street, Sebastian drove to the southwestern corner of Hyde Park. Once there, he left the horses in Tom's care and cut across the rough grass to the canal near which Rhys Wilkinson's body had been found.

The rain had been heavy during the night, leaving the long grass wet and sodden, and battering the last of the frost-tinged leaves clinging to the surrounding trees. There was a loneliness here that sank deep into a man, a yawning melancholy that seemed a part of the white empty sky and the tracery of branches and the haunting call of the geese lifting off the surface of the canal. He stood for a time beside the frost-nipped reeds, his gaze on the flat pewter expanse of the water before him. He thought about the laughing, devil-may-care officer he'd once known, and of the despair Rhys must have felt when he looked his last upon this scene.

Shrugging the image away, Sebastian began to walk along the edge of the canal, crisscrossing purposefully back and forth, his gaze on the cold, wet mud oozing up between the reeds at his feet. Lovejoy's constables had searched here before him, he knew, but he suspected their effort had been halfhearted, their explanation for the invalid officer's death already running to seizure or heart failure.

It was some minutes before he found what he was looking for: a light blue bottle some four inches high, its stopper gone, but with the dark yellow label proclaiming LAUDANUM: POISON still largely intact. Reaching down, he picked it up, the silt-laden water lapping cold against his hand as his fingers closed around the bottle, empty now but for a faint, reddish brown smudge in one corner.

There was no way of knowing how long it had lain here; an hour, a day, a week? It suggested everything but proved nothing. Sebastian felt his fist tighten around the heavy glass with an unexpected surge of raw anger. Drawing back his arm, he hurled the bottle far out into the waterway.

It hit with a plopping splash, then sank quickly out of sight. Sebastian stood and watched the ripples fade to stillness.

Then he turned and walked away.

꒦

"Do you blame him for what he did?" Hero asked.

She was seated in the armchair beside the fire in her chamber, with Sebastian on the rug beside her. "Wilkinson, you mean?" He leaned his head back against her knee and drew in a deep breath. "I'm still not convinced he went there to kill Eisler. He could have had some other scheme in mind."

"A way to bell the cat?"

"Perhaps. Only, events got away from him—as they have an unfortunate tendency to do."

"And then he killed himself," she said quietly. "To spare his family the shame of the trial, and to give his wife and child a chance at a better life without him." He felt her fingers playing with the hair that curled at the nape of his neck. "We don't take good care of the men we ask to risk their lives and health for us, do we? We use them, and then when they're no longer of value, we toss them away."

"'King George commands and we obey,'" quoted Sebastian. "'Over the hills and far away.'" He turned to face her, his hands coming to rest on the growing swell of her belly. "Lately, I find myself wondering what the world will be like when she grows up."

"He," said Hero firmly.

Sebastian laughed. "You're certain of that, are you?"

Her lips curved into a slow smile, and he thought she'd never looked more beautiful. "Yes."

Author's Note

The theft of the French Crown Jewels from the Garde-Meuble in Paris in September of 1792 was essentially as described here, although the involvement of Danton and Roland, while suggested, has never been proven. Napoléon's determination to recover the French Crown Jewels, as well as the ruthlessness of the methods he employed, was likewise real.

The identification of the Hope Diamond as the recut French Blue is now generally accepted. An old lead cast of the French Blue with a label saying it belonged to "Mr. Hoppe of London," recently discovered in a drawer in the French National History Museum in Paris, was donated in 1850 by a descendant of the Archard family. Interestingly enough, Charles Archard was both a close associate of the Hopes and one of the lapidaries tasked by Napoléon to recover the French Crown Jewels. How Hope acquired the diamond is not known, although multiple theories exist. I have chosen the one best suited to my story. It is significant that Napoléon, who surely knew more than we do about the events of September 1792, always believed that the Duke of Brunswick (father of the Princess of Wales, Caroline) had been bribed with the diamond not to attack Paris. There is also considerable evidence to support the belief that Brunswick sent his jewels to Caroline when his duchy was threatened by Napoléon, and that she sold them after his death.

Hope and Co. did indeed run into financial difficulties as a result of the war and was sold to Barings in 1813.

The recut blue diamond reappeared, briefly, in London in September 1812, exactly twenty years after its original theft, when a Huguenot lapidary named Francillon drew up a sales prospectus for a London diamond merchant named Daniel Eliason. Since that gentleman did not meet a violent death (and was as far as I know nothing like the nasty character here portrayed), I have changed his name to Daniel Eisler in making him my murder victim. What happened to the diamond after September 1812 is not known, although there is considerable evidence that it was acquired by the Prince Regent and was in his possession until his death in 1830. At that point it reappeared in the possession of Henry Philip Hope, although he always refused to divulge its origins.

Numerous books have been written about the history of the Hope Diamond; arguably the most useful and current are Patch's *Blue Mystery*, Kurin's *Hope Diamond*, and Fowler's *Hope: Adventures of a Diamond*.

Blair Beresford is of my own creation. However, Thomas Hope's marriage to Louisa de la Poer Beresford was much as described here. After Hope's death, she married her cousin William Carr Beresford, the illegitimate son of her uncle the Marquess of Waterford. A general under Wellington, he was eventually made Viscount Beresford. Interestingly, he was the commander responsible for the unauthorized, disastrous attack on the River Plate region in Argentina that played a part in *Where Serpents Sleep*.

The Walcheren Expedition and the deadly fever that resulted from it are both real.

The grimoire known as *The Key of Solomon* is real. Probably written in the fourteenth or fifteenth century, it became hugely popular, although it continued to exist largely in handwritten manuscript form until late in the nineteenth century, when it was finally printed. There was a very real upsurge of interest in grimoires, or magic handbooks, in the nineteenth century. Most of those that became popular dated back to the Renaissance, for reasons Abigail McBean explains to Hero.

London's vibrant molly underground—with its accompanying dangers of extortion and prosecution—was essentially as described here, although more vibrant in the eighteenth century than by the early nineteenth.

The Black Brunswickers were a real volunteer corps raised by Duke Frederick William, Princess Caroline's brother, to fight in the Napoleonic Wars after the French occupied his duchy.

The life of London's crossing sweeps was as described here, with these biographical portraits being loosely based on some of those recorded by Henry Mayhew. Mayhew's work, which appeared midcentury, also serves as the inspiration for the collection of articles Hero is writing. Some of the crossing sweeps did indeed go to the Haymarket after dark, where they played a part in supplying girls to gentlemen in carriages.

The Abbey of St. Saviour in Bermondsey, Southwark, had almost entirely disappeared by the beginning of the nineteenth century. Besides the lay church (which still stands), all other traces vanished somewhere between 1804 and 1812. Since there is some dispute as to when, precisely, the gatehouse and its attached structures were demolished, I have taken the liberty of using them here.

When a gravely injured Frenchwoman
is found beside the mutilated body of a
young doctor, Sebastian finds himself
drawn into a dangerous, high-stakes
web of duplicity even as he is forced to
confront the truth about a brutal wartime
act of betrayal that still has the power
to destroy him.
Don't miss the next
Sebastian St. Cyr Mystery,

WHY KINGS CONFESS

Available now in hardcover and e-book,
and in March 2015 in paperback.
An excerpt follows. . . .

Chapter 1

St. Katharine's, East London
Thursday, 21 January 1813

*P*aul Gibson lurched down the dark, narrow lane, his face raw from the cold, his fingers numb. There were times when he wandered these alleyways lost in brightly hued reveries of opium-induced euphoria. But not tonight. Tonight, Gibson clenched his jaw and tried to focus on the *tap-tap* of his wooden leg on the icy cobbles, the reedy wail of a babe carried on the night wind— anything that might distract his mind from the restless, hungering need that drenched his thin frame with sweat and tormented him with ghosts of what could be.

When he first noticed the woman, he thought her an apparition, a mirage of gray wool and velvet lying crumpled beside the entrance to a fetid passageway. But as he drew nearer, he saw pale flesh and the gleaming dark wetness of blood and knew she was only too real.

He drew up sharply, the dank, briny air of the nearby Thames rasping in his throat. Cat's Hole, they called this narrow lane, a refuge for thieves, prostitutes, and all the desperate dispossessed of England and beyond. He could feel his heart pounding; the stars glittered like shards of broken glass in the thin slice of cold black sky visible between the looming rooftops above. He hesitated perhaps longer than he should have. But he was a surgeon, his life dedicated to the care of others.

He pushed himself forward again.

She lay curled half on her side, one hand flung out palm up, eyes closed. He hunkered down awkwardly beside her, fingertips searching for a pulse in her slim neck. Her face was delicately boned and framed by a riot of long, flame red hair, her lashes dark and thick against the pale flesh of her smooth cheeks, her lips purple-blue with cold. Or death.

But at his touch, her eyelids fluttered open, her chest jerking on a sob and a broken, whispered prayer. *"Sainte Marie, Mère de Dieu, priez pour nous pauvres pécheurs . . ."*

"It's all right; I'm here to help you," he said gently, wondering if she could even understand him. "Where are you hurt?"

The entire side of her head, he now saw, was matted with blood. Wide-eyed and frightened, she fixed her gaze on him. Then her focus shifted to where the black mouth of the passage yawned beside them. "Damion . . ." Her hand jerked up to clutch his sleeve. "Is he all right?"

Gibson followed her gaze. The man's body was more difficult to discern, a dark, motionless mass deep in the shadows. Gibson shook his head. "I don't know."

Her grip on his arm twisted convulsively. "Go to him. Please."

Nodding, Gibson surged upright, staggering slightly as his wooden peg took his weight and the phantom pains of a long-gone limb ripped through him.

The passage reeked of rot and excrement and the familiar coppery stench of spilled blood. The man lay sprawled on his back beside a pile of broken hogsheads and crates. It was with difficulty that Gibson picked out the once snowy white folds of a cravat, the silken sheen of what had been a fine waistcoat but was now a blood-soaked mess, horribly ripped.

"Tell me," said the woman. "Tell me he lives."

But Gibson could only stare at the body before him. The man's eyes were wide and sightless, his handsome young face pallid, his outflung arms stiffening in the cold. Someone had hacked open the corpse's chest with a ruthless savagery that spoke of rage tinged with madness. And where the heart should have been gaped only an open cavity.

Bloody and empty.

Chapter 2

$\mathcal{T}$he dream began as it often did, with the sun shining golden warm and the laughter of children at play floating on an orange blossom–scented breeze.

Sebastian St. Cyr, Viscount Devlin, moved restlessly in his sleep, for he knew only too well what was to come. The thunder of galloping horses. A shouted order. The hiss of sabers drawn with deadly purpose from well-oiled scabbards. He gave a low moan.

"Devlin?"

Laughter turned to screams of terror. His vision filled with slashing hooves and bare steel stained dark with innocent blood.

"Devlin."

He opened his eyes, his chest jerking as he sucked in a deep, ragged breath. He felt his wife's gentle fingertips touch his lips. Her face rose above him in the darkness, her features pale in the glow of the fire that still burned warm on the bedroom hearth. "It's a dream," she whispered, although he saw the worry that drew together her dark brows. "Just a dream."

For a moment he could only stare at her, lost in the past. Then he folded his arms around Hero and drew her close, so that she could no longer see his face. It was a dream, yes. But it was also a memory, one he had never shared with anyone.

"Did I wake you?" he asked, his voice a hoarse rasp. "I'm sorry."

She shook her head, her weight shifting as she sought in vain for a comfortable position, for she was nearly nine months heavy with his child. "Your son keeps kicking me."

Smiling, he placed his hand on the taut mound of her belly and felt a strong heel grind against his palm. "Shockingly ill-mannered of her."

"I think he's beginning to find it a wee bit crowded in there."

"There is a solution."

She laughed, a low, husky sound that caught without warning at his heart, then twisted. As much as he yearned to hold this child in his arms, thoughts of the looming birth inevitably brought a sense of disquiet that came perilously close to fear. He'd read once that more than one in ten women died in childbirth. Hero's own mother had lost babe after babe—before nearly dying herself.

Yet he heard no echo of his own terror in Hero's calm voice when she said, "Not long now."

He felt the babe kick one last time, then settle as Hero snuggled beside him. He brushed his lips against her temple and murmured, "Try to sleep."

"You sleep," she said, still smiling.

He watched her eyelids drift closed, her breathing slow. Yet the tension that thrummed within him remained, and he found himself wondering if it was the coming babe that had sent his unconscious thoughts drifting back to a time he wished so desperately to forget. A cold wind stirred the heavy velvet drapes at the windows and banged an unlatched shutter somewhere in the darkness. There were nights when the high, arid mountains and ancient, stone-walled villages of Spain and Portugal seemed a lifetime away from the London town house sleeping around him. Yet he knew they were not.

He was still awake when an urgent message arrived in Brook Street from Paul Gibson, asking for Sebastian's help.